ISBN 978-1-5276-5872-1
PIBN 10878831

"'Go! my boy, go! in God's name'"

HARRY C. EDWARDS

M

BOSTON

"'*Go! my boy, go! in God's name*'"

M

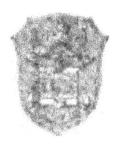

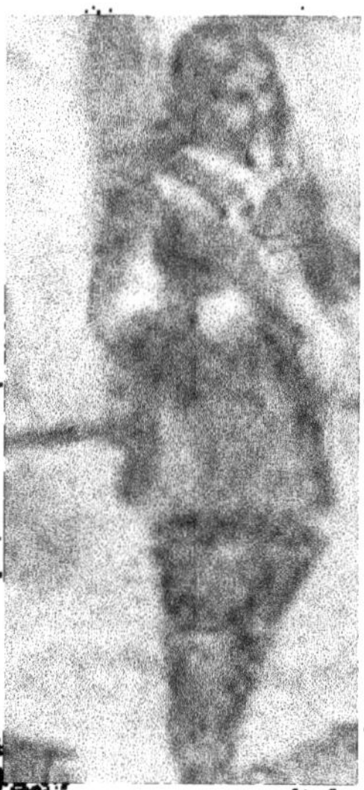 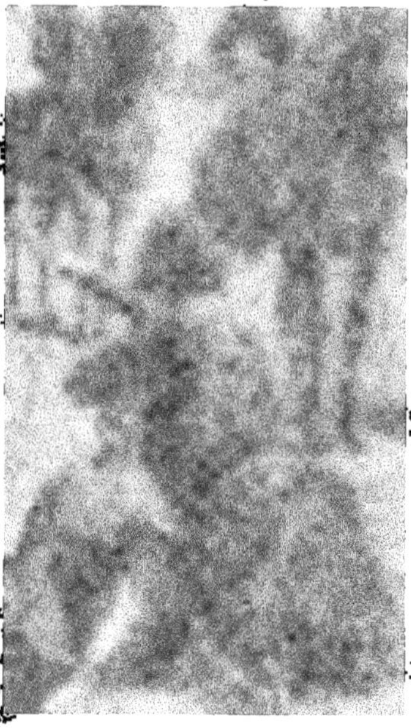

DAUNTLESS

A STORY *of* A LOST & FORGOTTEN CAUSE

By EWAN MARTIN

Author of "The Knight of King's Guard," etc.

Illustrated by

HARRY C. EDWARDS

"Their swords are rust,
Their bones are dust,
Their souls are with the saints, we trust."

BOSTON

L. C. PAGE & COMPANY (INCORPORATED)

M D CCCC

University Press · John Wilson and Son · Cambridge, U. S. A.

List of Illustrations

DAUNTLESS

I

AMONGST the swarm of bold adventurers who aided Strongbow in the Conquest of Ireland was a daring Norman pirate named Raymond Sans Peur, who succeeded in obtaining possession of one of the fairest manors in the County Dublin in a fashion which would be considered more creditable to his courage than his integrity in these more scrupulous days.

As soon as Strongbow had crushed out all spirit of resistance in the South and East, he proceeded to distribute the country among his followers in the same way as William the Norman had done in England after Senlac. In Ireland, as in the sister Island, a portion of the spoils found its way to the Norman monks and prelates who had followed close upon the heels of their military compatriots, and one of the Conqueror's piacula to Mother Church was the beautiful Valley of Shanganagh, which is situate between the bold headlands of Bray and Killiney. This delightful tract of land was ceded to the Cistercian Monastery of Dublin; but, owing to the dangerous situation of their property, the good Monks were unable to enjoy more than the empty title of ownership.

Strongbow had, indeed, triumphed over the walled towns on the sea-coast and wherever else his indomitable ships could push their way, but the Wicklow Mountains, and the two fierce Clans inhabiting them, taught him the sharp truth as to there being limits even to his victorious arms.

The O'Byrnes and O'Tooles of the Wicklow Mountains continued, long after Strongbow's time, to be a constant source of dread to the invaders until Perrott, the natural brother of Queen Elizabeth, broke their power forever; but, during the interim, very few of the settlers dared venture beyond the strong girdle of their fortresses round Dublin, inasmuch as "the air did not agree with them," as a Wicklow Chieftain once scornfully remarked.

As the Mountaineers harried the lands of Churchman and layman alike, with a broad-minded impartiality, the Abbot of Saint Mary's found himself in the position of one owning a treasure whereof he could make no use, and in this extremity he applied to Strongbow for a captain daring enough to undertake the dangerous duty of Warden of the Valley.

The Conqueror, thereupon, bethought himself of Sans Peur, who, throughout the struggle for the Island, had proved himself to be a master-mind even amid that band of daring resolutes. He had rendered sterling service during the Conquest, but he was nothing but a nameless adventurer in that titled host, and, consequently, his claims had been ignored during the season his master had been showering rewards among his other followers.

Somewhat ashamed at having forgotten so trusty an adherent, Earl Strongbow tendered this perilous wardenship to Sans Peur, and the adventurer accepted the offer with cheerful alacrity. There was some subsequent confusion as to the exact nature of the contract between the Abbot and Sans Peur, and it is now impossible to determine which of the two was to blame for the misunderstanding. Perhaps Sans Peur erred as to the exact nature of his trust; perhaps he may have made some mental reservation as to the Abbot's future claims; or it is possible the Churchman did not explain with sufficient clearness that Sans Peur was to regard him thenceforward as his over-lord: however, there is one matter whereof there is no vestige of doubt; id est, the appointment of Sans Peur to the Wardenship of the Valley was the last transaction wherein the worthy Monks of Saint Mary's had anything to do with their property.

Out on the Dublin Mountains the Warden took his post, and at a spot commanding the high-road to the city he built his first castle. It was a very rude, cramped structure — little more than a peel tower; yet, notwithstanding its size, it was one of the strongest fortifications, up to that time, erected in the country. Never was house founded under more trying circumstances. Twice was the uncompleted tower stormed and the workmen killed among the building material, and twice was the daring Norman obliged to retreat with a handful of his men before the Wicklow highlanders. However, Sans Peur returned after each repulse to resume the interrupted castle, and working with the bow in one hand and the trowel in the other, at last completed the tower which stands to this day as a monument to his determination.

And, surely, the ground it was built to keep was worth fighting for, as there is never a fairer or sweeter spot in the fair land of Ireland than that lovely Valley which runs from headland to headland with the mountains leaning over it as if to gather it into a jealous embrace. Yet, if the landward scene is fair, the seascape is, if possible, fairer. Southward, Bray Head wades out into the blue waters of the Bay like a great Lion carved out of granite. Northward, over the triple-cleft summit of Killiney, Howth appears like some sleeping sea monster, and Eastward, Dalkey Island peeps up like its truant offspring that has swum closer inshore to inspect the beautiful land they all sentinel. Yes, truly, it was a manor worth fighting for, and the grey old Castle of the Norman freebooter seems to nod over the Valley as if in grim approval of the long gone struggle wherein it was won.

Strong as the Castle was, it was subjected to many trying sieges by the Wicklow Mountaineers; yet Sans Peur and his little garrison, though often hard pressed and always outnumbered, frustrated every attempt to dislodge them. Even after they had learned that the skill and vigilance of Sans Peur were more than a match for their own rough methods of warfare, the Mountaineers never lost an opportunity of harassing their enemy; and the little tower continued to be the object of so many forays that it earned the name of "*Bearna Baeghail*" or the "Castle of the Gap of Danger," by which title it continued to be known until the Gaelic language gradually faded into the memory it has latterly become.

However, when Sans Peur had sufficiently proved his might among the Wicklow clans, he set about securing the Valley for himself by a method which contrasted strangely with the fashion whereby he had defended it for others. He made friendly overtures to the Wicklow chieftains, espoused one of their daughters (as his master Strongbow had done before him), assumed the dress and language of the country; and, in a stroke, not only guaranteed the Valley from molestations by his neighbours, but also secured them as powerful allies. He then strengthened his position by erecting two more castles, filled them with some of his warlike kinsmen, and, having thus firmly established himself in Shanganagh, he threw the tax-collector of the Abbot into the river that runs by Bearna Baeghail, repudiated his vassalage stoutly and announced his intention of holding fast to the land by the same method whereby he had won it.

At first, the Abbot endeavoured to temporise with the usurper in person, but Raymond shut his gates and refused to see him. Then the Abbot assailed him with letters containing mingled threats and remonstrances, but the recipient politely returned these missives on the plea of his inability to read them, which excuse, it must be acknowledged, had, at least, the merit of ingenuous candour. The indignant prelate next petitioned Strongbow for troops to aid him in regaining possession of his property, but that nobleman was too much engaged elsewhere to pay any attention to the wrongs of the Church, whereupon the Abbot disconsolately fell back on his last refuge, — namely, the spiritual power, — and solemnly cursed Raymond with bell, book, and candle, but without either getting back his ravished lands or causing the bold robber any visible discomfort.

In due time Raymond died and was buried in the ancient monastery of Saint Olaves. The Monks of Saint Mary's vainly petitioned his son, Gilbert, to make restitution for the impiety of the dead Warden; but Gilbert Sans Peur was possessed with ten-fold the unscrupulous spirit of his father and double the determination to hold on to whatever he had won. During the troubled reign of John, this unprincipled warrior still further added to the spoils of his father by dispossessing another free-lance like himself who had seized some adjoining land of the Carmelites Friars.

The Monks of Mount Carmel begged Gilbert piteously for the land which had been wrested from them, but that hard-hearted person bade them go forth and do their own killing themselves if they were in need of another estate, and swore vehemently that nothing on the earth or over it would persuade him to part with the land which he had robbed from his brother marauder. Accordingly, the Carmelites joined the Cistercians in piously consigning Gilbert to the same place in the next world, wherein they earnestly hoped his father was already domiciled, and, abandoning all further attempts to recover their property, left Gilbert Sans Peur and his descendants in undisputed possession of the Valley.

The descendants of Sans Peur, whose name in course of time became Anglicised into the patronymic of Dauntless, suffered or prospered according as the tide ebbed or flowed; but, during the jars and shocks that convulsed Ireland for centuries after the Conquest, they succeeded in retaining their hold upon the Valley with a grip, little less tenacious than that of their robber founder.

Once, in the reign of King Richard the Second, the then head of the Dauntless family went out into open rebellion with Art Murrough Cavanagh and, on being taken prisoner, was promptly beheaded for his trouble. The Valley was escheated to the Crown and remained out of the possession of the family until his son received it back from King Henry the V. as a reward for his heroic conduct in the French wars. Later on, in the reign of Henry the VII., another Dauntless of the Valley threw in his lot with the Pretender, Perkin Warbeck, with all that ardour for the House of York which animated the entire Irish people. On the suppression of the rebellion the greater part of the Valley was confiscated by the Miser King; but the remaining portion, in itself forming a considerable tract of country, continued on in possession of the family even through the dangerous reign of Elizabeth.

With the exception of the two enthusiasts before mentioned, the Dauntless family were a cool, level-headed race governed by a profound love for their possessions and a corresponding distrust of anything which might imperil them; and, in consequence of this prudent disposition, they succeeded in escaping the almost general confiscation of property, notwithstanding their conservative adherence to the ancient faith.

The sole representative of the house of Dauntless in the following reign was a young law-student, who, like many young Irish gentlemen of that period, had been sent to Oxford during the reign of Elizabeth in order to escape the perilous atmosphere of his native land. Shortly after taking his degree, he proceeded to Lincoln's Inn in company with the ill-fated Sir Phelim O'Neill; and, in the centre of a company more brilliant than learned and much more joyous than studious, the two young Irishmen spent several years studying law after their own fashion.

At one of the Masques given by the young Templars in honour of King James, Walter Dauntless met a beautiful young country-woman whose fair face, gentle modesty, and sad history had attracted the attention of the King himself. Some fifteen years before, this young gentlewoman's father, Sir Cathal MacMahon, a near relative of the MacMahon, Prince of Orgiall, had been engaged, like all his clan, in the rebellion of the two great Earls of Ulster. During the earlier part of the war, he attained a high reputation with both sides for military skill which he still further enhanced towards the close of the campaign by his intrepid conduct at the rout of the Earl of Essex at "The Pass o' Plumes." This character, however, stood him in bad stead afterwards, for, on the submission of the Earls, he was one of the few exempted from pardon and was accordingly sent to the Tower, where he was detained a close prisoner for the remainder of his life.

Some five years after his commitment, he begged permission to send for a page of his Clan on the grounds that such an attendant was necessary on account of his impaired health. The request was granted, and a young page shortly afterwards arrived from Ireland and was accordingly admitted to Sir Cathal's prison. The page continued to share his master's prison for nearly three years without exciting any suspicion of his being other than what he appeared to be until a slight fever, which necessitated the attendance of a physician, led to the discovery that the supposed boy was in reality a pretty little girl of thirteen.

The old soldier, thereupon, confessed that she was his daughter, who had assumed this disguise in order to be with him; and this filial devotion so touched the heart of the fatherly old King that it caused him to blubber freely when relating the incident to his son, Prince Henry, and to send his own physician to attend the little heroine.

On her recovery, King James gave orders for the provision of suitable apartments for her in the Tower, and moreover commanded the hitherto strict nature of Sir Cathal's imprisonment to be relaxed to that description of durance which was known as the "outer ward," which gave him liberty to roam about with his daughter in the gardens, walks, etc., that lay within the enceinte of the great Fortress. The young lady continued to watch over her father with unfaltering love, notwithstanding the trying irritability of temper that imprisonment developed during his latter years; but her filial devotion had its earthly reward after his death, inasmuch as the good-natured old Monarch settled a small pension upon her and placed her under the care of the venerable old Lady H——, one of the few noble families at Court professing the same faith as the young orphan.

Walter Dauntless was touched to the heart by the beauty and sorrow of Kathlyn MacMahon. He immediately fell in love with her in the headlong fashion of his race, and, shortly after their first meeting at the Masque, he asked her to become his wife. The aged Lady H—— approved highly of the young lawyer and warmly seconded his suit; but the poor friendless girl herself at first shrank from his advances and then hesitated in a maze of doubt and confusion. The recent death of her father, the sudden nature of this proposal of marriage, and a certain doubt as to whether she cared sufficiently for her lover made her pause in distressful indecision; but, whilst she hesitated and Dauntless pleaded, another sentiment than sexual affection was fighting his battle for him in her heart.

She loved her native land with all the passionate affection of her race and ever since her father's death had turned her eyes longingly to the West. The Court of London was a gilded cage to this young falcon of the North, and as she thought that a husband chosen from her own race would afford her the speediest means of escaping from it, she yielded at length to the prayers of her lover.

Such reasons for entering into the state of matrimony may not meet with general approval; and yet, poor Soul, although she made him a true and loyal wife, she saw many another woman, who had given her hand in marriage for far less worthy motives, lead a happier life than she deserved to have.

The fruit of this union was a boy, born two years afterwards in London on the feast of Saint Henry, and, according to the pious old custom of the time, named after the saint on whose festival he came into the world. After that event all the young wife required to complete her happiness was a speedy return to her native land; but, whilst she was weaving day-dreams of a journey to Ireland in company with her husband and babe, Walter Dauntless was, at that very time, mustering up courage to tell her that their future life was henceforth to be irrepealably bound to London.

He had been guided to this decision by very divergent reasons. In the first place he had been accustomed to the gaiety and splendour of a Royal Court, and the prospect of a dull country life on his property seemed dismal in comparison. Another reason was the depreciated condition of his Irish estate, for, in common with most of the young courtiers of the time, he had fallen a victim to the prevailing vice of gambling and the Valley had suffered in consequence. But the chief reason which made him dread a return to Ireland was his detection of a growing spirit of intrigue which was steadily laying the foundation of still further trouble in that unhappy land.

The terrible severities of the last war had completely crushed out all spirit of resistance, and Ireland, drained of her life-blood, lay weak, trembling, and spiritless at the feet of her conqueror. Moreover, the people looked patiently for some concession of religious liberty from the son of Mary Stuart, whom they regarded as the Martyr of their faith, and, consequently, nothing was further from their minds than a revolt against King James. But, just at that period, there was a large section of the English people who would have regarded a rebellion in the sister country as something in the shape of a blessed harvest.

It was an age of mad extravagance, and every official in England, from the Lord Chancellor down to the crier in the law-court, was alike venal, needy, and unprincipled. The King's pacific relations with France and Spain had cut off the source whence England had drawn so much wealth in the reign of his warlike predecessor, and all these spendthrift unconscionables were anxiously casting their eyes around to see whence they might obtain a renewal of supplies which foreign commerce had ceased to yield. The tracts of country in Ireland that had survived the Elizabethan forfeitures appeared to offer the readiest solution of the difficulty, and Walter Dauntless, himself a lawyer and a courtier, foresaw that such a scheme, once set afoot, would not take long to be developed and consummated.

The same tenacious ichor which dominated in the blood of

the old Norman freebooter also ran through the veins of his seventeenth-century descendant, and Walter Dauntless, therefore, coolly and resolutely made up his mind to hold fast to his property, come what might. Let his fellow-countrymen await the time when they would be either charged with sham plots or adroitly goaded into real conspiracies — it mattered little to him — but he himself was determined to ride peacefully at anchor, feasting, gaming, and singing, far away from the storm which would engulph the fools who were too thick-sighted to foresee its coming.

Although he had firmly resolved to settle in London, he had, so far, shrunk from communicating his decision to his wife; until Kathlyn, wearied by frequent evasions and postponements of their return to Ireland, one evening put the question of their journey to him in a manner that left no room for further subterfuge.

She was sitting in the pretty little parlour of the house in Fetter Lane which they had occupied since their marriage. The diamond-paned casement was latched back on its notched bar and through the open window floated the drowsy hum of bees in the garden without — for there were gardens and flowers in Fetter Lane at that period — and the warm spring sun smiled in on her babe, who lay sleeping at her feet in his quaint oak cradle. The street door opened and her husband entered, singing merrily and clicking his rapier against his heel. He stopped short at the door of the little parlour and instantly checked his song at the half playful, half reproachful gesture which she directed to the sleeping infant, who lay in the midst of his soft white coverings like a rosebud in a snowdrift.

He unbuckled his light walking rapier, laid it and his hat softly upon the table, and stole over to his wife on tiptoe. Then, kneeling down beside her chair and putting his arm around her in the fashion he was wont to do in the days of their courtship, he kissed her gently upon the cheek and regarded the sleeping child with a long look of contemplative affection.

At length he sighed and said softly, —

"Truly! the goddess of the cartwheel hath been constant to me in one matter even though she hath played the jade with me in others."

"Oh, Walter," said the young wife, with something like alarm in her voice, "I trust you have not been playing heavily again?"

"No! No! Sweetheart!" answered her husband, flushing slightly, "I pledge thee my word I have not been playing at all, since — since —this morning, and then it was but a few mains of dice I threw with that boorish Huntingdon clown, Cromwell of Lincoln's Inn, and his friend, young Master Wiltonholme. No! No! mouse, when I thanked Fortune it was for the sweet wife and babe I am blessed withal and not for any paltry gold pieces I may have lost or won this morning. But thou, Heaven gild thee, hast thou nothing pretty to thank Fortune for?"

"Everything, everything," said his wife, heartfully. "Everything that a good woman could pray for — everything — but — a home in our own dear country, where methinks our happiness would be complete. Oh, Walter!" she continued, speaking more rapidly as if she feared he would interrupt her. "Why not go home to our own land, where we can see green fields and blue skies once more and leave this murky city with all its wickedness, treachery, and sallow-faced mirth behind us? You must know that this life you lead among false London courtiers and gamblers cannot lead to good and that a peaceful existence among our own simple country folk across the sea is best for us both. Do not plead the burthened condition of your estate as a bar to our journey, for, remember, there is mine own kith and clan in the far North, where we shall find a home amidst true and simple hearts. Oh, Walter! Walter! come away with me to the North and never doubt to find a welcome there, for my Uncle Bryan, Lord o' the Dartry, my own dear Sept of Fermanagh, and all the others who form portion of Clan Colla, would divide their cloak and share their last *boinneog* with us twain for the sake of my father's memory."

Her husband frowned, bit his lip, and put away her clinging arms from his neck. Then he arose from his knee and pointed to the sleeping child.

"Methought, Kathlyn," said he, harshly, "that you did love your babe."

"Dear Husband," cried the frightened woman, starting back as though he had struck her and flushing painfully, "why should you question my love for him?"

"I also thought," he continued slowly, "that our home, albeit a city one, was not displeasing in your eyes, and I was also vain enough to think I was as dear to you as you are to me."

"What makes you ask such idle questions?" faltered his wife, tearfully. "God knoweth how thankful and appreciative I am of all these blessings."

"Why, then, so desirous to imperil thy treasures for such a summer-day dream as a home across the sea?" asked he, with a swift, incisive look into her startled face. "Thou, who hast seen one war pass over Ireland, shouldst know how neither age nor sex can protect the most innocent in that country when the sword is out? Ha! Wench, do I speak idly now?"

The hot flush faded from her cheeks and left them white as marble.

"Wherefore anticipate a return of those dreadful times?" said she, trembling in every limb. "The military power of the Clans is broken — the Chieftains are too much cowed to resent even further oppression and the entire land is at present as peaceful —"

"As the lamb in the hands of a butcher," interrupted her husband, grimly. "But, think you, Sweeting, the butcher will spare the lamb for the sake of its meekness? No! Kate, no! If Ireland is drowsing peacefully at present, there are busy brains in this country who have no intention it should remain in that state long. Even now, the lands of those dreamers in Ulster are being parcelled out here in London on mock charges of treason. Nay, more, Kate; I have known cases where the spoilers have already re-sold property to be confiscated for charges not yet determined on. Shall I, who walk open-eyed and observant amidst these plotters, deliberately leave shelter in order to swell their spoil? No, by my soul, no! Home may be sweet, but Hold is sweeter, Kate, and, therefore, resign thyself to London, for Ireland, henceforward, must be no more than a memory to us twain."

Kathlyn wept softly but heartfully at these tidings, but Walter Dauntless stood apart with a shadow of a smile on his face and made no attempt to console her. He was exulting secretly at the successful fashion in which he had raised an everlasting barrier to his wife's long-cherished scheme of a home in Ireland; and whilst he congratulated himself that she could not reproach him for being the cause of their remaining in London, looked forward with much complacent satisfaction to a continuance of the gay, dissipated life which had completely enthralled his careless, selfish, pleasure-seeking soul.

II

LITTLE by little, Kathlyn Dauntless resigned herself to the inevitable, and, as years went on, the increasing cares of her little household and, more especially, the loving observation of her child dulled the gnawing hunger for her native land.

One of the sweetest traits in womanhood is that solicitude wherewith a mother watches the early development of character in her little graft; but in the heart of that lonely, exiled daughter of Erin, anxiety welled up from a higher and even more noble passion than mere maternal affection. Kathlyn Dauntless was consumed with a secret but nevertheless glowing curiosity to discover what disposition lay dormant in her child in order that she might direct him from his earliest years into whatever path he might best serve that country to which she had passionately dedicated him.

Would he be a soldier, — one consecrated to free, or aid in freeing, that beloved land from the insolent soldiery of the Sassenach? Or would he be a great lawyer, destined to plead in the Hall of Westminster for justice for his oppressed country? Or would his path to duty lie to some higher calling wherein he would venture life and limb for the purpose of keeping the Lamp of the Ancient Religion aflame in the old land?

When such thoughts would cross her mind, she would hold her boy out at arm's length and cry aloud in Gaelic: —

"By which path, O Lord! By which path is he destined to lead his Country to liberty? Shall it be flower-strewn and triumphant, or beset with thorns and traced with his life-blood as was the Course of Thy Martyrs in the days of old?" and then she would fold the frightened child to her bosom and weep and pray over him by turns.

Vague, fantastic schemes of a simple, enthusiastic spirit; all built up on no surer foundation than the future of a little child of seven! Yet this lonely daughter of Erin, who piled up impossible plans, in the midst of the great dissolute capital which had humbled her beloved land, was not the first or only woman who had cherished similar delusive plots; such dreams as hers must have haunted thousands of Jewish mothers when Israel lay groaning in Egypt.

As her boy showed early inclinations towards one of the higher walks of life, she decided, through the artless system of logic whereby such simple souls arrive at previously wished for conclusions, that he was specially fitted for the priesthood; and, indeed, a more experienced judge of human nature, on being confronted with Master Harry Dauntless at that early age, might have made a similar prediction. He was grave and thoughtful and from his earliest years was invested with a solemn reserve which sat on him as quaintly as though it were a garment fashioned for a grown man, but which had been subsequently shrunken by magic on his childish form. Yet there were good reasons that the child should have possessed these unchildish qualities of gravity and reserve. The religion of his parents not only compelled them to rear him in lonely isolation, but obliged them oftentimes to entrust matters of life and death even to his young keeping. Before he could read, he knew well that one incautious word breathed out into the street might hand over to torture or death the mild, nervous old gentleman who taught him his lessons and sometimes celebrated Mass in the upper attic. As soon as he could speak, he was taught the importance of being silent as to the other strange visitors who flitted in and out of the little house in Fetter Lane; and, though these visitants puzzled his young brain exceedingly, he learned to exercise a discreet control over his tongue which would have done credit to a veteran statesman. Sometimes these strangers were country squires from estates so distant that no one else seemed to know of their whereabouts. Sometimes they were lawyers of such a retiring nature that their names were unknown in the Temple. Sometimes they were suspiciously white-handed sea-captains whose ships lay in other ports than London, and once there arrived a tall, thin woman who stayed one entire week in the back attic and whom the child heard his father address on one occasion as "My Lord."

Although young Master Harry accepted all these visitors as being what they professed, and never spoke of them even to his parents, it was not long before his observant little mind noted one peculiarity about them. They were all overwhelmed with a sense of shrinking modesty. Lady, squire, soldier, sailor, lawyer, or physician, all appeared to have a bat-like antipathy to daylight, and invariably arrived at the little house in Fetter Lane after nightfall, or departed thence at a like unseasonable hour for commencing a journey. Of all these birds of passage there was one, and one alone, who, on account of his singular divergence from the habits of his predecessors, puzzled the immature brain of Master Harry; but as this visitor considerably perplexed the more diplomatic head of his father also, the incident by no means demonstrated any lack of intelligence on the part of the child.

One bright summer day, during the absence of Walter Dauntless, a big, stout, handsomely-dressed soldier made his appearance in Fetter Lane, and rapped so violently that half the neighbours came to their windows in astonishment at the noisy summons. Kathlyn went to the door, and, on seeing whom her visitor was, turned pale, beckoned him hastily into the house, and, as soon as he was safely inside, bolted the door quickly, and then sank down on her knees with every symptom of intense agitation.

The big man tossed his plumed hat one way and his gauntlets the other, and greeted the frightened woman with a boisterous freedom that betokened long acquaintance or close relationship; but, notwithstanding the brave cut of his gilded leather buff-coat and his soldierlike mien, the child shrank from him in distrust, and stood back, marvelling greatly that his mother should kneel down before such a man and what motive she had in kissing the great ruby ring upon his forefinger.

The stranger drew Kathlyn Dauntless to her feet and kissed her warmly upon the cheeks, yet notwithstanding the affectionate way she returned his embrace and the look of trust and affection she bestowed on him, it was quite evident his appearance had disturbed her, inasmuch as she trembled all over and remained silent whilst the big man plied her with eager questions.

"What, Coz! Coz! my pretty little Coz!" said the soldier, after addressing several questions without eliciting a reply, "that's thrice, and thrice thrice, I have conjured thee by our relationship, and thou hast not vouchsafed me a welcome as yet. Have I changed so much in features, or thou in spirit, that thou canst not find confidence enow to cry in the good old fashion of the North, 'Ho! kinsman! green rushes to thy feet'?"

"Nay, Evir, nay, Heaven forbid!" answered Kathlyn, in Gaelic; "and yet I can hardly find it in my heart to say that I am glad to see thee. Tell me, in Heaven's name, what madness hath tempted thee to venture within the springs of such a death-trap as the gates of Clan London!"

"*Nabocklish!*" said the soldier, laughing. "Neither do I run any risk, and therefore put thy fears and curiosity alike into thy pocket, and leave off trembling like a kitten which fears the babe who would be its playmate. Why, Kate, ever since this match between the Infanta and the young Prince of Wales hath been set afoot, London is as secure an inn for a soldier of Spain as Madrid; and even if this alliance were not filling the town with Dons, I could scarcely choose a better couching spot than inside Temple Bar, for the hunter seldom looks for a deer in his own byre."

He put his arm around her and laughed so uproariously that she trembled once more, and brought him hastily into the little parlour, from whence she would have excluded Harry, had not the big soldier caught him up in his arms, and declared he would not allow her to break up a family party.

"No, he shall not leave, Coz!" said he, holding the boy out at arm's length and glancing from him to his mother. "It were an ill deed to part new-found kinsmen at so short a notice. He hath thine eyes, Kathlyn, — eyes as blue as Lough Neagh on a summer's day, — and with such a true token of his mother and her country in his face it were a strange matter if he should prove unworthy of either."

He set the boy astride his booted thigh, and asked him his name and from whence he hailed, but observing that the child, although perfectly self-possessed, was regarding him in puzzled silence, he shot a look, half-reproachful, half-comical, at Kathlyn, and repeated the question in English.

"My name is Harry Dauntless," replied the child, in the same language, "and my home is in Shanganagh in the Kingdom of Ireland."

"And where is Ireland and what is Ireland to thee, my pretty boy?" asked the stranger, with a wistful look at the grave little figure perched in horseman fashion on his muscular thigh.

"Ireland is not here," replied Harry, slowly. "It is far, very far away across the sea, and I have never been there, yet mother tells me I am to love it on that account the more dearly, because it is mine own country."

"Bravely answered, my pretty little man," said the soldier, with a wide-lidded stare of his steel blue eyes. "Bravo, Kathlyn! thou hast so far trained him well, and there is hope for Dark Rosaleen[1] since she hath such weans born to her even in the land of the Saxon. And tell me, Harry, wouldst like to wear a *skene* and *claidheamh*, and strike a blow for the land thou dost love so well under the colours of thy mother's clan? Nay, Kathlyn, never frown; I chatter in this idle fashion because I must talk lightly lest I sigh heavily. Never heed thy mother, child, never heed her, but answer me truly, — wouldst like to be a soldier and wear a long sword such as I carry?"

"My mother says I am to be —" commenced the child, but suddenly breaking off he bent forward to his mother's ear and asked, in an audible whisper, "May I tell him what I am to become when I grow up?"

The big soldier burst into a fit of laughter so violent that his whole body shook as if in an ague, and young Master Harry thought it prudent to slip from his knee to the ground lest he should arrive there in a more perilous and less dignified fashion, and taking refuge behind the petticoats of his mother regarded the stranger with the most intense suspicion.

"Yes, Harry," said his smiling mother, "you can say what you please before this gentleman, who is —"

"Captain MacMahon of the Clan Colla," interrupted the soldier, quickly. "Thy mother's cousin and thy own poor kinsman; and now come hither, my prudent little gossip, and tell me what thou wert about to say when suspicion scared thee to thy mother's knee. Wouldst like to wear a buff-coat and a Spanish blade upon thy hip, Boy, and carry both with a stout heart to the service of thy native land?"

Harry drew near to the Captain and stretching out his little fat hand shyly stroked the handsomely stamped and gilded buff-coat of the soldier.

[1] The name by which the exiled Irish of the seventeenth century were accustomed to designate their native land.

"I think I should like to be a soldier and wear a long sword as you do," said he, in a low voice, with his curly head on one side and his eyes fixed hard on the inlaid rapier hilt of the Captain. "But then I do not think that I ever can, as mother says I am to be a priest as soon as God makes me strong enough."

"Why not be both, Harry?" asked the Captain, regarding him with a strange smile.

"But do priests wear buff-coats and go to the wars?" said the child, fixing his innocent childish eyes on the keen ones set in the half jesting, half earnest face of the big man.

"Aye, that they do," said the Captain, with a gay laugh, catching him up in his arms and once more setting him astride his leg, "and their reverences, nowadays, are often to be found a-horseback, in back and breast and steel cap, in company with the boldest men-at-arms of them all."

Then the Captain drew his dagger and putting the long, glittering blade into the boy's hand taught him the points and guards of the broadsword while he conversed in broken snatches with his mother; and the three became so absorbed in one another's society that they did not observe how the evening had stolen on them until a loud knocking at the street door startled both grown members of the little party.

Kathlyn, white to the lips and trembling in every limb, rose to her feet and asked her kinsman feebly what she was to do.

"Put on a bold face and admit whoever it may be," said MacMahon in Gaelic. "But, remember, I have no further title than cousin even to thy husband himself."

"For shame, Evir," said Kathlyn, nettled in spite of her fear. "Dost entertain any fear of the good faith of my Walter?"

"No fear of mine own proper life," answered the Captain, speaking quickly but coolly. "But until such time as I deem fit, he must know nothing more of me than my mere relationship to thee. Do my bidding implicitly, Wench, for there is more than a man's mere life depends upon the observance of my secret—and now to the door with a stout heart."

The boy noticed that the Captain slipped the ruby ring off his finger whilst he was speaking, and as soon as his mother left the room he was still further surprised to observe him draw forth a pair of small pocket pistols from a slit in his buff-coat, and, after glancing at them for a moment, thrust them back into their hiding-place. Notwithstanding this startling precaution, the soldier continued to chat gaily with the boy during the few minutes his mother was absent, and when Kathlyn Dauntless returned to the little parlour, leaning on the arm of her husband, the Captain put down Harry from his knee and rose to his feet with a smile which would have become a courtier who had been unexpectedly gratified by some mark of Royal favour. Kathlyn presented her husband to the Captain with a strained air of gaiety in order to conceal her recent alarm; but the soldier, far from showing any trace of discomposure, addressed Walter Dauntless with such courtly grace as to instantly win the good opinion of that astute man of the world.

When he learned that MacMahon purposed remaining in London for some weeks, Dauntless, in the hospitable fashion of his countrymen, offered him a home in Fetter Lane. MacMahon accepted this offer with a charming air of mingled grace and gratitude, and that night transferred his modest luggage to his kinswoman's luxurious little house, where he took up his abode for a couple of weeks. On parting he declared his visit had proved the happiest period of his life, but it must be confessed that if the Captain's sojourn in Fetter Lane had been a pleasant experience to him, it most certainly did not prove a like pleasure either to his host or hostess.

His presence was a continual reminder to Kathlyn that she was acting with a certain amount of duplicity towards her husband, for the first time in her simple, truthful life. In addition to this uncomfortable sensation the Captain nearly drove her distracted with secret fears on his account, for, far from staying within doors and avoiding publicity, the big, loud-voiced man was in the habit of swaggering in and out of the house at all hours of the day with his great plumed hat flapping on his boldly carried head and his long sword clicking aggressively against his heel as if to challenge the attention of every passer-by. Nor was it long before his host learned to his intense dismay what a dangerous companion accompanied him about in the person of his guest; for the Captain was not only in the habit of speaking loudly and in public concerning matters which wise men discussed in whispers and within doors, but seemed positively anxious to introduce such perilous subjects whenever he met any of the few Irish friends of his host who formed a small circle of their own in the Temple. Although Walter Dauntless was one of the most courteous of men, he was also one of the most circumspect of courtiers, and after several ineffectual hints as to the danger of expressing such views he at length told the Captain of his dislike to these discussions in such plain terms that they undoubtedly led to the abrupt departure of his guest.

They were returning one evening from Lincoln's Inn, where MacMahon had expressed himself more forcibly than heretofore, when Dauntless took occasion to speak to him of the prudence of keeping his mouth shut on such subjects in the City of London.

"Why should I?" asked the Captain, airily. "Is it because yon wizened little mechanic views my Spanish rosette with a jaundiced eye that I am to hold my tongue unless I speak of naught but what is pleasing to such base paltry knaves? Troth, as long as speech is free and the Yellow and Red of Castile is welcome in England, I see no harm in speaking of what all Europe gossips about."

"By all means," answered Dauntless, hastily. "But you spoke of the likelihood of foreign arms appearing ere long in Ireland, and speeches of that currency smack too much of treason to be pleasing either to Londoner's ears or mine."

"Treason?" echoed MacMahon, with a loud laugh. "What mighty treason is it to say that your fat-brained old King over-reached himself in craft when he sent the broken Irish clans abroad for the purpose of getting rid of them? Why, any man with as much wit as would fit on a dagger's point might have foreseen that he was but sowing dragon's teeth in France and Spain which would ere long sprout up armed men in Ireland, for the whole world is well aware that the men of Ulster are not that lady-hearted, soft-palmed breed who are wont to bear exile abroad on their own account or injustice done their kinsfolk at home."

"It is no great matter to me whether they stay abroad or come home and be hanged," said Dauntless, contemptuously. "Their doings are nothing to me; but let me tell you frankly, Master MacMahon, that the one thing I do desire above all others is a blissful ignorance of them and their doings."

"What?" said the Captain, with a sidelong but watchful glance. "Hath wrong and persecution no power to touch thee? Hath this so-called Plantation of the North not stung thy sense of patriotism to the quick? Hast not been moved by this shameless act of unvisored robbery which all the world — yea, and many true-hearted men in this very land of England itself decry as an act of hellish cruelty and injustice? Fie, fie, Mr. Dauntless, for that scornful wagging of thy head! What value canst thou set upon thy country when thou canst afford to smile so wantonly upon her sufferings and persecution?"

"I do not care a single maravedi for my country," answered his companion, coolly, "but I do confess some love for my wife and child, and moreover have some foolish regard for my own life, which, notwithstanding its low value, is nonetheless mine own. Wherefore, give me leave to tell thee, Master MacMahon, that all this touch paper stuff concerning Ireland and foreign schemes is most distasteful to mine ears, and on that account let me beg thee from henceforward not to introduce such matters again."

The Captain bowed stiffly and assured his host he would not offend again, but notwithstanding his obvious discomfiture he appeared more cheerful than usual at the supper table that evening. The next day, however, he made some halting excuse for the termination of his visit, which was accepted by his host with scarcely concealed satisfaction and by his kinswoman with a feeling which nearly approached relief, and the only person in Fetter Lane who really regretted the departure of the big soldier was Master Harry, who, deprived of so entertaining a teacher before he had completely mastered the broadsword exercise, wept bitterly for nearly two days after he had gone.

III

THREE years passed before the Captain again visited Fetter Lane, and he ought to have been prepared to have encountered changes there as elsewhere, yet it was quite evident to Kathlyn, who opened the door for him, that he was much more startled by her appearance than she was by his.

The sudden apparition of her big kinsman was a surprise for her, but the robe of mourning black wherein she was clad was a much greater shock to him, for he saw at a glance that the Visitor Who Will not be Denied had been to and departed from the little house in Fetter Lane during his absence.

MacMahon held out his arms silently to Kathlyn, and with a little sob she dropped into them like a wounded bird and burst into a fit of weeping. He drew her gently within doors, where he was confronted by little Harry, also dressed in deep mourning, and at sight of him MacMahon's face lighted up for a moment and he uttered an ejaculation which sounded uncommonly like an expression of thankful relief. Embracing the boy tenderly with one strong arm and his mother with the other, he half carried them both into the little parlour, where he placed the sobbing woman in one chair and sat down himself in another with the boy upon his knee; then by degrees he learned from his afflicted kinswoman the story of her last and greatest sorrow.

Walter Dauntless, the careless, self-loving man of pleasure and fashion, was dead, — having left this world with a suddenness which was no doubt as great an inconvenience to himself as it was a grief to his widow.

Some six months before the Captain's arrival, the plague made one of its irregularly timed visits to London, and on its appearance Dauntless shut up his house and hurried off his wife and child into the country. He refused to accompany them on the plea of having to attend to numerous city engagements — many anything but creditable to his memory, but wherewith his wife, fortunately for her own peace of mind, never became acquainted. As soon as he got rid of his family ties, he went back to his bachelor rooms and ways in Lincoln's Inn. He enjoyed himself so thoroughly with his friends in London that he was, no doubt, extremely provoked at being obliged to part company with them after one short, joyous week; but that stern Sheriff, Death, who has as little consideration for the feelings of the happy as the miserable, sent his then most trusty Bailiff, the Plague, with a writ of attachment for the body of the gay profligate, and this service was performed with such startling promptitude that Walter Dauntless was a horrible swollen corpse six hours afterwards and was festering in his grave for a week before his horrified widow was acquainted with the intelligence of his being even indisposed.

Although the Captain was greatly moved by this recital, he was much more concerned on account of his kinswoman; for in addition to her six months' old sorrow, passed in a city which she abhorred and a house full of depressing memories, he learned she had been left an additional legacy of trouble in the tangled state of her late husband's affairs.

The poor soul had set herself the task of staying in London to personally supervise their settlement as a sacred duty owing to her boy, but as each day had seemed to evolve some fresh complication in their unravelment, she had sunk into such a state of broken-hearted despondency that MacMahon clearly foresaw unless she were speedily hurried away from her depressing surroundings, it would not be long before she joined her husband in Saint Dunstan's Churchyard.

Her kinsman volunteered to interview Mr. Quillett, the lawyer entrusted with the settlement of her husband's affairs, whereupon she thankfully accepted his offer and received a new lease of vitality from his assurances of being able to bring these long-delayed matters to an instant and satisfactory conclusion. Her face brightened and her heart beat with fresh hope as he assured her, with many stamps of his heavily booted feet and much minatory wagging of his bull head, of the way he would make the rascal stir himself; and when she had duly armed him with a power of attorney and sent him off to Lincoln's Inn in search of Mr. Quillett, she sat down and cried happily over her boy in the belief that her troubles were over.

In the meantime, the big soldier swaggered down to Mr.

Quillett's chambers in the Inns and, confronting that gentleman with little ceremony, slapped down his credentials as though they were a challenge and very bluntly demanded all the papers of his dead kinsman.

The lawyer, a nervous, studious little man, one of that species of forensic larvæ who never issue out of the musty cocoon of research which has enveloped them since they learned to read, was considerably disturbed by his big bullying client. He informed MacMahon nervously that he had nothing more than copies of the papers which were still in the chambers of Walter Dauntless, but showed considerable determination in his refusal to accompany him thither when his visitor expressed a desire to inspect the originals. He, however, offered complete possession of the chambers and their contents in return for a proper quittance, and exhibited a certain amount of decorous joy when the Captain made it out and informed him of his intention of taking over the uncontrolled management of the dead man's affairs from that forward.

As soon as MacMahon obtained the keys of the defunct lawyer, he sallied out majestically across the Square and, having ascended two flights of dusty stairs near the Gate Way in Chancery Lane, stopped at the chambers of Walter Dauntless and unlocked the door. He stood at the threshold for some minutes without venturing to enter, but it was a more generous feeling than the mere selfish dread of infection which held him spellbound, for there was an overwhelming sense of sudden death and desertion about everything in the apartment which would certainly have depressed if not terrified a bolder heart than his.

There on the table, which was littered with several packs of cards, dice-boxes, half-emptied flagons of wine and half-filled drinking glasses, lay the hat and sword of Walter Dauntless, just as he must have last laid them down. Everything lay as it had been left in that last merrymaking. No living creature had ventured to touch a single article in the room since its late owner had been carried out to the grave, except that, amidst the dust of six months which powdered everything, an enterprising spider had spun her web from the tip of the plume in the dead man's hat to the hilt of his rapier as if in a silver funeral knot. A chair, over the back of which was draped a cloak as though the wearer had just tossed it down, a handful of brown withered leaves in a bowl which had once been filled with roses, a shattered lute upon the ground, a music book, opened at a merry bacchanalian song, and propped up against a tarnished silver cullis bowl and a hundred other little indications of vanished ownership, one by one claimed the sorrowful attention of the big Irishman and held him in a trance of melancholy thought.

He collected his resolution with an effort, crossed himself devoutly and entering the chamber with a firm step proceeded into an inner room, which, from the appearance of the still disordered bed, the few empty physic bottles and a cup containing some half-dried, noxious-looking compound, was evidently the place where its late owner had expired. Here, in a corner, he perceived an iron chest which he instinctively felt was the strong box of Walter Dauntless; and on trying the lock with half a dozen of the keys came on one that opened it and found that his surmise was correct.

It contained neither plate nor specie, but was brimful with papers which he carefully removed into the outer room and, having cleared a space for them among the dice-boxes, cards, and other litter, he sat down to investigate their contents.

He was not long engaged in this work before he learned that the widow had far underestimated the confused condition of her husband's estate. Every available asset appeared to have been encumbered for some time past with charges and mortgages. Every negotiable source of income seemed to have been tapped and drained in turn by the dead profligate; and the Captain noted with a lowering brow that all the debts, without exception, owed their origin to the gaming table.

The light was waning in the room, and the Curfew bell was ringing in the Square before he had succeeded in doing more than making out a tabulated list of these debts and credits; and, with a heavy heart, he abandoned his labours for that day. Next morning at an early hour, he resumed his self-appointed task in Lincoln's Inn, and, on completing it by midday, found that his fears were but too well founded.

He had hoped, if not confidently expected, to have found that his kinswoman had been well provided for: but when he struck a balance between all that the dead man owed and the little owing to his widow, MacMahon saw, to his intense consternation, that the most she could expect from the ruin of a once fair fortune was a pittance barely enough to live on.

He returned that evening to Fetter Lane utterly depressed, and it cost him a pang of inward pain to assume an unnatural gaiety in order to hide his unfortunate discovery from Kathlyn. When he left her next morning for the purpose of going to the Inns, he looked cheerful and spoke cheerily to her at parting, but in reality his eyes had much to do to wink back his tears, and his heart was swelling to bursting point as he thought of her helplessness and poverty.

Once more he read through the mortgages and bonds in the faint hope of coming upon some more favourable conclusion than his first perusal had led him to adopt; but he was obliged to acknowledge to himself that the ruin of the House of Dauntless was complete and irremediable. The very plate and pictures in the little Castle in Ireland were hypothecated for gaming debts and the estate itself had been saddled with a second mortgage.

"He might have spared *that*, at least," muttered the Captain, with a groan, "I thought the traditions and pride of his race would have forbade such profanation. But, alas, what trust is sacred to either the Drunkard or the Gambler?"

On the back of one of the copies of these mortgages were carelessly drafted some directions in the handwriting of the dead man, and as they appeared to be the protocol of a will the Captain read them through with a certain amount of mournful contempt. In addition to the settlement of his Irish estate upon his wife for her lifetime with the remainder in trust for his son, were many nugatory and futile legacies which MacMahon knew well utterly exceeded the entire assets of the gambler's estate.

"Poor, weak fool," said he, with a touch of querulous scorn, "from what source didst thou purpose to draw these airy gifts —was it some long looked for turn of luck, some eagerly calculated law of chance, or some desperate hazard at the gaming table whereat thou didst lose all?"

He was about to lay it down sadly among the other useless papers when his eyes were attracted by the date which headed it.

"Strange!" he muttered, knitting his brow with a thoughtful frown, "and yet it is so recent as to be scarcely eight months old. Dauntless, although a gambler and a reckless one at that, was by no means a fool where actual property was concerned, nor would he have been likely to have mentioned bequests which his estate was unable to make good unless he left some hidden hoard which either covers or exceeds these mortgages."

With the shadowy hope of discovering such a provision, he carefully examined not only the strong box, the hangings, the furniture, the boards, the wainscotting of the rooms, but the very books, which he opened and examined leaf by leaf, but in vain. Wearied and covered with dust, he gave up the search, and sweeping up the parchments in his arms carried them into the inner chamber, where he flung them into the chest and slammed down the lid with a gesture of disappointment and anger.

The heavy iron fell with a noise that rang through the deserted house like the report of a gun, and the violence wherewith he had closed it caused the lid to fly up a few inches, where it remained gaping open as if in an attempt to tell its well-guarded secret. The Captain braced one muscular knee upon the top of the lid in order to force it down sufficiently to lock the chest once more; but, failing to effect his purpose, he discovered that a couple of the rivets which bolted the inner to the outer shell of the lid had started, and a small white object, hitherto concealed in some secret recess, was protruding between the two sheets of metal in such a way as to hinder the lock from engaging in the catch.

He drew this object from its hiding-place and was considerably startled to find that it was a small, buckram-covered packet, clumsily sewn up with different-coloured threads as if by the unskilful hand of a man. He ripped off this envelope with his dagger and discovered an inner case of leather of similar clumsy workmanship, which he stripped off in turn and within it found a single sheet of parchment which he proceeded to unfold with trembling hands.

It was a bond, drawn up in set legal terms which testified to the fact that Master Richard Wiltonholme, described as a Gentleman entitled to bear arms, was formerly indebted to Master Walter Dauntless, Esquire, Barrister-at-Law, in the sum of Ten Thousand Pounds, Sterling, money of England, and the interest thereon at Five per Centum per Annum.

The Captain was so much astounded by this discovery that he was obliged to sit down, open-eyed and breathless, for some minutes, whilst the significance of his find slowly percolated through his thick head. He read and re-read the document twenty times over, as if he hoped to discover by that means its actual value; but, although it was drawn up in terse, clear terms, which left no doubt as to its purport, and was attested by the signatures of no less than four witnesses, there was nothing to indicate its being worth the parchment whereon it was written. The Captain was utterly ignorant of the name, residence, or condition of either the surety himself or any single one of the four witnesses; and as he sat staring helplessly at the little sheet of parchment which lay between his outspread elbows, he felt a dull sickening feeling of despair steal through him like a narcotic. As his eyes wandered stupidly away from the document for a moment, they rested vacantly upon the bunch of keys which lay on the table before him, and he was suddenly struck by the similarity between the handwriting in the document and that on the parchment tags attached to them. He uttered an exclamation in Gaelic, jumped to his feet, thrust the bond into his pouch, and rushing down stairs and across the court, as though running for his life, burst into the chambers of Master Quillett like an avalanche.

The lawyer, who was wedged into the angle formed by a half-opened folio of immense thickness, raised his head at this abrupt intrusion, and recognising his visitor with a cry of horror, dropped his book immediately and bounded into an inner room, the door of which he clapped to and bolted. The big Irishman hammered vigorously on the panels and demanded an interview which was unhesitatingly refused by the man of law, who added still further emphasis to his refusal by barricading the door with all the available furniture he could drag against it. MacMahon stormed and entreated by turns, but Mr. Quillett remained obdurate, and failing to bring about an interview face to face, the Captain endeavoured to obtain the information he so much needed by cajolery. However, the lawyer proved himself more than a match in cunning for the impetuous soldier, and utterly foiled him by strenuously denying all knowledge of Mr. Wiltonholme, his circumstances, address, occupation, or existence. Discomfited in this attempt, MacMahon next tried to obtain the addresses of the witnesses; but Quillett professed an equal ignorance of them too, and piteously besought his visitor to leave him in peace and not to bring infection and death to one who had never injured him.

This last speech furnished the Captain with a powerful lever to work upon his prisoner's feelings. He pulled over a chair beside the door, sat down and announced his intention of spending the remainder of his existence there unless the lawyer furnished him with the information he required. Mr. Quillett once more piteously assured him of his ignorance of the entity of Richard Wiltonholme, but eventually persuaded the Captain to raise the siege on supplying him with the addresses of three persons who, he cautiously informed him, might or might not be the persons he was in search of.

Outside in the Gate-house Square the Captain stopped beside the fountain and considered the names and addresses, noted in his pocket-book, for a few minutes in deep thought.

"Ha! Hum! Nathan Nott, Feather Merchant, Blackfriars," he muttered as he stroked his closely-clipped beard. "Neither thy name nor thy residence hath favour in mine eyes, friend Nott; for thy Christian name smacks of the second book of Samuel, thy sirname bespeaks closeness in the grain, whilst thy trade and residence savour too much of the Puritan. Thomas Fairweather, Ancient, in the King's Life Guards. No! I do not think I shall trouble the soldier. Ha! Phelim O'Neill, Knight, Barrister-at-Law, that name cries 'Ireland' as loudly as 'Farragh' in a skirmish, and being a countryman, he ought to be the easier to pump. Wherefore, Sir Phelim! I shall do myself the honour of calling on thee and getting what information I can without showing the cards I hold in my own hand." Whereupon the Captain put his tables in his pocket, cocked his hat with a self-satisfied look and swaggered off majestically to the Temple. He had little difficulty in finding the address he sought, and was about to tap on the door of one of the chambers in the outer Temple when it suddenly opened, and two gentlemen, one of whom was big, blustering, and over-dressed, and the other slender and plainly clad, appeared, and, on seeing the big, handsomely clad soldier, stopped short and regarded him with a look of polite enquiry.

IV

THE Captain took off his hat, gave it a flourish in the Spanish fashion, in order to readjust its plume of feathers, and replaced it on his head; then, with a stately bow and a dip of his rapier hilt, he asked if he had the honour of addressing Master O'Neill.

"We are two poor cadets of that ancient and honourable family," said the younger gentleman, touching his beaver politely. "And we shall be glad to know in what manner we can serve you."

"My business is with Sir Phelim O'Neill," said MacMahon, glancing from one to the other interrogatively, "but as I have not the honour of knowing him, might I ask which of you two gentlemen is he?"

"I bear that name for want of a better," said the over-dressed gallant, playing with the strands of a thin gold chain linked here and there with emeralds and pearls, which hung round his thick throat like a daisy chain round the neck of a bull. "If there is any way in which I can be of use to you, I pray you command me as you would your own servant."

"My name is MacMahon, — a poor soldier in the service of Spain," said the Captain, in a hesitating manner. "And although I am unknown to you, I am a near relation of one who, I believe, was not wholly indifferent to your love. Wherefore I have taken the liberty of calling upon you in the hope that you would accord me the honour of appointing an hour when I might wait on you alone."

"You can claim it now if you will be so good as to walk into my poor chambers," said the exquisite, motioning him to enter with one hand whilst he extended the other to the slim young gentleman, who bowed politely to the soldier and descended the stair. "Adios! good Dan, Adios. Bear thyself with a sprightly favour and commend me to his Grace. Pray, Master MacMahon, walk into my poor lodgings, and use them as though they were your own. Ha! Cousin Daniel, one moment. I forgot to warn you, in case you should go to Westminster by water, to beware of Tom Whistle's wherry, for the villain's cushions are as greasy as a butcher boy's head, and I spoiled me a new cloak of maroon grain in his boat this day Tuesday it was a week — One moment, Master MacMahon! one moment more, I crave your indulgent patience. Cousin! Cousin Dan! I prithee forget not my commission to the goldsmith you wot of in Cheapside nor my messagè to the Duke, and so farewell, Dan! and may victory sit upon thy helmet like the raven on the crest of that rare Roman bully Corvinus."

During this disjointed speech, which was divided by hasty excursions to the head of the stairs and equally hasty returns to the Captain, Sir Phelim conducted his visitor by easy stages into a richly furnished apartment. He motioned MacMahon to a seat and, taking up a small perforated silver ball shaped something like a grenade, applied it to his own nose with an affected gesture and then sank languidly into a velvet-covered armchair. There was an embarrassing pause for a minute, during which the two men furtively regarded one another; and then the Captain, in the confidence of his ability to pump so shallow a vessel, plunged straight into the matter he was interested in.

But the Courtier, notwithstanding his affectation and apparent stupidity, baffled every attempt to extract information as effectually as the lawyer had previously done, and the Captain (who was unwilling to display his great trump card for fear the other should depreciate its value) began to think he had entered on a duel of wit with one who was either absolutely deficient of ordinary intelligence or who was vastly his superior in cunning.

"My good Sir," said the Knight, with a wave of his right hand, which was done as much for the purpose of adjusting a cloud of cobweb-like lace at his wrist as for displaying the splendid rings upon his fingers, "I do most sincerely assure you I have no knowledge of any bond such as you mention, for, although my poor late friend often honoured me with his company, he never had sufficient trust in my ability to make me a confidant in business transactions."

"But I understand," said MacMahon, "that your name was one of the witnesses to this document."

"As for my poor name," answered the Knight, with a wan smile, "that has been on so many pieces of paper already that if I had but a groat for each signature, by Saint Iago! I should be a richer man than the King himself. I pray you, Master MacMahon, have a glass of this Xeres wine, which some of my friends have assured me is indifferent good."

"I thank you," said the Captain, hastily, for he was anxious to get back once more to the subject nearest his heart, "but as I never drink wine — "

"A most remarkable admission in a soldier," said the Knight, with a wave of his left hand for the purpose of drawing attention to the large diamond which dangled from a bracelet round his wrist. "Then, if you will not drink, I pray you do me the honour of partaking of some of these apricocks which I have specially brought from Saint Helen's every week."

"I thank you again," said the Captain, "but the matter to which I have referred hath so pressing a claim upon my rest that it hath left little room for such trifles as eating and drinking. Wherefore I — "

"Now permit me to say, my dear Sir," said the other, with a gesture wherein polite horror and affected solicitude were blended in a grotesque manner, "that such matters as eating and drinking are of far greater moment to our poor souls and the still poorer frames wherein they are encasketed than the wearying concerns of makings and spendings; for, look you, Sir Captain, as there was never a soldier who could fight his best on an empty stomach, so was there never another man, of any condition in life, who was fit to attend to any matter of moment unless he was in the habit of taking good care of his body for his soul's sake."

As if to give assurance to his belief in this doctrine, the Knight very daintily ate two or three of the apricots and dropped the stones deliberately one by one on a small silver salver on the table, whilst the Captain mopped his forehead and boiled inwardly with vexation.

"Surely, Sir Phelim," said he, appealingly, "surely a bond drawn up for so large an amount, in the presence of so many witnesses and executed within so short a period as seven months ago must have left some shadow of memory in the mind of a barrister like yourself."

"True! True! I have been called to the Bar," said the

Knight, spreading his jewelled hands abroad as if to deprecate some folly of his youth which his visitor had charged him with. "True! I am, as you yourself very justly say, a member of the Inns of Court, but, I assure you, I do not practise the profession. I protest, Master MacMahon, I am but a poor simple gentleman who hath the whim, or the weakness, or whatever you may be pleased to term it, of liking to inn here in this abode of learned men with whom I, alas! have nothing further in common—"

The Captain bowed and looked as if he fully believed this statement, but nevertheless maintained a discreet silence while Sir Phelim continued, "As to this bond or writ, or whatever it is to which you refer—I regret exceedingly my forgetfulness of ever having seen such a deed either made over to or received from my poor late friend as I could not recall to memory, although offered a prince's guerdon for the act, a single one of the few legal instruments I have had to do with during this time past—I regret this inability all the more, since you appear so anxious to know about this particular bond; but what can I do, Master MacMahon? my poor silly memory is a Lethe, a perfect Lethe, and its condition must plead my apologies for not being able to serve you in this matter."

Having delivered this polite and non-committal speech, the Knight selected another apricot with an air of nice discrimination, and rose as if to hint that the interview was over; but the Captain rose, too, and with a face ruby red with excitement and baffled anger produced the precious bond and laid it on the table with a trembling hand.

"Surely, Sir Phelim," said he, choking in his anxiety, "you will not deny your signature, if, as I am creditably informed, this is your own handwriting."

In an instant all the listless affectation disappeared from Sir Phelim like the vapour of one's breath from a mirror in summer-time. The apricot dropped from his hand just as he was about to pop it into his mouth, he rapped down the silver pouncet box on the table, and regarded the red and excited face of the Captain with a look of sharp intelligence and suspicion.

"I do not deny mine own handwriting, Master MacMahon," said he, in a harsh, metallic voice; "but may I ask you in the fiend's name why you come here asking questions about private bonds, given by one friend to another, whilst you yourself not only know of them as well as I do, but carry them in your pocket?"

"Because," said the Captain, with a shamefaced look, "I was acting not for myself but for my kinswoman, Mistress Kathlyn Dauntless, and feared to tell you, who might be an interested party in the concerns of the surety, that I had found this document among the papers of her husband. I wish to find out the real value of this bond before I acquaint her with its existence; and now that I have truly stated the reasons why I was unwilling to show you the bond at first, I hope you will act straightforwardly with me, and tell me truly what you know of the condition of Master Wiltonholme."

"A very simple and candid statement," remarked O'Neill, coolly, "which I have no doubt is founded on truth. As for the bond, I have tolerable eyesight, and can see for myself that you have that in your possession; but how am I to know, Master MacMahon, that you are acting in the best interests of Walter Dauntless and his widow?"

The Captain looked him fixedly in the face for a moment or two in some hesitation, then he breathed one word spoken in Latin into the other's ear, and traced a sign upon the table with the forefinger of his right hand, whereupon the courtier started violently and changed colour.

"My Lord," said he, with a respectful bow, "you can command me in what fashion you will."

"Then tell me, Sir Phelim," said MacMahon, anxiously, "is this bond so much money, or is it but a folio sheet of idle words, fine writing, and bright sealing-wax? Answer me truly, Sir Phelim, as you must some day answer the widow at a higher tribunal than the King's Bench,—is it worth its face value or not?"

"That must be as you yourself shall steer the ship," answered the Knight, shrewdly; "for the young gentleman who signed that bond, in his present state of fortune, would not fetch more than the value of the clothes on his tall person if you shut him up in the Counter to-morrow."

"Then it is a worthless promise," cried the Captain, with a frown and a groan.

"Why, yes and no," said O'Neill. "If you wait your time, it will be worth its full value on the death of a certain old gentleman down in Kent. But if you put young Wiltonholme to the touch o' the Law before that time comes, you will not only destroy all hope of his ever coming into what he is but heir to on good behaviour, but you will also kill at the same stroke your goose with the golden egg."

"Is the youth of such good family and expectations, then?" asked the Captain, with a meditative look.

"What, have you not heard of Sir Jonah Wiltonholme of Strood?" asked Sir Phelim, with a stare. The Captain shook his head. "He is the wealthiest and bitterest Puritan in England," continued O'Neill, "and is uncle to this young springald Dick Wiltonholme, whose bond you hold. "The old gentleman is one of those crabbed beings who consider themselves specially endowed with a charter from their Maker for the purpose of making every one miserable who prefers to live merrily and look jollily. His house in Kent is a veritable city of refuge for all the sour bigots who think as he doth, and he hath so many of these gloomy friends and lovers to whom he is like to leave marks of his affection, that, by my faith, his rakehelly young nephew would be likely to have but a small portion in his will, in case he should learn how he has been anticipating his fortune."

"I presume the young gentleman is an unconscionable gambler and a spendthrift," said MacMahon. Sir Phelim laughed easily and shrugged his shoulders in a deprecating manner.

"He is as fond of the bones and pasteboards as another," he replied, "but whether he deserves so hard a character as you give him is more than I can say."

"And I dare say," continued the Captain, thoughtfully, "that this bond was given for some gambling transaction wherein he stood indebted to Walter Dauntless. Can you tell me if this is so, Sir Phelim?"

"That, my Lord, is a question which I am unable to answer," replied the knight. "But as the young squire is one of those who prefer the Song of 'Merry Companions All' to the Hundredth Psalm, you may rest assured he did not borrow a sum like that in order to build a church with it. There is one thing certain, however, and that is that Richard Wiltonholme will neither repudiate nor endeavour to shuffle out of the debt, for he owes the head upon his shoulders to Walter Dauntless, who saved him from smelling the block when Scots Jamie sat upon the throne. He hath other reasons also to feel grateful to the memory of Walter; besides, to do the young fellow justice, he is as straight and honourable a youth as you might wish to meet withal; and make him or break him, I will warrant him to stand by his word, whether the bond be for a debt of honour or a mere matter of business."

After asking a few more questions, the answers to which afforded little more information to the Captain, he took his leave of Sir Phelim and walked back dejectedly to Lincoln's Inn, where he sat for some time immersed in profound thought.

"The time is not yet come to put the matter to the essay," he muttered slowly, "and, even if it were, I doubt very much if Kathlyn would accept so large a sum derived from such a questionable source. If thou wert rich and well to do, Kate, I would not hesitate to tell thee of my find and let thee take or leave it as thou wert pleased, but thy lot is too beggarly to permit me to leave the matter at the chance disposal of a simple, narrow-minded soul like thyself; wherefore, Kathlyn, I must practise on thee somewhat. Yes, come what will, I shall keep this scrap of parchment from thee until I can turn it into its proper equivalent in gold pieces, and in the meantime shall keep as affectionate a watch over this young Kentish Squire as he doth over his proper life."

That evening was a period of severe trial to the Captain when he revealed to Kathlyn Dauntless the true condition of her fortune. She had fondly believed, up to that moment of disillusion, that she held a considerable property in trust for her child, and her kinsman's clumsily broken story of ruin filled her with so much anguish that the Captain had great difficulty in restraining his inclination to blurt out the whole of his secret. A dread that she might enquire too closely into the nature of the bond and his inability to turn it into money just then, however, acted as a powerful gag upon his tongue; so he choked and fidgeted in his chair and furtively touched the precious document in his pocket from time to time, whilst his cousin wept over the vanished fortune of her boy.

Next day, however, Kathlyn Dauntless was quite herself again; and she faced her ordeal of poverty with so brave a heart, that her stout kinsman, who, worthy man, was wholly unversed in the ways of women and consequently unaware of their superior fortitude in encountering financial misfortune, was completely stricken dumb with amazement. She was almost cheerful during the time she was completing the last few preparations for her departure to Ireland, and the only moment she faltered was on the summer evening when she bade farewell to the Captain, below London Bridge.

As she and Harry stood on the lofty poop of the ship which dropped slowly down the river with the tide, she alternately pressed her kerchief to her eyes and waved it to her kinsman in the wherry astern. But when the ship's main course, which up to then had been flapping lazily against the mast, slowly swelled out before the evening breeze and the Captain stood up solemnly, hat in hand, in the wherry, which the ship soon left astern, she leaned up against the stem of the great gilt poop-lantern and sobbed as if her heart would break, and Harry, who did not exactly know why, cried lustily with her for company's sake.

The last view they had of London was the dark shadow of the Tower which loomed sullenly up through the river fog on their left. It seemed to Kathlyn Dauntless to be some vast monster that rose up in the evening mist to remind her of her father, lying in his narrow grave in the Tower Chapel, and she thought of the long, sad years they had mingled their sighs and tears within those gloomy walls.

Once more her tears flowed like rain; but there was balm mingled with their saltiness this time. She caught her boy tightly to her swelling bosom and pointed to the four-peaked shadow of the White Tower.

"Look, Harry! Look, child!" she cried. "There goes the last of London town. Note it well, my boy, note it for the last time, for, please God, we shall never look upon its walls again."

V

THE voyage of Kathlyn was uneventful, for the weather was fine and England was then at peace with all the world; so there is nothing more to be said of her nine days' sea-journey round the coast and up the Irish Sea than its being one of the usual tedious passages of the time. But it would be a harder task to describe the feelings of the poor exile when she caught sight of the mountains of her beloved land on the morning whereon the ship skimmed merrily over the blue waters of Dublin Bay.

She had come on deck at an early hour when the first shout of the watch announced that Ben Edair and Ireland lay on the lea; and she stood on the poop for more than an hour without uttering a word, with one arm leaning on the quarter rail and the other clasped round Harry, her heart brimming over with thankfulness, her eyes dimmed with tears, and her soul feasting itself greedily on the brown swelling hills and purple mountains that peeped up through the sea mist.

As soon as she landed, she took such steps as were necessary to obtain possession of her husband's ancestral estate. Although her own inclinations prompted her to return to the home of her childhood in the far North, she resolutely stifled her longings for the sake of her boy, and therefore established herself in the lonely little castle in the Dublin Mountains. She believed it was her duty to personally supervise the dilapidated estate in the Valley. The restoration of the shattered patrimony of her son claimed priority to all other considerations, and moreover she felt that one half of the dream of her simple life was already fulfilled. She was once more back in her native land, and the other half of her mission was now ready to be undertaken; namely, to teach her boy to love his country as fiercely as she did herself, and to train him up to do something for it when his time should come.

The Castle of Bearna Baeghail, if so small a building deserves the name of Castle, at that time consisted of the stout, square tower which the founder of the family had built so courageously, and several rambling buildings which had been added from time to time to the parent tower by its successive occupants. There was no outer rampart such as one finds in the noble residential castles of England or the great military fortresses of Trim, Limerick, or Carrickfergus; but there was a strong, high wall, known in Ireland as a Bawn, adjoining the tower, which afforded a secure place wherein to collect the flocks and herds at night. This enclosure was a very necessary adjunct on account of the neighbouring marauders of the Wicklow Mountains and the scarcely less lawless riders of the Pale; for the former were accustomed to look upon the cattle of the Sassenach as a blessed provision of Providence for their special benefit, and the latter had scarcely less scruples in lifting the cattle of their fellow Palesmen with whom they did not happen to be on visiting terms. A strong iron clenched door, which was in turn protected by a heavy movable grate, afforded the only entrance to the tower, and as all the surrounding outbuildings communicated with this refuge, the tower in itself formed the key and citadel of the little fortress.

In this small but strong dwelling the widow took up her residence, and assuming the double duty of Châtelaine of Bearna Baeghail and Bailiff of Shanganagh, set to work to restore the long-deserted rooms and equally neglected farm surrounding the Castle. The improvement of the estate and the reduction of the outstanding mortgage upon it were heavy loads upon her peace; and to enable her to carry on the fight with poverty which she was waging on her son's behalf, she kept a meagre table and a small retinue for some years.

The only garrison the little fortress boasted of was a stout old soldier named George Ledwidge, who acted as butler, reeve, and warden; his daughter Maureen, a stout, comely little damsel of fifteen, who was cook and maid to Kathlyn; and a semi-idiotic youth named Con MacGauran. This last person, who, though very nearly as big as an ox, was as cowardly as a child of five, acted as herdsman and general drudge to Maureen and had a double claim upon the protection of Kathlyn. In the first place, he was a member of one of the septs which help to swell the great family of Clan Colla,—in itself a strong bond on the heart of his mistress,—and, secondly, the circumstances of his birth and misfortune were particularly melancholy.

Some twenty years before Kathlyn took up her abode in Shanganagh, Lord Deputy Falkland sent a party of his soldiers into Ulster for the purpose of clearing out some of the Clans in order to make room for the first consignment of the lately established planters. Amongst the many other wretched creatures whom they flung out into the bitterness of a winter night was a poor woman then on the eve of her confinement, and the barbarity with which she was treated was the immediate cause of her own death and the idiotcy of the male child to whom she gave premature birth. His poor useless life, unfortunately for himself, was preserved by some of the other unhappy outcasts, amongst whom he grew up into a great, powerful, silly creature; and as soon as he attained a man's stature and strength, he stole away from the kind-hearted wretches who reared him up, and, after the manner of so many of his kind, tramped aimlessly through the country until chance led his footsteps to Bearna Baeghail, where the pitying Kathlyn established him as a permanent retainer.

Notwithstanding his infirmity, the poor fellow made himself useful in many ways besides herding the small drove of cattle which it was his duty to look after; and, though it was very difficult to make him understand the most ordinary communication, yet once it had been impressed on his weak mind by dint of repeated commands, he never forgot an injunction, which peculiarity, although in some ways a gleaming virtue, was nevertheless the cause of considerable embarrassment on some occasions. For instance, he had been duly impressed with the necessity of driving into the bawn all cattle on the approach of any suspicious-looking persons; but although this in itself was a prudent precaution, the advent of any chance visitor to Bearna Baeghail was invariably heralded by the hurried arrival of the widow's score of cows, followed by Con himself crying out with all the strength of his cavernous lungs that "de O'Tooles or de Sassenach Soldiers was come upon us."

As visitors of any kind were rare, such mistakes of poor Con did not often cause consternation in the little household; yet Bearna Baeghail was by no means out of the track of danger, even in that time, and still continued to justify its title; inasmuch as no fewer than five marauding parties passed the little fortalice during the first year in which Kathlyn had taken up her residence there. On one of these occasions — it was in the still, dead silence of a November night — the raiders approached so close to the walls that for a long anxious minute stout old Ledwidge, who was standing arquebuse in hand on one side of a loop-hole, and Kathlyn, who was leaning against it at the other side with Harry beside her, thought that their last hour was come.

Never could Harry forget that incident of his early childhood. Never could he forget the deep silence, which was broken only by the low growl of their big deer-hound and the smothered whimpering of the idiot, who crouched trembling like a sick animal at the bottom of the winding stairs. Never could he forget the darkness and loneliness throughout the building (for all the lights had been extinguished at the first alarm), nor the red glow of the arquebuse-match that lit up the grim, worn face of old George Ledwidge, scowling out into the darkness, nor the white countenance of his mother turned upwards to the black sky, — all, all, were indelibly stamped upon his mind. Recollection would bring back to him vividly the sound of the soft but heavy tread of the raiders as they passed on over the wet heather with an occasional clank of arms or a smothered laugh or remark in Gaelic; and then he would close his eyes and seem to see again the sickly winter moon as it waded out feebly through the watery clouds and shewed the mountaineers passing along with a faint shimmering of spear-heads and a few red sparks dotted among them that marked the lighted matches of their snaphaunce men.

On another occasion, a party of Lord Wentworth's buff-coated soldiers, returning from a sudden dash into the territory of the O'Tooles, knocked at the door in the early grey of the morning and imperiously demanded meat for themselves and fodder for their horses.

Kathlyn was very unwilling to receive such guests, but she dared not exhibit any symptoms of dissatisfaction at their visit, and accordingly laid all the slender resources of the Castle at their disposal with the best grace she could assume. They had evidently been engaged in hot work, inasmuch as several of them were wounded, and though they drove back no prey of cattle, dragged with them a score of fierce and sullen-looking captives secured with thongs to their stirrup-irons. Amongst the prisoners, who had been left outside in the bawn under the lax charge of a tired and hungry trooper, was a young freebooter, whose handsome countenance bore some trifling likeness to Harry; and on account of this fancied resemblance to her boy, Kathlyn resolved to aid him in a dash for his life. She contrived to drop a knife into the folds of his mantle when the sentinel's back was turned; and she experienced a greater sensation of pleasure from the sharp, swift look of silent gratitude which the youth shot at her from under his shaggy brows than from all the graceful compliments paid to her during her sojourn at the Court of England.

Waiting his opportunity until the hungry trooper had ventured somewhat nearer to the kitchen door than the limit of his beat warranted, the boy suddenly cut through the leather thong which bound him and slipped out of his mantle as a serpent casts his skin. Then, clad only in his saffron-dyed shirt and striped truis, he dived under the bellies of the horses next him, scrambled over the wall of the bawn like a mountain cat, and disappeared amid the heather as suddenly as if the earth had swallowed him up. As his fellow-prisoners were the only persons who witnessed his escape and the sentinel was unconscious of being one prisoner short, Kathlyn escaped the serious consequences which would have undoubtedly visited her if she had been detected in this act of Quixotic chivalry; so the troopers paid her some rough compliments on parting and resumed their march, utterly unconscious of the trick which their hostess had played upon them.

Such instances were of common occurrence in the Dublin Mountains during the early period of the reign of King Charles, and serve to shew how affairs then stood in Ireland; yet, notwithstanding the lawless condition of the Pale at that time, the property of the widow was unmolested by both sides even in the midst of such perils. The Palesmen, with a chivalry which was as remarkable a characteristic of their rude nature as their unscrupulous methods of raising money and provender, had an understanding amongst themselves that any attempt upon the kine or Castle of Bearna Baeghail would be requited by the remainder as a personal affront; while the Mountaineers, perhaps on account of her well-known lofty birth and helpless condition, or on account of the many acts of kindness which she shewed to the wandering Harpers of the Mountains, also preserved an inviolable respect for her property.

I ought perhaps to mention one solitary exception.

One of Maureen's petticoats, which had been hung out to dry on a neighbouring hedge and forgotten during the night, excited the cupidity of a boy who accompanied one of these marauding expeditions, and was carried off in triumph. Even this insignificant booty was restored next day by the culprit, in propriâ personâ, who arrived in charge of a wild-looking gentleman in a rusty breastplate and morion. The latter presented the offender to Kathlyn and intimated to her easily that as the Clan of the offender had decided upon handing him over to the Mistress of Bearna Baeghail for judgment, she might, if it would do her any satisfaction, hang him from the top of the Castle for the benefit of his morals and in reparation of the insult offered to her.

Kathlyn, however, hastily but decidedly refused to avail herself of this very kindly offer, and, having refreshed the two, dismissed them both with much good advice and a couple of warm plaids, whereby she increased the very high repute in which she already stood with the Mountaineers.

One evening, towards the middle of the fourth year in which the widow had taken up her residence in Bearna Baeghail, she received a visit from the Captain. He arrived in company with four stout peasants and a herd of fifty head of cattle, with which, he affirmed, he was travelling to the summer fair at New Ross. MacMahon informed his cousin, with a roguish twinkle in his eyes, that he had turned husbandman since their last meeting, yet Kathlyn, although sufficiently well acquainted with her kinsman's character to know that this rôle was an assumed one, was little prepared for the surprise he had in store for her.

He appeared to be greatly surprised and delighted by the appearance of Harry, — who by this time had developed into a fine, straight boy of fourteen, — and on being solemnly greeted by that young gentleman, vowed he would never have recognised him, but laughingly reproached him for having forgotten his old teacher of the broadsword exercise.

"No, Sir, I have not forgotten you," said the boy, with a

puzzled look, "I remember you quite well. You are Captain MacMahon, my mother's cousin, but you are so much changed."

"Changed, Harry?" said the Captain, visibly disconcerted, for there were a few wrinkles visible at the corners of his eyes and some grey streaks had lately become apparent in his beard. "Changed, boy; in what way am I changed?"

"Why, Sir," said Harry, with a wistful look at the frieze doublet and leathern small clothes of the Captain, "when I saw you last, you had such a brave hat with a Yellow and Scarlet riband in it, and a soldier's coat of gilded leather and a sword and dagger, and now—you are dressed like Tam Haggis, Sir Thomas Merryl's Scots farm bailiff; are you then no longer a soldier?"

"Prut! tut! Harry," said MacMahon, laughing. "It is not the coat that makes the soldier any more than the cowl maketh the monk. What though my coat be changed, the heart beneath it is the same; and in earnest of its beating as lovingly as ever towards thy mother and thyself, I have taken this opportunity of coming hither in order to prove my love for ye both."

Then the Captain, with a great amount of humming and circumlocution, explained to Kathlyn that he had discovered a debt due to her late husband which amounted to a considerable sum. It was a debt which had been owed for years, he said, and the debtor was, at the moment, unable to discharge his full liability to Mistress Dauntless; but as he was an honest man and was anxious to reduce it by as much as was in his power, he had begged the Captain to hand her £600 on account of the overdue interest and to assure her at the same time of his intention to repay the whole of his obligation ere long.

This communication threw Kathlyn into a wild state of astonishment and thankfulness. She had eked out a pinched existence for nearly four years on less than one third the amount of this sudden windfall, which in itself was but the interest on a sum too large for her simple mind to realise. To her tear-swimming eyes the heavens seemed to be raining down gold, and through this wondrous shower she pictured to herself a great and glowing future for Harry. With such immense wealth behind him, she thought, he might command the world. There was no power upon earth which could withstand the might of one owning such a fortune, no height so ambitious but he might aspire to climb; but in all this flashlight dream she assigned no place for herself, — it was all to be her boy's domain alone.

When she became calm enough to speak coherently, she plied her kinsman with a hundred disjointed queries as to the source, certainty, condition, and extent of this hitherto unsuspected fortune! and the Captain, who was sweating with fear lest she should suspect his secret, stammered, mumbled, and contradicted himself so freely that his manner would have assuredly aroused the suspicions of a more worldly person than the simple widow. Fortunately for the peace of the bluff Captain, she either anticipated his replies or paid little attention to them, and, when the full flood of her questions was exhausted and the current of her joy swept into a more temperate channel, he very gravely advised her not to buoy herself up with hopes, which, though fair and reasonable, were by no means certain.

He advised her to husband well the first instalment of her good fortune and recommended her to devote a third of it towards paying off some of the mortgage on the estate, to put by one third of it in view of Harry's education, and to expend the remainder upon improvements in the Castle and the introduction of more servants and comforts in her meagre household. Kathlyn very readily agreed to the first two proposals, but she obstinately opposed the last as an unnecessary outlay. One part of her kinsman's proposal found special favour with her, and that was her boy's resumption of his long-neglected studies; and accordingly a young theological student, who had been recommended by the Captain, arrived a month or two after this interview and took over the duty of instructing Master Harry Dauntless in all that was good for his mind and soul.

It would be hard to determine how far pupil or teacher was responsible for the little store of knowledge which Harry laid up during the five years his tutor remained in Bearna Baeghail. The master was a gentle, spiritless young man over whom a perpetual sadness hovered like a cloud, caused perhaps by his delicate health or a dim foreboding of his own bloody end (for he was hanged, drawn, and quartered at

Tyburn by Desborough in the first year of his priesthood). He was completely wanting in the firmness of character so necessary in a teacher, and, consequently, although himself a very well-read man, conveyed very little of his learning to his pupil, whom he permitted to range at his own sweet will. As for the boy himself, although by no means wanting in either intelligence or energy, he was one of those impatient spirits who are utterly unable to concentrate their thoughts on any subject which does not claim their interest on first sight. He was a voracious reader of books, or rather a hoverer over them, because he flew from subject to subject and page to page much in the fashion that a bee flies from flower to flower in order to sip the sweets which are hidden in them. Yet, to do his errant taste justice, he plunged into grave as well as pleasure-giving reading with equal interest, and among the various theological books of his tutor discovered one, written by Duvergier de Hauranne on the Jansenist theory concerning Freewill and Necessity, which he read through with the deepest interest and which made a powerful impression on his young mind.

But the boy's best teacher was Nature herself. The great lonely mountains amid which he loved to prowl, gun or rod in hand, and the sea, by whose border he wandered alone but never lonely, did more to develop in him a simple nobility of character and purity of mind than either books or teachers by themselves could ever have brought about.

The Mountains, with their perpetual calm and silence, in addition to inculcating habits of thought and contemplation, also fostered in him that spirit of freedom and independence which is the birthright of the mountaineer; whilst the Sea, which either sparkled azure and silver along the coast-line or came curling shoreward in black and leaden breakers, filled him with that spirit of self-reliance which is so dominant a feature in those who dwell by its borders.

Yet these good qualities were discounted by other traits due to the same surroundings which were far from a benefit to him in after life. His mountaineering life invested him with a haughty shyness towards strangers, and the evidences of the former greatness of his family which confronted him on every hill-top in the shape of Castles which no longer owned their sway, imparted a slight tinge of bitterness to a naturally sombre mind. Notwithstanding these defects, he was by no means an unlovable youth, and the few friends whom he had made by the time he had attained his twentieth year were in the habit of expressing an opinion amongst themselves that when Harry Dauntless was ground down and polished up by contact with the outer world, there was little doubt that he would develop into a very creditable member of those of his rank in life.

He was a straight, handsome, high-spirited youth, profoundly ignorant of the ways and almost unconscious of the existence of the world beyond the Valley. He was silent, active, and hardy as one of his neighbours the Wicklow freebooters, a dead shot with fowling-piece, musket, and pistol, an excellent horseman, and as full of the lore of the river, wood, and heather as a naturalist and gamekeeper combined. In short, he was one of a class of young Irish Squires who were as plentiful at that time as they are to-day, and, as I trust, shall continue to be two hundred years hence.

VI

About this period of his life Harry Dauntless entered wilfully on the first trouble of his existence by falling desperately in love; and by a not uncommon accident which often directs the affairs of young gentlemen in their first attack of that disorder, had fixed his affections on a young lady eminently unsuitable to him in age, disposition, and fortune.

She was the only daughter of old Sir Thomas Merryl, his near neighbour, who was the sole person of consequence with whom his mother and he were on terms of intimacy, and was therefore the first and only woman except his mother and Maureen, with whom he had exchanged over fifty words in his life. The young lady was about five years his senior and was moreover of an extremely lively and frivolous disposition. She had set her heart upon a life in the Court of England and had quite made up her mind at an early age that she would yield her pretty, blooming self to the first suitor who should promise her such a prospect. As Harry's nature was a perfect antithesis to her gay, butterfly one, she entertained nothing more than a good-natured and somewhat contemptuous friendship for her shy young admirer; and, without holding more serious sentiments herself or intending to awaken them in him, alternately petted and scolded the love-smitten boy, who day by day felt more assured that his future was indissolubly bound with that of Barbara Merryl.

Harry wore her picture round his neck, wrote very bad verses after the style of Sir Philip Sidney in her honour, and (not having the good sense to hide them from her) got heartily laughed at for his pains; but notwithstanding such discouragement, he was so completely in the thrall of his enchantress that he accepted her ridicule meekly, drank in her commendations greedily, obeyed her capricious commands eagerly, and, in a word, was as much in love as a healthy young man could very well be. Perhaps, unknown to himself, some strain of the craftiness of his old Norman ancestor may have tempered Harry's love; and there was no lack of unkind people in the Valley who whispered that the heiress of Carrickmines was sought by young Dauntless for the sole purpose of restoring once more to his family that portion of their ancient estate. But, if such thoughts were ever harboured in Harry's mind, the suspicion of such a scheme never for a moment entered the head of the good-natured old Knight, who entertained a genuine affection for the proud, quiet youth and very readily forgave and made light of his slightly pompous manner.

The old gentleman encouraged the frequent visits of the boy for the sake of the genuine pleasure he derived from his company. He was by no means a well-read man, but took a great delight in controversial debates with any one whom he considered worthy of his steel, and he therefore loved to draw Harry into an after-dinner argument over a bottle of sack every time he visited Carrickmines; whilst Harry, for his part, was always ready with the headlong ardour of youth and inexperience to attack or defend either side of a subject, provided it was one of the very many at which he had nibbled during his desultory course of study.

After the fashion of many imperfectly educated men, who accept as a token of erudition in others what is merely a superficial acquaintance with many subjects, the Knight, vastly impressed with the extent of Harry's reading, formed a very high opinion of his young neighbour's talents. He considered that a youth of such erudition and sound sense (for Harry invariably worsted the good old man, although he would never acknowledge his defeats) was one eminently fitted for public life; and, shortly after Harry's attaining his majority, the Knight suggested to him that he should seek one of the public offices which the recall of Strafford had left open.

His ideas exactly coincided with those of the young gentleman; and Sir Thomas, who happened to have some influence with the Earl of Ormond, applied for and very easily obtained for his young friend the Commission of Constable of the Barony, in which post he was accordingly installed, to the unspeakable gratification of himself and the satisfaction of Sir Thomas.

Not long after this event which so flattered Harry's youthful vanity, Kathlyn discovered through that instinct common to mothers that her son was in love, and, suspecting on whom his affections were set, was greatly shocked and startled.

Some time before, she had observed with a feeling of hidden disappointment that Harry displayed an increasing dislike to enter the calling to which she had devoted him in his early childhood. She had reluctantly sacrificed all his prospects as far as any of the learned professions were concerned in order that he might retain the faith of his family, and now her simple, narrow soul was racked in finding that after all her jealous care he snould be in love with an Englishwoman and a heretic.

Since the first instalment of the bond seven years before, the subsequent payments, though varying in amount and irregularly transmitted, were invariably brought in person by the Captain, and on the next visit of that bluff personage she instantly communicated to him her suspicions and tearfully asked his advice.

The Captain bit his lip and looked extremely vexed.

"There is only one thing to be done," said he, curtly; "and that is to get him away from the Valley and out of the influence of this girl, who, you tell me, is in every way unsuited to mate with him."

Kathlyn sighed heavily and reminded her cousin that Harry had long since displayed a decided aversion to enter the priesthood, and that all the learned professions were closed to him on account of his religion.

"I am in some degree to blame for not having spoken to you ere this concerning Harry's future," said the Captain, gravely. "But I trusted that a Monarch like ours, wedded to a Catholic Queen and himself the grandson of a Catholic Martyr, would have taken some of the burden off our shoulders ere now and thus permitted Harry, in common with many thousands of other well-born young men, to serve the State without offence to their religious belief or dishonour to themselves. However, all that hope is now gone by, for the King, poor soul, hath his hands too full with his rebel subjects to do more than wish us well; wherefore, I see no other employment for Harry save service under the Cardinal in France or the Spaniard in the Low Country, to which courses I am personally averse — unless — " here he paused, looked fixedly on the ground and then continued very slowly, "unless — the cruelties now being framed against the Faith here should drive men to do what the Scots have done across the sea; in which event Harry should find a cause wherein he might draw a worthy sword."

He regarded his kinswoman with a steady gaze that conveyed more than his mere words, and she returned his look with one of wakened intelligence. The blood of the old rebel, who had wrought such havoc among the gay soldiers of Essex in the Pass o' Plumes, leaped madly from her heart and throbbed in her neck and temples; her eyes flashed with the light of battle.

"The Old Cause?" she whispered in a low, tremulous tone. "Is it the Old, Holy Cause? If *That* should once more call for sword-blades and men to wield them, though he is my son, — my only son, — the pulse of my affections, and the sole joy of my eyes, I willingly devote him to its service, provided you can induce him to embrace it."

The Captain that evening very cautiously sounded Harry on the subject of taking service abroad, but the young gentleman gave a very decided refusal to fall in with any such suggestion. He declared he possessed no desire for military glory, and vowed that, even if he had, he certainly would never run the risk of being knocked on the head for the sake of a foreign prince whose sole love for Irish soldiers was summed up in the trite consideration that they were very cheap, very plentiful, and could be depended on to fight like devils.

Discomfited in this attack, MacMahon then artfully drifted on to the subject of the dearth of Catholic young ladies in the Valley. He deplored the temptations whereto young gentlemen of the true faith were exposed, whereby they were often entangled in the siren charms of fair heretics, spoke guardedly of poisonous berries so very, very fair without, so deadly foul within, and finally wound up what he himself complacently felt was a powerful argument, by dwelling with intense satisfaction on the unavoidable wretchedness which followed those who mated with others of a different religion.

Harry listened to this lay sermon with a scarcely repressed yawn. MacMahon himself felt quite assured that no sensible man could be otherwise than convinced by his reasoning; but the only effect it had on Harry Dauntless was to create a huge contempt for the meddling Captain and a firm resolution that he would offer his hand to Barbara Merryl immediately.

Accordingly, the next day after dinner, he mounted his horse and rode through the Bride's Glen to Carrickmines, where he arrived a couple of hours before sunset.

At the Castle lodge he encountered a horseman so vigorously engaged in abusing the old porter that he was unaware of his approach until his horse stirred restlessly and neighed a welcome to Harry's bay mare, whereupon the cavalier turned his head, and Harry recognised him with a curt nod as a certain Captain Hooter whom he had frequently met at the hospitable table of the old Knight.

This gentleman was one of that type of persons who, in their efforts to be agreeable to all above their own position in life, succeed in making themselves cordially detested by the majority with whom they come in contact. He was moreover possessed of an evil spirit that prompted him on all opportunities to pay compliments of the most fulsome description, which, being patently devoid of sincerity, were seldom taken for true metal except by such dull souls as the worthy old Sir Thomas Merryl. This genial creature had been formerly a buccaneer, or, as he more euphemistically put it, "had sailed in Spanish waters," and, perhaps, on account of the valuable experience he had gained in that pleasant trade, had been appointed an Assistant Commissioner to the Court of Forfeited Estates by the Lord Justice Parsons.

On recognising Harry, Captain Hooter stopped short in the steady stream of oaths which he was rattling down on the head of the old porter (for it was one of his pleasing idiosyncrasies to address all servants with a brutal rudeness that was in direct inverse ratio to the adulation which he paid to their masters) and a beaming smile broke over his wine-blotched face as suddenly as sunshine in the middle of a Spring shower.

"What! Master Dauntless, upon my soul," he cried with an assumed start of pleasurable surprise. "Ah, my dear young Sir, I protest that it requires the advent of such a one as yourself to console me for the disappointment which I have just experienced; for I have just learned how I missed our noble friend, Sir Thomas, by taking the shorter but more arduous route across the mountains from Dublin instead of having jogged comfortably hither by the high road whereon he travelled."

Somewhat disconcerted by this news, Harry asked the old porter if he knew Sir Thomas Merryl's destination, and if he could furnish him with his address; but Hooter, who could never resist the pleasure of hearing the music of his own voice, took upon himself to answer these queries.

"He set forth this morning at nine o' the clock," said he, with a knowing leer of familiarity, "for the purpose of joining his sweetly beautiful daughter in Dublin, which city, as perhaps you are aware, Master Dauntless, hath been illuminated with her goddess-like presence during the last fortnight. Sir Thomas inns at the sign of the 'Golden Fox' in James Street, in which den he is like to remain a week or two, and as we have both drawn a blank in his old cover, — ha! ha! ha! a poor conceit, but a ready one, — I suppose, Master Dauntless, that there is nothing more for us to do but e'en whistle off the hounds and shog home again."

The Commissioner claimed a share in his company towards Dublin, which companionship Harry would have very gladly declined if he could have done so without giving offence, as he bore no liking to the ex-buccaneer; but, as their roads were identical and as Hooter was moreover an esteemed friend of Sir Thomas, he could not very well refuse, so the two rode slowly along the bridle-path towards Bearna Baeghail.

As Harry was silent and preoccupied, his companion, who had talked incessantly from the moment of their meeting without eliciting more than monosyllables from him, concluded that the young man required some interesting topic to awaken his attention. Accordingly he plunged into a recital of many incidents connected with his former lucrative but precarious occupation which made his hearer's blood run cold.

Without observing the look of mingled disgust and horror which gradually spread over the face of his companion, the honest gentleman cheerfully recounted many incidents of hideous cruelty wherein he had taken a leading part, and then proceeded to lament the decay of the buccaneering industry, which he attributed to the degeneracy and harsh tendencies of the times.

"Alas!" said he, sorrowfully, "these are muling days wherein all enterprise is discouraged — There is no chance now for a young fellow of a sanguine temperament and a stout heart, for it is well known that if any gentleman were to hoist the Jolly Roger for a cruise in the South Seas and should by any misfortune fall in with a King's ship, he would be most certainly consigned to his own yard-arm by the very hands of those to whom he might reasonably look for sympathy and protection. Nor is this cramping of bold hearts confined to those who make the sea their profession, for we have instances ashore. Aye, even here in Ireland, Master Dauntless, where you may find a notable instance in the collapse of the late noble Earl of Strafford's attempt to prove the Crown's title to the Counties of Galway and Mayo. Ah! Master Dauntless, I tell you that that was a mighty project, worthy of the masterly brain which planned it, and would have been of immeasurable benefit to the commonwealth, but, look, Sir, how ill it ended. The land, which is of no use to the inhabitants, as they know not how to take care of it, is still lying fallow — hundreds of honest gentlemen of London and elsewhere are defrauded and disappointed — the noble Earl hath lost his head — and the entire business is fallen through, never, perhaps, to be revived again — Alack! alack! I tell you, Sir, that for my poor part I would not have taken £5000 for my share of the commission that would have been due to me in virtue of my office if that great stroke of statecraft had been consummated."

A sudden turn in the bridle-path which brought them in full view of Bearna Baeghail turned the current of his very rapid flow of language into another channel.

"Upon my sacred honour," he said, "a very fair and excellent dwelling, Master Dauntless, and pitched in the best possible position. I warrant you it was set up by one conversant with the art of war and the conduct of leaguers — Builded, I presume, by your late worthy father, whom I regret never having been so fortunate to have met?"

Harry very briefly informed him of the date and circumstances of its erection by his ancestor, Sans Peur.

"'Swounds!" said the Commissioner, in an ecstasy of admiration, "he must have been a rare bully, that same Sam Power." (Then he continued, utterly ignoring the scorn in Harry's face): "He must have been a rare good judge of pasture land, too, if I may judge by the fresh greenness of the grass beneath its walls. Why, Master Dauntless, I do protest I consider it better cattle meat than that of Carrickmines — Not that the lands there are not fair and sweet and all that a gentleman could desire, and speaking of Carrickmines, Mr. Dauntless, *there* is a chance for a strapping gallant like you; the two estates march side by side, and sweet Mistress Barbara would make as fair a wife as any man could desire. Ha! Master Dauntless, ha! have I struck home? The maid is almost sick with love for you, as my worthy gossip, Captain Copperthroat, assured me last week at the 'Boar's Head' over a tankard of spiced Canary, and I am sure there is many a youth in the County who would gladly risk his life for the sake of winning the fair maid and fortune which is ready to pop into your arms for the mere asking."

Perhaps one of the most galling stings to human vanity is to find that one's dearest secret has been divined and made common property by another, and Hooter's insolent speech set the young man's hot blood fairly boiling.

He reined up his horse and asked Hooter in a voice that trembled with suppressed passion by what right he dared couple his name with that of Miss Merryl's. The Commissioner, surprised but by no means disconcerted by this question, reined in his horse, too, and looking back easily over his shoulder, replied with great coolness that he had eyes, ears, and a tongue and lived in a land where speech was free.

"Then let me tell you, Sir," said Harry, furiously, "that, notwithstanding such freedom, I shall chastise you if you presume to mention the young lady's name and mine again in the fashion you have done — Do you take my meaning, Sir? I shall chastise you if you ever dare repeat your late remarks."

Mr. Ephraim Hooter, although by no means a coward and at all times prepared to put his body, life, and soul to the hazard of the sword when any material interest was involved, had a most decided aversion to imperil these valuable possessions when any such shadowy phantom as a threat or the offended nicety of another man's feelings was concerned; so he bowed slightly and continued to regard Harry with the greatest composure.

"Now, understand me, Sir," said Harry, gathering up his reins and turning his mare's head towards Bearna Baeghail: "if ever you venture to soil Miss Merryl's name by making her the subject for your alehouse wit; if ever you dare to repeat your late speech or venture to address me again, — I shall cudgel you soundly."

And with this parting shaft the angry young man clapped spurs to his beast and galloped up the bridle-path.

The Commissioner remained for a few minutes where he had left him, with his hands crossed easily on the pommel of his saddle and a bland smile upon his face.

"Ha! my young friend," said he, softly, as he eyed the back of his late companion with an ominous look. "Is that the stuff you are made of? Fie! Fie! Fie! you will spoil your horse's wind and your own good looks if you give way to such fits of ill temper — If you had guessed but one half of what I know concerning Dublin Castle, you might have pitched your tone towards me in a much less haughty spirit. I forgive your ignorance, my dashing young Constable, but I will not forget your kind offer to cudgel me, and I heartily promise that if I ever have an opportunity of clipping your wings, I shall take a few extra feathers from you as a memento of our pleasant ride this afternoon."

With a comprehensive glance towards the Valley and an amiable nod addressed to the unconscious subject of his soliloquy, Captain Hooter shook his bridle merrily and resumed his journey.

In the meantime, Harry spurred his horse up to the Castle in a state of suppressed anger, and his temper was by no means sweetened on his arrival by finding his mother's kinsman still there. It was the usual custom of MacMahon to take his departure on the same day on which he paid one of his irregularly timed visits, and Harry learned with secret annoyance that on this occasion he was to be a guest for some days to come. Of late years a growing distrust of the Captain had taken root in Harry's mind; for MacMahon, although intimately and accurately acquainted with the inner life of every one, continued to shroud his personality in a mysterious fashion from Harry in a way which was alike irritating and incomprehensible to that young gentleman.

This distrust, which had been still further increased by some seditious hints which the Captain had lately dropped, coupled with his disappointment of the afternoon and his recent quarrel with Hooter, rendered Harry more than usually reserved that evening. The Captain observed this preoccupation with secret satisfaction and concluded it was the result of the conversation he had had with him on the previous evening. Anxious to complete the partial victory which he fancied he had gained over his young kinsman, the Captain resolved to vigorously follow up his advantage whilst his convert was wavering, and therefore suggested a walk on the battlements after supper, to which proposal Harry tacitly agreed.

A narrow, winding stair built in the thickness of the wall led up to the flat roof of the tower, which was bounded by a machiolated battlement of great thickness from which in olden times the Norman bowmen had rained down arrows on many an investing army; and this spot, which was a favourite resort of Harry's, afforded a view of the entire Valley which was of surpassing loveliness. It was an evening well suited to view such a scene, for there was not a single cloud in the still blue sky which was brightened by a suspicion of crisp frost; and as if to rival the blue of the sky, the sea lay far below them like a vast sapphire crescent set in the pale gold of Killiney's sands. The brown, black, grey, dark green, purple, and bright emerald hues on the soft swelling hills melted and mingled their shades in soft combinations beneath the mellow October sunshine; and, with the exception of the distant lowing of the cattle as they were being slowly driven homeward, the occasional whistle of a passing curlew and the clucking and murmuring of the little river at the foot of the hill, there was not a single whisper to wound the stillness of the evening air.

For some time the two, filled with the languorous beauty of the evening, remained silent, and even the Captain, who had come there with other intentions than to admire the landscape, was intoxicated with the splendour of the sunset.

"Truly! truly!" he murmured softly. "It is a land worth going far into the battle for."

"Aye, truly," remarked Harry, with a sidelong look of bitter meaning at his companion, "and if it is so well worth fighting for, how much more is it not worth the keeping!"

"Ha! think you so?" said the Captain, with a piercing look; "then be advised of me and join those who, wise in their generation, arm against the Tyrant ere he wrests all from them."

Harry, who had been leaning with folded arms upon the battlement, stood up and, regarding the other with a steady gaze, pointed to the smiling Valley which lay beneath their feet.

"Once, that stretch of country," said he, coldly, "from the confines of the Three Sisters[1] to the Wicklow Mountains yonder, was the birthright of my fathers. They held it in peace so long as they paid their King that obedience which is accounted by all earthly and divine authorities to be his due; but there was one of my ancestors who thought differently to the majority, and, lo! how shrunk and cabined are the lands of the Dauntless family now — wherefore I ask you, Master MacMahon, is it likely I should prove myself an arrant fool by entering into any treasonable undertakings when I have such an impressive warning for ever before my eyes?"

"Now, may God be my judge," said the Captain, with great earnestness, "but thou dost utterly misjudge my meaning and wrong the single-hearted motives of thousands of others as loyal as thyself. I say, as loudly as any swaggering Cavalier and a great deal more sincerely, 'God Save King Charles'" (here he raised his felt hat solemnly), "and I swear that our object in taking up arms is as much for the purpose of defending the King as ourselves."

"Your schemes may be based upon the highest principles of loyalty," said Harry, superciliously; "but for my part I fail to see the purity of the motive. I am well aware that the members of the governing body in Dublin are inimical to his Sacred Majesty; but, even though I believe them to be rogues and traitors, they are none the less our fellow-subjects, and no law-abiding hand would dare to point a sword at them without the King's express command."

"The King is little better than a shadow in England at present and less than a shadow's shadow in Ireland," replied MacMahon, with a keen glance at his companion. "The English Sectaries have of late joined forces with the Scots pack and they hem him in so close that he can neither save his friends nor bid them do what is best for him and themselves. Mark you, Harry, how Strafford fell, and judge from his fate what power is mightiest in England at this moment. Surely, the King had good cause to feel beholden to so faithful a servant. Although Strafford was a tyrant to this unhappy country, — an impartial tyrant, I grant you, inasmuch as he would have none of the lesser dogs mumble what he had set

[1] Killiney Hill.

apart for the Royal Lion's share, — yet he was a devoted steward to his Master and deserved a better recompense at his hands than the block. Alas, poor King! dead shade of Royal power, thou wert no more able to save him than thou art competent to take the only course which may yet save thyself."

The Captain ceased speaking, and for a few minutes regarded his young kinsman with a sidelong but watchful glance, but, as Harry remained staring moodily over the darkening landscape without uttering a word, MacMahon continued on in the same strain.

"Amongst those who hold the reins of state in England," said he, "the King can count a few zealous partisans, a few half-hearted friends, and a few passive dissonants, so he hath some comfort in knowing that his parliament is not all banded against him; but here, in Ireland, he hath no friends among the powers of the land. The Executive Committee is to a man against him, Parsons and Borlase are Puritans to the backbone, and every official is the King's enemy; wherefore, unless the landed gentry take prompt measures to clip the power of these smooth traitors, the King's cause and the already tortured country must pay the penalty of this indifference. Come, Harry, it is a glorious cause I offer you. We are about to draw our swords on behalf of a Monarchy which the rebel Scots have pledged themselves to overthrow; we are promised aid from abroad and countenance at home; our plans go on apace, and, ere many months are past, we shall strike a blow that will ring the knell of the malignant faction in Ireland. Say, Harry, does not such a prospect charm you?"

"Once more I tell you, Master MacMahon," said Harry, sternly, "I shall never take up arms, even on the King's behalf, against my fellow-subjects without the King's expressed command. If it should ever seem good to his Majesty to issue such a command, then, but not till then, shall I prove my readiness to support his authority. In the mean time, Cousin, I prithee, spare me further discussion on this matter."

Harry made an excuse to retire to bed on the plea of being compelled to rise early next morning; but when he was alone in his own little bedroom he sat down in a profound reverie for over an hour before he thought of undressing.

"If this upheaval whereof MacMahon hints is coming," he muttered thoughtfully, "how can I avoid being sucked into the whirlpool? Should the King raise his standard here in Ireland as, they say, he intends to do in England, no loyal subject could disregard such a summons; and yet — and yet I would I could escape such a call. MacMahon is right, — the odds against the King are greater here than those in England. In the North are the lately planted Undertakers, — all bitter Puritans; down South are the great Lords, resolved to fight to the death for their spoil in Munster; and here in Dublin are a swarm of cunning city merchants and courtiers watching like corbies round a sick lamb, and waiting for a pretext to wrench more spoil from us wretched Catholics."

The curtain of his open window blew back, and a grouse, startled by the light which issued from the window, crowed and rose whirring up from the heather close below the Castle wall.

Harry crossed the room, drew aside the curtain, and leaned out. The night, though moonless, was full of the luminous haze of the stars, which glittered in the dark blue sky overhead, and under their soft light the outlines of the hills lay around the Castle, distinctly visible. The sweet mountain air blew gently on his heated face and waved his hair about his temples, and all the love for his home, the mountains, and the life and pleasures they afforded, rushed into his heart and stirred him intensely.

"No! no!" he cried, "this home I love so dearly must not be risked in any cause, be it ever so just. God ordained that I should be a peaceful and slothful member of the commonwealth, and I cannot enter on any cause wherein I may imperil all I hold so dear — I cannot help myself — I cannot help myself — it is destiny."

Then he undressed, and, getting into bed, almost immediately fell fast asleep.

VII

ON the following morning, when Harry had dressed and descended to the bawn, he learned with secret satisfaction that, early as it was, he had already been forestalled by the Captain, who had left the Castle some hours before daylight. The young gentleman, accompanied by Ledwidge, rode down the bridle path, crossed the rough wooden bridge which lay in one rude span over the mountain torrent, and slowly toiled up the steep ascent of Tullagh, upon whose summit the tiny ruined church of Saint Olave, with its surrounding tombstones, is perched like a sleeping hen with all her chickens around her.

Close by this old Scandinavian place of worship is an ancient stone cross, one of the four which had been placed in far-off ages for the purpose of marking the bounds of sanctuary wherein many a trembling fugitive had couched in safety from the slaughter weapon which had chased him thither. And at the foot of this rude memorial of a dead time the two horsemen drew up for a while in order to breathe their panting animals.

Harry turned half-way round in his saddle and looked back lovingly on Bearna Baeghail, whose weather-worn tower and bartizans shone as yellow as gold in the early morning sunshine. A lark sang gloriously in the blue sky overhead, and the song which swelled from her throat in an irregular crescendo of vigorous sweetness seemed to him like a hymn of the joy of possession, and caused his mind to revert to the conversation he had had with the Captain on the previous evening.

"Yes! Brave little bird," he murmured, as he strained his eyes upwards, in order to follow its course. "I accept thy message. To thee and me the mountains and the pure, sweet air; to others the wrangles of the creeds and the stifling atmosphere of plots and counter-plots. Let others make or mar great fortunes in these seething times, but we twain shall continue to live our quiet lives according to our natures,— not molesting others and unmolested ourselves."

He gathered up his reins again, and, nodding to Ledwidge as a sign to follow, touched his bay mare lightly with the spur and resumed his journey. They trotted forward briskly towards Killiney, skirted round the base of the hill, and soon came to Dalkey, with its seven ancient Castles. Clattering through the ill-paved streets of this quaint old townlet, they took the road along the seacoast through Dunleary, and, crossing over the slob and heather which at that time surrounded Dublin, struck the main road close to the College, just as the bells of Christ Church clashed out the hour of noon. Here, travelling, by no means good at any time, was rendered worse than ordinary by an unusual number of city-bound carts, which, on account of the heavy way they were laden and the careless fashion they were driven, frequently choked the narrow road in front and thus hindered advance every hundred yards or so. As they crossed Hoggin Green, Harry saw that the narrow streets in front were so densely thronged as to forbid passage to horsemen; so, accordingly, he dismounted at the corner of Dames Street, and, handing over his horse to Ledwidge, bade him await his return at the Haggard Hawk Inn.

With a malediction on the crowd which compelled him to make his way afoot, and a rueful look at the muddy streets, he walked through Dames Gate, which then formed the Eastern boundary of the City proper, and strode up the steep ascent of Castle Street, on past Christ Church, the Tholsel, and along High Street. He observed that there was the same unusual throng of people within the city as without, and among the crowd he noticed a great number who, on account of their half military dress, their great height, and the contemptuous manner in which they shouldered the citizens, appeared to be, or to have been recently, soldiers.

"Some of Strafford's disbanded troopers," thought Harry, half carelessly, half pityingly, for, notwithstanding the insolence of their bearing, many of them looked nearly starved. "Poor devils! It was a cruel stroke of policy to disband them so suddenly, and a still more cruel deed to ask them to volunteer for the King of Spain's army and then refuse them permission to go at the last moment. They must have a hard lot in store for them a few months hence, for I do not suppose they can have saved much, and when the few dollars in their pouches are run out, it seems to me as if they must choose between honesty, coupled with starvation, and the highroad and the gallows, inasmuch as the old saw holds ever true which affirms that 'No Irishman will ever return from the pike to the plough or relinquish the sword for the spade.' "

Too much absorbed in the object of his own journey to pay further attention to these stalwart outcasts, Harry shouldered his way impatiently through the crowd until he arrived at the house wherein Sir Thomas Merryl and his daughter had taken up their residence. It was a small but handsome dwelling, with a beautiful oak front, which was carved and gilded in the fashion so dear to the Dublin citizens of that period. The "Golden Fox" which hung from a delicately wrought iron support projecting half-way across the sidewalk, did not indicate by any means that the house was an inn, but was the then existent method of distinguishing private residences in the city; and, as if to disassociate any such character from its austere respectability, its windows were more closely latticed than those of the neighbouring houses, and its street door, unlike their hospitable ones, was fast closed.

With a final twitch at his point-lace collar and a frowning glance at his muddy boots and spurs, Harry knocked at the door, which was presently opened by one of the Knight's serving-men, who, on account of the young gentlemen's frequent visits to Carrickmines, was well acquainted with his appearance. The man informed him that the Knight was not at home, but added, parenthetically, he had received instructions from his young mistress that, in case Master Dauntless should call, he was not to suffer him to depart without seeing her; whereupon Harry allowed himself to be ushered without further ceremony into the parlour, where he found Barbara engaged at a large piece of embroidery.

The young lady received him with such unusual manifestations of pleasure that he was not only surprised, but was considerably disconcerted, into the bargain. All the fine speeches which he had so often rehearsed for this particular occasion fled out of his mind instantly, like cowardly soldiers who desert their general at the moment of a projected assault, and left him in a state of tongue-tied embarrassment which would have disgraced the veriest chaw-bacon in the country. But Miss Merryl did not afford herself an opportunity of observing the manifest confusion of her young admirer, for as soon as he had seated himself in a chair close to hers she bent over her embroidery frame once more, and chattered on for nearly five minutes without pausing for breath. She rallied him gaily on his recent neglect, and reproached him with a mock sigh for having deserted her. She told him that his conduct had been that of a recreant knight, and poutingly recounted the numerous commissions which he should have considered it his duty to perform, but which she had been obliged to intrust to the unsympathetic care of menials in his absence. She informed him dolefully how dull she had been in the city, and how much it had changed since her last visit; and, finally attacking the late puritanical movement among the citizens, she unwittingly paid an eloquent tribute to Harry's vanity by comparing him with them.

"'T is oh for the days of poor Wentworth!" said she, "He was a tall and proper deputy, and I feel ashamed of my King that he should permit his majesty to be clowned by such weavers as Borlase and Parsons. I tell thee, Harry, I did look on thee of late as a very dull companion with thy interminable controversies with my father concerning freewill and destiny; but, since I came to Dublin, I have come to regard thee as a very gentle, perfect, and accomplished cavalier, — that is, in comparison with these psalm-singing Dublin folk. Ah, woe is me! but Dublin, which was wont to be at one time the sprightliest city in the Three Kingdoms, hath become so dull, so muddy, and so sluggish, that, I pledge thee my word, Harry, thou hast come into my life to-day as welcome as a ray of sunshine to a prisoner in the Black Dog."

Whilst the young lady spoke she continued to ply her needle without once glancing towards her companion, until Harry, whose heart was beating fast, drew his chair closer, and, stretching out his hands, took both of hers from the embroidery frame, and looked straight into her startled eyes with that expression which can never be misunderstood by a woman.

"Why not let me be that sunshine for ever?" said he in a pleading voice, "or, rather, be that blessed gift to me. Oh! Barbara, thou canst not misunderstand me. Be my life's sun and earth and heaven in one, for I love thee! I love thee! more than I can tell."

The young woman changed colour, and a sudden pang of remorse shot through her as she realised for the first time what feelings she had awakened in Harry. She struggled in evident confusion to withdraw her hands from his, and, when he slipped down on one knee close to her feet and burst into a passionate declaration of love, she turned to him with such an expression of unaffected trouble on her face that it caused him to pause in his headlong speech.

"Stop! Harry, stop!" she said with a note of pain in her voice. "You do not know how much you hurt me by what you say nor how sorry I feel for the folly and thoughtlessness I have been guilty of. We should both have known from the first that such feelings were utterly impossible between us, and if my foolish conduct has misled you, I am not wholly to blame, as your own good sense should have estimated it at its proper value."

"Oh, Barbara!" cried poor Harry, with all the anguish of despair, "is it possible you have never cared for me after all the years you permitted me to hug this delusion to my heart?"

"Indeed, Harry, you do me an injustice," answered the young lady, gently, "for I have always regarded you with the kindliest feelings. You have been my earliest playmate and most valued friend; you have shared my childish plans and accompanied me in all my walks and excursions in the Mountains; you have supplied the place of the brother I never had, and for all these reasons you have ever been dear to me; but, Harry! Harry! we are man and woman now, and, as you know very well, there is every cause why you should not regard me ever in the character of a possible wife."

"Do not dismiss my love as though it were the growth of a night," said Harry, pleadingly. "Do not forget, Barbara, that from childhood you, and you alone, have been my sole love—"

"That was because you never saw any other woman but myself," said she, withdrawing her hands from the slackening ones of her lover and gaining fresh self-possession in proportion to the despondency which was settling down over his heart. "But that is no reason that you might not fall in love with another woman than myself later on, even if we two fools were mad enough to marry. Think how jealous I should be of you, Harry, when you discovered that there were many thousands of such creatures as myself in the world who wear petticoats likewise. Think how incensed I should be whenever you dared look out of the corner of your eye at a prettier face or a trimmer and more youthful figure than mine. Ah, you shake your head now, Harry, but you would stamp your foot then and cry 'Out!' on the headstrong folly which shackled you to me. Besides, Harry, — it is all so ridiculous, — I am not only older by some five years than you, but am moreover so full of humorous fancies and so utterly unsuited to play the part of a mate with one of your temperament, that if we two flew straight hand in hand into the face of common-sense in the way you are so anxious to do, the remainder of our lives would not be long enough to bewail our folly."

Continuing on in this light strain, Barbara Merryl succeeded in taking from her speech more than half the bitterness which a rejection, no matter how gracefully worded, must necessarily inflict on a discomfited suitor. She assumed the character of one many years older than himself, made Harry feel somewhat like a small boy who had said something very foolish to a benign, grown-up sister; and, having received a double pledge from him never to refer to his suit again and a promise to regard her as an affectionate friend, dismissed him in a very confused state of mind.

When he was gone she sat down and cried for a little while, and then she dabbed her eyes with her lace-edged kerchief and laughed. "Poor boy!" she said to herself, "I suppose I have wounded his proud, gloomy heart by bidding him wear the willow, but he will soon get over his disappointment. What other answer could I make to his earnestly proffered offer of a living death among those desolate hills with no better company than himself and that prim, elderly female-rebel, his mother. Odds my little life! I would rather be a chambermaid in the Fleet prison in London and live and die a maid within its walls than be the beloved and worshipful mistress of his tumble-down old sheep-pen. Poor, foolish Harry! I feel some tweaks of conscience on your account, for I fear I have used you for lack of neighbours as a cavalier, just as archers do a stuffed figure to practise their shafts upon; but, well-a-way! a little chastening is good for us all, and I warrant your heart shall be lighter than mine on the night I beat a slipper sole at your wedding dance."

In the meantime Harry Dauntless, with his chin bowed down dejectedly on his breast, retraced his way slowly through the city, which appeared to have become even more crowded than it had previously been in the earlier part of the day. The fair, which was to have taken place on the morrow, had already asserted that spirit of excess and conviviality which then, and until quite recently, was one of the main features of such institutions throughout Ireland; and here and there Harry encountered many country people whose maudlin friendship or noisy quarrelsomeness displayed the different stages of intoxication through which they had already progressed. The citizens, who might have been easily distinguished from the country folk by their austerity of countenance and superiority in dress, cast many glances of dislike and anger at the latter; but the townsmen yielded place on the sidewalk to the strangers with a sullen alacrity which was still further accelerated whenever they looked at all like any of the disbanded soldiers of Lord Strafford.

Passing down Cork Hill, Harry observed two big men, whose soiled buff-coats and swordless shoulder-belts indicated their association with the latter class. They were both very much the worse for drink and were standing at the foot of the Castle drawbridge criticising with drunken gravity the bearing and unsoldier-like appearance of the sentinel on duty.

"How grim would Wentworth look," said one with a drunken hiccup, "if he could come back to life and see such a guard mounted for duty where so many pretty fellows were wont to stand in his day! I tell thee, Padrig, I would engage to knock over yonder sentinel and capture the Castle single-handed, with no better weapon than the stem of this tobacco pipe, if any one were to offer me a good crown piece."

The disbanded soldier spoke in Gaelic, and, though Dauntless was but very imperfectly acquainted with his mother tongue, he could not fail to comprehend the drift of his remarks, inasmuch as the sentinel, a very feeble-looking old man, leaned so wearily on his pike that it seemed as if a gust of wind would have toppled him over. Notwithstanding his depression, Harry could not refrain from smiling at the drunken man's shrewdness; and though the incident vanished from his mind by the time he had reached the city gate, he often ruminated on its significance in after years.

He struggled through Dames Gate and into the street beyond, where a noisy multitude of peddlers crying their wares, porters staggering under their loads, and drunken men reeling about among the prim-looking citizens, formed a confused and surging sea of humanity through which a string of country wagons tacked from side to side like heavily-laden ships in a gale of wind.

As he slowly wriggled through this motley throng, a young man, clad in the close cap and flowing robe then worn by all students of the learned professions, issued out of a neighbouring tavern and pushed up against him so rudely that he was within an ace of being tumbled into the kennel. Harry was about to make a fierce retort, but one glance at the aggressor convinced him of the folly of resenting his rudeness, for the student was too much intoxicated to be aware of having given any offence to the young Constable of Shanganagh, and moreover was intent on seeking a quarrel with another passer-by whose cloak he had laid violent hands on.

"Hallo! Teague," said he, in a thick, vinous tone, as he swung heavily out of the stranger's garment. "Tell me, who gave you permission to come masquerading into Dublin in that garb?"

The object of this unprovoked insolence spun round on his heel with an angry exclamation, and Harry saw that he was a tall, fine-looking youth some two or three years older than himself. He wore the distinctive, voluminous Irish mantle (which so much excited the anger of poor Edmund Spenser) and was clad in the short, close-fitting jacket and truis, which, even so late as that period, many of the Irish country gentlemen still retained in defiance of the Sumptuary laws of Henry VIII. He was evidently a person of rank, for he wore a plume of egret feathers in his light blue barrad and had silver spurs on his soft, grey riding boots; but what most attracted Harry's attention was the dark, wild beauty of his face and the singular gold clasp which secured the feathers in his cap.

"Let me go my way in peace," said the stranger, with an

evident struggle to keep his temper, " or it may be the worse for you. I have no wish to interfere with you and should be sorry to treat you ungently; but, by Saint Bride! I shall lose the small amount of patience wherewith I am blessed unless you release my cloak."

" Keep your patience or lose it, as you will, and be damned to you in any case for a rapparee," was the polite rejoinder. " But you go not hence until you explain to me why you come into the peaceful haunts of quiet citizens, tricked out in such outlandish and forbidden garb wherein you are an insult to our well-bred eyes. Know you not Poynings — Ha! and, if so, down upon your marrowbones and crave the pardon of the much-offended laws of me, their youngest nursling!"

The crowd, which had quickly become congested round the centre of this exhibition of drunken buffoonery, applauded loudly, and one gentleman in a butcher's apron remarked to another wearing a porter's shoulder-knot that it was as good as an interlude of the players in Smock Alley.

" When I was at the University," said the stranger, still endeavouring to keep his temper and to extricate his mantle from the gripe of his tormentor, " I was always taught that, in the event of a gentleman being overtaken in his wine, it was more seemly for him to keep his rooms, than to go about the streets thrusting insults upon inoffensive strangers."

" By Pollux's foot and Hector's hand!" hiccupped the student. " Am I to be schooled in deportment by a saucy Irisher? Nay! by the rood, nay! take that, you bog-trotter, to your chops, and a wannion on you."

He released the other's mantle in order to aim a slap at his face, which indignity the stranger avoided by stepping back a pace in a sudden blaze of anger, at the same time clapping his hand, upon his sword. The hilt and blade quivered beneath his hand, and his handsome features were for a moment distorted into an awful expression of vindictive fury; but, instead of drawing his weapon, as all the bystanders fully expected he would do, he struck the student such a heavy blow on the chest that he knocked him senseless on the cobble-stones.

A dead silence followed this feat, and while the young stranger looked furiously round the crowd, as if to challenge criticism, a decently clad citizen who, from his leather apron, appeared to be an iron-worker, remarked in a sepulchral voice that it served the swaggering young companion right. The sympathy which the iron-worker expressed for the stranger excited the quarrelsome disposition of a weaver who was standing on the opposite side of the crowd.

"It's easy seeing that the College gentlemen are some of your *back* just now," said he scornfully, "for every one in Dublin knows it is the custom of your Guild to abuse any of your friends when they are down."

The jealousy which at that time existed between the different trade guilds in Dublin was of such intense bitterness that it often occasioned the most murderous street fights. The students of the College, with that love of adventure which has been one of their unchartered rights since the foundation of the University, invariably joined in on such occasions; and, notwithstanding that the young gentlemen were in the habit of regarding the individual members of all the Guilds with the most supreme contempt during the piping times of peace, yet, on the first sign of a street riot they never failed to throw themselves into the thick of the battle, wherein they lent their powerful aid to whatever Guild their capricious fancy happened to attract them to for the occasion.

The man of the bellows and tongs answered him of the beam and shuttle in as sharp a fashion as he was addressed, and a member of some other guild threw in a still further apple of discord by roundly abusing both the smith and the weaver. Threats and oaths were followed by blows, and blows were succeeded in turn by the war-cries of the Weavers and Iron-workers, and the fallen student, who had by this time partially recovered his senses, put the cap on the situation by bellowing out "Trinity" at the top of his voice. The last war-cry brought out a couple of dozen students from the surrounding taverns and by-ways with drawn swords in their hands. Immediately on the appearance of the students, knives and hangers were drawn among the crowd, a country cart laden with heavy billets was stopped and emptied in a twinkling, in order to supply weapons for those who were unprovided with them; and, in a single minute, the unlucky stranger found himself surrounded by a savage ring of scowling faces and brandished swords and clubs.

The object of this sudden outburst of hostility whipped out his sword, unclasped his mantle, and, rolling it round his left arm in the fashion of the Irish kerns when about to engage an enemy, glared round on his assailants with the expression of an angry lion. Some of the students cried out for "fair play" and "one at a time," but, as they were at that moment considerably in the minority, and as the greater part of the crowd seemed to have been inflamed with an unreasonable but none the less murderous animus against the bold stranger, matters would have gone hard with him in a few minutes if it had not been for the presence of mind of Harry. He drew his sword, stepped up beside the stranger, and, bidding him follow on his life, hurried up a flight of wooden steps to a half-opened door from which a young servant girl was looking forth on the scene below. Thrusting his companion into the house, and, turning round, himself, for a moment to drive back those who came rushing up the steps, Harry sprang in after him, flung to the door, and then drew the bolts and bars before the crowd could follow them.

It was a sudden impulse on his part, mingled with a chivalrous desire to save so gallant a life, and a vague sense of affinity, roused by no more powerful token than the stranger's cap-clasp, which was fashioned in the badge of his mother's clan; yet, even while he stood listening to the thundering blows which the mob rained on the door, with the full consciousness that its yielding meant instant death to them both, he could not feel any other sensation than that of satisfaction. The poor girl, whose curiosity had so opportunely served them, fled screaming upstairs, where she bolted herself into an upper room, and the two fugitives stood breathing hard and listening to the crash and tinkle of falling glass, which the mob were playfully demolishing in the front of the house. Presently, a series of heavier blows than those which had hitherto rattled on the door caused the frame and panels to start inwards like living things from the violence without; and Harry remarked coolly to his companion that the crowd were using sledge-hammers, and probably dash in the door about their ears in a minute or two.

"Oh! for ten broadswords of my sept," said the other with a groan. "I would save them the trouble by opening it, and would treat these mechanical hounds to such a specimen of an Ulster hunting party that some of them would carry the tokens of it to their graves. Nevertheless, I have that in my belt which shall stop the barking of half a dozen of them at least."

He produced two small but beautifully-wrought steel pistols from his belt, and, handing one of them to Harry with the remark that he had but three charges apiece, entered a little room adjoining the hall-way, where there was a small oriel window projecting some four or five feet over the street. Every vestige of glass had been already dashed into the room, and the very diamond-shaped frames wherein the panes had been set had also shared the same fate, and now lay scattered about the floor, twisted up into all manner of fantastic shapes; but the paneless window afforded an excellent vantage-ground from which to direct a flanking fire on those engaged in battering the door, and into this redoubt the two young men stepped, pistol in hand.

Immediately the two appeared a howl of execration went up from the crowd and a shower of paving-stones came rattling into the room; yet, in spite of the heavy missiles which came whizzing viciously around him, the stranger covered the wielder of the sledge-hammer with his weapon and bade him drop the implement as he valued his life. The man recoiled hastily from the door, but another member of the mob, either more reckless or less sober than his companion, picked up the sledge and prepared to resume the attack. In another moment blood would have assuredly flowed, for there was an ominous look in the eyes of the stranger as he glanced along the pistol barrel; but before either the one could swing his sledge or the other press his trigger aid came to the besieged from a wholly unexpected quarter.

A big, roughly dressed sailor, who had been staring open-mouthed at the two young men for some minutes past, at this point forced his way through the crowd and struggled up the steps by sheer force of his great bulk and strength. As he drew near, Harry was astonished to recognise in him his ubiquitous kinsman, Captain MacMahon, and was still more astonished by his subsequent proceedings.

"Come! come! my lad," said he, in his blustering, important fashion, at the same time pulling back the man from the door, and taking the sledge from him as though he had been a child and his weapon a toy. "This will never do, for you are wasting time and labour in endeavouring to effect an entrance in that way. I shall show you a much more expeditious fashion for opening a bolted door. Here, take this crown piece and fetch me a barber's brass bason, a few screws, and a pound of powder, and I shall make you a petard which shall blow that door into the middle of the house whilst you are saying Hem!"

This proposal, which seemed to promise the mob a cheap and amusing pyrotechnic display, was received by a loud cheer, under cover of which the Captain managed to say to the two fugitives in a low but very distinct voice, "*Ad Scalas ad inferum hortuli*," and, as soon as he perceived that his communication was understood, he made some plausible excuse to those around him and instantly disappeared in the crowd. The two young men made their way to the back of the house and found themselves in a small but well-cared garden full of flowers and a sense of nodding peace which contrasted strangely with the scene then raging in front of the house. At the end of this peaceful retreat they perceived a stone-flagged terrace guarded by a marble balustrade, and, hurrying down to this spot, discovered a flight of stone steps leading to the river. They instantly descended to the lowest flight, where they listened anxiously for some minutes to the low, hoarse murmur of the crowd, which at last burst out into a dull bellowing roar of impatient anger, doubtlessly caused by the tardy coming of the self-appointed general of their siege train.

Presently they heard a mighty shout of "*Trinity, Ho! Trinity*," which was answered by another of "*Hooragh for the Boys of the Liberties*," and mingled with these street slogans came the clash of military arms as the City Guard joined in the fray, which now appeared to have become general. Above all this disorder they suddenly heard the crash of the falling door, followed by the triumphant shouts of the mob, who came pouring into the house. The noise they made in rushing from room to room sounded so distinct to the two fugitives that they were on the point of stripping to their shirts and taking to the river, when such a course was rendered unnecessary by the appearance of a small boat (one oar of which was pulled by the Captain and the other by a preternaturally stunted and cunning-looking boy), which swept round the corner at that moment and grated up against the steps on which they were standing.

VIII

THE two young men required no invitation to jump into the boat, which no sooner received them when the Captain and his companion immediately pushed off, and rowed out straight into midstream. The cries of "*Trinity*" and "*The Liberties, Ho! the Liberties,*" sounded so close, that Harry was impelled to turn his head from time to time to see if they were being pursued, and through the dusk of the October evening he perceived two crowds, each hemmed in by a line of halberdiers, who were being pushed back towards different points, one in the direction of the College and the other towards the City Gates. The Captain appeared too much agitated to question them, either upon the cause of the disturbance or the means whereby they had become embroiled in it, but his partner at the oars was more curious or less disturbed, for, with a jerk of his matted head towards the shore, he asked Harry with an elfish grin if he knew "what *back* de young nobs of Trinity was for dis evenin'."

Harry professed his unacquaintance with the names of the rival factions and the cause of the affray, but the answer appeared to amuse the oarsman.

"Jus' so," said he, with a look of supreme cunning. "Dat is de same guff dat any of yees give whenever ye have run yeer toasting irons tro' somebody's guts: but don't ye be afeerd of me, Master—I won't split as I have rowed many a tidy gintleman over de water of harm's way afore dis. Why, it was only last Chewsday week I brought a young College nob across to de Pill who gev one of de City Watch a han's bret of his dagger tro' de tripes an' I never said nothen more about it dan it served de Blue Coat right, for I tink it is a murdherous shame, and a pity it is, dat gintlemen can't have a little piece of honest divarshun widout dese same bullying blades of de Watch comin' in an' spoiling de sport."

On arriving at the other side of the river the Captain threw the boy a piece of gold and immediately hurried the two young men ashore. He urged them quickly along through several streets, whose meanness and narrowness bespoke the decay and antiquity of the portion of the town they were traversing, and, finally leading them up a very dark and noisome lane, rapped on an iron-clinched door in a peculiar fashion. Not receiving an immediate answer, he repeated the summons with a louder application of foot and hand, and presently a slide over a grating in the door was withdrawn and a man's voice behind it asked in quavering tones what they wanted, to which query the Captain replied in a low voice, "*Pax Domini omnibus Domi.*" The grate was immediately closed and the door opened, and Harry was astonished to perceive that it was held open by a monk, clad in the grey habit of the Cistercian order, who closed the door immediately they entered. Harry found himself in a very narrow passage, which, on account of the great height of the walls and the garb of the monk, he surmised formed that portion of the ancient Cistercian Abbey of Saint Mary which was known as the Slype.

By no means surprised at the fear and caution of the monk, and only wondering how any of that persecuted order had contrived to linger on in a city where the Puritan faction was so strong, he followed his companions through the Slype until their conductor stopped before another door set in a deeply-splayed arch. The monk turned a key, and swinging back the door, motioned them to enter with a nod, in accordance with the rigid rule of his order which imposes gestures in substitution of all unnecessary speech, whereupon the three fugitives stepped one after the other across the threshold.

They entered a lofty arched chamber, the roof of which seemed to be carved out of one vast piece of stone, from whose apex several beautifully proportioned ribs of groined masonry curved down to meet the capitals that rose in four graceful brackets from the ground.

The beauty of the chamber and the perfection of its proportions filled Harry with admiration; but, beyond its architectural grace, the vast apartment possessed little else to attract attention inasmuch as a few rush-bottomed chairs and a common deal table constituted all the furniture. He was well aware of the austerity of the Cistercian order, their vow of perpetual poverty, their enforced silence, and the invariable absence of everything approaching comfort in their dwellings; but he was painfully struck by an all-pervading sense of ruin and neglect which seemed altogether out of harmony with the magnificent appearance of the great room.

The niches in the walls were empty, the beautiful stone mouldings round the windows and the old oak panelling which ran breast-high round the room were defaced with the marks of axe and sledge-hammer, whilst a graceful statue of the Virgin and Child, which had been carved by the magic hand of Albert Dürer, looked down sadly on a still more melancholy scene of wanton desecration below.[1] The tombs had been brutally grubbed up or destroyed, the masterfully-carved faces of saints and bishops which had formerly decorated the bases of the pillars had been ruthlessly hammered off, and the very tiles under foot, which had at one time shone in the richest shade of green, red, and purple, had not been spared, for any wherein the mad fury of the Iconoclasts had detected a fancied resemblance to sacred emblems, had been rigorously pounded into atoms.

During their walk through the streets, the Captain had gathered in a broken fashion from Harry the part he had taken in the late disturbance; but, beyond one or two fervent ejaculations, he had made no comment on his behaviour until they were safe within the Chapter House, where he took the right hand of each of the young men in either hand of his and then looked from one to the other in such a solemn fashion that both his companions started.

"The ways of Heaven are wonderful," said he in a full voice full of emotion, "and the means whereby It effects our best ends are a never-ending marvel. Little did you think, Harry Dauntless, when you risked your life on behalf of this youth, that you were preserving my beloved nephew, and still less did you know, Florence MacMahon, that your preserver was no other but the son of my beloved cousin; but, thus did Providence accomplish at the one time a signal act of all-seeing wisdom, wherein It was pleased to make use of one kins-

[1] This statue, at present on the right-hand side of the high altar in the Carmelite Church in White-Friars Street, Dublin, is the identical one from which the crown was taken for the coronation of Perkin Warbeck, when he was crowned King of England in Christ Church.

man as the instrument of saving another in order that the two should be more closely brought together."

"Let heralds settle among themselves the exact degree of relationship we stand in, Mr. Dauntless!" said the younger MacMahon with his handsome face all aglow. "It is nothing to me how they decide such matters, but you have this day bound me to you by a bond as powerful as though we had been suckled at the same breast. I entered Dublin, this morning, in the belief that I was the sole surviving son of MacMahon of Glencairn; I shall leave it convinced I was mistaken. Mr. Dauntless, let me beg of you the affection of a brother, for, if you will accept me on such terms, I shall consider I am bound to you in that degree from henceforward."

The young gentleman spoke with all the fire of his race. His great grey eyes, brimful of dewy feeling, were so much dilated that they appeared almost as if they were blue, and his voice faltered with genuine emotion. He looked so gallant, generous, and handsome, that Harry's heart went out to him from that moment, and he instantly clasped his proffered hand and assured him of his joy upon gaining such a relation. Harry endeavoured to make light of his services; but the Captain, who had observed with the greatest delight the seal of friendship set upon the two young men, declared that fighting and fasting went badly together, and vowed that neither of them should venture to speak another word until they had some supper.

He accordingly opened the door and called the monk, to whom he spoke a few words in an undertone, whereupon the religious made a silent gesture of intelligence and withdrew. In a few minutes a shock-headed and very ragged boy, who might have been the twin brother of their late ferryman, made his appearance, and, with one hand on the door and one eye twinkling round it, stood half-way in the room and half-way in the passage and asked their honours how he could serve them. The Captain bade him go to a neighbouring tavern and fetch what he had written down on a leaf torn from his tablets, which he handed him along with a piece of gold. The boy thrust the paper into his ragged doublet and the gold into his mouth with such celerity that it made the beholders fear for the moment that he had swallowed the latter, but as he disappeared almost immediately they had no opportunity of setting their fears at rest until he reappeared, about a quarter of an hour later, in company with a great square, willow-woven basket. He set his burden on the table with a pleasant grin of anticipation, and raising the cover produced in turn, a clean, coarse table-cloth with the concomitant knives, and what was, then, a rare luxury in Ireland, some two-pronged forks, some tall wine-glasses, a straw-colored flask of Canary, a loaf of excellent white bread, and last of all a pie dish containing a venison pasty of such liberal dimensions that it took away the breath of the beholders.

The three kinsmen soon made an alarming breach in this noble trophy of pastry-cook's art, and Harry, who had been fasting since early morning, paid so devout a tribute to its excellence that he had no eyes for anything beyond the circumference of his plate, and consequently did not observe that the two MacMahons had twice raised their glasses to their lips and had twice laid them down untasted after exchanging a glance and a smile in his direction. But when he had been helped twice and had sorrowfully but firmly declined a third plateful, Evir MacMahon caught his eye, and he noticed that the Captain was regarding him with a strange questioning smile, as though he were endeavouring to gauge his disposition at the moment.

"I had a toast, Harry," said he, after a little hesitation, "which I would have wished to have proposed were I not fearful of giving offence. However, let it pass, as I shall substitute one that is dear to you and which your new-found brother will not refuse to honour. Harry! Florence! I drink the King and Eire and confusion to all traitors."

The three gentlemen stood up, and Harry, raising his glass and saying with marked emphasis, "My King and My Country," emptied it at a draught, whereupon his companions, exchanging a swift look, repeated the toast and followed his example.

When the three had reseated themselves and the Captain had filled the glasses once more, the younger MacMahon looked across at Harry with a friendly but a meaning smile.

"I would your toast had been 'Country and King' instead of 'King and Country,'" said he, "and I should have liked it all the better. Yet shall I say 'God save the King' as heartily as you do, Mr. Dauntless; but methinks if you had added a prayer that he might deliver himself from evil counsellors you would have asked Heaven for the surest blessing his Majesty stands in need of."

"The King, like ourselves, is but a man," said Harry, gravely, "and his will, like that of other mortals, is controlled by wills as mortal as his own. For my part I believe he can do no wrong, yet as he is obliged by the circumstances of his state to rely on the advice of others, he is often directed by evil or foolish counsellors to lay the ship of state upon a course which is as distasteful to himself as it is to some of his subjects."

"*So dorn don a dubh fuiltibh!*"[1] cried Florence, impetuously, and there was a gleam in his eye that gave token of the fiery spirit which lurked skin-deep within him, "and that is my motto and maxim, Mr. Dauntless. If the King is so much under the influence of wicked or foolish men, do you not think it were time for some of us to lay our hands to the axe in order to lop away these poisonous tendrils ere they choke the fruit tree?"

"Florence," said the elder MacMahon, uneasily. "Florence, you evidently forget that Mr. Dauntless holds different political views to ours. Fain would I have him regard matters as we do, much would I give to have him leagued with us; but remember another time and another place were more fitting to plead our cause with him."

"Good Uncle, where can we find a fitter place than here?" cried the other, flushing with excitement and indicating the groined roof and venerable walls with a wave of his hand. "Where can you find a fitter place than in this ancient house where Lord Thomas Fitzgerald dashed down the Sword of State and hurled defiance at that bloody tyrant, Harry of England? When can you find a fitter time than now —"

"Stop! I beseech you, stop!" said the Captain, with a look wherein fear and anger struggled for mastery. "If you have no regard for your own safety, remember that the lives of others hang by a gossamer thread on your lips;" and he indicated their late attendant, who was at that moment crouching in one of the recesses of the Chapter House.

But the ragged Ganymede of the Abbey, far from being

[1] "Here is an armed hand for the black-blooded." The motto and slogan of the MacMahon family.

interested in their conversation, was too busily engaged in devouring the remains of the venison-pasty to pay any attention to what they were doing, far less to what they were speaking of; and the Captain had to shout thrice to him before he was able to attract his attention in order to send him to the "Haggard Hawk" for Ledwidge and Harry's horse. As soon as the boy had left, Harry, who was in dread that the young Chieftain would resume the perilous theme he had been interrupted in, asked Evir MacMahon if the room wherein they sat was the same where the unfortunate young Earl of Kildare had formally renounced his allegiance before entering on his fatal step of rebellion against Henry the Eighth.

"Yes, Cousin," replied the Captain, with a sigh, "in this very hall, over one hundred years ago, that unhappy youth flung down the sword of state ere he plunged into his ill-advised but honourable enterprise."

"And brought himself and his five uncles to the gibbet and quartering-block at Tyburn," remarked Harry, drily. "I fail to see where the honour accrued, for, if there was much honour to be gained by being strangled like a felon, methinks I could obtain such distinction by crying '*Torre*' to the first traveller I met on my way home this evening."

"His own hot-tempered inexperience and the leasings of that treacherous period brought shame and death upon him," said the Captain, gravely. "He had no higher motive than mere personal revenge upon his father's supposed murderers, no more organised support than the following of his own single clan, no better leader than his own gallant, reckless spirit; yet an ignominious death in itself by no means entails a heritage of disgrace on the memory of a good man who has suffered in a good cause. As for my own poor self, if I were offered a great and noble undertaking under the leadership of a wiser and more temperate Chief than poor Silken Thomas —I tell thee, Harry Dauntless, I would cheerfully embrace such a cause even were the Devil to rise up and foreshew me the gallows as my ultimate portion in it; and when my time came to die, I would place my head upon the block as calmly as ever I laid it on a down pillow, with the happiness of knowing that I had attempted to further such an undertaking."

The Captain's voice, which had unconsciously deepened into more sonorous tones than usual, rolled impressively upwards amid the groining of the roof, like the mellow notes of an organ being softly played in a distant chapel. His broad chest swelled, his eye dilated, and he sat up straight in his chair with such a look of majesty that his seaman's rough serge dress appeared to assume the dignity of a kingly robe. Harry became conscious of an insidious feeling of mingled awe and fear, which in some subtle fashion also infected Florence MacMahon; and, when the Captain ceased speaking, a solemn silence fell upon the three kinsmen, which was intensified by the extinction of the winter light which by this time had faded away and had left them in total darkness.

For some time they sat as silent as if they were members of the order whose guests they were, until the same monk who had admitted them appeared, bearing a lighted lamp which he left on the table and then withdrew as silently as he had entered. The appearance of this poor illumination served in some degree to enliven the spirits of the party for a while; but, notwithstanding that they talked on various subjects and once or twice joined in a rousing laugh, it was not long before a vague sense of depression settled down upon the spirits of the three. Both the MacMahons appeared to be preoccupied, and Harry fancied that when they spoke their voices had lately taken a sepulchral note and now rolled ominously through the arches overhead. The pulsating flicker cast by the lamp into the cavernous angles of the Chapter House peopled each far-off recess and embrasure with nodding shadows which seemed to him to be the silent ghosts of the dead Kings, Princes, and Bishops, whose remains lay beneath the broken floor at their feet, and who now rose to look with displeased and reproachful eyes on those who dared to intrude their petty stories and intrigues of a world which they themselves had so long done with.

It was therefore an intense relief to Harry when the shock-headed boy thrust one half of his face into the apartment and announced that his honour's horse and "*own* man" were waiting for him in Capel Street, and, before the boy had the words out of his mouth, he was on his feet and was bidding farewell to his two hosts. Florence accompanied Harry as far as the Slype, but the Captain, making him a sign to remain there, walked with his other kinsman as far as the street where they found Ledwidge anxiously waiting with the horses. Before

Dauntless put his foot in his stirrup, the Captain gave him implicit instructions to avoid the city on his way home to Bearna Baeghail, giving as a reason for this injunction that his appearance among the citizens might lead to his being recognised by some of his late assailants and being perhaps treated with violence; but, no sooner had Harry parted from MacMahon and got clear of the narrow streets round the Abbey than he turned his face towards the only bridge, which at that time spanned the river on the site of the now existing Essex Bridge, and trotted across it without giving another thought to the Captain's warning. The only other means whereby he could cross the river was two miles further up, and as the winter night had already closed in and as he had no intention of adding four miles to his journey in order to humour the whims of his elderly kinsman, he accordingly took the shorter route through the city.

As he passed by the Watch House, near Wormwood Gate, he met three halberdiers dragging along a drunken man, who violently protested that he was a personal friend of the Lords Justices and was endeavouring to persuade them to bring him to his friends immediately. The Watchmen and their noisy prisoner passed on one way and Harry and his companion went the other, without thinking further of the ravings of the drunken reveller; but little did Harry think, and still less did the Watchmen surmise, that this drunken fool carried in his muddled brain the fate of the Irish Royalists and the future history of the entire Island.

IX

ON his return to Bearna Baeghail that night, Harry, like many thousands of others, lay down tranquilly to sleep, without suspecting what that memorable St. Ignatius, day would bring forth ere the dawn broke again over Ireland. In the same spirit of peaceful ignorance he rose on the following morning, and, taking his fowling-piece, went out across the mountains, according to his almost daily custom. But his mind was full of depressing thoughts, and the grouse, which whirred up from beneath his feet, and the black cock, which whistled overhead, were only marked by the good red spaniel that accompanied him and that turned from time to time a wondering and reproachful look on his young master. During the following three days he wandered aimlessly through the woods of Cherrytown, or down Glen Druid, or along the banks of that little torrent which, having its source in a deep ravine in the Three Rocks, picks its wanton, laughing way through that beautiful spot known as the Bride's Glen. But in whatever direction he happened to wander in the morning, towards evening, he invariably sought some spot from whence he could see the stately towers of Carrickmines; and there, leaning pensively on his gun, he would stand for some time regarding the home of Barbara Merryl before he turned his depressed countenance towards Bearna Baeghail.

Thus, avoiding all companionship except his own gloomy thoughts during the next few days, he remained utterly unconscious of the events which had torn the country in two since his last visit to Dublin. The first intimation he received that anything unusual had happened was from Ledwidge. The old man had been sent into the city on some trifling commission, and on his return to the Valley told such a tale of closed gates, doubled guards, and universal terror that Harry, recollecting with a sudden start the mysterious hints dropped by the Captain and his nephew, was considerably alarmed. He said nothing to his mother, but his countenance wore so troubled a look that evening that she evidently guessed there was something weighing on his mind, for she kissed him more tenderly and invoked a blessing more impressive than usual on his head when she was about to retire for the night.

His sleep was disturbed by terrible visions, which, no doubt, had their source in the startling news brought by Ledwidge that afternoon; but Harry himself, during the remainder of his life, had no hesitation in attributing them to a supernatural origin. His dreams were of rout and battle amidst which he seemed to stand always alone, always vanquished, yet ever unhurt, although all around him appeared to swim in blood. Then, at intervals, amidst these scenes of violence, he saw the dead and gone members of his ancient family pass one by one before him like the Kings in the Glass of Banquo.

Now it would be the figure of old Barry Dauntless, his grandfather, with his white hair and flowing beard, and dressed in his sombre physician's garb. Now it would be the shade of Thomas Dauntless in plate armour, he who died in Dublin Castle for his participation in the attempt to establish the cause of the impostor of the House of York, that House so strenuously supported and beloved by the Irish people. Now it would be the huge form of Sans Peur, the gallant but unscrupulous founder of his race, clad in the rude, mascled-leather armour of the first invaders, with his mighty two-handed sword on his shoulder and a look of triumphant scorn in his eye, and now it would be Almeric, he who followed Cœur de Lion to Palestine, with the Red Cross on his shoulder and his hands crossed on his breast. Last of all came his father, clad in his sober dress of black velvet and his barrister's gown floating round him. In one hand he held a book secured with silver clasps, to which he pointed with an impressive gesture, and then, to the dreamer's horror, human blood oozed out from between its leaves and fell drop by drop upon the ground.

Terrified beyond description, yet possessed with an overmastering desire to know the contents of the book, he stretched out his hands; but his father shook his head in sorrowful refusal, and at the same moment the blast of a trumpet, which sounded as dreadful as the last call to judgment, ripped the night in two, whereupon the figure raised its hand with a warning gesture and faded away.

Harry started up in bed, weak and trembling, with every limb clammy with the sweat of mortal fear. He muttered a prayer of thankfulness as his eyes were greeted with the thin light of morning which streamed in through his open window, and he drew in with a gasp of relief the pure, sweet air which blew across the heather. He was congratulating himself that he had experienced nothing more dreadful than a disordered dream, when he was startled by the clear, piercing tones of a cavalry trumpet, which blew so noisily that every vault and room in the Castle vibrated with the summons. The sound seemed so intimately connected with his late vision that he could scarcely restrain a cry, but recovering his self-possession on the conviction that such a sound was caused by human agency, he hastily dressed himself and proceeded to the battlements.

Looking down from a projecting bartizan, he perceived a single horseman, dressed and armed after the fashion of a trooper of the time, close to the door, and half a dozen yards from him stood the trumpeter who had so lately blown this startling summons. A pistol shot away on the highroad was a strong body of cavalry who stood in file formation with their horses' heads turned South, as though they had made but a temporary halt on their way. Their armour and steel caps glittered through the mountain mist in the first rays of the sun, which was at that moment rising over the unruffled horizon of the sea, and their file leader bore a guidon of white and green, which hung in dripping folds in the still, moist air.

The horseman below struck an impatient blow with the butt of a heavy pistol on the door, and then turned round to the trumpeter.

"This mountain air must be a sovereign remedy for sleeplessness," said he, in a voice which sounded strangely familiar to Harry. "Ho! Rory, sound another flourish, and see if you can bring any one out of bed."

The trumpeter inflated his lungs and handled his instrument preparatory to another ear-splitting performance, but, before he could clap the mouthpiece to his lips, Harry leaned out of the bartizan and asked the horseman who he was and what he wanted at that extraordinary hour.

"It is I — Evir MacMahon," was the reply. "Open quickly and bid thy mother come down immediately."

Greatly astonished by his kinsman's appearance and companions, and wondering blankly whether he himself was not the subject of some delusion of the senses, Harry made his way downstairs to his mother's room and tapped on the door. She had, however, by this time risen and dressed, and had descended to the gate, where her son found her engaged in conversation with her kinsman, who still retained his saddle.

MacMahon's face wore a troubled and yet a triumphant look, such an expression as one might assume who had won a great victory at the cost of some dear friend's life, and Kathlyn, although weeping silently, displayed a gleam of the same sorrowful pride through her tears.

"In Heaven's name," cried the bewildered Harry, "tell me the meaning of this disturbance, and what has happened that should bring these armed men and yourself here at this hour of the morning."

"It means to the Parliament of Westminster," said the Captain, "that we are in arms for our sovereign, King Charles of England, and our rights and liberties. It means, that our native land from Malin Head to Cape Clear is in our hands. It means, that Charlemont, Newry, Mountjoy, Dungannon, Cavan, and Tanderagee are ours; and, though the babbling of a drunken coward has betrayed my cousin, Colonel Hugh MacMahon, and Lord MacGuire, and lost us Dublin Castle, with arms for 20,000 men, it means we shall have Dublin and its Arsenal before another moon looks down on them."

"Where have they confined poor Hugh Oge?" asked Kathlyn, weeping afresh. "Oh, Evir! is there no hope of a rescue for him and the young Baron of Fermanagh?"

"They are already on their way to London," answered the Captain, gloomily. "Their fate is as certain as if the grave had closed over them, but they have left ten thousand fighting men behind to demand a life for every hair upon their heads."

"And was it to tell me of this mad uprising against the constituted authority of the land," said Harry, scornfully, "that you have taken the trouble of riding here with sixty troopers, Mr. MacMahon? or do you purpose to garrison Bearna Baeghail as well as Dublin Castle?"

"Last time we met, my lips were sealed, and I could not offer what I do now," replied the Captain, sitting up very straight in his saddle. "I have come, Harry Dauntless, to offer you a guidon in my troop of horse, service under the command of one who is esteemed the topmost leaf in the proud laurel wreath of Spain's military glory, companions in arms who are the noblest on both sides of the Pale, and the fairest and holiest cause that ever a man drew a sword for. Come, Harry, come, and do not hesitate to mount the green and white scarf of your country and ride with me to Kilkenny."

"Master MacMahon, if that be your real name," said Harry, sternly, "when first I saw you, you professed yourself to be a soldier in the army of the King of Spain. Since then, I have met you in the assumed character of merchant, farmer, sailor, and peasant by turns; but there was one garb wherein you ever dressed yourself, and that was your treasonable nature. Nay, mother, nay, — take your hand from my arm, — I am no longer a child, and will say what I think to this mysterious man. Now, Kinsman, if kinsman you be, or, if your relationship be not of the same easy sort which you don and put off with your other disguises, take my answer and ride your ways. Seek other dupes further afield, and, if your time is of any value, do not waste it in trying to snare me in any of your plans."

"Foolish boy," said the other, with a look of calm dignity; "even if I entertained any wicked scheme to lure thee into treason against thy lawful sovereign, dost think so basely of thine own mother to deem her capable of being a partner in the cheat? Fie on you, Harry, fie! Know then, boy, that I am Evir MacMahon, son of Turlogh, brother of Sir Bryan, Lord of the Dartry, and true kinsman and loving friend to thy mother, who is my second cousin. I am neither soldier, sailor, merchant, peasant, nor traitor, but a priest of God and the Catholic Bishop of Clogher. Nay, Kathlyn, never wring thy hands nor look wildly about thee, for I can well afford to stand in my true character in the light of day since I gathered such bedesmen in my train."

He indicated the troop of cavalry with a proud smile, and then looked inquiringly at Harry, who, greatly discomposed to find himself in the presence of the redoubtable Bishop of Clogher, and fully conscious of the esteem in which this remarkable man was held by Queen Henrietta, stood silent and confused beneath his steady gaze.

"And now, Harry," said he, smiling quietly, "if thou art satisfied as to my identity, what answer am I to have?"

"My Lord of Clogher," said Harry, with an uneasy bow, "I humbly thank you for your proffered cornetcy, but I cannot reconcile my conscience with the assumption of arms against the King's ministers on no better warrant than a profession of good will for his person."

"In other words," said the Bishop, somewhat contemptuously, "thou art one of those very loyal folk who will hold back until his Majesty comes personally to give thee leave to defend thine own life and aid him. Well! well! I know how common is such cheap zeal; but beware, Harry, that it does not undo thee! The day is at hand when thou and others like thyself must take one side or the other; and on the dawning of that Armaggedon, look to it, that thou art not found sleeping when thou shouldst be watching in thy girded harness. Farewell, Kathlyn, farewell. Farewell, Harry, and remember thou my warning."

He raised his hand, on which the great ruby ring shone like a gout of blood, and solemnly blessed them both, and then turning his horse's head cantered down the bridle path to his companions. The trumpet sounded cheerily the signal to advance, the party moved forward with a merry jingle of accoutrements, and, after riding for some short distance down the road, they struck abruptly in a westerly direction across the mountains. Harry Dauntless leaned against the gate-jamb and looked silently after them, and Kathlyn, with the spirit of her martial race aflame within her, stood beside him with flashing eyes and dilated nostrils. They watched them flounder through a marsh, pick their way across the heather, and resolutely breast the steep hill before them, and mother and son continued to regard them silently until the crest of the mountain ridge shut out the sparkle of their armour from their eyes and the tramp of their horses from their ears.

. . . .

To detail the causes which amalgamated so many opposing interests, so many hitherto hostile families, and so many shades of political parties into that great organisation which was known as the Confederation of Kilkenny, is a recital which properly belongs to history; and the student who cares to read all that has been written by both sides on that subject shall find enough material to bewilder him for the remainder of his life. Modern research has by this time settled all doubt as to the loyalty of the movement, and, although there are still some historians of these times who continue to refer to it as the "Bloody Rebellion," the fact that such renowned Irish Royalists as the Earls of Fingal and Castlehaven, Lords Louth, Gormanstown, Slane, Dunsany, Trimbleston, Netterville, and a host of other gallant and noble names were associated with it from the commencement, ought of itself to dispose of such a ridiculous charge.

As far as numbers went, it was one of the most powerful organisations which had ever been got together in Ireland, for it embraced not only the nobility of the Pale and the landed gentry, but also included the warlike Clans of the North, who up to that time had been consistent and powerful enemies of all preceding Monarchs of England.

If Charles, instead of temporising with the Puritan party in Ireland, had boldly acknowledged at the outset his treaty with the Confederate leaders, or if the Confederation itself had possessed more unanimity at the time of its initiation, it is probable, considering the length of time the Royal Cause was upheld in Ireland after its suppression in England, that a great portion of the history of the two countries would have to be re-written. But Charles, fearful of offending the Puritan faction in Ireland, refused, on one pretext or another, to acknowledge his secret treaty; and the Confederates, after being twice disappointed by the non-fulfilment of his promises, grew suspicious not only of the King, but also of one another.

As all Ireland was at this time openly arming for the coming struggle, it was absolutely obligatory for every man capable of bearing arms to make public profession as to his political faith. During this period Harry, deluged with conflicting advice from without, and rent asunder with selfish fears within, contemplated in helpless indecision each of the various factions which claimed loudly for itself the exclusive title of the Royalist Party. Whilst in this state of irresolution, he heard that his old friend, Sir Thomas Merryl, had returned to Carrickmines, and, eager to have his views on the state of affairs, he rode across to the Castle on the same day that he was acquainted with the Knight's home-coming.

He found Carrickmines in a great state of bustling activity. Outside the walls, he encountered quite a small army of stout fellows engaged in felling trees and removing anything which might afford cover to a hostile force. At the lodge, he was met by one of the Knight's serving-men in buff-coat, steel cap, and bandoleers, who conducted him into the interior of the Castle, which exhibited a like scene of military activity. A light wooden platform had been erected for the convenience of musketeers in manning the loopholes. In the centre of the bawn, Tom Roche, the cobbler of Cabinteely, sat on a heap of bandoleers and old buff-coats, repairing with a palm and a needle any which required his attention. In the courtyard, he encountered a smith overhauling a great stack of pikes, partisans, muskets, petronels, and such weapons, and close beside the latter, found Sir Thomas himself, who was fumbling about among a heap of mould bullet-pouches and morsing-horns.

The Knight stopped short in his fussy occupation and exhibited some signs of confusion when Harry asked him, with a smile, if he were making preparations against the rebels.

"Yes, boy, yes," said the old gentleman, with a furtive glance at his young friend, "that is — against all rascals who are really against the King; but there are so many fellows who shout loudly for him, whilst they strike hardly against his Sacred person, that it takes a wise man in these days to distinguish between the knave and the true man."

Harry ventured to remark timidly that there ought to be little doubt in a question of that nature.

"There ought to be no doubt at all, Sir," answered Sir Thomas, explosively, "but the country is full of jacks-in-office who will not acknowledge plain, hard facts like the abominable treason and rebellion of Sir John Hotham at York. That scoundrel, Hotham, who is a type of one of your lusty-voiced loyalists — notwithstanding that he dared to shut the gates of York in the King's face, and talk sweetly to him from behind the breech of a loaded culverin on the wall — is accounted a very honourable person by the Parliament of England, who commend him for his loyal behaviour. On this side of the Irish Sea there are many such hypocrites, in whose hands the Lords Justices would commit places for the King, on the same terms as Hotham held York; but there are also left in the country some honest men who will not permit such scurvy knaves inside their doors, and I take some pride in declaring that I will not permit my house being garrisoned to the prejudice of my King."

"But, Sir Thomas," said Harry, blankly, "the Lords Justices possess the perfect trust and confidence of the King as well as the Parliament, and they would, surely, discountenance anyone whose loyalty was not above question."

"That may be as it is," answered the old man, stoutly, "but, for my poor part, I shall not allow any crop-eared son of a tinker inside my walls on the strength of a Parliament commission and an avowal of love for King Charles. I have resolved to maintain Carrickmines, against all comers, on behalf of his Sacred Majesty; and in proof of my determination to hold it to the last drop of my blood, I have sent Barbara as a maid of honour to the Queen at Whitehall."

"It is hard to say whom one can trust in these times," said Harry, with a look of great perplexity, "and on that account I have ridden over to ask your opinion. I was debating with myself as to the propriety of offering my sword to the Earl of Ormond, who is raising forces to meet Lord Mountgarret, now reported to be at the head of a mighty power of the rebel Confederates in Kildare; and I should therefore like to have your advice on my taking such a step."

"The Earl is a very worthy gentleman," said the old Englishman, drily, "but he is full of the most childish suspicions of those who wish him well, and is completely ruled by those who love his Royal Master after the fashion of Sir John Hotham. No one doubts Ormond's good-will, but, in these days, good-will for His Majesty seems to be the cheapest article in the Three Kingdoms. Look to the matter yourself, Harry Dauntless, and then answer your own question. Ormond holds his Commission from the King, but is subject to the immediate authority of the Parliament; therefore as he can turn in no direction but what they are pleased to point out, he is nothing more than his title — Captain General of the Horse and Under-lackey of the worshipful Lord Justice Parsons."

Utterly bewildered with this last speech of Sir Thomas Merryl's, Harry remounted his horse and rode home in an unenviable state of perturbation.

"Are they all going stark mad," he muttered to himself, "that each one should arm against the other, and strike at his neighbour who shouts the same watchword as himself?—At one time, I would have thought the banner of Mountgarret a safe one to follow; but, Lo! on this side of the Pale the cry is, 'Down with the rebel Mountgarret,' and he answers it back with his watchword of 'God and the King and down with the traitor Parsons.' Now comes the Earl of Ormond, duly accredited with the King's commission, to raise troops on his behalf in Ireland, and behold! The Lords Justices doubt even him, and command him on his allegiance to hold them idle; and last of all my old friend Sir Thomas tells me, as plainly as he can, that the Lords Justices themselves are suspected. A plague light upon them all for a pack of crafty conspirators! However, as I must needs make choice among them, methinks the Earl's commission will afford me the most secure means of testifying my loyalty and preserving Bearna Baeghail, and therefore I shall ride to Dublin to-morrow and offer Ormond my sword."

X

HARRY'S decision filled his mother with the most poignant anguish, inasmuch as she was well aware that the Earl of Ormond's troops were destined to be employed against the Confederate army. She strenuously endeavoured to dissuade him from his purpose by representing to him the fratricidal nature of the campaign he was about to engage in of his own volition; but the quiet determination with which her son encountered these entreaties and arguments, convinced her very soon that it was a hopeless task to make him alter his mind. Accordingly, she sorrowfully watched him set out for Dublin on the following day, and, as soon as he was out of view, she returned to her chamber, where she offered up a heartful prayer that Heaven would keep her son and her kinsmen apart in the impending campaign.

In the meanwhile, Harry, accompanied by Ledwidge, arrived at Dame's Gate, which they were permitted to pass after a searching examination by the Guard. As soon as they entered the city, they made their way immediately to the Castle, which was at that time approached by a drawbridge flanked by two small towers; and between these towers, which stood almost on the spot now occupied by the existing gateway, they perceived the guard being mounted for that day.

They numbered ten file of men, and were of a very different type of warders to the decrepit old man whom Harry had last seen on duty, for each one of the twenty was a fine, stout fellow who had been drafted thither from the lately raised regiments of the English Parliament. Each was strong and active looking, each was completely harnessed in breastplate, morion, and buff-coat, and looked as if he were well acquainted with the use of the pike, musketoon, and sword he carried. While Harry and his companion were observing these stern, clean-shaven soldiers with great interest, their drummer suddenly beat a long roll, and at that moment the whole twenty sprang up sharply into a position of rigid precision, each one with his pike advanced and his right hand as high as his chin. A sort of under officer, known as "a gentleman of the round," made his appearance from one of the adjoining towers, and having minutely inspected their arms and harness, posted his sentinels and marched off the relief, dismissed the remainder of the guard to their room in the Cork tower.

As soon as this military ceremony was concluded, Harry turned his horse towards the bridge, but was not permitted to traverse it, inasmuch as the sentinel, presenting his pike at him in a threatening manner, asked him in the nasal drawl so much affected by the London Puritans what was his business there.

"Admission to his Excellency, the Earl of Ormond, or his troop adjutant," answered Harry, regarding his questioner with great interest.

"If you mean Colonel James Butler, he whom the profligate of this town of Beth-Shan term Earl of Ormond," said the Londoner, with an unfavourable glance at the long, brown curls and gaily laced dress of the young cavalier, "you will not find him in the Castle; but if you seek that vain and carnal man, you will probably find him in the quarters of his Horse Guards."

Harry asked him where they were situated.

"On the far side of the street," answered the Puritan, with a jerk of his helmeted head, but without relaxing the position of his weapon for a moment. "He keepeth his troop of Life Guards in yonder Court which resembleth the Cave of Adullam in respect of the company gathered therein; if you must needs see the man Butler—yonder tailor's soldier, who standeth in the gate with his eyes red with wine and his mouth full of lewdness, can very likely tell you where his ungodly master may be found."

Glancing in the indicated direction, Harry observed a very splendidly dressed young soldier lounging at the entrance to a large court which was surrounded by overhanging galleries similar to those existent in that fine old inn—"the George" of Southwark. He thanked the man, and crossed over to the Lifeguardsman, who presented a remarkable contrast to the grim, plainly-dressed sentinel of the Castle. Although he was far more splendidly-apparelled than the Puritan soldier, the Royalist trooper lacked the soldierlike air and bearing of the Londoner. He was leaning up against the wall with his arms folded on his chest and his carbine resting negligently in the jamb of the gate; and the Puritan had done him no injustice in saying that "his eyes were red with wine," for it was quite apparent to Harry that he was at that moment, either on the highroad to inebriety, or was in an interesting state of convalescence from the effects of a recent debauch.

"I cannot tell you whether his Excellency is within the Court of Guard or not," said this easy-going sentinel, in reply to Harry's enquiry, "for, rat me! my eyes are so heavy he might have passed my post half a dozen times without my noticing him, unless he spoke to me. However, if you are a volunteer for His Sacred Majesty, I suppose it is all right, so pass in and ferret him out for yourself."

Harry glanced hopelessly at the numerous doors which looked forth on the court, and asked the Guardsman if he could give him any hint as to where he would be likely to find the Earl.

"Go in under that gallery," said the Guardsman, "and try the room on the right of the passage, if you do not find the Earl within, you are very likely to encounter his troop-adjutant, inasmuch as that room is his office, and he will very likely serve your turn as well as his Lordship."

Harry dismounted, and, leaving his horse with Ledwidge at the gate, sought the indicated room, and tapped on the door with the butt of his whip. A voice within bade him enter, and, on turning the handle, he found himself in a very barely furnished room wherein a neatly-dressed gentleman and a private soldier sat at a table with writing material before them.

The room was noticeable by reason of the spareness of its equipments, inasmuch as a couple of uncased cavalry guidons, with their standard poles arranged crosswise on the wall, a few chairs, the table at which the two men sat, and a small military travelling chest comprised all its furniture and ornaments. With the exception of the two guidons, whose small and gorgeous squares of silk were weighed down with the gold bullion on their devices, fringes, and tassels, everything about the apartment bore an air of meagre shabbiness; for the walls were as bare as those in the quarters of the private troopers, the common deal table was unhonoured with a cloth, and was splashed with inkstains of various hues, the few chairs were mean and rickety, and the uncarpeted floor was strewn with white sand like the floor of a public inn.

The personal appearance of the gentleman who sat at the table was also in keeping with these simple surroundings, for, notwithstanding that his dress was of the finest broadcloth and was scrupulously neat, it was so severely deficient of ornamentation as to give its wearer the appearance of one of the Parliamentary party. He raised his face, and Harry perceived him to be a young man, some few years his senior, on whose very handsome features courtesy and sweet-temper were mingled with great firmness of character; and assuming from his simple dress and quiet demeanour that he was either the troop-adjutant or Quartermaster of Ormond, he took off his plumed hat with a stiff bow, and lost no time in stating his business.

"My name is Dauntless of Shanganagh," said he, curtly. "I have come for the purpose of offering my poor services to his Excellency, the Earl of Ormond, and should therefore feel much beholden to you if you would acquaint him on his return with my desire of serving His Majesty under his banner."

"And right glad am I to hear such tidings from your own lips," said the other, standing up and offering his hand with a frank and winning smile. "Not that the traditional loyalty of your family is unknown to me; but it is gratifying to learn in these days of mere lip-loyalty that there are some of His Majesty's subjects who are willing to prove what they profess by taking the field for him in person."

"Dan," said he to the trooper, who rose and stood with an air of respectful attention, "I shall not require you for the next half hour, therefore stroll down the High Street as far as the Tholsel, and, in case you happen to fall in with any of our light dragoons returning from exercise at Kilmainham, bid the rascals not to strike up a tucket and beat their kettle-drums on passing the Castle guard, as though they were about to charge a stand of pikes. The rogues seem to regard as a part of their duty to His Majesty, never to pass by these London bull-dogs of Parsons without having a snap at them; but see that they go by in an orderly fashion henceforward, for there is little to be gained by chafing sore heads just now, inasmuch as we may have quite enough cracked crowns among ourselves to rub later on."

The trooper made a respectful, but by no means servile bow, and withdrew; and, when the door was closed behind him, Ormond motioned Harry to the vacant seat, and, bending forward, asked him eagerly how many men he brought with him to the King's banners.

Harry flushed to the roots of his hair as he realised for the first time that he would be compelled to make an open confession of the poverty of his family.

"I regret, your Excellency," said he, in great confusion, "that my means do not permit me to bring more than my own poor self and my serving man for your acceptance, as two volunteer troopers, and as I can afford nothing worthier, my poverty must plead for my inability to offer to do more for his Majesty."

It needed all Ormond's self-possession to conceal his disappointment. "What!" he thought with a feeling of inward dismay, "only two swords! Is that all the Valley of Shanganagh can muster now? Ah! I forgot. He is a Catholic — poor devil — and fines and confiscations have very likely reduced him to this low estate." Concealing his disappointment with an admirable smile, he made a courteous inclination of his head, and said aloud.

"Accept my sincere sympathy, Mr. Dauntless, for the existing misfortunes of your honourable house — It is an unmerited state which is the common lot of many others like yourself in these hurly-burly times, and was a condition wherein I myself, as you are doubtless aware, was plunged in my earlier days." He caught Harry's eyes with his winning smile; and his recruit (who, like most men of the day, was well acquainted with the history of the Earl's former poverty ere his romantic marriage with his lovely cousin restored him to his position) recovered his self-wounded vanity and smiled back too.

"Ah! you smile, Mr. Dauntless," continued the Earl, nodding and smiling, "but, I can assure you, I have known a degree of poverty which you have never experienced, nor ever shall, I trust; and I can therefore feel for those who have suffered too. But, *Corregio*, as the Spaniards say — Mr. Dauntless, you shall not find the King either a niggardly or an ungrateful paymaster, and who knows but that when this ruffling time is straightened out, you may find your house re-established in its old position. At present, I shall offer you no worse a rank than a saddle in my own troop of Life Guards, wherein, I promise you, will be found none but the best blood of Ireland; and, as we have both suffered, will you allow me to claim that brotherhood which such experiences give me a right to exact, and so permit me to supply you with whatever outfit you may require. Believe me, Mr. Dauntless, it will be you, and not I, who will confer a favour if you will honour me by treating me as your banker."

The tone of genuine kindness with which this was said completely took away any sting of humiliation which such an offer would have conveyed, if made by a less tactful speaker, and the kindly look which accompanied this speech made Harry Ormond's servant from that forward.

"My Lord," said he, with some feeling, "I most sincerely thank you for your very generous offer; but, as I and my servant are already well-mounted, my fortunes, reduced as they are, can very lightly bear such small outlay as the equipment of two private troopers."

"Well, Mr. Dauntless," said Ormond, laughing, "if you will not allow me to be your banker, at least permit me to be your armourer and quartermaster." He wrote a few lines on a slip of paper which he handed to his volunteer, and continued, "If you will give that billet to my orderly, who was here when you came, and whom you will probably find outside in the Court of Guard, he will help you to pick out some harness and weapons from my own collection, which you will oblige me by wearing for my sake. And now, Mr. Dauntless, farewell! Our troops shall muster in the Castle yard on this day fortnight, — that is, God and Sir William Parsons willing, —and as I do not expect to see you before that time, I shall therefore wish you good-luck and good-day."

He held out his hand in a friendly fashion, which Harry accepted with a profound bow, and, having assured the Earl of his gratitude, he bowed again and left the bare little orderly room.

In the Court he found the Earl's orderly, to whom he presented the billet, and, while the man glanced over it, Harry could not help being impressed with his quiet air of superiority and the strange, middle-aged look on his beardless, ruddy face. When he had finished perusing the billet, he crumpled it up carelessly, and thrust it into his belt, and then, in a well-bred accent, which contrasted strangely with that of any of the troopers whom Harry had hitherto encountered, he bade him follow him. He crossed the Court and, opening one of the many little doors which surrounded it, ushered Harry into a room where there were a number of cuirasses, helmets, swords, and other weapons of various makes and workmanship.

"About thirty-eight inches round the chest," said he, brusquely, after he had glanced at Harry up and down as though he were a wooden figure. "I think this light cuirass of his Excellency will about fill your requirements, — not that you are compelled to take that one if you do not care for it, — for his Lordship hath mentioned in his billet that you were to have your choice of all his gear."

Harry professed himself as being perfectly satisfied with the first piece of harness, and also expressed his approval of a fine steel-cap with a movable triple-barred face guard which the orderly next handed him. He however demurred about accepting a valuable pair of wheel-lock pistols which the soldier next presented to him.

"Take 'em if you like 'em," said the other, carelessly, "or choose another pair if you list; but, if you will take the advice of a poor soldier of fortune, you will take these plain, twenty to the pound, as being a more serviceable brace of tools than yonder silver mounted gauds of thirty to the pound; inasmuch as one requires a weapon in a hand to hand ruffle which will lift his adversary off the ground and not a pretty little toy which will make a wound the size of a dried pea."

Harry yielded to the superior experience of the soldier, and accepted the costly weapons without further protest. He was about to take his leave, but the man informed him shortly that there was another part of his equipment which was as yet incomplete.

"You want a coat of the Earl's colours," said he, "and if you will accompany me as far as Warber Street, I think I can obtain you one. There was a tunic made, some little while back, for a young gentleman volunteer of Sigginstown, who discovered, to his very great regret, that a distressful colic, or his grandmother's consent, or some such obstacle hath prevented him at the last moment from joining, and as he was about your build, I have no doubt the tailor can fit it to your back with very little trouble."

Accordingly the young Lifeguardsman accompanied the soldier to a tailor's shop in Werburgh (or as it was then called Warber) Street, where he was accommodated with a handsome coat of fine white cloth richly embroidered with gold; and, having disposed of these weighty matters concerning arms and uniform, the two retraced their steps towards the Court of Guard, where Ledwidge was waiting patiently with the horses.

As they walked through the streets, the soldier asked Harry, amongst several other apparently innocent questions, many queries as to the numbers, disposition, worldly position, and political tendencies of his neighbours; and, notwithstanding his natural reserve, Harry found himself entrapped on one or two occasions into replies which had revealed more of his own and his neighbour's affairs than he would have cared to communicate to a stranger. He was extremely mortified at being so easily pumped; but, notwithstanding his determination not to afford him any further information, this strange trooper, in whose ruddy face youth and age met and blended in so extraordinary a fashion, appeared to have some occult power of extracting unwilling answers to any skilfully put question he chose to ask.

Once, and once only, Harry caught him tripping, and that was by some casual reference to his kinsman, Evir MacMahon, to whom the soldier referred by his old military disguise.

"Pardon me," said Harry, with a quick glance of suspicion, "I did not mention the gentleman's name, and do not know, therefore, how you come to connect me with him."

But the self-possession of the soldier was not to be shaken even by so apparent a slip of the tongue.

"Did you not?" said he, with a guileless look of surprise. "Well, I must have heard of your relationship from himself, — I am in some way a distant cousin of his, — for, as you know, all we poor gentlemen of the North are one of the same web by reasons of inter-marriages and clan ties. He very likely mentioned your name to me when I last met him in the Low

Countries where I served with the Spaniard before I donned the cassock of a private trooper of King Charles."

By this they had reached the Court of Guard, and his companion lingered a moment at the gate, while Harry mounted his horse.

"*Hasta otra vez*, as the Dons say, Mr. Dauntless," said he, cheerfully, "and when you next see Captain MacMahon tender him the greetings of his poor kinsman, who bids him remember that there are twenty sides being formed in these coming troubles, but there is only one to choose."

"From whom shall I say this message came?" said Harry, shortening his reins.

"Subtle is my name," said the trooper, with a smile and a nod, "Daniel Subtle, and on account of my poor qualities, which can afford me no higher grade than the saddle of a private trooper, I am termed by my facetious friends, Infallible Subtle,—do not forget, Mr. Dauntless, Infallible Subtle, *Adios*."

As they rode down Castle Hill, honest George Ledwidge ventured to spur his horse alongside his master's for a moment.

"I beg your honour's pardon, Master Harry," said he, with an apologetic touch to his hat, "but I do not like that fleering jack-a-napes you were speaking to just now. I saw his eyes follow your honour with a look which was own brother to impudence, and if your honour but says the word, I shall go back, pick a quarrel with him ere he knows where he is (for I have a marvellous gift that way), and I will crack his crown for him in the shake of a duck's tail."

Although he had formed a strong dislike to his new comrade, Harry was very careful to conceal this disposition from his sturdy old follower. He assured Ledwidge that trooper Subtle, although a strange and somewhat eccentric person, was at heart a very honest fellow, and wound up a very long and didactic speech by bidding him beware of engaging in a quarrel with any of the followers of the Banner under which they themselves were now enrolled.

XI

THE muster of the Earl of Ormond's troops took place on a fine spring morning under the walls of the Castle. The Puritan sentinels on the battlements looked down with scornful contempt on the gaily dressed Cavaliers below, and the Dublin citizens who lined the fosse cheered themselves speechless in the way they usually do when they see any of their own countrymen under arms. Yet the appearance of that fine army was worthy of more thoughtful interest than the silent contempt of the Puritan soldiers in the Castle, or the idle admiration of the citizens who were gathered beneath the ramparts, inasmuch as it afforded a melancholy illustration of the lamentable state of disunion in which the country was at that moment.

Amongst that army of ten thousand men there was scarcely one, from the highest to the lowest, who had not some near relative, some close connection, or some dear friend enrolled in the opposite army; for one half of the noble families of the Pale were in arms under Ormond, and the other half, against which they were about to march, was marshalled under the banner of Lord Mountgarret, who was no more distant relation of the Earl of Ormond than his maternal uncle. However, if there happened to be any heavy hearts in Ormond's army there were no faces which betrayed any outward expression of gloom, when the Earl, giving the signal to advance, put himself at the head of his Life Guards, and rode slowly through the city with the trumpets and kettle-drums playing a stirring cavalry march before him.

Behind Ormond clattered his Life Guards — a splendid picture of military splendour in white and gold, bright steel-caps and breastplates, drifting plumes and sparkling accoutrements. After them followed the more soberly clad but soldierlike light horse; and, last of all, with the thunder of their side-drums drowning even the cheers of the crowd, came the infantry, rank upon rank, in blue or grey or green, according as the personal taste of each colonel had prompted him to clothe his regiment. The latter troops marched, arquebuse on shoulder and lighted match in hand, with that sturdy step so long the peculiar attribute of the Irish infantry soldier; and they passed on with the light-hearted indifference of their race, utterly oblivious to the melancholy possibility that the crime and after agony of Cain might be their own portion before many days were over.

They passed down James Street, and taking the Naas road, marched ten miles eastward, where they bivouacked for the night, without tents or shelter, in the open country, with a bitter east wind blowing on them.

This first night told severely on the spirits of the guardsmen, who, unused to such hardships, suffered extremely from this first rough experience of military life; but Harry, inured to such trifles as sleeping out of doors, found it nothing more trying than what he had often voluntarily undergone on many a deer stalking expedition.

There were many chattering jaws and muttered oaths among the Life Guards when the trumpet roused them from the damp heather to "saddle up" in the early morning, and it needed all the sternness of old Major Ogle, who commanded them, and the winning personality of Ormond to restore them to something like discipline.

That day they reached Athy, but, while they were congratulating themselves on the prospects of sleeping for one night at least under cover, their advanced guard sent back word that the Confederates were advancing in overwhelming force; and, shortly after this message was received, the sound of a scattered firing, gradually increasing in loudness and intensity, told them that their advance guard was engaged with the enemy, and was retiring on their supports.

Ormond, deeming it imprudent to risk an engagement with so large a force, ordered his troops to retire slowly on Dublin, and accordingly they fell back on Rathmore, where they bivouacked again. In the morning they found that Mountgarret had crept round their outposts during the night, and had taken up a strong position on that desolate spot then known as Blackhale Heath, and daybreak showed the forty standard of the Confederates stretched across their front, as if to dispute their march to Dublin.

A hasty council of War between the Earl and Sir Thomas Lucas, his General of Horse, and Sir Charles Coote the elder, who commanded the infantry, resulted in a decision to give battle to the enemy. Accordingly the Royalist army commenced the battle by a heavy cannonade on the right wing of the Confederate army, which was under the immediate command of Lord Purcell of Loughmo. As the Confederates were totally unprovided with cannon, it was not long before they exhibited signs of unsteadiness in this rather one-sided engagement, and, on observing this confusion, Ormond bade Sir Charles Coote charge their main body.

"As for myself," said he, in that winning manner which endeared him to all his followers, "I shall fall in as a trooper under the command of my good old friend Major Ogle, in case it becomes necessary for my Life Guards to support you, Sir Charles; and the only privilege I shall claim of him is my right to ride in the first rank."

Coote's regiment advanced steadily over the intervening ground until they got within striking distance, when, suddenly rushing forward with a wild yell, they threw themselves with such fury on the Confederates that the latter instantly broke and fled. Scarcely had the cheer died away, which announced this success to their comrades with the main body, when a strong body of cavalry, led by a man on a white charger, appeared unexpectedly on their right, and wheeling round, advanced straight on the Royalist guns posted on that flank.

"Mountgarret in person," muttered Ormond, with a groan, "God keep us asunder in the mêlée," then, turning to his companions, he said in a loud, clear, ringing voice, "Draw swords, Gentlemen, and follow Major Ogle and myself, for, by Heaven, we must n't let these fellows have our guns."

The Life Guards and light horse formed rapidly into line, the trumpets sounded the charge, and, with their gallant leader in the front rank, the cavalry of Ormond dashed forward on the Confederate horsemen, as though they were charging a stiff fence in the hunting field. Much lighter horsed and worse armed than the Earl's cavalry, the Confederates were unable to withstand the impact of this overwhelming charge, and consequently broke at once and fled in every direction, as their infantry had previously done. Although they were completely broken by this charge, the Confederate cavalry only lost some dozen or two in killed and wounded; for Ormond, perhaps conscious of the unnatural character of the engagement, forbade any further pursuit of the discomfited emeny. But if such mercy was being meted out to the Confederate cavalry in that quarter, their broken infantry was being subjected to a merciless slaughter at the hands of Coote's soldiers in front. Twice did Ormond order the trumpets to sound "the retire," and twice did he despatch messengers to stop the butchery; but it was not until he himself galloped up to Coote, and ordered him to personally recall his men, that he was able to arrest this horrible work.

"Your Excellency," said the savage old man, saluting Ormond with his bloody sword, "You are in supreme command here, and I shall obey your orders implicitly; but I think it would be a lasting honour to your name if you were to permit me to continue the good work, and not to suffer one of these men to leave the field alive."

"We have gained enough honour for one day, Sir Charles," said the Earl, with a sad look at the black-coated figures which lay wallowing in blood in every direction on the heath. "Let the remainder of the poor wretches go unharmed, for I consider that the most glorious victory in the annals of warfare is but a sorry triumph when gained at the expense of the blood and lives of one's fellow-countrymen."

Thus mercifully ended the battle of Kilrush, the first engagement between Ormond and the Confederates, which cost the latter over three hundred men in slain alone, among whom was the unfortunate brother of Lord Dunboyne. Scarcely a dozen of Ormond's men were killed, and Harry, like many of his comrades, went through the charge without giving or receiving a blow. George Ledwidge was not, however, so fortunate as his young master. He had received a wound from a pike, which, although slight, was sufficient to prevent him from accompanying the Earl 's troops on their homeward march to Dublin, and was consequently quartered in a neighbouring house of Lord Castlehaven; but, as the old man's hurt was of a trifling nature, and, as he was perfectly happy and in good hands, Harry left him behind without feeling any great anxiety on his account.

The return of the victorious army was made an occasion of

general rejoicing among the Dublin citizens, for they were delighted to welcome their soldiers back from a successful campaign, and thought little, or cared less, of the fratricidal nature of their triumph. The Earl was raised to the dignity of Marquess of Ormond, by Charles, and received the thanks of the Irish House of Commons. He was received on all sides with loud acclamations, his army was fêted as though they were preservers of the state, and, for the moment, it seemed as if the ruin of the Confederates had been completed and was being approved of by the nation at large. But there was one all-powerful being in the Irish Government who, although bitterly inimicable to the Confederate League, indirectly contributed to its preservation. Lord Justice Parsons, the then virtual ruler of Ireland, by no means shared in this general spirit of rejoicing over Kilrush, and openly stated that he wished the number of the rebels had been increased instead of having been diminished, on the principle of the more rebels there were, the more property there would be to be confiscated later on. He was at heart a zealous Parliamentarian, eager to increase the power of his own party at the expense of the King's, and as he hated Ormond, with an intensity which was little inferior to his detestation of the Confederates, he lost no opportunity in strengthening his own faction and thwarting his enemy at the same time. The result was that Ormond, who was the sole member of the Irish Government devoted heart and soul to the King, fretted himself into a serious illness in consequence of the malicious opposition of the Lord Justice. And as soon as the Marquess was declared to be in such a state of prostration as to be unable to attend to public business, the crafty Puritan seized the opportunity he had been so long waiting for. He instantly disbanded Ormond's army, and dispersed its soldiers to their homes, established strong garrisons of Scottish Covenanters throughout the country, and then initiated a system of galling oppression and extortion for the purpose of furthering his own dark schemes.

In consequence of these political changes, Harry found himself at liberty to return to his home some six months after Kilrush, and, wearied of the inaction and licentiousness of garrison life in Dublin, lost no time in turning his face towards Shanganagh. As he rode round the base of Killiney Hill on his way home, the peaceful calm of the mountains contrasted so refreshingly with the stifling air of intrigue wherein he had lately been compelled to live, that the change seemed to him like a delicious mental banquet. On the South side of Killiney he left the main road, and, taking a short cut over the heather, cantered along with a slack rein, delighted to find himself once more among rivulets, hillocks, brakes, and undergrowth. He was so full of that wild animal joy of living which a ride across the mountains so often evokes in even the most phlegmatic natures, that, before he was aware of his proximity to the bridle path, he burst through a light screen of dwarf ash-trees and dropped down on it so suddenly as almost to jump on a trooper who was standing by his horse.

The stranger's horse plunged violently, and the man, hanging on to the bridle with one hand, swore with great fluency and vigour at Harry for frightening the horse of a wounded man, and added a gruff request that he would mend his manners by catching the animal and helping him to mount. Harry made a very ready and sincere apology, and, on dismounting and coming to the other's assistance, was very much astonished to recognise Hooter, very pale, very weak, and apparently very helpless. His face was haggard and smirched with powder, his clothes were smeared with blood, his morion was chipped all over, and two cup-shaped dints in his cuirass marked the recent impact of a couple of musket balls. Although the circumstances of their last meeting were fresh in his mind, Harry could not restrain a generous feeling of compassion, and observing that the Commissioner's right arm was rudely bandaged and was hanging limply by his side, asked if he could do anything for him.

"If you will bind this bandage a trifle tighter round my arm, and fill my pipe for me," said Hooter, coolly, "I do not know of any other favour you can do, except to help me on my horse."

Harry stripped off the bloody rag from the Commissioner's arm, and whilst rebandaging the injured limb with his own sash asked, incidentally, how he had come by the wound.

"A thrust through the ribs of my gauntlet," was the unconcerned reply. "Methinks the bone is broken, for I could not use my sword to finish off him who inflicted it, and had, therefore, to have recourse to my petronel; but, in good sooth, I got the best of the encounter, inasmuch as I blew off his head with a couple of ounce bullets at half-arm range."

At that moment the deep boom of a cannon, fired at no great distance from the two, rent the air with a startling peal, and its sullen thunder was tossed to the hills around, where it was caught by the echoes and flung from rock to rock in a succession of varying repetitions. The horses plunged violently, and Harry, dropping the arm of the wounded man with a suddenness which drew forth an oath of agony from him, sprang at their bridles just in time to prevent them bolting.

"Good God!" cried the young Cavalier, as he endeavoured to soothe the terrified animals. "What does that cannon shot mean in the Valley? Can you, Captain Hooter, explain why it was fired?"

"Oh! Aye!" muttered the Commissioner, nursing his wounded arm, which had been jarred by the hurried manner in which his surgeon had lately dropped it. "I forgot, they were waiting for a shovelful of scrap iron in order to wipe off a dozen of the rascals who had taken refuge in a cellar; but, I warrant, that charge of langrel has settled them in their quarters forever." He fumbled awkwardly in his pocket with his left hand, and at length succeeded in fishing out of it a little silk bag, which he handed to Dauntless. "You will find a small Devonshire clay in that, along with the concomitant Trinidado," said he, pleasantly, "and if you will kindly fill my pipe and set it going for me, I shall be as happy as one in my crippled condition can very well be."

"Tell me quickly, Captain Hooter," said Harry, as he complied with this request, "in what part of the Valley is this dreadful deed being done? Surely, none of the rebels have ventured to make their appearance within its quiet confines!"

"I expect there are no rebels left in the Valley by this time," answered Hooter, enigmatically, as he lit his pipe at the burning tip of his musketoon match, "inasmuch as (Puff) when stout old Sir Simon Harcourt fell (Puff), Gibson (Puff) his second in command (Puff—puff) swore (Puff) he would not leave a flea (Puff) alive upon their carcases, and, by my sacred honour (Puff), he is not the man to break his word. Would you mind giving me a leg up into my saddle? Softly! softly! I prithee, Mr. Dauntless! One never knows the use of the most trifling joint in his body until he injures it, and then, by my soul, he seems inclined to lean on it more heavily than on any of his other sound members."

Harry commenced an earnest entreaty that the Commissioner would explain his speech more fully, but was interrupted by the sound of a second cannon shot, which boomed heavily on the quiet mountain air.

"What!" said Hooter, raising his scorched eyebrows with an expression of quiet surprise. "A second dose? What a clumsy set of rogues they must be! They ought to have settled a generation of Egyptian cats with one charge. However, I trust they have at last finished off the remainder of the malignants in Carrickmines, inasmuch as they fought desperately and inflicted shrewd loss on us before we got inside."

"Carrickmines?" cried Harry, in dismay. "Carrickmines? why in the name of reason should the King's troops have been sent against the dwelling of a peaceful subject like Sir Thomas Merryl?"

"The old gentleman was pleased to refuse scutage for the King's service," said Hooter, calmly puffing a cloud of tobacco from beneath his long moustache, "and very insolently denied the right of the Lord Justice to send a troop of horse to be quartered upon his estate, wherefore it was deemed necessary to teach him a lesson in good manners, which he has learned too late to benefit him further in this life."

"Now, God between me and harm," cried Harry, paling visibly, "but I trust, Captain Hooter, you do not mean to convey that Sir Thomas has met with any personal mishap?"

"I thought I had already mentioned to you," said the Commissioner, suavely, "that I, myself, accounted for him when he gave me this farewell gift through the bones of my forearm. Sorry and sad was I to do it, for, alas! many a pleasant evening have you and I had with him with our legs tucked snugly under the same table; but, Treason, you see, Mr. Dauntless—Treason will lurk in grey hairs as well as amidst young lovelocks."

"You bloody-minded villain," cried the horrified young man, shrinking back and trembling all over, "Is it possible that you—you who have received so many benefits from that good old man—could have nerved your hand sufficiently to murder your benefactor in the very spot where you so often enjoyed his hospitality?"

"Wild words, Mr. Dauntless, wild words," said Hooter, with a stern, steady look in the white face of the young Lifeguardsman. "It is ill speaking thus of what hath been done by command of the Lords Justices; and you, who hold the King's commission as Constable of the Valley, should use more respectful language concerning services which have been rendered His Majesty by even such unworthy hands as mine."

"Silence, villain, and do not couple the King's name with such infamy," answered Harry, furiously. "If such deeds were done by the King's command, I would trample his dearly-prized commission underfoot, throw off my allegiance, and take to the hills as the bitterest rapparee of them all; but, as I know full well that such ravening acts of blood are contrary to the King's expressed desires and the Constitution of England, I shall trust to the law to avenge my friend, and, I tell you, Mr. Hooter, that high as you stand with Lord Justice Parsons, I shall carry you to judgment for this foul murder if there is either law or justice left in this unhappy country."

Hooter laughed softly and blew a long, spiral whiff of tobacco into the pure, cool air, and Harry, overmastering a strong inclination to strike the life out of him on the spot, flung himself into his own saddle and galloped off with his heart almost bursting with grief and indignation. He rode on scarcely conscious of where he was going until he came to a place where the road forked abruptly, in one direction upwards to Bearna Baeghail and in the other down hill to the Bride's Glen. At this angle, which afforded an uninterrupted view of the lower part of the Valley, he had often lingered in happier days for the purpose of feasting his eyes on Carrickmines; and, at this well remembered spot, he reined in his panting horse and turned his eyes with a wild and haggard look upon its walls.

Viewed, from where he stood, the Castle did not present the appearance of a building which had sustained an assault, but a long column of infantry toiling up the hill with a couple of siege guns lumbering behind them, proved the truth of Hooter's statement, inasmuch as the soldiers moved leisurely, and had all the appearance of men who, having toiled hard, were returning from the completion of some weighty task. Half way up to the bridle path they halted as if to rest, and faced about towards the Castle. Whilst they stood motionless on the heather below, Harry endeavoured to ascertain their number, but before he had counted half the party, he was interrupted by a terrible phenomenon.

A sudden flash of straight-tongued fire issued from the basement of the Castle, and stabbed the sky with a lurid glare for a moment. It was followed by a report like circumambient thunder. The roof opened outwards, a flickering light played for an instant along the topmost battlements, huge stones and solid portions of masonry shot up high into the air, a dense column of greasy smoke curled up lazily into the blue sky and hung over the doomed building like a funereal plume of feathers; and then, with a deep, long, murmuring roar, Carrickmines slipped down in a mighty cascade of rubbish to its foundations.

The soldiers on the hillside gave three ringing cheers, which the evening sea breeze carried merrily over the heather to the ears of the horror-stricken young Cavalier. He sat stupefied in his saddle for a few minutes, whilst he mechanically patted the neck of his trembling horse, and murmured such commonplace terms of assurance as horsemen use towards a frightened animal. Then, as he realised the full significance of the terrible sight below, the tears came slowly into his eyes, and he removed his hat and stretched out his hand towards the spot where Carrickmines had stood one short hour before.

"Farewell!" he said in a faltering voice. "Farewell! Sir Thomas. May God have mercy on thy soul and may He visit thy murderers with the red rod of His vengeance in His own proper time."

He turned his horse up the bridle path, and rode home overwhelmed with emotion. On approaching the gate he observed three figures standing in the porch, and gazing so intently on the dreadful sight in the Valley that they were unaware of his presence until he clattered into the bawn, whereupon they turned their faces toward him with a startled look. One was his mother, who regarded him with an expression of mingled joy and alarm, the second was honest old Ledwidge, who shuffled forward sheepishly to take his bridle, and the third was a pale, thin, gentlemanly person in a plain riding-suit, who shrunk back hastily into the shadow of the porch at the first glimpse of his white and gold uniform.

When the first affectionate greetings between mother and son had been exchanged, Kathlyn introduced the stranger, with a nervous smile, as Mr. Acton, and added parenthetically that he was a former friend of his dead father. Harry shot one reproachful glance at his mother, and then turned a look of such searching intuition on the stranger that Mr. Acton's pale face grew visibly paler under the steady gaze of those clear blue eyes.

"My Lord Castlehaven," said Dauntless, gravely, "I am heartily glad to see you at my poor house of Bearna Baeghail, but my pleasure is marred by the fact that, not only your lordship but my mother should deem it necessary for you to assume another than your own honoured name whilst my guest."

"Do not think so poorly of my faith in your honour, Mr. Dauntless," said Castlehaven, appealingly, and the look of dumb entreaty in his eyes reminded Harry of the expression of a tired hare beneath the jaws of the gazehound. "I assumed another name than mine own in order that I might save you from the charge of knowingly affording shelter to a hunted fugitive who is flying for his life to the Confederates. I thought I would have given you conscientious grounds hereafter for swearing that my true character was unknown to you; and, indeed, as I do not remember having had the pleasure of meeting you until this moment, your recognition has considerably surprised me."

"We have met before this," said Harry, smiling, "but I suppose your lordship has better reasons to have forgotten me than I should forget you. You stayed in my father's house in Fetter Lane for a fortnight when I was but a child of nine, yet I remember your face and figure distinctly, although you were on that occasion dressed in woman's apparel. Your lordship is as secure here in Shanganagh as you were in my father's house in London; but, may I ask, what misfortune has compelled one of such well known loyalty as yourself to seek shelter in the Confederate ranks?"

"Loyalty," echoed Castlehaven, bitterly, as he pointed to where a thin stream of smoke rose up among the trees where Carrickmines had formerly stood, "Loyalty! You have not to stir far abroad from your own door, Mr. Dauntless, to see what a poor bulwark is afforded by loyalty in these days. There fell one whose loyalty was as high above question as that of Lords Fingal, Mountgarret, Dunsany, or Louth; yet what hath loyalty availed him or them? Trumped up charges, as monstrous, as unnatural and transparent as the Devil's mock of Majesty who begot them, hath disposed of them all one by one: this one to the Block, that one to the Rack, yonder to the Confederates. My fate would have been the first of the three, had it not been for this good fellow," (here he indicated Ledwidge) "who, in requital for some small kindness which my lady showed him after Kilrush, effected my escape from the sheriff's lodgings, and thus afforded me the only refuge left in Ireland for thousands as unhappy as myself."

At this moment Maureen appeared at the door and timidly announced that supper was ready. In the little banqueting room, which was feebly lighted by two small windows whose ten foot splays indicated the great thickness of the wall, was laid a frugal supper to which mother, son, and guest sat down without further ceremony. The room was small and the viands scarcely better than such as might have appeared on a farmer's table; but if the first was scantily furnished and the latter were simple, the pictures of ten generations of the Dauntless family on the wall, and the specimens of that antique silver tableware (which is so highly prized by the Irish people) gave an air of dignity to the little apartment and the plain fare.

During supper, the Earl recommended Harry to accompany him to the Confederate camp, and cast in his fortunes with that party. He gave as his reason for such advice that it was better to meet an impending evil half way, than to await its coming, and this counsel found a warm supporter in Kathlyn, who added her entreaties to the more temperate opinions of their guest.

"Oh! Harry," she cried with suffused eyes, "Are not Lord Castlehaven's misfortunes a warning as to what the tyrants will assuredly do unto the lesser land-owners when their turn comes? Cast off, I beseech thee, these wretched delusions wherein thy imagination hath clothed the brutal old sot Borlase and his fox-like co-partner in tyranny, William Parsons. Away with such shams of Royalty! and hearken to the voice of thy afflicted country calling out for her lagging sons in this hour of affliction."

"My Lord and you, my beloved mother," said Harry, in a troubled tone of voice, "The Lords Justices, unworthy ministers as they may be, are still the representatives of the King. I know full well that they have wrought much evil in the land, but they have so far done me no harm, and, therefore, as I have received no pretext for turning my sword against them, I cannot join with those, however well-meaning they may be, who are now in arms against their authority."

The Earl sighed deeply, but made no further attempt to persuade Harry to follow his fortunes. Shortly afterwards, Castlehaven retired, on the plea of fatigue and a desire to be astir before daybreak, and as soon as mother and son were left to themselves, Kathlyn made one more effort to induce Harry to join the Confederate party. She knelt down by his chair and represented, with all the eloquence of her enthusiastic nature, the sanctity, patriotism, and loyalty of such a cause, but in vain. Harry only shook his head sullenly, and for some while confined himself to ejaculations of subdued irritation; but, notwithstanding this discouragement, she continued her entreaties until a hasty answer from her son wounded her heart as though it had been pierced with a splinter of ice.

"What is all this prate of Ireland to me?" said he, angrily. "What do I care about its sorrows so long as I am permitted to live in peace? I tell thee, Mother, that Bearna Baeghail is a sacred trust which has been confided to me by my ancestors, and, rather than imperil one square yard of it, I would see the remainder of the country sunk into the nethermost pit."

His words shattered the one great hope of her simple life, and she bowed down her head for a moment to conceal the anguish she felt. Nevertheless she kissed him tenderly on the forehead, and walked out of the room proudly; but when she reached her own sleeping chamber, she broke down and wept bitterly over the discovery that her son was possessed in a greater degree with the selfish caution of his father's race than the martial patriotism of her own. In the meanwhile Harry continued to sit where she had left him, with his eyes staring widely at an open book in his lap, and his mind in a state of painful agitation.

The prophetic words of warning uttered some time back by Bishop MacMahon, and which were now confirmed by his unhappy guest, the recent disbandment of the Royal army and the triumphant attitude of the Puritan faction, the dreadful event in Carrickmines, which proved the strength of the latter party, and, over all, a haunting sense of some undefined personal misfortune about to come, weighed down his heart with an oppressive feeling of melancholy. He tried in vain to shake off these gloomy thoughts, and to fix his attention on the book which lay open before him, but again and again his mind reverted to the same depressing subjects. At length, when the night was waning into day, the gloomy doctrine of predestination with which he was permeated brought its own sombre consolation as a recompense for the agony it had inflicted on his jaded soul. He flung down his book upon the table, and stood up straight and defiant.

"What avails regret for the past or fear for the future," said he, grimly, "I must endure my weird, whatsoever it may be, and I trust I shall not be the first of my race who either rushed to meet it or tried to avoid it."

The faint, grey light of early morning was stealing through the barred window; so, remembering his guest's anxiety to be on the road before sunrise, he quietly aroused Ledwidge from his bed in the basement and ordered him to saddle Lord Castlehaven's horse. Then, softly ascending the turret stair, he knocked gently at the door of his visitor's room, and, receiving no answer, turned the handle and entered the apartment.

By the light of the wasted candle, which guttered redly in its socket, he perceived the Earl kneeling, fully dressed, at a small court-cupboard in the centre of the room, with his arms flung across it and his head between them, face downwards. His sword and pistols lay beside his right elbow, and, observing a gold rosary knotted round his left hand, Harry concluded he had fallen asleep at his devotions, for the bed had not been disturbed. He advanced lightly towards the kneeling figure, and laid his hand upon his shoulder, whereupon the supposed sleeper started instantly to his feet with a cocked pistol in his hand which he replaced on the table upon recognising his host.

"Pardon me, Mr. Dauntless," said he, in a tremulous voice, "but I did not hear your approach, and one so unhappy as myself hath cause to tremble if a fly should light upon his shoulder."

Harry saw that his eyes were wet with tears, and a rising

feeling of compassion swelled his own heart as the Earl, with a gesture of despair, held out his hand, on which the rosary sparkled, and continued: —

"When wife and child are in God's keeping alone, when home means a heap of blackened ruins, and the enemy are hot on the track, it says something for the consolation which religion can afford, when it can keep one, like myself, from fainting to death beneath the sheer weight of their misery. I had a brother, once, Mr. Dauntless, who should have borne my title; but he thought that the grey cowl of a Cistercian monk sat lighter on his peace than the pearls and strawberry-leaves of an Earl's coronet. I laughed at his taste, whilst I availed myself gladly of his choice; but methinks now that he was wiser far than I."

They descended to the bawn, where Ledwidge stood with the saddled horse, and when Castlehaven had mounted, he shook hands with Harry, and said: —

"The thanks of beggars, Mr. Dauntless, in this land of dispossessed men are cheaper than grains of sand, and, therefore, I shall not weary you by attempting to express what gratitude I feel to you and your mother. As for you, my good fellow," he continued as he forced a slender purse into the reluctant hands of Ledwidge, "I trust I shall be enabled to reward you for my preservation in a more fitting manner, if God should ever send us better days. Good-bye, Mr. Dauntless, once more, and my best prayer is that you shall be saved from such bitter sorrow as mine."

As Harry watched the lonely figure as it proceeded on its solitary way across the heather, a grim hard look drew his features into an expression as though he were trying to pierce the impenetrable future.

"There goes one," said he, in a low voice to himself, "who should have weathered the storm, if cautelous circumspection could have saved a fortune in these times; I wonder — I wonder if I shall ever be compelled to take the same desperate road as he hath gone."

XII

ALTHOUGH the Great Civil War raged furiously for the next nine months in England, it produced little corresponding activity in the Sister Island for the following reasons. Sir William Parsons, owing to his Machiavelian policy of driving prominent men into the Confederate League in order to attach their estates, had permitted that party to attain a power which was fully equal to his own; and the startled Puritan found himself in the position of a necromancer who has raised a spirit which he is unable either to dismiss or control. The Marquess of Ormond had succeeded in bringing about a Cessation of arms between the two factions, in order to induce some of the Confederate troops to cross over to England to support the King. As this move had considerably weakened the strength of their party without gaining any open acknowledgment of their treaty with Charles, the Supreme Council of Kilkenny resolutely declined to send further aid; and thus, for nearly a year, both Confederates and Parliamentarians in Ireland stood inactive but watchful, like two tired wrestlers who have mutually agreed to grant each other the breathing time they both require.

During this lull in the political tempest, Harry Dauntless recovered his spirits and once more wandered gun or rod in hand over the country, revisiting each well-known haunt among the mountains, and avoiding only Carrickmines, on account of the painful memories which lay buried beneath its ruins. The most profound peace brooded over the Pale, and Shanganagh, in particular, presented all the smiling aspect of a Valley in Arcadia. Consequently, he experienced no unpleasant shock, on one summer afternoon when he was returning from the Bride's Glen with a basketful of its dainty little trout, on being suddenly hailed by one of two horsemen who trotted up from behind. He turned round and perceived his ubiquitous kinsman, Bishop Evir MacMahon, habited like a merchant and followed at some distance by a tall, melancholy-looking serving-man. Since their last meeting in the early dawn at Bearna Baeghail, when his kinsman had brought him the first news of the insurrection, a considerable number of Harry's political views had been either modified or radically changed, and amongst them was his former estimation of the Bishop's character. Harry still retained a certain puzzled fear of him; but, as the Bishop was by this time the openly acknowledged agent of Queen Henrietta, the young Constable's former distrust had been latterly converted into a feeling of respectful awe, and he consequently saluted his kinsman with more cordiality than he had hitherto exhibited. The Bishop was not slow to observe this change in Harry's manner, and his keen eyes brightened visibly.

"Well, Harry, well," said he, cheerily, "I am right glad to see that thy campaign against us hath not spoiled thy love for the river nor soured thy temper against us. I confess I was somewhat grieved when I heard that thou wert in arms against us, but, as Ormond is now our very good friend, I don't suppose thou shalt find anyone among us who will bear malice for the dusting thou didst help to give us at Kilrush. Nevertheless, Harry, I am sorry, truly sorry, that, even when thou dost ride stirrup to stirrup with us later on, when Ormond and ourselves join hands, thou shalt be then too late to claim the glory which shall belong to those who followed the green and white banner from the commencement."

"Why, my Lord," said Harry, a little maliciously, "I was not aware that your party had won any considerable victory lately."

"*Nabocklish,*" said the Bishop, with a shamefaced laugh, "our hands are tied at present, owing to this Cessation, but, the moment it expires, Ormond and ourselves shall pack off thy friends Borlase and Parsons to their sour colleagues in Westminster. Ah, Harry, Harry, if thou hadst only joined us when I offered thee a troop of horse, thou couldst have gratified every desire for dallying with death in the King's service, inasmuch as thou couldst have gone with the five thousand volunteers, whom we poor rebels sent under Lord Biron to Chester last August, in case the peace of the Cessation had sat heavily on thy stomach."

Harry asked his kinsman with a smile why he himself had not gone.

"Because," answered the Bishop, with a knowing look, "I

hold opinions similar to those of my servant, Roe, who is a very superior person for one of his class. Being, as you may see, one who would be likely to make a good dragoon, he was offered a considerable bribe to join the Chester army; but when he heard that the English rebels made it a matter of religion to hang every prisoner who speaketh with an Irish accent, he thought the conditions of service somewhat hard and decided like an honest fellow that he would serve the King and Ireland at the same time."

By this time they had arrived at Bearna Baeghail, where the Bishop and his man dismounted. Ledwidge came forward to take the Bishop's horse, and was on his way to the stable, when Evir MacMahon called him back and ordered him in an off-hand way to look after his servant's animal as well, as he required his attendance within doors. The old man immediately complied with this request, but, the moment the Bishop was out of ear-shot, he muttered a curse below his breath upon all rapscallion serving-men who shifted their proper work upon other people's shoulders. Kathlyn greeted her cousin with her usual warmth, and then almost immediately flew off to Maureen in the kitchen, from whence came a delicate perfume of broiling trout mingled with a suspicion of roast venison collops a few minutes after her disappearance.

The Bishop, as full of spirits as a school-boy who has been granted an unexpected holiday, stamped about the room, with his spurs jingling and his sword clicking, just as Harry remembered him years before in Fetter Lane, and addressed the seemingly endless flow of his raillery alternately to his kinsman and his servant. The latter stood silent and thoughtful with a rather dejected look on his fair ruddy face, and answered his master only in monosyllables. He appeared to be about thirty-five, although the red-golden hair which curled on his well-shaped head, chin, and lip, gave him perhaps the advantage of looking five years younger than he really was. His dress, though coarse and suitable to his rank, displayed a well-set figure with a great length in the leg and an unusual depth and breadth in the chest, and Harry instinctively thought what a perfect trooper this sullen, dejected serving-man would have made, if he had been taken in hand by such a one as old Major Ogle of the Life Guards.

Meanwhile, Evir MacMahon paced backwards and forwards,

altering the current of his high spirits at every turn, and hardly allowing either of his companions time to answer the questions he put to them.

"Shut that door, Harry, I prithee," he said as the first suspicions of Kathlyn's absence were confirmed by the odour of Harry's trout broiling. "If I am a priest, you must not forget that I am also a man, and that cooking of thy mother would have very sorely tried the resolution of Saint Anthony himself. For, by my word, Harry, I am nearly famished and travelled to death, what with journeying yesterday from Athy and riding round and round the walls of Dublin this morning, looking for suitable places for setting up our battering trains when — What, Roe, what, hath thy rheumatism caught thee in the knees again, that thou shouldst look so gloomy? sit down, man, sit down, and never require a second bidding."

"Now may the devil take thee, Mr. Roe," thought Harry, "for the coolest sort of serving-man I have ever met withal.— In the name of reason why doth my cousin endure and encourage such familiarity on his part?"

"Cousin Harry," continued the Bishop, "I think you might open that door again. I remember me of several venial sins, for which the tantalising odour from the kitchen might well serve as a fitting penance. For instance, do you remember, Roe, that crop-eared Roundhead officer we met at Kilgobbin, and whom I sent off on a wild-goose chase? Why, man, dost wrinkle thy countenance so — if that chair is hard, take yonder one with the cushioned seat. Harry, my lad, we encountered a Roundhead patrol this morning near Kilgobbin, and were suffered to pass them unmolested on producing our permits, but shortly afterwards were again stopped by another party in charge of an officer who was very desirous of knowing if we had passed any suspicious persons on our way. I suppose I must have taken an unreasonable time in turning up mine eyes and tuning up my voice to the same whine as his own, but, in any case, I annoyed this honest gentleman so much that he dropped all his pious jargon and swore so lustily that he would slit my throat if I did not come to business, that his speech would have stricken the hardest swearing trooper of King Charles dumb with envy. So, in punishment for his profanity, I told him that we had lately overtaken a party of the rebels (which was quite true, for they were the other half of his own patrol), and consequently set him and his party off helter-skelter at a pace which I presume I helped to quicken by riding back to the other half and telling them that a party of the malignants were on the road in front, and so set one party of the cut-throats running away from the other. Oh, it was a sweet jest! was it not, Roe?"

"Your Grace seemed to enjoy it mightily at the time," answered the man, tersely, "but, as we have no assurance that we shall not fall in again with the same party on our way back, it is quite possible that your Grace hath not yet heard the last of the jest."

The reckless Churchman burst into a fit of boisterous laughter, and was about to make some jesting rejoinder when his attention was directed to Ledwidge, who at that moment entered, bearing half a dozen covered dishes on a beechen tray, and followed by Maureen, carrying a silver cup and pewter plate, both of which were so highly polished that it was difficult to say which was the more precious metal. The old soldier placed the dishes on the black oak table with becoming solemnity, whilst his daughter, stealing an occasional sidelong glance at the visitors, arranged the single cup and platter and straightened a few of the other articles on the table in the swift, deft fashion of a woman.

"What, my little girl, what!" said the jolly Bishop, regarding the single plate and cup with a comical expression of mock fear. "But one knife and fork to all those dishes! Why, I am but of mortal girth, and even if I feel I have the appetite of Gargantua when he ate up the six pilgrims in the salad, I know very well that I have not his capacity. Fetch another platter and cup for my man, and Roe, even though he be a poor trencher-man and a silent companion, shall keep me in countenance."

This arrangement by no means pleased Harry, who secretly thanked his stars he was not enrolled in an army where such terms of familiarity existed between all ranks; and Kathlyn, who shared something of the haughty spirit of her son, also felt some annoyance when she observed the servant take a seat opposite his master. However, as Harry was too well-bred to offer any objection to his guest's wishes, and as Kathlyn was in the habit of regarding any whim of her cousin's as partaking of something of the nature of a religious ordinance, neither mother nor son betrayed any outward symptom of displeasure.

The knives clattered merrily on the platters as the pink trout, brown venison, and yellow griddle-cake succumbed beneath the attack of the two travellers; and if the servant, either on account of the awkwardness of his position or natural abstemiousness in diet, ate and drank sparingly, his master made up for any deficiency on his part by giving free play to an appetite which would have done credit to three stout, hungry men. The big Churchman, however, did not permit his attention to his plate to interfere either with his natural high spirits or his conversation, and he rattled on in such a precipitous torrent of fun that he quite carried away his hearers with him. Presently Harry lost his natural reserve and laughed long and heartily, Kathlyn became infected with her kinsman's high spirits, and her usual patient smile gave place to a merry look of animation, old Ledwidge caught himself on the verge of joining in with an explosive guffaw once or twice, and in consequence assumed an increased austerity to make up for this lapse in decorum, and even the dejected serving-man assumed a shadow of a weary smile. When the meal was finished, the Bishop filled out a bumper from the flask at his elbow, and rose up, cup in hand.

"Cousins," said he, "we have claimed the ancient Irish rights of *Sorn* and *Coshering*, and you have sustained the charge in the good old Irish fashion. I owe ye both a toast to the honour of Bearna Baeghail, but ere I drink it there is another to which it must give place: 'Here is to our tenants, the Puritan Parliament of Dublin, and a quick and pleasant journey to them to their own kith in Westminster.'"

Just as he raised the cup to his lips, a hurried step was heard in the passage, and Con MacGauran, with his shock of hair on end, his eyes nearly starting out of his head, and his lower jaw agape, appeared at the door of the banqueting room, and held out one trembling hand as if to forbid the toast. The idiot clawed wildly at the air once or twice like a drowning man, and after one of those long gurgling utterances so common to persons of his afflicted class managed to gasp, —

"*De Sider! De Sider Derg!*[1] Tree, Six, Tirty. *Sider Derg* are riding up to kill us all!"

[1] *Sider Derg, i. e.*, The Scarlet Soldiers.

The cup fell untasted from the hand of the stout Bishop and rolled empty over the oak floor, his face grew ashy white, his knees trembled under him for a moment, but, recovering himself immediately, he snatched up his sword and pistols and ran to the door, closely followed by Harry and Roe. Down below upon the bridle path, with their horses' heads set in the direction of the Castle, was approaching a party of horsemen whose red cassocks and sparkling arms were sufficient to proclaim them at first sight as Parliamentary cavalry; but even this startling sight, far from dismaying Evir MacMahon, appeared to recall all his native courage and resource.

"The horses! the horses!" he cried, starting towards the bawn. "Leave the saddles behind us, Roe, and by Saint Hubert, the patron of all good sportsmen, we shall beat the Roundheads in a race across the mountain."

Half way across the bawn, the Bishop stopped with an exclamation, for at that moment six mounted troopers appeared upon the crest of the hill above, and, descending the slope as if to meet their comrades on the bridle path, completely shut off all escape in both directions. The two confederates exchanged a grim look of consternation, for there could be no doubt as to the hostile intentions of the two parties, and the servant, regarding his master with an enquiring look, said something to him in Spanish which Harry thought sounded like an expression of assurance.

"The Cessation!" replied the Bishop, fiercely, in English. "What do these ruffians care for Ormond and his paper treaties? I tell thee that these cut-throats would not miss an opportunity of fleshing their swords upon us if we came to them with a safe-conduct signed by Charles himself."

"Then they are very likely to have as pretty a ruffle as the stoutest blade among them could desire," said the man, very composedly, as he hitched his sword belt so as to bring his hilt well forward. "There are but three file and a half approaching from below, and, if your Lordship and myself could account for a brace apiece with our petronels, we would have but three to encounter with our swords ere their comrades came up. Unless" (here he glanced towards Harry) "we stood them off behind the battlements, which I suppose is not your Lordship's intention, for fear of compromising Mr. Dauntless."

This last remark fired Harry's blood on the instant and

roused him to action. He caught the Bishop and his man, dragged them inside the door, which he instantly barred and chained, and then enjoining perfect silence and inaction on their part, took down from the wall a long-barrelled fowling-piece of Spanish workmanship, which he proceeded to load with ball ammunition. Then he went up alone to the battlements, where he stepped into a bartizan and scrutinised the Parliamentarians, who by this time had drawn up about a hundred yards from the walls. Six of them immediately dismounted, whilst the seventh, who, from the plume in his morion, appeared to be their leader, trotted easily up to the gate, where he reined in his horse, and glanced up at Harry with a jaunty nod. Dauntless immediately recognised the cruel, smiling face of Hooter under the shade of the upturned steel cap, but collecting his presence of mind, he rested his piece in a corner of the bartizan and, leaning forward from an embrasure, regarded him steadily.

"Mr. Hooter," said he, sternly, "to what reason am I to attribute your presence here in company with armed men? Surely the terms on which we stand to one another and my own position with the Lords Justices are sufficient to demand an explanation for so extraordinary a proceeding."

"My young Constable of Shanganagh," answered Hooter, with a malignant grin on his coarse face, "you need have no fear either of me or the good fellows who accompany me; inasmuch as we have come for the purpose of affording you that protection which one of your well-known loyal principles is so likely to stand in need of in these days. Very many rascals come and go along the Pale in such subtle disguises as to hoodwink one even as clever as yourself; and, as our quarters down in Cherrytown were none of the best, and as I heard that a couple of suspected malignants were seen heading towards the Valley this morning, I, therefore, determined to make Bearna Baeghail my inn for a while and thus protect you and pleasure myself."

"I am beholden to you for your proffered protection, which I do not stand in need of," said Harry, pale but scornful. "As for your taking up your quarters here, unless you can show me a warrant from the Lords Justices empowering you to change your billet, I must decline to receive either you or your companions."

"My warrant, my young Cock of Shanganagh,' said the ruffian, touching the hilt of his sword insolently, "is contained in this good sheath of sharkskin, wherein you shall find many powerful and trenchant reasons to convince you that when the King's men knock, doors must open. Perhaps you may remember the lesson which I helped to teach our lamented friend, the late Sir Thomas Merryl; and, notwithstanding the slender force at my disposal, you may find they are sufficient to teach you a similar reproof, unless you hop down briskly from your perch and open the door immediately."

"If you can show me no better warrant than that," answered Harry, steadily, though his frame shook with passion, "you may sit outside my gate all night; and, if you attempt to force an entrance, I warn you that my people are well armed and I will defend my property in the manner that the law permits."

If Hooter had known that two desperate and well-armed men were standing within ten feet of him at one of the lower loopholes, he might have acted differently; but, as he was as well acquainted with the number of domestics in Bearna Baeghail as he was with every other homestead in the Barony, he assumed that Harry was the only person in the house who would be likely to offer resistance, and he immediately proceeded to put his own simple plans into execution.

"Thank 'ee, my young blood," said he, gleefully, "you are one after my own heart, inasmuch as you appear to dislike wasting time, which I consider is too valuable a commodity to be frittered away in 'ifs' and 'buts.'"

He turned in his demi-pique and waved his gauntletted hand to the troopers on the bridle path below.

"Stottart, my good fellow," he shouted cheerfully, "bring me that petard and madrier along with the other trinkets which I bade you put in your saddle bags this morning."

One of the soldiers mounted, rode up to Hooter, and handed him a couple of slender iron bars, a screw-driver, a small block of hollowed wood called a madrier, to which the petard was attached, and, last of all, the petard itself, which consisted of a small, metal cone fitted with a time-fuse and loaded with a couple of pounds of blasting powder. Dismounting from his horse, and setting to work with great diligence, Hooter braced both madrier and petard to the door with the light iron bars, secured them with half a dozen long screws, and then stepped back a pace or two to admire his work.

"A very excellent piece of oak in this door of yours, Mr. Dauntless," said he, pleasantly, as he glanced up at the white face of the young man above him. "I have very nearly twisted my two hands off at the wrists in driving the screws into it, but now let us see how it shall stand the shock of a couple of pounds of blasting powder."

He blew on the match of his musketoon preparatory to lighting the fuse, whereupon Harry snatched up his piece and, cocking and shouldering it in one motion, bade him stand back from the door or his blood would be on his own head. As Hooter's only reply was a low chuckling laugh and a threatening movement nearer the petard, Harry, with a vengeful look in his eye, took aim at the Commissioner's head and pressed his trigger. The Castle rang to the discharge of the gun, and, while the smoke hung wavering in the air, Hooter lurched to one side and then dropped heavily into the angle of the gate-post with his head twisted to one side and to all appearance lifeless. The man who had assisted him to lay the petard, rammed spurs into the flanks of his horse and galloped towards his companions, crying out at the top of his voice that their leader was slain.

"And may the devil take his soul into the bargain," added he, angrily, "for bringing us out of where we were so snugly quartered. Turn and ride for your lives, lads, ere they pour their shot among us, for I caught sight of others with lighted matches at the lower loopholes."

"Nay, brother Stottart," said another, more loyal to his fallen leader than his companions, "shall we leave his dead corpse behind, to be, perhaps, the object of their devilish popish charms, cantrips, and such heathen abominations?—Turn back, brother, and help me to carry him off, lest they hang his dead body from the walls, even as the Philistines did that of King Saul at Beth-Shan."

"Go back by yourself, then," said the man addressed, with an oath, "and carry him off if you like; but, for my part, I think my own live bones are worth more than a ton of dead men's, and that young gallant on the top of the tower holdeth a gun-barrel too straight to permit my accompanying you.—

Come on, lads, and let us join the others on the hill above and leave Hooter to rot where he is."

The other men agreed emphatically with the last speaker, and accordingly they made a circuit of the Castle, taking care to keep well out of musket-range, and, as soon as they had joined their companions on the hill above, the whole party set off at a brisk trot in a Southerly direction.

When the first flush of indignant anger had passed from Harry, and he saw his enemy lying motionless on the pavement, all the stern resolution, which had up till then nerved his heart and hand, melted away with the thin smoke which curled lazily from the muzzle of his gun; and, resting the butt of the weapon on the embrasure, he leaned forward and remained for some minutes staring vacantly on the limp and huddled figure beneath. Presently he was roused by the sound of the bolts of the gate being withdrawn and the hinges creaking noisily; and then, as the door swung open, the body of Hooter, which had been lying with its face crushed up against it, rolled slowly over and he heard the supposed dead man give utterance to a deep groan. Evir MacMahon stepped out of the gate, and, bending over the prostrate man, unbuckled his gorget, removed his helmet, and closely examined his head and neck. Then he made a sign to those within, and Ledwidge made his appearance with a pitcher of water, which the big Churchman emptied over the face of the Commissioner, who gasped, groaned, opened his eyes, and regarded the other's face with a look of the utmost terror.

"What!" he gasped. "*You* here? for God's sake do not let these people murder me, *Señor Brâbant*."

"There is no fear of your coming to harm, either here or in Dublin," answered the Bishop, with a significant look, "provided you will do what you are bid, and will answer truthfully such questions as I am about to put to you."

"Carry me within doors and see to my hurts first," said the wounded Roundhead, feebly. "I can scarcely speak or think at present, for I feel as if the half of my head were shot away, and my chest stings as though a shovelful of hell fire was burning there."

The Bishop and Ledwidge raised Hooter and carried him within doors, and as soon as they disappeared under the arch, Harry dropped his gun into a corner of the bartizan and leaned forward again on the battlements with his eyes fixed moodily on the sparkling sea.

"Please God, I have not wounded the ruffian mortally," he muttered sullenly to himself, "not that it would lessen my offence in the eyes of that malignant old Make-traitor Parsons, but I feel that the slaying of such a wretch as Hooter is rather the office of an executioner than a soldier and a gentleman. Yet it doth gall my soul to think that such a one should be the immediate cause of the confiscation of the last poor possessions of my house. How I have striven, plotted, struggled, and humbled myself to keep them! How I have endeavoured up to the last to avert such a fate! but how relentlessly hath the Spinner contrived to twist my thread into the long string of the dispossessed in spite of all my struggles.—Tush, Harry Dauntless, why should you repine? Laugh while you may and sigh when you must; for such poor puppets as we mortals are, had better resign ourselves passively to the strings which direct our fortunes than pull vainly against them."

Just then, Evir MacMahon made his appearance on the battlements, and, observing the grave expression on his face, Harry anxiously asked him if Hooter's wound was likely to prove mortal. He was greatly relieved when his kinsman assured him that, so far from the Commissioner's hurt being serious, it was likely to prove to be of so light a nature that a few weeks' rest would suffice to effect a cure.

"The bullet of your gun," said the Bishop, "struck him on the cheek-piece of his helmet and glanced down on his gorget, and, in consequence of the excellence of the rascal's harness, he hath sustained nothing worse than a broken collar-bone and a lump on the side of his head the size of a potato. But there are more weighty concerns in my mind than the hurts of a paltry ruffian such as he, and the chief of my troubles is, to know what course you yourself intend to pursue."

"Methinks, after I have wounded the trusty Commissioner of the Lord Justice," answered Harry, bitterly, "there is no other choice left me than to seek shelter immediately under the banners of the Confederates."

"God knoweth," said the Bishop, with a wistful look in his eyes, "that my heart yearneth to see thee allied with us; but, lest thou shouldst accuse me in after days of having dealt with thee in a half-faced fashion, I shall now unfold to thee more than, perhaps, I have warrant for telling. This brute, Hooter, is one of those dogs who hath been for some while running on both sides of the hedge. He is a secret agent of the Marquess in addition to being the open instrument of the Puritans and (on what account does not matter to thee) knoweth to his fear that I hold him in the palm of my hand like a wounded hedge sparrow. The villain hath just acknowledged to me that he held no higher warrant for his recent outrage than his own malignant desire to insult and humble thee by quartering his brother cut-throats here in despite of thy protest; and he hath moreover assured me that there is no scheme afoot in Dublin Castle against thyself or property. Thus far, thou hast no cause for fear, — for I am convinced that the fellow spoke the truth (not for love of it, but for his own sake), for well he knoweth what would happen to him if he were to deceive me in the smallest tittle of a word. A short term of imprisonment, a moderate fine, or, perhaps, a mere rebuke, may be all which Parsons may award thee when he hears the account of the matter which I shall compel Hooter to deliver; and now it remains with thee to decide whether thou wilt abide the issue here or adhere to thy first plan of joining the Confederates."

"I know too much of Parsons," answered Harry, "to trust even so small an estate as Bearna Baeghail to his mercy, no matter what statement you may compel Hooter to make. My mind is made up to join the only party left in Ireland who support my Sovereign, and I would set out this very hour if I could place my mother in some safe asylum."

"She cannot find a more secure place than here," answered his kinsman. "Nay, Cousin," he continued very earnestly as Harry shook his head with an impatient frown. "I pledge you my word as a priest that this scurvy ruffian shall render Bearna Baeghail a spot of greater security for her than any in Ireland."

"What trust can you place in the assurance of such a villain?" asked Harry, with a touch of incredulous scorn.

"The best in the world," replied Evir MacMahon, drawing himself up with pride at the thought of the intrigues wherein his entire existence was enveloped. "His life, the love of his own wretched carcase, and, what he loveth even more, the unconsidered trifles filched from his brother robbers. I hold every one of these at my disposal, and he knoweth I could rend any-one or all of them from him at will. Rest assured, Harry, that, if thy mother had an army at her disposal, she could not have such security as I can exact from this same trembling wretch."

"If you can so securely engage my mother's safety, then let it be the North for me, in God's name," cried Harry. "I am sick of all this juggling with those who are resolved upon hav-ing my property, in the face of all my wiles. I have nothing left me now but my sword, my honour, and my horse; yet, if I join your army like a beggar, Evir, I promise you that I shall not make the worse soldier on that account."

"Do not say beggar, Harry," said the Bishop, embracing him warmly and flushing hotly at the thoughts which raced through his mind like a pack of hounds in full cry. "Do not say beggar, for I have that of thine up my sleeve which shall set up the fortunes of thy house at their apex when the sun shines bright again. Wend thou to Cavan at once by the main road; I and Roe shall journey thither by the Kilkenny route, as we have business to transact in that city, and in any case it were wiser for us to travel by divers roads. Down to thy mother, Boy, and gladden her heart with thy resolution. My blessing on thee, but she shall be a happy woman on hearing the news, and then, Boy, to horse! to horse! and Ho! for the North."

XIII

AFTER a brief but affecting interview with his mother, Harry dressed and armed himself for his journey. Having little fear of meeting any of the Parliamentarian troopers on the lonely upper road, he took that course through the mountains, and, riding boldly in a Northern direction, arrived a couple of hours before sunset at that spot just above Saggard where the last ridge of the Dublin Mountains slopes gently down to the fertile plains below.

Before him, stretching in one unbroken carpet of green pasture-land, lay the beautiful counties of Kildare, Meath, and Louth, with every river, field, and hedgerow clearly defined in the bright evening sunshine. Fully seventy miles away, rose the deep blue outline of Slieve Donard and the Mourne Mountains distinctly visible even at that immense distance; and away in the East the towers, churches, and pinnacles of Dublin shone dimly yellow through the halo of smoke which enveloped them like a sea mist. The beauty of the scene was not without its effect on the mind of the young fugitive, and a hitherto dormant feeling of affection for his country awoke within him, and filled his heart with a share of his mother's enthusiasm.

"Dear, distressed land," he murmured softly, "I have too, too long stopped my ears to thy pleading, but henceforth I devote myself to thee. Dear country, receive me in thy service, and may Heaven send thee happier days than these and better sons than I."

Descending the hill, and avoiding all villages lest he might fall in with any of the Puritan garrison of Dublin, he proceeded cautiously over the fields until he struck the main road North of Dunboyne. From thence he rode on at a brisk trot until he arrived at Navan, which town he reached late in the evening, and put up for the night at an obscure inn in Friar's Lane. In the morning he learned to his consternation that a party of Coote's Horse was reported to be then scouring the country North of Navan for the purpose of harassing the outposts of the Confederate Army. These ruffians, whom Coote has been accused of using as instruments of vengeance against his private enemies, had a character for ferocious brutality which Harry, on account of his previous acquaintance with them under Ormond, knew but too well they had deservedly earned. To fall into their hands meant instant death to anyone unprovided with a pass, inasmuch as they never encumbered themselves with prisoners; and those travellers who were furnished with permits invariably gave Coote's Horse a wide berth, as they had an unenviable reputation of making little distinction between rebel and loyalist in case the object of their suspicions happened to be mounted on a good horse.

Consequently, Harry was obliged to spend a week in his wretched lodgings until a passing farmer brought the welcome news that Coote's regiment had suffered a signal defeat at the hands of a strong body of O'Neill's cavalry, and had fallen back on Trim, thus leaving the road to the North once more open. Next morning he started at an early hour, rode steadily on in a North-westerly direction towards Cavan, and by midday reached the border of the County and headed towards the pretty little village of Virginia. The district through which he passed was wild, hilly, and lonely in the extreme, and the few country people to whom he addressed enquiries as to the whereabouts of the Confederate Army afforded him little information. They either could not or would not understand his imperfect Gaelic, and invariably assumed that air of stupid simplicity wherewith the Irish peasant so easily baffles any attempt to extract information which he is unwilling to impart. Notwithstanding his mountain training, the loneliness of the hills had a depressing effect on his spirits, and his thoughts in a proportionate degree trended into a gloomy channel.

He pictured to himself, half-scornfully, half-sadly, the rabble wherewith he was now irretrievably to be associated, and the contemplation did little towards restoring his good spirits.

"A few thousands of naked, ignorant wretches armed with scythes and rusty skenes," he muttered, "led by some score of noisy, robber chieftains; and this is what my cousin Evir terms an Army! An Army, wherein my brother officers will be a turbulent company of so-called gentlemen, their education nothing more than a barbarous acquaintance with their own tiresome genealogies reaching back to Noah; their ambitions bounded by a wrangling jealousy for precedence at the board and in the field, and their military skill a mere brute courage which prompts them to rush upon a platoon of musketeers and get shot like rabbits for their pains. The men of my command, a savage mob like their cousins, the Scots Highlanders, their discipline, their own unfettered will to do what they list. Their terms of service, their right to join or leave their standards whenever it pleaseth them, and their method of expressing disapproval of an order which does not fit their humour, the insertion of a palm's length of a skene dhu into the bowels of the officer who is hardy enough to insist upon their obedience. An Army! Heaven save the mark! an army which should scarcely warrant the despatch of a half squadron of dragoons in order to send it flying in every direction like Mountgarret's rabble at Kilrush."

With his mind full of such despondent thoughts, he reached the Southern shore of Lough Ramor about sunset, and was proceeding slowly along the forest road which skirts its beautiful crescent, when suddenly a stern voice, which seemed to proceed neither from the fern which bordered the road, nor the woods which skirted it, but from the air overhead, commanded him sharply in Gaelic to stand and declare for whom he was. Somewhat startled by this unexpected summons, which appeared to come from no particular quarter, Harry drew rein and looked about in every direction, but without encountering a human being.

"I know but little Gaelic," he said uneasily, "and would rather answer you, whoever you may be, in Saxon, and therefore, if you can understand so much of that tongue, I tell you that I am for God and King Charles."

A bitter, mocking laugh was the reply, and the voice said in perfect English:—

"So say all the red-coats too; they are all for God and the King, and, if one were to judge from mouths alone, Charles of England had every one of his subjects overflowing with love for him. Take thy hand from thy holster, young Sir, for thou art covered with my musketoon, and I tell thee in a friendly way that I am not one of those jerkers who shut both of their eyes when pressing a trigger. State truly what is thy business in this part of the country."

"I am on my way to the camp of General O'Neill," answered Harry, "and if you are one of his soldiers, as I assume you are, I beg you will direct me what road to take, and let me pass in peace."

"I cannot allow thee past my post on mine own authority," replied the voice "but I shall get down on the road, and keep thee company until the Corporal walks the round to relieve me."

There was a rustling in the leaves of a great oak-tree which flung its gnarled boughs half-way across the road, and, with a clinking of armour, a well-appointed trooper suddenly dropped down on the road, snaphaunce in hand, and bade Harry, in a bluff but not unfriendly fashion, to dismount and unsaddle. He was a sunburned, soldier-like fellow, and the harness on his well-built figure, the piece in his hand, and the pistols in his belt bore a glittering tribute to the care he bestowed on them.

Whilst Harry was unsaddling his horse, the man carried on an amicable conversation with him, but, notwithstanding his friendly attitude, the soldier did not relax his vigilance for a moment, and continued to keep a watchful eye on Harry and the road he had come by.

When the young Cavalier had turned his horse loose to graze, and had himself taken a seat at the foot of a great mountain fir, he indicated the oak-tree with a smile, and asked the soldier if his commanders were in the habit of posting their sentinels in such airy watching places.

"Oh, no, your Honour," replied the trooper, with a laugh, "my post is on the road between the scaur and yon burn which flows into the Lough; but I saw thee two miles away, and was nonplussed not only because thou wert alone, but on account of that," pointing with a puzzled look at the scarf of Royalist Blue which Harry wore across his cuirass, "and as I knew thou wert not one of Coote's nor Munroe's, I e'en climbed up where I could watch the better, and stop thee if necessary."

The excellence of his English, and the soldier-like bearing of the man suggested to Harry that he must have served under the English banners, so he put the question to him directly.

"Yes," said the Confederate, frankly, "I was one of Strafford's men, and wore a Red Cross in my hat before I changed it for this," pointing to the green and white tuft in his morion, "and though my pay is less than what it was, and my general even stricter than the Earl, yet my present duty is more to my liking than my former service."

"Is your general so severe in his discipline," asked Harry, "that you give him the character of exceeding even Wentworth in strictness?"

"Severe?" echoed the man, with a stare. "Aye, one may well term Red Owen O'Neill severe. Why, Sir, it is scarce a month since he had a poor fellow of Art Dhu Colkitto O'Neill's regiment executed for nothing more than shooting a Puritan weaver in Newry."

Harry ventured to remark that the man probably deserved his fate, and that O'Neill's sentence was in accordance with justice.

"Perhaps it was, and perhaps it was not," said the man, sullenly, "and perhaps, if you had been in Rory O'Neill's place, you would have acted as he did. The psalm-singer had killed poor Rory's mother and father at the Massacre of Island Magee, and as Red Owen said himself, he would have hanged the weaver if he had been found guilty by a properly constituted court of law, wherefore Rory only anticipated the hangman. But, notwithstanding the provocation he had received, and the fact that Art Dhu Colkitto and Sir Phelim O'Neill, the general's own cousins, went down on their knees to beg for his life, Red Owen ordered him for death as resolutely as though he were a mere Saxon *boddagh*, instead of one of his own name and clan. It was in vain that Art Dhu pleaded all the good services of poor Rory, for the only reply of Owen was that his cousin should not make his own burden harder to bear by reminding him of his clansman's good qualities. He swore that he should die if he were his own brother, inasmuch as he had taken the law into his own hands, and had slain the wretched murderer without giving him a moment for repentance; but, as Rory had proved himself on many occasions to be a good soldier and a brave man, he spared him the shame of a felon's cord, and ordered him to be shot to death by a platoon of his own clan, which was accordingly done on the following morning."

"Good God!" cried Harry, greatly moved by the recital of this grim history of retributive justice, "Why should O'Neill have added to the unhappiness of the poor fellow by ordering his own kinsmen to act as his executioners?"

"You gentlemen of the South do not understand us men of the North," said the trooper, proudly. "A common murderer would not have been accorded the honour of having six of the best blood of Hy-Niall act as his executioners; and poor Rory O'Neill said, just before he faced them, that death at their hands was robbed of half its bitterness. As for the firing party, — when it was made absolutely certain that no prayers would avail their kinsman, — I warrant you, it would have been a dangerous duty for any one not belonging to Hy-Niall to have undertaken the duty."

Both men relapsed into silence. The trooper was, perhaps, overcome by recollections of similar instances of the unbending justice of his great general, and Harry Dauntless, for his part, was deeply affected by the sentinel's story, which afforded him material for a hundred reflections as he sat silent and thoughtful on his mossy seat at the foot of the rustling fir-tree.

"What mysterious power can this man possess," thought he, "that he can visit these breaches of discipline with such severe penalties, and yet retain the blind devotion which, report says, not only his own clan yield him, but which the other hitherto discordant elements of his army also offer him freely? How is it he succeeds in keeping together an army of rival clans, which every one of his predecessors failed to maintain in one camp for longer than a month or two? He must be a shrewd-brained politician, — a very master-mind of subtlety, — or he would not have triumphed where so many others have failed. As for his military skill — I myself have heard from old Major Ogle that Francis of Pavia had accounted O'Neill to be the first soldier in Christendom on account of his defence of Arras against Richelieu; and his nine months' defence of a city with but a poor fifteen hundred men against thirty thousand, very fairly substantiates such a reputation."

He regarded the stalwart figure of the trooper, who stood some dozen yards away, with renewed interest, and a fresh stream of conjecture slowly percolated through his mind.

"Perhaps some of O'Neill's army are armed with better weapons than broadswords and sciaths,"[1] he thought musingly, "Perhaps they are not the rude mob which I have heard they are. The men who held Arras so resolutely against the Frenchman were Ulstermen like yon fine fellow; and if O'Neill has succeeded in arming the rest of his men as well as yonder sentinel, it is very possible that the Army of the North may yet give a very good account of itself."

The shadows of the pine-trees were stretching in gigantic streaks across the turf, when a party of four men, dressed and armed in the same fashion as the sentinel, wheeled round a corner of the road and advanced rapidly in the direction where the latter stood guard over Harry. They halted within a few paces of the sentinel, and one of them, who wore two feathers in his morion in lieu of the horse-hair tufts of his companions, advanced and held a brief parley with Harry's friend. They spoke in Gaelic, and, though the purport of it was unknown to the young prisoner, there was no doubt it had reference to him, for the man who had been relieved nodded to him, and said, —

"My corporal, who speaketh no Saxon, bids me say thou art to come with us."

Harry rose, and was about to resaddle, but the trooper shook his head, and intimated that he would not be permitted either to mount or take his horse, which one of the soldiers led into a narrow fissure between two rocks which seemed to swallow them up immediately.

The man very civilly offered to carry his saddle, and walked by his side, conversing in a friendly fashion, but, nevertheless, Harry observed that the Corporal and the remainder of his party, as they fell in behind, blew on the matches of their snaphaunces in a very significant way, as if to intimate that any attempt to part company would be followed by very prompt and unpleasant action on their part.

About a quarter of a mile down the road, Harry's friendly guard led the way up a steep bank densely covered with ash and hazel trees, and, pulling asunder two drooping ashes, revealed a cup-shaped dell surrounded by a thick curtain of hazel and young beech trees, which not only concealed the

[1] *Sciath,* — the leather roundel or target which formed the sole defensive armour of the Irish kern.

existence of such a spot, but also afforded a shelter little inferior to a marquee.

A soldier, on his knees beside a charcoal fire over which a small, iron pot hung on a pliant willow slip, raised his head on his companions' entrance, and having greeted them with a few words in Gaelic, again devoted his attentions to the pot, which gave forth a pleasant odour of supper; and the troopers, piling their musketoons, but retaining their swords and pistols, sat down and invited Harry, with word and gesture, to do likewise.

There were several blankets and six saddles scattered about the dell; and observing that the ground had the dried, crushed, sickly yellow appearance which grass assumes when human bodies have couched on it for some length of time, Harry asked his friend how long they had been keeping guard in that spot.

"The cavalry picket is always mounted in this dell," was the reply, "but we ourselves have been only two days here; and shall leave it to-morrow, when relieved by some of O'Donnell's regiment of horse."

"What regiment of horse do you yourself belong to, friend?" asked Harry.

"The O'Reilly's of Clough Oughter," answered the man, proudly. "Than which there is no better regiment of horse in Ireland or England, and I, who have served in both countries, know of what I speak."

"And are there many in Mr. O'Reilly's regiment as well equipped as you and your comrades?" continued Harry, who was becoming interested in these evidences of discipline in the Confederate Army.

The man addressed spoke a few words in Gaelic to the Corporal, who laughed loudly, and, regarding Harry with a look of contemptuous amusement, said something in the same language, which Harry asked his friend to translate for him.

"He says that Mr. O'Reilly, as thou termest the chief of our clan, whom we call Clough Oughter and his friends the O'Reilly, hath five hundred better men at present in his regiment; and when the next consignment of saddles and harness cometh from abroad, there will be a rare scramble among five hundred more as good, who are waiting for them."

"And the infantry regiments of General O'Neill," continued Harry, "are they all as well armed and manned as thy regiment appears to be?"

"That is a question," said the soldier, drily, "which you can easily resolve for yourself when you see them to-morrow; but it is not a matter which one of my degree could venture to tell you of to-night."

At this point the soldier by the fire lifted off the little iron pot, and placed it down in the middle of the company, who were immediately greeted with a fragrant steam which gave promise of a better supper than Harry had supposed these wild regions could have afforded. The pot contained a mixture of beef, mutton, potatoes, barley, and ramps, or wild onions, all boiled in that species of rich, appetising compound which is best known to English mouths and ears as Irish stew.

The Corporal poured forth the broth into a tin porringer, which was passed from one to the other of the company like a loving cup, and divided the remainder of the contents of the pot into six messes; and, notwithstanding that the only plates used at this simple meal were fresh, green chestnut leaves, no party of aldermen ever enjoyed a civic banquet better than Harry and his companions.

When this satisfactory business was over, the Corporal produced a large stone jar from a little spring which bubbled up in the middle of the camping ground, and, having rinsed the tin cup which had done duty as a soup tureen, filled it from the big jar, without qualifying it with any other liquid, and handed it, with many polite expressions in Gaelic, to the prisoner.

It proved to be a raw, brimming measure of Poteen, that awful concoction of liquid fire which is to this day distilled in the North and other remote parts of Ireland, in defiance of the Police and the Excise authorities. The very fumes from this dreadful stuff brought tears into Harry's eyes; but, unwilling to give offence to his good-natured guards, which a refusal might entail, he took a mouthful, handed the cup back to the Corporal, and, overcome by the potency of the fiery liquid, burst into a paroxsysm of coughing.

His neighbour, raising the cup and glancing towards his prisoner, remarked, "*Slainthe agus Failthe*,"[1] and transferred the contents at one draught into his own person without any

[1] "Health and Welcome."

outward symptoms of injury or discomfort; and each man of the guard, with a bow to Harry and the approved salutation of "*Slainthe*," drank a cupful of the same dreadful spirit with apparent composure and satisfaction.

The aldermanic stone jar was corked up again, whilst the party drew sociably round the fire, and Harry, who had never heard of the immense quantities of raw whiskey which these active men of the North can drink without effect, could not have believed that the big, quiet soldiers who sat smoking peacefully and chatting quietly had drunk anything stronger than water, had not his own scalded throat kept reminding him at intervals of the mighty strength of their after-dinner grace-cup.

When the last faint topaz of the twilight was succeeded by the darkening shadows of evening, the Corporal, in a blunt but civil fashion, intimated to Harry it was time to retire, by pointing out to him a bed of heather which had been considerately gathered for him by the English-speaking trooper.

The man, wishing him good-night, lay down close beside him, having first taken the precaution of putting the aldermanic stone jar out of the way of temptation to his guard, by snugly stowing it away under the flap of the saddle which served him as a pillow. The other men, with the exception of one left on sentry, rolled themselves in their cloaks, and soon after they lay down, their heavy breathing, succeeded by a tempest of snoring, testified the profundity of their slumbers.

For some time Harry lay awake with his eyes fixed on the dark figure of the sentinel, whose movements he could follow amid the hazel-trees by the glowing spark of his snaphaunce as he paced to and fro. The young man's thoughts dwelt on the events of the day. The lonely though beautiful country he had traversed, this first encounter with the Confederate forces, of which he was now virtually a member, and the soldier-like appearance of their outpost, until, gradually lulled into drowsiness by the softness of his heather bed underneath, and the langourous rustling of the beech and hazel saplings overhead, he fell into a sound slumber.

XIV

BEFORE daybreak the Corporal roused his prisoner and, intimating by a sign that he was to rise and follow, led him out of the dell in an opposite direction to the way he had entered it on the previous evening. He conducted Harry through a dense thicket where the two men were compelled to scramble over fallen pine-trees or dive under low-growing oak boughs at every yard or so. Each step they took sank them hip-high in a perfect sea of tall, rank fern, trailing sweet-briar and lush flags and grasses, so that their progress was necessarily slow and toilsome, and Harry was not sorry when they emerged on a road where five of the guard were already standing by their horses. The men were engaged in saddling six of those sturdy little horses which are known in Ireland as *garrans*, a breed of animals which appear to thrive under hardships that would assuredly kill finer-looking and handsomer cattle, but Harry looked in vain for his own bay mare.

He was startled by the sudden appearance of his English-speaking friend, who rose up from a fern-shaded hollow leading his mare by the bridle; and, while the man aided him in saddling, Harry learned from him that a secret pass from the road below led to a cave beneath their feet which the picket of Lough Ramor were in the habit of using as a stable. He was admiring the skill evinced in the selection of such a watch post when a party of six mounted men came trotting towards them through the early mist and on drawing nearer proved to be the expected relief. On approaching the old guard, the relief halted, the Corporals of each party exchanged a brief conversation between themselves, and then returned to the heads of their respective commands, and that with which Harry was concerned set forward at a brisk, swinging trot over the hills.

After two hours' journey through a country which rose and fell in hills and hollows like the regular waves of an ocean after a mighty storm, they clattered into a little town lying in a deep bowl-shaped hollow which gave the place the appearance of having been scooped out of the bottom of an extinct crater. In the centre of the town, close to the market cross, the Corporal halted and dismissed his little command and then made a sign to Harry that he was to accompany him. He brought him into a house in the Market Square wherein he encountered a number of stout fellows in steel caps and buff-coats lounging about in what appeared to be a guard-room. One of the soldiers offered him the only chair in the room, and, addressing this man in very imperfect Gaelic, Harry asked if there was anyone present who spoke English. The man, guessing at rather than understanding his enquiry, roused up one of his companions who was lying asleep on a broad wooden shelf that did duty for a guard-room bed and presented him to Harry, who immediately asked the fellow to bring him before his commander.

"Hoogh, Aye," replied the linguist, with a nod of intelligence, "De Taioseach, yis, yis, de Taioseach — de Taioseach will be here — a minnit — ten minnit — yis, yis, — Her honour sit down and content herself — de Taioseach here in ten minnit."

Harry had not the faintest idea as to who or what the word Taioseach signified, but as he was unable to elicit any other speech than the foregoing from the interpreter, he sat down and resigned himself patiently to whatever time should bring. At the end of an hour he heard the click and jingle of armour and the quick tread of a couple of men descending the stairs; and, presently, a fine, straight young fellow in a leather jacket and blue truis and wearing a barrad surmounted with a cock's feather, entered the room and shouted at the top of his voice, "*An Taioseach.*"

Every soldier in the room sprang to a posture of respectful attention as a young officer, with a sash of green and white thrown lightly across his cuirass and a plume of the same colours nodding on his helmet, entered the room with a quick, firm step and stopped short on beholding Dauntless. The oreillets or hinged ear-pieces and the triple-barred face-guard of his half-casque almost concealed his features, yet Harry thought there was something familiar in the appearance of the supple, graceful figure and the blue-black lustrous hair which curled from under the rim of his helmet; but, before he could assure himself of the identity of the officer, the latter caught both his hands and the voice of Florence MacMahon welcomed him joyously.

"*Cead Mille Failthe*,[1] Kinsman," he cried with sparkling eyes; "thou art as welcome as Spring flowers. My uncle told me of thy coming eight days back, and for this last week we were in dread lest thou had fallen into the hands of Coote's fellows, whom we sent packing back on Dublin a short while after you started. Tell me, Harry, how didst thou manage to evade them?"

In as brief a fashion as he could Harry informed the young chief of the events of his journey from the time he had parted from the Bishop in the Dublin Mountains down to the hour he had arrived at the Confederate outpost at Lough Ramor. On hearing that his comrade had not yet breakfasted, the impetuous young Chieftain hurried him upstairs, two steps at a stride, to a small apartment which from its furniture appeared to be devoted to the double duty of a sitting-room and a bed-chamber.

"The quarters of the officer on duty in the town of Cavan," said Florence, with a laugh and a comprehensive gesture, "are not very magnificently furnished, as you may see, but if O'Neill does not lodge us sumptuously, he at least feeds us well; and my page and foster-brother, Cormac, shall provide you with a breakfast which ought to assure you that the Confederate Army does not starve its soldiers."

He gave some directions in Gaelic to the young fellow who had announced his appearance in the guard-room, and the page, making a deep obeisance, withdrew. In a few minutes, Cormac re-appeared with a very substantial round of spiced beef, a loaf of brown bread, a flask of good red wine, and a silver-mounted ram's-horn, all of which he carried on the concave side of a leather buckler, and, without appearing to be conscious of the grim nature of his service, laid this novel tray on the table in company with a murderous-looking skene dhu.

Dauntless was much too hungry to consider whether the skene had ever been used for less agreeable uses than carving spiced beef, and, sitting down immediately, took it up and applied himself with a very stout appetite to the good things

[1] "A hundred thousand welcomes."

before him, whilst Florence strode up and down the apartment with that quick, springing step peculiar to his excitable nature.

"I expect, Harry," said he, stopping short in his walk, "that it will not be long ere you are taking your own turn at such duty as you have found me employed on, inasmuch as O'Neill is not one of those Court o' Guard soldiers who believe in their recruits idling themselves to death with inaction, preferring rather that the sword should wear out from constant polishing than it should consume itself away in its own rust."

Harry, on whom the trooper's story of the previous evening had made a deep impression, paused as he was pouring out a glass of claret and asked Florence with an enquiring look what manner of man was his new General.

"Such a one as for years we have hoped for to lead us into the field," was the reply, "and yet" (here, the mouth of the young Chieftain twitched nervously as if at the recollection of some unpleasant memory) "not all that our hopes had pictured the nephew of the Great Earl should be. The thirty years he hath spent abroad have crushed out of his nature all the feeling that should animate an Ulster Chieftain; and the service of Spain hath stamped its harsh discipline upon his methods of war, his policy, his manners, nay, on his very soul. In short," added the young man, flushing hotly and dropping down into a seat opposite his companion, "we had hoped and longed for a Chieftain to head us, and — and — "

"You have got a very perfect soldier who hath been trained in the best school of his trade," interrupted Harry. "I fail to see the hardship of that."

"Nay," replied the other, quickly. "You men of the Pale, who are not strung to one another by our mighty bonds of clan and kin, cannot understand how much love and hate influence us. What antiquity hath rendered sacred to us might appear ridiculous to you, and when I tell you that this silent, moody soldier does not care a tester whether a man be of his own clan or another which hath been at feud with Hy-Niall since the Deluge, it may cause men like yourself to smile broadly, but it wrings our hearts to weeping point."

"Upon my life," said Harry, "I must confess, if he holds an even scale, I see no reason why either of them should feel aggrieved."

"It may be very acceptable to those who have been the deadly foes of his clan," answered Florence, with a darkening brow, "but it beareth hard on those who have supported the banner of his house on many a bloody field; and, for my part, it galls my heart to see this Spanish-Irishman serve out praise and blame to this and that and t' other just as he would deal out provant bread and ammunition—and yet he is so perfect a soldier that I could forgive him for this indifference to clan feeling if he did not break into our dearest traditions."

Harry enquired with some curiosity as to what way O'Neill offended in this particular.

"It may mean nothing to an Englishman that his place is on the right or the left of the line," said Florence, with his grey eyes dilating with fire. "Nor would he greatly care whether his family had claimed from time immemorial the privilege of leading the van in attack or the rear in retreat. Place him in what part of the battle you like, and he will care nothing for his position so long as his General sets him there; but we men of the North regard the transfer of such places to strangers or any chance company as the deprivation of laurels, which we had so hardly won centuries ago. Such apparently trifling, but none the less dearly-prized rights, have all been swept away by our General, and now it is 'MacMahon to the right, or the left, or the rear,' with as much indifference as I would order my page, Cormac, to lace my buskins."

"Now, Heaven be praised for such a general," thought Harry. "With such a man at the helm, utterly superior to these petty jealousies and absurd tribal privileges, there ought to be good hopes for the Army of the North."

At this moment, the deep roll of a drum sounded in the street below, and its echoes rumbled tremulously in the room where they sat.

"Come, Harry," cried Florence, springing to his feet, his eyes sparkling and his breast swelling with pride. "Come with me, and I shall shew you what sort of men we Chieftains of the North lead into battle."

Outside in the street, Harry encountered sixty stout musketeers in back and breast plates, and an equal number of pikemen in buff-coats, who were already drawn up in well-ordered ranks awaiting their chief. Two pipers in close-fitting scarlet jackets and blue hose, who were standing in front of their companions, inflated their instruments on the appearance of Florence, and with a prelude of one, long, blood-curdling note, burst into the "Royal Hunt," which was the gathering march of their Clan.[1] The ear-piercing screams of the war-pipes, which were rendered more discordant by the narrowness of the street, nearly deafened Harry; and the deprecatory explanation Florence made for the smallness of his command was utterly lost upon the Palesman. He scarcely heard his companion giving the word for the party to march off, and was greatly relieved when they left the town and reached the open country where the sound of the pipes was less clamorously offensive.

The Chieftain and his friend, marshalled by the two pipers, who preceded them with that swaggering step peculiar to the brethren of their craft, marched at the head of the arquebusiers, and about a mile from the town the party entered a beautiful forest, where the lilt of the pipes instantly assumed so subdued a tone as to render them almost melodious. They marched on under great trees, where the deep blue of the pines, the dark green of the sycamores, and the brighter shades of the beech and ash were pierced here and there by shafts of sunlight which made golden wounds in the bordering fern and luxuriant underbrush, and, as they passed on through this charming district, Harry could not help being impressed by the great, but not altogether unfavourable, contrast between his new comrades and his late fellow-soldiers in Ormond's army.

Ormond's infantry, heavier armed and booted, moved with a deep and rhythmic tramp, which contrasted in a marked degree with the quick, soft tread of these mountain soldiery, who, shod in light buskins of untanned deerskin laced with thongs of leather, moved with the noiseless steps of panthers. Now and then, Harry was obliged to turn his head, in order to assure himself of the actual presence of nearly two hundred men marching close at his heels; and, if it were not for the

[1] The Irish war-pipe is a very different instrument to the feeble bellows-inflated contrivance which is met with in the country parts of the Island. It was of the same pattern as those in present use in the Corps of Pipers of the Royal Irish Fusileers (87th Regt.) and the Leinster Regiment, and differs from the Highland pipe in having two instead of three drones, while its reeds are much longer and its tones softer than those of the latter instrument.

faint smell of the burning matches of the arquebusiers and the occasional jingle of steel against steel as some soldier changed his eighteen-foot pike from shoulder to shoulder, he would have felt convinced at times that Florence, the two pipers, and himself had outmarched the remainder of the party and had left them out of sight and hearing.

He asked MacMahon why so large a guard was deemed necessary for a town which appeared to be so insignificant as Cavan, and was astonished to learn that another guard of two hundred men was also mounted at Killeshandra, and that a chain of these watchful and hardy sentinels were stretched from one end of the country to the other, which rendered it impossible for a single person to slip into the district wherein the Army of the North lay encamped. Harry was about to express his admiration for this evidence of the prudent nature of O'Neill when he and his companions, issuing from the woods, surmounted a verdant little hill beneath which lay the waters of Lough Oughter, and the vision of its placid loveliness checked the half-spoken sentence on his tongue.

Down before him, in the middle of the lake, which spread its glittering expanse among a hundred sinuous bays and wanton curves, he saw a noble castle on a tiny island which appeared to be composed wholly of flowers. From the machiolated battlements the Green and White banner of the Confederates and the Bloody Hand of Hy-Niall waved side by side, and beneath their folds a couple of sentinels paced backwards and forwards with fluttering mantles and glistening arms. Along the shore of the mainland, as far as the eye could reach, rows upon rows of tanned leather tents were pitched in admirable order, and a thousand fires along the water's edge and a deep hum of many voices bore very obvious tokens as to the strength of Owen Roe O'Neill's army.

Opposite a row of tents, which was marked by a pole bearing the standard of the MacMahon sept, Florence dismissed his guard, and bidding Harry accompany him, led him down to a level stretch of green turf where an officer in a plain suit of brown velvet was explaining to a little knot of gentlemen the use of one of those curious field-pieces then known as boiled leather guns. One of the group was Evir MacMahon, whom Harry saw for the first time in his life attired in a fashion befitting his calling; namely, in a simple, black rochet and the white bands of a clergyman. Next him stood a big, fair man in a splendid suit of grey and maroon velvet which fairly glittered with precious stones. The latter person wore a look of bored inattention, and, from the impatient fashion in which he fingered the gold chain round his neck and the furtive way he directed his looks in every direction but the field-piece, bore a ludicrous resemblance to a huge school-boy who had been compelled to attend a lecture on a subject in which he had not the slightest interest. Leaning on the wheel of the gun was a grave, middle-aged gentleman in a riding suit and long, black morocco riding-boots; and, close behind the instructor, with their backs to Harry, stood two young men, one in a buff-coat and the other in a full suit of cavalry armour, who were both attentively regarding every gesture of the instructor as he spun round the little brass wheel of the elevating gear on the trail-piece.

Taking advantage of a pause which the instructor made in his lecture, Florence stepped forward and touched the rim of his helmet in a military salute.

"Your Excellency," said he, respectfully, to the officer in brown velvet, "Mr. Dauntless has arrived safely from Dublin and is now come to report himself."

The officer addressed turned about, and the eyes of the two men encountered one another, — the one with a look of quiet welcome, the other with a stare of silent astonishment; for, in the man in brown velvet, Harry recognised Evir MacMahon's dejected serving-man and the far-famed Soldier of Arras.

XV

THERE was the same look of dejection on his countenance which Harry had observed at their last meeting, and the young Cavalier felt it hard to realise that behind those quiet, weary eyes lived the gallant soul which had caused one wretched little town in Flanders to be associated with the memory of one of the most famous military achievements of the time.

He took the hand of Dauntless with a smile, and, after the Bishop had in turn greeted him, introduced him, one by one, to the other chiefs and officers whom he had been instructing.

"My kinsman, Sir Phelim O'Neill," said he, indicating the huge cavalier in grey and maroon, who offered Harry a hand very nearly as large as a ham, whereon so many jewels glittered that he could scarcely bend his thick fingers.

"My dear friend and lover, O'Reilly of Clough Oughter, who is at once my brother and my host." The gentleman in the riding suit and the black morocco boots made a bow of Spanish punctiliousness.

"This is my nephew and clansman Hugh," presenting him to the young officer in buff. "And, last, but not least, your future Colonel, Manus O'Donnell, in whose regiment of Horse I propose to appoint you as Cornet, unless you would prefer a company of foot."

The gentleman in armour bowed, and remarked frankly that he was glad of so promising an officer; but Harry very humbly replied that, on account of his reduced fortunes not permitting him to offer anything worth the consideration of the Confederate Army, he was quite willing to serve as a private gentleman in whatever capacity it might please his Excellency to appoint him. The young Palesman was very much surprised to observe a faint smile of incredulity flit from face to face at this speech, and he directed a swift glance of puzzled enquiry at the Bishop, who flushed and coughed nervously.

"You served in the Cavalry of my good friend, the Mar-his recruit's heart to warm insensibly towards him. Young Hugh O'Neill, who appeared to share some of his uncle's melancholy, which a long sojourn in Spain had perhaps accentuated in both of them, and Phillip O'Reilly spoke but little; but Evir MacMahon and the stout Sir Phelim O'Neill made up for a dozen conversationalists in the hot duel of words which they maintained throughout dinner, and O'Donnell and Florence MacMahon, though by no means so fluent, made no bad seconds in this controversy, the one taking the big Churchman's part and the other the big Courtier's.

The Bishop and Sir Phelim scarcely ever sat down for five minutes together before they were involved in some wrangle which, though it never went beyond a mutual avowal of contempt for the other's intellect, appeared to afford them both the most profound satisfaction. No matter what his subsequent conviction might be, the Bishop was accustomed to maintain with stubborn obstinacy whatever opinion he happened to express on his first view of a subject; and Sir Phelim, partly because he delighted to stir up his antagonist, and partly because he steadfastly believed that it was impossible for the Bishop ever to be in the right, consistently and conscientiously disagreed with him on every occasion.

During the heated argument which raged between these two excitable disputants throughout the meal, they made frequent appeals to O'Neill, but failed to elicit anything from him beyond a few soothing remarks which reminded Harry of the efforts of a grown man to pacify two quarrelsome children. But the young Palesman was beginning to feel very weary of them both by the time they had arrived at that point in their argument, where each had based the soundness of his reasoning on premises which the other would not grant, and he heartily wished them both a hundred miles away when they came to Owen Roe for the purpose of referring their dispute to him, and thus cut short a very interesting account which O'Neill was giving of the siege of Frankfort.

The disputed question between Evir MacMahon and Sir Phelim was on the efficacy and mobility of the boiled leather gun, a subject which the ignorance of the two controversialists rendered them eminently unfitted to discuss.[1] Nevertheless,

[1] The boiled leather gun, although invented so long ago as the time of Gustavus Adolphus, who used it with deadly effect in the Continental

Owen Roe listened first to one and then to the other with a grave, patient smile which betrayed nothing of the contempt he must have felt for both, and was proceeding to give an account of the terrible execution which these light artillery had wrought in the Saxon ranks at Leipzig, when Harry felt his sleeve pulled and discovered Florence standing beside him with a somewhat bored and wearied look upon his handsome face.

"Come with me," he said in a low voice, "and I shall introduce you to my sister, who is in the rose arbour, where we shall at least have some respite from this interminable talk of guns, leaguers, Tilly, and Pappenheim."

Harry would have much preferred listening to the general's account of Leipzig, but as he perceived that both the younger O'Neill and O'Donnell had left the apartment, and moreover Florence had him firmly by the arm, he reluctantly accompanied him.

"Confound this impatient fellow and his sister along with him," thought Harry, irritably, "I expect she is some strapping piece of rusticity clad in a linsey-woolsey sack tied round the middle with a yard of bright-coloured sash. I wish he would have left me in peace."

"Hath my worthy but somewhat tiresome uncle already saddled thee with a heavy burden of duty that thou shouldst look so gloomy?" asked the young chief, as they descended the stair arm in arm.

"Thy uncle?" repeated Harry. "Is O'Neill as well as the Bishop thy uncle?"

"Yes, in sorts," was the careless reply. "You see, my grandfather married one Eva O'Neill, aunt of this iron-sinewed general whom we have both the honour of serving under, and though such relationship would go for nothing in the Pale of Dublin, yet we of the North allow, claim, and cherish such ties up to the thirty-second degree, to our own great gratification and the eternal confusion of heralds and sennachies.

"But tell me, good Harry, hath Owen Roe already set forth

wars, has within recent years claimed the grave attention of modern artillerists. It was composed of a steel tube closely lapped with raw-hide, which was in turn covered with mastic, and formed a wonderfully light and effective weapon.

thy terms of duty, or hast thou been ordered to undertake sentinel duty on top of the hill for practice; for I am ready to stake my life for warranty he hath not given thee long space to recover from thy journey."

Harry smiled at the shrewdness with which Florence had guessed the purport of the general's conversation with him, and told him that he was to be handed over to the care of O'Donnell's adjutant on the morrow, for the purpose of undergoing a month's preliminary drill before joining his troop.

"I thought he would not suffer thee to loll about in idleness for long," said the young Chieftain, laughing. "However, as thou dost not assume the yoke until to-morrow, why, *Carpe Diem*, and in any case we shall not be very far from one another, as our line of tents adjoins those of O'Donnell."

So saying, he led the new-made Cornet under the Castle arch, and round the wall by a narrow, sand-strewn path which was bounded on either side by a carefully trimmed hedge of roses. Their feet made no sound on the fine white sand, and as they followed the windings of the path, Dauntless became gradually conscious of the subdued murmur of women's voices and a clear, ringing peal of unrestrained laughter somewhere close to him in this wilderness of flowers. An abrupt turn conducted them to the entrance of the arbour, where the two men halted instinctively until it should please those who occupied it to bid them enter, and though it was scarcely a moment before they were perceived and welcomed, yet it was quite sufficient to enable Harry to take in a comprehensive view of the arbour and its inmates.

It was a tiny space walled in on three sides by a fragrant screen of red and white roses which had been trained by cunning hands into the form of an arched roof overhead. The floor was composed of fine, smoothly-clipped turf which was as soft and level as a velvet carpet; there were a couple of rustic benches made of unbarked sycamore, and a little ebony table, and amidst these surroundings were two women who seemed fitly established in such a charming retreat.

One was a middle-aged lady, tall, stately, yet kindly-looking who was dressed in a handsome gown of black velvet slashed with cherry coloured satin. She was standing up and regarding a young girl clad in a white robe who sat at her feet on a low bench with a rich piece of white silk and gold embroidery in her lap. The younger lady's head was bent over her work, and her needle was twinkling busily through the silk, whilst she talked to her companion; but, perceiving the double shadow of the new comers on the green turf at her feet, she stopped her embroidery and looked up, and Harry had little difficulty in indentifying her as his comrade's sister.

She had the same type of perfect features as Florence, the same little bow-shaped mouth, the same round chin, short, straight nose, and that same species of changeful eyes which melt from dusky grey to sapphire according as the lightning spirit within moves them to express different emotions. Her hair, which like her brother's was blue-black, lustrous, and curling, was confined about her shapely head by a golden circlet wherein shone one great emerald, but, beyond this splendid jewel, her white round neck, arms, and fingers, and her short-sleeved, white gown were absolutely devoid of ornament.

Florence, with a low bow, presented his comrade to the elder lady, whom he addressed as Aunt, and who was no other than that courageous and remarkable woman Rose O'Neill, the sister of Phillip O'Reilly. She extended her hand to Dauntless with a grace and dignity which might have been expected from one of her high birth and her long sojourn in the Court of Spain, and as the young man touched the tips of her fingers respectfully with his lips, he thought how well-mated was this stately woman with the gallant Owen Roe O'Neill. The young Chieftain then introduced him with less ceremony to his sister, and as the young lady rose to offer him her hand, the soft drapery of her gown settled so gracefully on her straight, lithe figure as to bring to his mind the Hamadryads he had read of in his boyhood.

"You both laughed loudly as we came through the rose garden," said Florence, seating himself on the grass as soon as the two ladies had established themselves on the rustic bench and the younger had resumed her embroidery. "It was thy voice, dear Aunt, I heard laugh loudest of the twain. Tell me, I prithee, what was the jest?"

"I bade Aileen tell you to look for a stouter *Fear Brataighe*[1] than your foster brother, Cormac," answered Madame O'Neill, smiling, "for I maintained that there was

[1] Standard bearer.

not a man of Glencairn who could sustain the weight of the standard of your newly raised company, if she put another ounce of gold thread into the workmanship."

"And what answer did Aileen make to that attack upon her Chieftain's foster brother?" asked Florence, smiling back at the elder lady.

"She averred stoutly," said Madame O'Neill, "that Cormac would not only carry the new standard with triumph, ease, and satisfaction to himself, but that she would engage him to bear his Chieftain, if necessary, slung in a basket from the cross bar of its pole."

MacMahon laughed, and rising lightly from the ground stepped over to his sister's side.

"Largesse, Aileen, Largesse," said he, gaily. "I shall tell Cormac of the brave way you defended him, and I warrant you that he will be as proud of the compliment, as I am of her who made it."

He bent down and drew the piece of embroidered silk from his sister's hands, notwithstanding an ineffectual remonstrance on her part.

"Tush, Girl," said he, laughingly, as he spread the rich work over his outstretched left arm. "Odds basting stitches and embroidering needles — I do not intend to rend it into pieces. Come hither, Dauntless, come hither, Sirrah, and let me put thy knowledge of heraldry and thy courtly skill to the proof by reading me this device aright, and making a speech pretty enough to vie with the workmanship."

Harry confessed his slight acquaintance with the Science of Dexter and Sinister, and felt much more inclined to praise the beauty of the needlework than to study its details, but the Chieftain gave him little time to say much on that subject.

"See, Harry," said he, in the approved jargon of heraldry, "A Naked Arm, embowed, holding a Falchion, all proper, the point pierced through a Fleur d' Lis, with the motto, '*So dorn don a dubh fuiltibh,*' — the meaning of which thou art doubtless acquainted with. In the Dexter corner you will perceive a Right Hand displayed — Gules."

Here he stopped with a sudden wince, and dropping the flag once more into his sister's lap, wrapped up his hand in a corner of his flowing mantle.

"You spoke sooth about the needles, Aileen," said he, with

a grimace, "for I came on one a moment ago which was nearly as long as and as biting as a Connemara-man's skene."

His sister laughed merrily, and took up the flag in order to resume her interrupted work, but a paleness over-spread her face, and the silk dropped through her fingers as she observed a small stain of fresh blood on its shimmering folds.

"A bad omen, Florence," said the young lady, trembling, for superstitious as the North is in these days, it was much more superstitious in those times. "A bad omen to see blood on what hath not yet waved in the battle's breath."

"Pshaw, Aileen," answered her brother, scornfully, "Is it possible thou canst believe such mumbling folly which is more suitable to an ignorant old peasant woman than an educated young lady who hath read Plato and all the other tiresome and long-winded heathen philosophers. Upon my life, girl, thou dost make me blush for thy intelligence."

The young lady, however, was not to be crushed by mere ridicule, and she quickly cited half a dozen well authenticated cases of prescience and forebodings whereby she displayed an unusual acquaintance with classical and ethical writers. Florence disposed of each of her instances with totally irrelevant and contemptuous explanations, and Madame O'Neill lost no time in skilfully directing the talk into less sinister channels; but, when the remainder of the company had recovered their spirits, and were chatting gaily on other subjects, Harry Dauntless stood silent and wonderstruck as a result of the previous conversation. He was by no means surprised that an active-minded man like Florence should scoff, or affect to scoff, at the ethical and philosophical works which he had flung away the moment he left his University; but he was utterly astonished to learn that this beautiful girl who appeared to him like a water lily which had never breathed another air than that of Lough Oughter should be conversant with subjects which the gravest men of the outside world had long considered their special domain. And with all her beauty and intelligence she was so frank, so natural and unaffected, that while Harry admired the charms of her mind and person, he wondered greatly at her composure and transparent innocence.

"Surely," he thought, "this girl, notwithstanding her womanly modesty, must be conscious of her own beauty and intelligence. Her own glass would tell her of the first, and observation of others of her sex would convince her of the second, even if there were not a hundred tongues to assure her that she possessed both qualities in no ordinary degree; and yet she speaks so simply, and looks so demure, that I cannot but believe that she is at heart a fool or a coquette, or perhaps indeed a combination of both."

It did not take Harry long to discover how much mistaken he was in his first estimation of her character, and the revelation dispelled the very excellent opinion he had hitherto had of his own discrimination.

Aileen MacMahon was as conscious of her beauty as she was of her own intelligence; but the pride she took in her face and figure was no more than that which she took in her own splendid health, which she regarded as a Heaven-sent gift, for which she had every reason to feel very grateful; and as to her education, it caused her but little self-esteem to think that the French convent which had done so much for her, could have effected as much in thousands of others if they had been afforded such opportunities. Wherefore, on account of such matter-of-fact ideas, the young lady's inner self was clothed in a garment of sound, simple common-sense which was as white and candid as that which garbed her outer being.

The generous nature which had united so much beauty, intelligence, and good sense, had also excluded that haughty spirit which a stranger could not help noticing in her brother. But that she shared something of the fire of his nature in a softened degree, much in the fashion as the fierce rays of the sun are transmitted with a softer, mellower tint through the coloured glass of a Cathedral, was quite evident to Harry by her reply to the half jesting remark which he made about her having left no room for the King's Cipher on the banner she was working.

"Pray, Mr. Dauntless," said she, with a flush on her neck and cheek, "what claim hath the King to have his arms embroidered on the banner of Glencairn?"

Harry replied, in rather a confused manner, that as the arms of the Confederates were engaged in his service, it seemed only natural to suppose that his Cipher should be used in conjunction with those of the leaders of the Ulster army.

"The King's cause and that of Eire happen to be identical at the moment," answered the young lady, flushing still more, "but that does not give the King a right to claim anything beyond the use of our swords. Charles Stuart pledged himself to grant our country what was either not in his power to grant or his wish to fulfil, and he is therefore either treacherous or weak. If he is one or the other or both, he is in any case not blameless, and as the Banner of Glencairn shall never bear the device of any name that is not stainless, it were better that it should have no further blazoning than its own crest."

"Bravely spoken, little sister, like a true daughter of Clan Colla," said the Chieftain, laughing, "thou hast been uncontestably answered, Dauntless. I shall bespeak a suit of light harness from Shane Ruadh, the hereditary armourer of our clan, for Aileen and, I beseech thee, dear Aunt, if anything should happen me in the field, that thou wilt dress her up in the most bewitching doublet and truis, and set her at the head of Clan Mahon, where I promise thee she shall prove herself a second Jeanne d'Arc; but hark, Dauntless, the trumpets are blowing for the evening watch, and if you would sleep comfortably to-night, I would advise you come with me and see your home put in order to your liking.

"I expect the rough fashion in which my page hath very likely pitched your tent may hardly meet with your approval, and while it is still light, it were as well if you inspected it ere retiring."

The two young men accordingly made their adieux to the ladies, and getting on board the barge at the pier were quickly rowed ashore to the Confederate camp by the lake side, and it is only common justice to the memory of Harry Dauntless, to state that when he lay down to rest that night in his little, tanned-leather tent he pondered long on Barbara Merryl until he fell asleep, and not even in his dreams did a single thought of the strange and beautiful sister of his comrade flicker across his mind.

XVI

ON the following day Harry's preliminary drill commenced, and, long before he was released from it, he discovered for himself that Florence MacMahon had not exaggerated the discipline of Owen O'Neill's army. During his previous service under Ormond, the young Palesman had been a keen observer of the different systems of organisation in the Parliamentary army and his own side. In the one, it was conducted with an iron severity which was calculated to depress any but religious enthusiasts, and, in the other, with a slackness of discipline and a contempt for the observance of military form, which the Cavaliers were in the habit of associating with a sugar-loaf hat, a stern, clean-shaven face, and a rebellious spirit. But in the Army of the Northern Confederates, the drill was conducted with a happy combination of strictness and cheerfulness; and, whilst there was an absence of the riotous carelessness of Ormond's regiments or the gloomy stiffness of the Puritan levies, there was a minute observance of detail which was the result of the unwearying interest which Owen Roe took in the military education of his young army.

Every morning at daybreak he was rowed ashore from Clough Oughter, and, as soon as he had mounted his horse, he would canter from regiment to regiment observing, encouraging and personally explaining different points in the several kinds of drill they were engaged in. Sometimes he would illustrate, by word and example, to an awkward cavalry-recruit how he should rise and swing in his stirrups when delivering a cut in order to add weight to the blow. Sometimes he would dismount and kneel among the pikemen with an eighteen-foot pike quivering in his strong hands, and the butt braced against his knee, in order to show them the best position to repel an attack of cavalry. At other times, he would pass in among the ranks of the musketeers as they went through the platoon-exercise, or he would personally examine them in the use of the complicated weapons with which they were armed; and in such occupations the indefatigable O'Neill was accustomed to spend the earlier part of the day. O'Neill devoted the afternoon and very often the best part of the evening to writing such letters as were necessary to one of his position,[1] and many a night the tired sentinels in the camp observed the solitary light in the third story of Clough Oughter burn until morning, and when they were dismissed yawning from their guard, they would marvel to see their General come forth to his other duties, looking as though he had but risen from a refreshing sleep.

During the two months' drill which Harry underwent, he had little time to himself, and with the exception of Florence and his own immediate comrades he encountered scarcely any other company. On two or three occasions, when riding to or from parade, he caught a glimpse of the white robe of Aileen MacMahon fluttering amidst the rose bushes of Clough Oughter, and once he saw her alone in a little skiff which she was pulling easily up the lake. She was directing her course towards a miniature island which was so thickly planted with young hazels and willows as to seem to be a portion of the lovely woods of Killykeen which the Fairies had detached and set adrift for their own special abode in the middle of the Lough.

The young lady recognised him, drew her oars inboard, and, resting one white, round arm on their crossed looms, waved her disengaged hand in that particularly pretty fashion which is so common among Frenchwomen. Harry acknowledged the greeting by bowing in his saddle until his own brown curls mingled with the flowing mane of his charger; and then, with a nod and a smile, she reshipped her oars and resumed her course, whilst the young Cornet, with something like a sigh, moved on slowly to the parade-ground.

The last week of his initiatory drill arrived, and, as its days passed slowly by, Harry Dauntless looked forward with increasing eagerness to his release from the drudgery of morning parades and the prospect of renewing his acquaintance with Madame O'Neill and her pretty niece. He was already far

[1] The multitudinous correspondence of Owen Roe O'Neill, ranging from letters to King Charles and Queen Henrietta down to notes to obscure marauders, is all preserved in the State Paper Office, and is an eloquent testimony to his energy and intellect.

more interested in Aileen MacMahon than he himself was aware of; and his daily intercourse with Florence, whose wonderful resemblance to his sister continually kept her personality before his eyes, thus gradually and unconsciously caused her to become a subject of his inmost thoughts. However, if Harry Dauntless was becoming more and more interested in Aileen MacMahon, his estimation of her brother was also undergoing a considerable change about this period.

From the first day of his arrival at Clough Oughter, Florence MacMahon had come to regard his friend as a species of confidential sink into which he was never tired of pouring either bitter diatribes against O'Neill and his discipline, or wearisome histories of slights to his own fretful dignity. The young Chieftain very much over-estimated the sympathetic nature of the Palesman, who, for his part, was much too polite to undeceive him or to yawn openly at his stories. And the consequence of this misunderstanding between the two young men was that Florence assailed Harry on every possible opportunity with apparently interminable narratives of his family's wrongs, and Harry gradually conceived an intense dislike to the company of Florence and a hearty hatred for the very name of Glencairn and all the genealogical history of that unlucky clan.

The source of these real and imaginary wrongs dated back to some hundred years or so before the fiery and restless soul of Florence MacMahon had come into the world, and had its origin in the claim which one of his ancestors had laid to the Chieftainship of Clan Mahon and the concurrent rank of Prince of Orgiall and Baron of Dartry. The reigning chief of Orgiall had been slain in one of the trifling, internecine skirmishes characteristic of that time, and his position usurped by one of less direct proximity to the title, but of uncontestable superiority in arms to the ancestor of Florence MacMahon. The ousted candidate, who happened to be connected by marriage with the Maguire, Prince of Fermanagh and Baron of Enniskielen, fled to his powerful relation and entreated him for aid; and Maguire, full of sympathy for his kinsman, assigned him a fine castle on the beautiful shores of the Upper Lough Erne as a temporary stronghold, and set to work to raise an army to support his claims.

The sudden invasion of Ulster by the English forces compelled all parties to lay aside their private differences in order to unite for mutual protection, and the long wars which continued without intermission throughout the reign of Elizabeth prevented the descendants of the exiled chief from making further efforts to establish their rights. In consequence of this state of affairs they gradually sank into that inferior grade of chieftains, then termed *Taioseach*, who held their possessions from those of a higher rank, on the understanding that they supported their over-lords in the field and assumed their names. But the MacMahons of Glencairn, as they were called from the name of the valley wherein their castle was situated, though they followed the banner of Maguire with unwavering loyalty for close upon a century afterwards, nevertheless steadily refused to accept that name and continued to maintain their nominal right to assume the senior title of their own clan. The father of Florence and Aileen had been slain at Armagh, in the terrible battle wherein Bagenal and the flower of Elizabeth's army were destroyed, and the then-reigning Chieftain of Fermanagh had assumed the care of his dead vassal's infant children, in accordance with the unwritten Brehon law, which assigned such patriarchal duty to one of his position.

The girl was sent to a French convent at an early age, and her brother in due time was despatched to Magdalen College, Oxford, in company with his patron's son, the ill-fated young Baron, who was destined to lose his life for his share in the plot to seize Dublin Castle. A strong affection, commenced in early childhood, continued in boyhood and established permanently by that enduring bond which college life knits between friends, had constituted young Hugh Maguire to be a portion of Florence MacMahon's very existence; and as soon as the young Chieftain was made acquainted with his friend's arrest in Dublin, he was instantly seized with a feverish desire to march upon the Capital and attempt his rescue, at all hazards. This wild scheme was, however, decisively negatived by his cool-headed General, who had no intention of marching on a walled city with an army which was, as yet, imperfectly drilled, and the refusal to fall in with his own views grievously offended the impetuous young man. The sharp way in which his great kinsman enforced discipline on all ranks of his little army was also privately resented by the young Chieftain; but the main grievance which chafed his restless spirit was Owen Roe's refusal to permit him to summon more men to the field than he could equip properly. Florence, who considered his dignity as a claimant to the Principality of Orgiall should have been supported by the attendance of at least four hundred men, had been deeply mortified because O'Neill had compelled him to dismiss nearly half the ill-armed rabble which accompanied him when he first joined the Confederate army; and this last grievance, in particular, was one on which he was never tired of dilating.

Dauntless had conceived such an intense horror of all these subjects that on the last day of his initiatory drill he felt his heart sink within him when Florence MacMahon suddenly accosted him and begged him to guess the good news which he had that moment learned. Harry, fully expecting to hear something more about Glencairn, shook his head dolefully and resigned himself to his fate, whereupon Florence clapped a hand upon either of his shoulders and regarded him with sparkling eyes.

"We are for the front, Harry," he cried joyfully, "yes, truly, you and I. You with half a squadron of O'Donnell's horse, and I with half a company of my clan. My uncle has at length awakened to the six-months-old fact that our enemies have been suffered to pillage the country within a few hours' march of Clough Oughter, and we twain are detailed to pounce down on Coote when next he rides forth from Enniskillen to take the air and anything else which is not too hot or heavy for him to carry off."

Harry eagerly asked his friend when the proposed expedition was to start.

"We cannot say what time Coote purposes to set forth," was the reply; "but our spy informed us that he cannot be longer than ten days at the utmost, as beef is running short within the town. Already our scouts and videttes have been pushed out along both sides of Lough Erne; so we may hear the trumpets sing Boot and Saddle and the pipes of Clan Mahon scream the gathering at any moment."

An invitation to sup that evening with O'Neill at Clough Oughter added another to the many emotions which filled Harry's mind. He was pleased at the prospect of meeting O'Neill again on less formal terms than those which their daily military relations had imposed on both for the last two months, and, moreover, hoped to see Aileen MacMahon, to whom his feelings were ripening unconsciously into something warmer than admiration.

But, in the banqueting hall of Clough Oughter, he looked in vain for either Madame O'Neill or Aileen, and was moreover placed at the lower end of the table, where he was deprived of the pleasure of hearing what few remarks O'Neill made during the meal. He was also compelled to be an unwilling listener to a fierce battle of words waged between Evir MacMahon and his usual antagonist, Sir Phelim O'Neill, on the momentous question as to whether a fourteen to the pound snaphaunce was more effective when charged with a single bullet of the full size of the calibre or when used with a brace of half-ounce balls sewn up in a piece of silk gauze.

When the two disputants had thoroughly exhausted not only their subject, but their hearers, they rested, figuratively speaking, on their arms, and Sir Phelim, assuming a lofty indifference to the Bishop, condescended to address Dauntless in what was intended to be a very friendly fashion. He entered upon an affecting eulogy on the virtues and charms of his deceased father, whom he described as a "sweet bully" and a most "perfect rake," and then proceeded to give a very racy account of the many court intrigues, gambling bouts, and questionable gallantries in which he and Walter Dauntless had borne shares.

This highly delicate attention on the part of Sir Phelim, which would have pained any ordinary young man (for there is something in our nature which revolts from hearing of the frailty of one's parents), caused the most exquisite anguish to poor Harry. He had been brought up in a moral atmosphere which was as pure as that of the mountains in which he had lived. His mother had sedulously taught him to regard gambling and low intrigue as the basest of vices, and he was not only absolutely uncontaminated himself with the gross breath of Court life, but was also accustomed to make little allowance for such faults in others whose early surroundings had been less innocent than his own.

What added an additional poignancy to the misery which Sir Phelim inflicted on his unhappy auditor was the brutally truthful ring of each of his stories. Harry was slightly acquainted with the reputation which his father bore for a libertine and a gambler, and each new story tightened the screw upon his shame and anguish; and it is impossible to say how long Sir Phelim might have lingered lovingly over these tales, or to what pitch of distraction he might have driven his listener, had not his speech received a check by the appearance of Madame O'Neill, who entered, leading Aileen by the hand.

It seemed to Harry as if their entrance brought a purer atmosphere into the room. The coarse story of Sir Phelim broke off at the half-finished word which hovered unspoken on his tongue, the angry frown with which the Bishop had been regarding the stout libertine across the table gave place to a pleasant, beaming smile, the loud voices at the upper end of the table were hushed, the half-raised goblets were laid down untasted, and, with one accord, all the gentlemen arose from their seats.

The two ladies walked slowly to the head of the table followed closely by Cormac, bearing a light and beautiful little harp in his arms. Rose O'Neill moved with a stately step, acknowledging with a graceful inclination of her head the courtesy paid her, while Aileen MacMahon walked beside her, with a slight colour in her cheek and her eyes cast down at the admiration with which all saluted her.

O'Neill received both ladies with an affectionate embrace, two serving-men brought chairs for their accommodation, and at a signal from the General the page advanced, and with a respectful bow tendered Aileen the Clairseach which he bore in his arms.

As she held the delicate little harp on her knee and adjusted the velvet cushion of her chair before she addressed herself to it, she appeared so graceful yet so unaffected, so spiritual and yet so humanly beautiful, that Harry was at some difficulty to determine whether she looked more like a Greek statue or Saint Cecilia herself, who had come down from heaven for the express purpose of delivering him from Sir Phelim's offensive stories.

With no more prelude than one or two rippling chords in order to obtain the pitch of the instrument, she commenced the following ballad as simply and naturally as a thrush bursts into song, and she sang it in a voice which, if not powerful, was at least sweet and true, and succeeded in stirring more than one heart around the table.

"Rede me where are the Sons of the North, of the Scaith and
Skene and Blade,
Who started up at the trumpet's call,
Took the lance from the thatch and the steed from the stall,
The buckler and blade from their hook on the wall,
And went forth as daring as they were true
When Eire cried to her sons for aid,
Lu Lu-Ullu Lu.

"Their bones lie East, — their bones lie West, in sea and silt and
sand, —
In the blood-warm depths of the Spanish Main,
In the Flemish mud and in Acquitaine,
In the sun-baked dust of the land of Spain,
And some — ah! they count but few —
Have mingled their clay with their native land.
Lu Lu-Ullu Lu.

"Wards of your Father's fame, of which for ages Bards have sung,
The Ship of your Country's hopes doth bide
But the turning point of the rising tide,
And the ghosts of your valiant fathers ride
On the wings of the winds, and they cry to you
With the sounding tone of the tempest's tongue,
Lambh Derg Ula' Abu!"[1]

There was an impressive silence until the last vibration of the harp strings had died away, and then a wild storm of applause greeted the pretty, blushing singer and stirred the tattered flags which drooped among the antlers and trophies on the walls. Some of the Chieftains drew their skenes, kissed the blades, and then, stretching forth their goblets, vowed to do great deeds in the combined honour of Eire and Aileen MacMahon; and Sir Phelim O'Neill, pouring out a bumper of Madeira, roared out, "*Lambh Derg an Uachtair*," and having drained the glass dashed it on the ground, and then trod it into fragments, lest it should ever carry wine for a less honourable toast. Owen O'Neill filled his own little silver cup with claret, and then offered it with a smile and a bow to Aileen. She barely touched it with her lips, and returned it to him, whereupon he pledged her in the courtly Spanish fashion, with his left hand on his heart, and then handed her back the empty cup.

[1] "The Red Hand of Ulster for ever."

"Aileenita," said he, adding that tender little diminutive to her name which the Spaniard uses when he addresses a woman he loves, "it was an ancient custom of the Chiefs of Uladh to requite a minstrel who had given unusual satisfaction by giving him a cup of wine or a golden armlet or collar taken from his own royal person. But thou wilt have none of my wine, little cousin, and as such trinkets as golden armlets and collars do not obtain among men-folk in this age, I prithee take my soldier's goblet in guerdon for thy pretty Rosg Catha and keep it in memory of thy gossib, Owen Roe."

The young lady accepted the gift with sparkling eyes, and while she was thanking the donor Harry contrived, amidst the bustle occasioned by some of the Chieftains rising to assume their cloaks and barrads, to approach the fair singer and compliment her on her skill. O'Neill, with a quiet twinkle of mischief in his eyes, advised Harry to learn Gaelic as soon as possible, as he would thus save Mistress MacMahon the labour of translating Gaelic songs into Saxon for his benefit on every occasion he supped there.

"Because," he added, glancing from the frank, simple countenance of Harry to the blushing face of his pretty niece, "I would otherwise be at a loss to know why she should have gone to such pains to sing in English to-night, — unless it were for the gratification of my courtly cousin, Sir Phelim, who, in my opinion at least, very wrongly protests that the Saxon tongue lends itself more readily to music than ours."

The flush which had deepened in Aileen's cheek at this banter caused some corresponding confusion to become manifest in Harry's face; but Madame O'Neill very good-naturedly came to their assistance at this point by telling the young Cornet of the beauty and softness of the Gaelic language and how easily it could be mastered. Harry replied with a light laugh that some unknown defect in his tongue had so far mocked his efforts to learn his native language, which he desired above all things to become acquainted with. Florence, who had joined the group at this moment, with his cloak on his arm and his plumed barrad in his hand, caught the last words.

"Eureka," he cried gaily. "I have then discovered a way to pay the debt I have owed ever since that day thou didst so ably second me in Dames Street and that without being a maravedi out of pocket. Why, Harry, if thou art so anxious to learn Irish, I shall make Aileen teach thee, and I myself shall examine thee from time to time to see thou art making due progress," and then, with what Harry thought a most unnecessary laudation, he recounted the circumstances of their first meeting, which O'Neill and his wife listened to with many marks of approval, and which Aileen, although she uttered no word, drank in with every outward symptom of intense interest.

It is true that Florence MacMahon had an unusually strong brotherly affection for his sister, but it was a mere feeble spark compared with the ardent passionate love and admiration which she entertained for him. He was no ordinary human being in her eyes. He was her Lord, the head of her Clan, the protector of her orphan state, and the sole surviving hope of her race. She was too natural to attempt to conceal what she felt towards her brother's preserver, and during Florence's narrative Harry was conscious that her splendid eyes were fixed on him wide open and shining with gratitude, and that her bosom was swelling and falling with pent-up emotion.

When the two young men departed that night from Clough Oughter, the farewells interchanged were no more than those which hosts and their departing guests ordinarily express, nor was a single word of more than formal politeness breathed from the lips of either the young lady or the new Cornet. Nevertheless, Harry experienced a vague but powerful feeling of emotion which took no tangible form until he was undressing for the night in his leather tent, when his hands accidentally touched a little miniature which hung round his neck by a frayed ribbon. He drew it forth from his shirt and regarded it with a rising flush on his brow as he remembered that he had worn it with unwavering fidelity for three years, but the reign of her it represented was from that moment over for ever.

"Yes, Barbara, yes," he murmured softly as he nodded to it with a faint smile, "thou wert in the right — thou wert in the right — but women are always right in these matters."

And then he walked softly down in the moonlight to the edge of the lake and threw the pretty little bauble as far into its shimmering waters as his arm could hurl it.

XVII

DURING the month which followed the supper party in Clough Oughter, Harry's duties brought him on many occasions to the Castle. He was generally the bearer of letters addressed to O'Neill, which were frequently brought by messengers whom it was not considered desirable to admit inside either the walls of the island stronghold or the limits of the camp; but, as he was almost certain to encounter Aileen MacMahon whenever he crossed over to Clough Oughter, he never experienced any great inconvenience at the length of time he was often detained there awaiting an answer.

Another month passed on without any attempt on Coote's part to make the long expected raid, and during this peaceful interval Harry's admiration for Aileen MacMahon, which had by this time matured into undisguised affection, had become quite apparent to all the inmates of Clough Oughter. The Bishop watched its growth with the keenest pleasure, O'Neill with quiet approval, and Madame O'Neill with that motherly interest which good women, who are happy in their own married life, never fail to exhibit when they see two young and handsome people in the incipient stage of courtship. Florence MacMahon was also pleased at this turn in affairs, inasmuch as he was sincerely fond of his sister, and was fully conscious of the good qualities of his friend, whom he looked upon as a man well calculated to make her happy. There were other reasons why the young Chieftain welcomed this prospect of a match between his sister and his comrade. Long before Harry's arrival at Clough Oughter, the Bishop had spoken in no doubtful terms of the great wealth which his young kinsman would some day inherit; and, in consequence of these hints, the younger MacMahon had come to regard Dauntless as one with whom an alliance would be likely to further some ambitious schemes of his own, wherein the House of Glencairn and himself figured prominently.

The only person in this little Lough side comedy who seemed unwilling to accept the part which had been assigned her by common consent, was Aileen MacMahon herself; and Harry had enough tact to perceive that her attitude towards him, although gracious and friendly, was by no means one which gave him much encouragement to make the tender confession he so ardently desired.

"She is much too grateful," he thought ruefully, "because I was lucky enough to be of some use to her brother; and, I have no doubt, from the way she is always referring to that subject when I would speak of other matters, she would just as readily laud some fat constable of the City Watch if he had undertaken the same chances which fate happened to throw in my way."

His former experience of the bitterness of a refusal, and a haunting dread that her affections were already engaged, deterred him from risking a declaration of his love at so early a stage, and thus another month drifted slowly by, during which the two young people met almost daily.

About this period one of the outlying cavalry pickets who were guarding the Upper Lough Erne brought back a stranger who had fallen into their hands in a similar way to the fashion wherein Harry had encountered the Lough Ramor picket, some months before. He was a tall, thin, powerful-looking man apparently about forty years of age, and, though excellently armed and mounted, was clad in garments which had so long passed the most hopeless stage of threadbare make-believe as to have resigned all pretensions to be anything but the tattered rags which they really were. A doublet he apparently did not possess, for the biceps of his thin, sinewy arm appeared in the intervening space between the top of his greasy gauntlet cuff and the sleeve of his tattered buff-coat. His once black felt hat, of the Puritanical sugar-loaf pattern, was worn white on the crown from the combined effects of sun and rain, a wisp of ventilated rag hung from his shoulders in lieu of a cloak, and his patched and broken riding boots, which were of that pattern then worn wrinkled below the knee in order to display the silk stockings of the wearer, were pulled high up on his muscular thighs for the same reasons which compelled that notable soldier, Captain Bobadil, to adopt a similar fashion.

However, if this tattered gentleman was dressed in garments which a beggar might have refused to accept as a gift, he possessed a calm assurance which a King in his robes and full regalia might have envied on his coronation day. When he arrived at Lough Oughter, O'Neill happened to be examining a regiment in the manual exercise, and the escort accordingly halted a little distance from him, to wait until he should be disengaged. This detention, however, appeared to be irksome to the prisoner; for, having cocked his battered hat as rakishly as though it were a silk beaver, and tenderly adjusted a very soiled wisp of muslin at his throat, he slipped off his horse, before the escort were aware of his intentions, and swaggered up to O'Neill. A couple of paces from the general he halted abruptly pulled off his hat with a profound flourish, and, dipping the hilt of the immense, four foot spadroon which he wore at his belt, protested to his Maker, in a very strongly marked London accent, that he was the most fortunate man on this planet in making the acquaintance of his Excellency.

O'Neill regarded this friendly apparition for a moment in profound amazement, and then asked him sharply to state his name and business in as few words as possible.

"Your Excellency," said the ragged cavalier, kissing the tips of his shabby gloves and bowing profoundly, "I am a man of few words myself, and I shall therefore not detain you long. My name is Cuttard, John, Jack, or Jolly, Jacky Cuttard, and to some I am known as Cut-and-Thrust-and-Come-again Cuttard; but the latter are only mine enemies whom I freely forgive as I hope to be saved. My Condition is that of a Captain of Horse or foot, with which branches of an army I have an equal acquaintance, having held a charge of one or the other in no less than five different countries; and my business here is to offer your Excellency the use of my sword in the campaign which I understand you are about to undertake against my late paymasters the Scots and English Parliamentary forces of Enniskillen, who are at present under the command of Sir Charles Coote."

O'Neill stared, open-eyed, at this cool personage for some moments, before he could recover enough breath to ask him if he knew what way Coote would probably treat him if he caught him in the service of the Confederate army.

"Hang me from the steeple of Enniskillen," was the unconcerned reply, "as soon as he could get a rope over the cross of the spire; for I am well aware that my late commander is an exceedingly quick and choleric gentleman, and, in the hurry of the moment, would be very likely to forget my manifold good services to him in the past."

"And what will you do," asked O'Neill, sternly, "in case I act in strict accordance with the articles of war. What will you do, Sirrah, in case I send you straight back under an escort to Sir Charles Coote at Enniskillen with a request that he will reciprocate my compliment by sending me any of my own rascals who should dare to make a similar proposal to him?"

"As I know your Excellency hath not the slightest intention of doing anything of the sort, there is no use in telling you what I should do," said the renegade, with unruffled composure, "my only anxiety is that you can offer me a saddle suitable to my birth or, at the least, a Corporal's rank; for, though I will uphold my title to gentility with my heart's best blood, I do not take it any shame to acknowledge that at times I have sunk my rank of Captain and 'have trailed the puissant pike,' as Will Shakespeare says."

"But you have not yet told me what you would do if I were to send you back to Coote," said O'Neill, fixing his grey eyes on the other.

"If I had any suspicions that your Excellency had meditated such a proceeding," replied this singular person, in a tone of friendly confidence, "I should have poniarded you five minutes ago; and now that I have trusted myself so much to your Excellency's good-faith, I hope you shall be able to see your way to appoint me to either a century of foot, or perhaps a troop of horse, with the corresponding pay and allowances of my rank."

The naïve simplicity with which this request was tendered caused O'Neill to laugh with more heartiness than any of his staff had ever observed in his usual, subdued manner; but this display of merriment did not appear to find favour with Sir Phelim, who asked his commander angrily in Gaelic if he contemplated taking such a runaway scareerow into his army.

"Why, Certes," answered O'Neill, in the same language, with a slight touch of contempt, "and if you want my reasons, they are briefly these. This same ragged fellow is not devoid of courage, and is just the sort of seasoned soldier I can make use of as a drill instructor or a troop adjutant. He is a rascal I have no doubt, for hardy insolence is writ large over his mouth and eyes; but as his own terms of service engage him with a rope about his neck, I have no fear that he will not be faithful, as long as he is paid."

He turned his back abruptly on Sir Phelim, and addressed himself once more in English to the renegade.

"Hark ye, my friend," said he, sharply, "and I warn you it were best you tell me the truth. Tell me the banners which you followed, their order according to roster, their generals, the length of time you served with each, and the several reasons that you left them. And take my word, Sirrah, that if I catch you tripping in the slightest detail, wherein I myself may happen to be acquainted, I shall discredit all the rest, and send you back to Coote, even if you were to produce credentials from every monarch in Europe."

"Commencing with the first, most honoured Sir," said Mr. Cuttard, as he checked off each period on the finger-tip of his worn glove in the fashion in which children play that interesting game of "this little pig went to market," "My first Master was Tilly, under whom I served in Germany and Poland for four long years; but as the recompense was too small for such hot work as Magdeburg, I left him to shake a leg with Louis of France. A year of the French service proved enough for me, because, although the pay was excellent, the work of slitting the throats of the poor devils of Huguenots was too much for my Protestant stomach, so I bade good-den to the Fleur d'Lis, and took on my own sacred Monarch, King Charles, for my third paymaster. I served him with great honour, but little profit, in Colonel Thompson's regiment of White-Coats, and though there was the most delightful religious tolerance in His Majesty's service — every gentleman being at perfect liberty to go to Hell in his own way — yet, alas! the pay barely sufficed to keep body and soul together, so I mounted the orange sash of the Parliament. I served the Constitutional forces of my country for two years in the Earl of Manchester's celebrated regiment of Horse which is better known as the Eastern Associates, and what with the King and the Earl, I was enabled to take an humble share in most of the affairs that took place in England, commencing with the glorious victory of Roundway Down, and ending with the late crowning mercy of Naseby. However, if the Earl was an excellent paymaster, he was a glum preceptor, and your Excellency can very easily understand that a cavaliero like myself, who had served in such merry company as the French, should have desired to try his fortunes elsewhere. But, Alack! Alack! in mine innocence I took service with the Scots under Coote, who half-starved and wholly over-worked me, and as my pay consisted chiefly in assurances that it was being laid up for me in that place where the rust doth not consume nor the moth devour — we e'en parted company, and so here I am at your Excellency's commands."

"You have referred to Roundway Down and Naseby, as two glorious victories," said O'Neill, with an obvious effort to keep his gravity, "but I was under the impression they were gained by different sides in these English wars — am I to understand that you refer to them merely as great military achievements, or do you speak of them from the experience of a partisan?"

"Both, your Excellency," answered the adventurer, serenely, "for I was on the side of His Sacred Majesty at Roundway, and I fought for the Parliament at Naseby. In fact my greatest trouble in recounting the battles, leaguers, and engagements wherein I have taken part is to remember on what side I was at each particular ruffle, in order that I may with propriety apply the term of 'glorious victory vouchsafed by Heaven' or sigh and say, '*Marte Iniqno*,' according to the circumstances."

"And now, I prithee, tell me," said O'Neill, with a keen searching look into the other's eyes, "what has induced you to honour me with an offer of your services?"

"The best of reasons," was the unblushing reply, "because I have already had the honour of fighting against you, and, therefore, feel I have some sort of claim upon your consideration."

"How, fellow," asked O'Neill, in great surprise, "where did you serve against me?"

The ragged Cavalier made a profound bow, and kissed the tips of his dirty gloves with a gesture of French affectation.

"At the intaking of Arras in the year of Sixteen-Forty," he

answered, "I served under Meilleraye, and am not likely to forget either you or Arras, so long as I carry the marks I received on the night you swooped out on old Rantzau. Ah! Sir, it was a beautiful piece of work on your part; but we were too many and too watchful for you, and yet we were but barely in time to prevent your making collops of the old barbarian and his Croatian irregulars."

Perhaps some weak spot in O'Neill's nature was touched by this subtle tribute to his fame, for he smiled faintly and muttered something about it being a hot night's work.

"And the next day, your Excellency," continued the soldier of fortune. "Do you remember our attempt on the Eastern rampier? I myself had not the honour of taking part in it, inasmuch as I was under the chirurgeon's hands for treatment of a wound I had received the previous evening; but I saw the entire business from our trenches. At daybreak our fellows advanced softly on the town in the full belief that you were all worn out with the late hard work, and that they were about to have a cheap market of you. They had crept up as far as the glacis without as much as a feather stirring on the walls — when — Puff! I saw the stone-work fringed with fire and smoke in a twinkling, as though Hell itself had popped boiling over the rampiers — and — and I cannot bear to think of what followed."

O'Neill asked the soldier, with something like compassion, if he had lost much on that occasion.

"I lost eighty louis, and the best friend I ever had," said the adventurer, regretfully. "He was a young French gentleman who was possessed with a commendable desire to learn the noble English game of Brag from me; and, as he invariably lost, I had come to regard him as a certain source of income. But, alas! he formed one of our forlorn of hope on that occasion, and the poor young man went to death owing me nearly two years' pay."

"And can you tell me," said O'Neill, curiously, "what induced your commanders to make so many desperate and disastrous assaults for nearly six months upon a city which they must have known was so scantily provisioned? How was it that they did not sit down and wait for another month or two, when they must have assuredly starved us out without loss to themselves?"

"I can explain that," said the soldier, with a knowing wink, "inasmuch as I was sentinel outside Chatillon's tent on the night that Richelieu's letter came from Paris. I heard the Marshal read every word of it to Meillerye, Chaulnes, and young D'Enghien; and, by my stainless honour, I can assure you that after they had mastered its contents they had as good reasons for wishing to get into Arras speedily as I have for desiring immediate employment."

"Dost thou remember, friend, what the Cardinal said?" asked O'Neill.

"Aye, that I do," replied Mr. Cuttard, with a grim smile. "Aye, as well as they do, for there was never a man who chanced to be brought in contact with Richelieu who was likely to forget the most trifling word he wrote or spoke on that occasion. They had evidently written to him asking for advice, inasmuch as his letter informed them very civilly that he was not a soldier, and was therefore incapable of giving them counsel in such a matter as the leaguer of a town. He then went on to tell them very sweetly that it was a case of each one to his trade,—his was to govern France, theirs was to fight the King's battles, and he finished up a very polite letter by assuring them all three that he would take off their heads if they did not get into Arras within a month of the receipt of his letter. The Cardinal was an incisive speaker and correspondent, your Excellency, a very incisive person indeed, and even when he condescended to put a jest on paper, there was always a library of wisdom and meaning underlying the most trifling communication he penned."

The words of the ragged deserter appeared to affect O'Neill in some inexplicable way, for he turned away abruptly from his staff, and for two or three days afterwards displayed such an unwonted air of irritable impatience as to surprise all his officers. He appointed Cuttard to be Riding Master and Troop Adjutant to O'Donnell's regiment of horse; and, although it was not long before the adventurer betrayed the fact that he was imbued with a weakness for fermented drink, and an innate vulgarity of disposition, he proved himself to be so efficient a soldier as to justify the good opinion which O'Neill had formed of his military qualities. Mr. Cuttard adopted an intimate and friendly disposition towards Harry, who had completely won him over at an early stage of their acquaintance by the opportune loan of a couple of shirts and an old laced coat. A chance reference on Harry's part to his father, also increased Mr. Cuttard's amiability in an even more pronounced degree. He swore with a most portentous oath that he had been one of Walter Dauntless's dearest friends during the time they had been both inmates of Lincoln's Inn, begged Harry to consider himself as heir to the great wealth of affection which he professed for his father, and insisted thenceforth upon attaching himself to the society of his young Cornet with a friendly obstinacy which it was impossible to withstand.

One morning Harry entered the little shed which O'Neill used as a camp orderly room, and was astounded to find it occupied by no other person but his late comrade, trooper Subtle, who confronted him in the scarlet uniform of a Parliamentary officer. It was quite apparent that Mr. Subtle had changed sides since their last meeting, as such defections were by no means uncommon in that treacherous period; but what struck Harry dumb with amazement was the presence of his former comrade in such a place and in such a garb.

"Good-morning, Mr. Dauntless," said he, with a cool nod to his astonished ex-comrade. "I am sorry that you have left the banner of the Marquess; but since you have thought fit to join the Confederate Army, let me congratulate you upon having elected to serve under the only general in it who is likely to do his party credit."

"I thank you for your good opinion of my general," said Dauntless, coldly, "and I wish I could say as much for your consistency. If my present service doth preclude my joining the standard of the Marquess, remember I shall still wield a sword for King Charles whilst you, Sir, are a renegade to the monarch whose bread you have eaten."

Instead of being offended by this plain speech, the Parliamentary soldier threw himself down into a chair and laughed so heartily that Dauntless, nettled by his apparent insolence, was on the point of shouting out angrily for the guard, in order to place him in custody, when the entrance of O'Neill and Evir MacMahon put a different complexion on matters. Both men, addressing the seeming Parliamentarian as nephew, embraced him with every symptom of affection, and Subtle producing a packet handed it to Owen Roe, who instantly ripped it open and read its contents with every indication of interest and excitement.

The Bishop introduced Harry to his nephew, and the young Cornet felt something like a reverential awe stealing through him when he learned that the beardless, youthful-looking, ex-trooper Subtle was no other than Daniel O'Neill, the most skilful and trusted confidant of King Charles, and the man whose reputation for diplomatic nerve, daring, and acumen was known and respected throughout every court in Europe. However, before the two young men had exchanged many words of a heartier nature than those which had passed between them a few minutes since, Owen Roe interrupted their conversation by asking his nephew abruptly if he were acquainted with the contents of the letter he had brought. His nephew bowed, with an uneasy side glance at Harry, who, divining immediately that the conversation was about to assume a private character, stepped to the door of the orderly room; but Owen Roe stopped him with a gesture.

"Stay, Mr. Dauntless," said he, with more animation than he was in the habit of exhibiting, "I may require your presence in a moment." Then he turned to his nephew and continued, "You are aware of the conditions he offers, Dan. Surely, Ormond is not so fond as to imagine I will continue to withhold my hand when the terms he offers are no more than a mere hope?"

"I told his Excellency that I anticipated such an answer," was the reluctant reply, "but he bade me inform you that he could not offer you better conditions than those, if it were to save his own life."

"Tush, lad, do not trifle with me," said his uncle, angrily. "Such talk might have passed current at the time when his hands were fettered by Borlase and Parsons; but now that he hath been invested with the Vice Royalty, he should be ashamed to take refuge in evasions which may ruin not only our cause, but that of his Royal Master."

"Dear Uncle," said the young man, earnestly, "fain would I be the bearer of conditions which would be more pleasing to you, in order that we might win your aid against the common enemy. Ormond and I, though we both profess the faith of the Church of England, acknowledge that it is only reasonable that you should demand tolerance for yours; but it is quite beyond the power of the King himself to grant what you demand."

"In other words," said Owen O'Neill, bitterly, "Ormond still clings to a hopeless trust. He will rather temporise with Monroe, Coote, Lesly, and Broghill, who are all avowed rebels to his Majesty, than accept the certain aid of those who claim no more than the right to worship God in their own way. Good God! Dan, is Ormond mad that he should hope to win such questionable allies? Go! bid him whistle the haggard hawk from the first quarry which she hath struck down, or endeavour to cajole the lion with fair words from the prey he is about to feed upon, and they will come sooner to his call than these Parliament men will relinquish their advantages. Well, be it so, Dan, — I shall no longer look to Ormond; but the day shall come when he must come to me, and then he will plead for acceptance of the terms he now daffs away so lightly."

He despatched Harry in search of O'Donnell, and when the Cornet returned in company with his Colonel, he found Daniel O'Neill sitting apart with a very gloomy expression on his face, and Owen Roe engaged busily in writing.

"Colonel O'Donnell," said the latter, without pausing for a moment in his writing, and yet speaking in the brief concise manner of one whose attention was undivided, "you will assemble the party which have been under orders this last two months for the Lisnakea road. Each man to carry seven pounds of powder-beef, and such ammunition and match as they are like to require for a week's expedition. Strengthen them with a troop of your own horse and a century of well-beaten soldiers taken from Art O'Neill's regiment of foot, and await my final instructions on the parade grounds an hour before sunset."

O'Donnell bowed, and O'Neill then turned to his nephew, and asked him in a kindly fashion if he would dine with him that afternoon, and rest a day or two in Clough Oughter.

"No, I thank you, Owen," answered the young man, with a heavy sigh, "nothing more for me than a cup of bonny-clabber,[1] a plate of bread and beef and a change of horses within an hour. My heart is too full to think of either rest or fine victuals, for God knoweth alone, Uncle, what misfortunes this move of thine may bring forth upon us both."

[1] The name by which butter-milk is known in the North of Ireland.

XVIII

JUST as the sun was sinking, the special service party which had been carefully reviewed by O'Neill in person moved off without sound of pipe or trumpet and marched slowly along the winding margin of Lough Oughter until they arrived at the shore of the Upper Lough Erne. Here O'Donnell detached a party of infantry scouts, which, spreading out into a fan formation through the woods, stole on like a pack of foxes in advance of the main body, which followed them with scarcely less stealthy movements.

In this formation they advanced in profound silence along the lovely shore of Lough Erne, whose hundred islands were mirrored in the unrippled water by the clear starlight of a cool, cloudless night in April. They crept on without hinderance for some six or seven miles through the dense belt of trees which girdle the lake, when suddenly the scouts in front halted, and the main body, passing the word to one another in tones lower than those of the night wind which sighed through the trees overhead, instantly drew up and rested on their arms. Presently a scout on foot crept back to whisper that he had fallen in with some of their own outposts in front, who had warned him of the near presence of a party of Scots Parliamentarians, encamped in the ruins of one of the many old castles by the Lough side; accordingly, the line of march was changed, and by the position of the Great Bear, which hung in the sky like some splendidly jewelled battle-axe, Harry judged they were proceeding in a westerly direction. Half an hour later they came upon the high-road, where they again halted. The infantry scouts were silently withdrawn and a strong cavalry advance guard, under the joint command of Harry and Cuttard, was substituted for the lightly armed clansmen who had heretofore preceded the little force. Just before they set forward O'Donnell, as if struck by a sudden inspiration, despatched one of his troopers for Florence MacMahon, who was some distance behind with his clan in the rear guard; and the man had departed on his errand scarcely five minutes before the young Chieftain made his appearance, silent, breathless, and eager.

"Glencairn," said O'Donnell, in a whisper, "I suppose thou art well acquainted with this part of the country."

"I ought to be," was the reply in the same guarded tones, "inasmuch as I am a Loughsider, born and bred, and I know every pass, ford, and togher for ten miles around as well as I know the four corners of the guard-room in Cavan."

"Dost know of a spot near the high-road where the ground is sufficiently well wooded to yield cover for the infantry," asked his commander, "and yet where there is sufficient room to afford a career for our troop of horse? Chance hath favoured us beyond our expectations, inasmuch as a body of Coote's horse with a goodly prey of cows are now encamped by the lake and must take this road on their homeward march to Enniskillen in the morning."

"There is such a spot as you describe," said Florence, in a panting whisper, "at the very entrance of Glencairn. A thousand men might couch in the bracken on either side of the road undetected by the keenest scouts among these Scottish reivers, and I will engage the plain on this side of the pass to be wide enough to manœuvre a regiment of cavalry in."

"Then take my horse," said O'Donnell, dismounting, "and ride along with Mr. Dauntless until you come to the spot you mention. If you happen to fall in with any of the Scots' outposts fall back at once, and if by any mischance they should discover you, mark you, use the broadsword and skene alone, for a musket-shot would assuredly upset my plans."

The party once more resumed its midnight march and in three or four hours' time arrived at the spot indicated by Florence, where O'Donnell disposed his infantry on either side of the road, placed a ring of sentinels through the woods, and posted the cavalry and the MacMahon clan at a turn of the road where they could wheel into position at a moment's notice. He then passed the word round for all to take what rest they could; and the cavalry, rolling themselves in their cloaks and keeping close to their picketed horses in the roadway, and the foot soldiers, folding their woollen mantles over their heads in the unhealthy fashion of their countrymen, lay down very composedly to sleep in the heather, apparently indifferent to the strong probability that within a few hours many of them were likely to sleep beneath it until the crack of doom.

Harry and Florence sat side by side on a fallen pine-tree, both silent, both too excited to think of sleep, and both occupied with very different thoughts. The prospect of immediate action, wherein he was about to aim a blow at the standard which he had lately followed, presented a solemn object of contemplation to the young Palesman; and, though he reconciled himself to the fact that that flag was now being borne by openly declared rebels to their King, he could not shake off an uncomfortable feeling of depression. As for Florence MacMahon, the close proximity of his ancestral home appeared to act on his excitable nature as a blast of wind into the embers of a smouldering fire, and the consciousness that the first blow in the Northern war was about to be struck within the defiles of Glencairn had set his fiery soul into a white heat of passionate hatred against the Sassenach soldiers who had driven him and his clan from that very spot.

When the faint, pearl-grey light of early morning stole slowly over the lake as though the very sun, aware of what was about to take place, was withholding its light reluctantly from the scene, the young Cornet saw a graceful castle appear amid the trees about quarter of a mile from where the ambuscade was posted; and Florence, indicating it with a bitter smile, informed him that it was Glencairn. It was a beautifully proportioned building, whose carefully laid courses, symmetrical battlements, and graceful turrets invested the entire edifice with an airy lightness seldom observable in castles of its class in Ireland. Its own graceful lightness and want of military strength had proved its best defence, for it had been abandoned by both sides as being too frail a stronghold for the establishment of a garrison; and therefore it stood in widowed loneliness, perfect but deserted, and with no other sentinels but the great, dark peaks of Knockninny Cuiltragh and Swaddlen Barr, which regarded it solemnly from the other side of Lough Erne. The appearance of this silent witness to wrong and persecution stirred a chord of sympathy in Harry's nature, and he almost forgave Florence for the long stories of Glencairn and the consequent weariness he so often inflicted on him. Florence pointed to the turrets which glittered like silver among the delicate green foliage of the woods which encircled them, and set his hand tightly in the hilt of his straight two-edged broadsword.

"There is room for only one more coffin in the MacMahon vault on Devenish Island," said he, in a low voice; "and I shall fill that place before another year passes, if I do not set the banner of the embowed arm with the sword and Fleur d' Lis over those walls in the meanwhile."

At this moment a scout came hastily in and informed O'Donnell that the marauding party had already mounted and were at that moment approaching along the high-road, whereupon O'Donnell reiterated his orders for silence, bade the infantry hold their fire until the signal agreed on, which was to be one long, shrill note on the bagpipes, and then took up his own position with the cavalry at the turn of the road. In about half an hour a small advance guard of the Roundhead cavalry came trotting cautiously down the glen and went on unsuspectingly until they were confronted by the Irish horsemen. Immediately they perceived the latter, they acted as all well-trained cavalry scouts should do, and galloped back to their comrades, firing their carbines on the way for the purpose of giving the alarm.

The report they made of the small numbers of their enemies apparently encouraged their commander to try bold measures, for in a few minutes a strong body of Parliamentarian cavalry came trotting down the glen with the evident intention of charging O'Donnell, and were just on the point of breaking into a gallop when suddenly the pipes screamed the signal amid the dense fern which bordered the road, and the startled Puritans were saluted with a volley which emptied a dozen of their saddles. For a moment there was the wildest confusion in their ranks and every man among them looked to see in what direction he could fly; but before the handful of Irish horsemen could complete their overthrow, the very impetuosity of their enemies saved them from total destruction. The clansmen who had been ambushed in the woods lost their heads on the first symptoms of unsteadiness among the Parliamentarians. They shouted their war-cry, flung down their pieces according to their old-time custom, and rushing down broadsword in hand on their enemies in the road, completely masked the charge which O'Donnell had intended to deliver at that instant.

As the impetuous Ulstermen were incapable of inflicting much punishment with their broadswords and skenes on steel-clad horsemen, they only succeeded in slashing a few horses and a trooper or two, and were themselves very severely handled in return; but they received a greater blow to their pride than the mere loss of comrades by the quick and skilful fashion in which their foemen profited by their rashness. The Puritan leader, who happened to be Captain Cartaret, the second in command in Enniskillen, instantly withdrew his horsemen from the disordered crowd of swordsmen, who effectually screened his retreat, and, retiring his forces by alternate half troops, he abandoned his booty on the high-road and fell back into the plain at the entrance of the glen.

In the meantime O'Donnell, although greatly mortified by the way in which his scheme had been overthrown, made one more effort to regain his former advantage. He quickly re-formed his scattered infantry, seized the abandoned cattle, and drew up his pikemen and musketeers on the plain facing his enemy. Then he endeavoured by every artifice to induce Cartaret to act on the offensive, but the Parliamentarian, notwithstanding that his horse greatly outnumbered the Royalist cavalry, was too prudent a soldier to charge unbroken pikemen and musketeers, and continued to fall back warily whenever O'Donnell advanced. Unwilling to permit so renowned an adversary to escape without further punishment, O'Donnell resolved upon a desperate scheme. It was nothing less than charging the Roundhead horsemen with his own slender force of cavalry and then retreating round the flank of his musketeers in the hope that Cartaret might be tempted into following him so far in pursuit. It therefore caused considerable astonishment among the Roundhead troopers when they saw O'Donnell's handful of cavalry abandon the strong protection of their pikemen and advance towards them at a trot; and they were still more astonished when they heard his trumpets sound the charge and perceived his horsemen coming straight for them at full gallop. Before they could realise the seriousness of their enemy's intention, the Irish horsemen burst among them with such violence that they were seized with a second panic and scattered immediately into irresolute groups; and if it had not been for the gallant Cartaret, who rallied them for the second time as valiantly as he had previously done in the glen, they would have fled from the insignificant force which had so demoralised them.

Dauntless heard the trumpets of his own party sound "the retire," and he turned around in order to follow his comrades, who were retreating in good order upon the infantry. Suddenly he was seized with giddiness, and, observing that a steady stream of blood was issuing from beneath his gorget, he realised stupidly for the first time that he had been wounded. As he struggled manfully against the deadly faintness which was overpowering him, he encountered one of Coote's retreating dragoons, and the Roundhead, observing his condition with a malicious grin, checked his horse and aimed a thrust at that space under his armpit which was undefended by his cuirass. The wounded man made a feeble effort to turn his enemy's point, but the trooper's sword slipped over his weak guard and ran through his ribs until it was stopped by the inner shell of the cuirass itself. Harry instantly dropped from his saddle with a faint prayer on his lips; and the Roundhead, not satisfied by this cowardly blow, leaned forward in his saddle and was about to deliver another thrust, which would have closed Cornet Dauntless's career on the spot, had not fate dropped on himself from a wholly unexpected direction.

Captain Cuttard, who had behaved on that day with the most remarkable bravery, had, for reasons best known to himself, ridden further in the charge than any of his companions. The fact was, the gallant soldier had observed a young Parliamentarian Cornet who wore a very handsome riding coat of blue velvet, and he had been seized with an ardent desire to possess it at all hazards. He had therefore hunted this unhappy young gentleman through the mêlée with the untiring patience of a bloodhound on the track of a runaway slave, and after a keen and exciting chase had succeeded in closing with his victim and disarming him in a pass or two. Deciding that a sword-thrust would be likely to injure the coveted riding coat, he stunned him with a blow of his musketoon, and having dismounted he stripped off the fallen man's cuirass in a twinkling and shook him out of the

"Harry instantly dropped from his saddle"

coveted garment with a dexterity perfected by many such experiences.

He was galloping back with his spoil, pursued at a discreet interval by two of his quondam comrades, when he perceived Harry lying on the ground with the dragoon in the act of giving him the coup de grâce. Notwithstanding that the spot was deserted by all of his own side and that three more dragoons had just then reinforced his pursuers, the troop-adjutant did not hesitate for a moment. He rode straight to the rescue of his officer, and brought down his musketoon on the dragoon's head with such force that the butt flew into pieces and the barrel nearly bent in two in his tingling hands. The steel helmet crumpled up like tin beneath that mighty blow, and the wretched trooper, with his skull fractured in a dozen places, dropped dead from his saddle without knowing what had struck him. His five companions, who came up at this moment, gathered fiercely round Cuttard; and although that gentleman defended himself, Harry, and the velvet riding coat with lion-like courage, it would have gone hard with all three had not Florence and half a dozen of his devoted clansmen rushed forward at this juncture and brought them into a place of safety behind the musketeers.

On account of the severe handling which both sides had received, neither Cartaret nor O'Donnell appeared inclined to renew the engagement, and accordingly the Irish fell back on the Lough with the captured cattle and left the road open for the Parliamentarians to resume their march on Enniskillen. At Butler's Bridge O'Donnell halted his command, inasmuch as his orders from O'Neill had placed that village as the Southern limit of the country he had given him instructions to patrol. He therefore detached a small party to convoy such of the wounded as could hobble along with the cattle by road to Clough Oughter, and he sent Cuttard in a small boat by water to the same fortress in charge of the still insensible Harry and three of the more severely wounded. Florence MacMahon, with a sorrowful expression on his face, watched the little boat glide down the Annalee, which at this point rushes in a strong and sinuous current to swell the waters of Lough Oughter and the Upper Lough Erne; and long after the boat and its melancholy freight had dwindled into a mere speck on the Lough, Cuttard observed his armour twinkling and flashing on the spot where he had left him.

A couple of hours' rowing brought Cuttard and his helpless charges to Clough Oughter, where Madame O'Neill and Aileen MacMahon were instantly summoned to attend to the wounded men. Madame O'Neill, calm and resourceful, and yet full of womanly tenderness, received her charges one by one in the guard-room, and Aileen MacMahon, who was not less courageous than her aunt, assisted her in her trying duties. The bloody necessities of the Civil War imposed on the women of that period a familiar acquaintance with shocking injuries which is now relegated to the trained hospital nurse; and Aileen, gentle and sympathetic as she was, behaved as bravely as one of her latter-day sisters of the Red Cross Association would have done under similar circumstances. But when Harry Dauntless, smeared all over with blood and clay, was silently carried into the guard-room and laid insensible at her feet, the poor young creature felt such a dreadful sensation of mingled weakness and anguish that she nearly fainted on the spot; and in that dire phase of agony she realised that her heart until that moment had cherished a hidden secret from her understanding.

However, she fought bravely against her weakness, and in obedience to her aunt's commands proceeded to dress the wounds of the three inferior soldiers with steady hands, notwithstanding the ghastly pallor of her face. Madame O'Neill, who considered the Cornet's wounds by far the most serious of the four men, devoted herself exclusively to Harry. She ordered him to be carried upstairs on a litter, hastily constructed out of a cloak laced on a couple of pike shafts, and, bidding Aileen and Cuttard follow her upstairs as soon as they had finished attending to the others, withdrew to look after her own charge.

Cuttard, although long accustomed to regard scenes of bloodshed and wretchedness with the most callous indifference, was deeply moved at the agony of grief which was manifest in the young girl's face. Whilst he assisted her to spread lint and roll bandages, he endeavoured to reassure her, and with that charitable object in view proceeded to give her a cheering account of the many horrible wounds he had seen throughout his varied military career. He entered into such minute and sickening details of these cases and weighed the possibilities of Harry's recovery with such delicate exactitude that if the young woman had been capable of hearing or understanding one half of what her assistant recounted, it is probable that she would have swooned outright. Fortunately for herself, Aileen had been so stunned by the ghastly appearance of Harry Dauntless and the discovery of her own secret feelings towards him, that the troop-adjutant's words made scarcely any impression on her sense of hearing; and, when she had finished dressing the wounds of the three men, Cuttard was obliged to speak twice to her before he could make her understand that Madame O'Neill required their presence above stairs. She declined the clumsily proffered assistance of his arm and ascended resolutely to the apartments where Harry had been conveyed; but once or twice on the way the sharp eyes of the adventurer observed her manifest symptoms of faintness, and he quietly spread out his arm behind in readiness to catch her lythe straight figure.

However, the moment she entered the chamber where Harry lay, she seemed to recover all her self-possession, although his appearance was even more ghastly than when she had first seen him in the guard-room. He was lying on a bed with his eyes closed, his arms stretched limply by his sides, and apparently insensible. His armour and coat had been removed, and his shirt had been ripped open already by Madame O'Neill, who had by that time succeeded in staying the effusion of blood from his wounds; but the blue mark of the musket-ball in his throat, the raw, red hole in his side, and the naturally fair skin of his breast which had turned as white as snow from loss of blood, gave him all the appearance of a corpse about to be laid out for the burial. Notwithstanding this trial to her fortitude, Aileen MacMahon executed such orders as her aunt issued with every outward symptom of composure; but a chance question that necessitated a reply on her part resulted in an incident which betrayed the highly strung state of her nerves.

At the sound of her voice Harry opened his eyes and looked on her with such an expression as one on the threshold of the grave might direct on some beloved object he was about to part from for ever. He struggled hard to utter some word which his white lips were unable to express, and, overcome with the effort, he sighed faintly and sank back unconscious. As his head rolled over on the pillow with a limp motion which struck a cold and ominous chill into the hearts of the three watchers, Aileen sank trembling on her knees beside the bed, and, gasping out, "Good God! he hath gone," instantly subsided in a dead faint upon the ground.

Cuttard, with the quick instinct of one accustomed to deal with military injuries, slipped his hand into Harry's shirt and laid the tips of his fingers over the heart of the unconscious man.

"No, my lady," said he, with a knowing wink at Madame O'Neill. "He liveth, and methinks will live long enough to thank this pretty lass for the interest she hath taken in him." Then he continued with a delicacy scarcely to be expected from one of his rude nature and training, "Of the two methinks the young lady is in greater need of attention than the soldier; and as your ladyship is more accustomed to attend to such gear than I, I shall retire until such time as it shall please your ladyship to send word that the coast is clear, whereupon I shall do myself the honour of taking your place by the bedside of my comrade."

XIX

IT was six weary months before Harry Dauntless was able to leave his bed; and long before that time arrived, O'Neill had fulfilled his threatened promise to Ormond, and had marched South against the Irish Parliamentary forces. When Harry was fit to leave his room and hobble about the pleasant little garden of Clough Oughter, he found that the peace of Eden had settled on the old Castle and the surrounding Lough side. The woods of Killykeen no longer resounded to the sounds of the pipe and trumpet, or the clank of arms and hoarse shouts of drill-instructors, nor was there a single vestige of the late encampment by the water side, for every fighting man of the Clans was away with O'Neill at the investment of Dublin.

The tide of war ebbed and flowed far away from the Northern Lakes, and the echoes of its storms came but faintly to the young soldier, who was in that pleasant state of convalescence which precluded his taking an active part in such stormy scenes, and was yet sufficiently restored to health to enjoy his peaceful surroundings and the delightful society of his two gentle nurses. During this period Harry commenced his long deferred lessons in Gaelic, which he received daily from Madame O'Neill and Aileen in the little rose arbour; and, if his teachers laughingly reproached him with the slow progress he made, perhaps they were in a great measure to blame for the inattention of their pupil. Given, a handsome and susceptible young soldier whose languor is rendered sufficiently interesting by two scarcely healed wounds, a pretty garden warmed by an autumn sun and full of the hum of the bees and the sensuous odour of woodbine and roses, a very beautiful young woman as a teacher, and any subject you please except love is not easily assimilated.

As time went quietly on, and Harry grew visibly stronger, the ever-increasing passion of his heart prompted him daily to declare his love for this young girl who had become so dear to him: but the days drifted on without his making an avowal of his love. This delay was not caused by any lack of opportunity on his side, nor by any shrinking avoidance of his society on the part of Aileen.

The good-natured Madame O'Neill left the two young people alone as often as they pleased; and Aileen, who had been always accustomed to that freedom which is alike the guardian and charm of young Irish ladies, would as soon have thought it necessary to have a duenna accompany her on a walk with her brother Florence, as to require the continual presence of a third party in the lively little wit combats which she engaged in with her convalescent patient. The very wealth of Harry's love was the source of his hesitation, and as each day augmented his passion, he dreaded more and more to put it to the hazard of a yea or nay, much as a vacillating gambler pauses ere he stakes his fortune on one colour of the roulette table. When a man loves in this fashion, his is no transient infatuation or mere summer-weather fancy; but strongly as he may treasure his love, and greatly as he may fear to risk its loss, an hour is bound to come when he must put it to the assay.

Harry's time came one warm September afternoon, when the overhanging woods around Clough Oughter were nodding gently to their own reflections in the placid waters of the Lough. The two young people were standing on the little stone pier below the guard room, and Harry, indicating the tiny islet which lies between Eonish and Dernish More, remarked laughingly to his companion that he wished he were king of such a spot.

"Then," said Aileen, merrily, "you would have to first dethrone its rightful monarch who is mine own unanointed self, inasmuch as that place hath been long since assigned to me by mine uncle as mine own kingdom."

Harry bowed deprecatingly, and expressed a hope that the Queen of the island would some day accord him permission to visit her dominions.

"Your admiration for the property of others betrays your descent from the Conquerors," said the young lady, smiling, and taking a couple of light paddles from the oar rack by the guard-room steps, "and on that account, perhaps, I should be chary of showing such confidence in you, inasmuch as confidence in Norman faith — Alack-a-day — hath ever been the undoing of us poor Irish. Yet, shall I not only give you a passport to my dominions this very day, but I shall myself conduct you thither in mine own royal barge; and in requital of this courtesy, I trust you will not return with drum and banner in order to dispossess me afterwards."

She stepped into the light *currach* which she was accustomed to row about the Lough by herself, and, imperiously declining Harry's offer to take the oars, rowed him away down the lake with strong, graceful strokes. On arriving at the islet, she ran the boat in among some weeping willows, and, brushing them on either side, disclosed a little stone staircase that was completely screened by the green branches which drooped over it. She made fast the boat to an overhanging bough, and, before Harry could rise from his seat, sprang lightly up the mossy steps, and then turned round to confront him with a mock-heroic attitude, and a look of dancing merriment in her grey eyes.

"The Queen bids you welcome to her island, bold Norman," she said. "But ere you land you must promise her that you will not return with dogs, hawks, guns, snares, or such engines for the purpose of playing havoc with her peaceful subjects."

Harry very gravely gave the necessary pledge, whereupon she offered him her strong, firm little hand in order to assist him up the stairs; and, as soon as he gained the topmost step, he found himself in a drowsy little clearing around which the hazel, birch, and willow trees had grown in such a way as to form a perfect bower. They sat down side by side on a moss covered bank, and Aileen whistled softly, whereupon an aged grey hare hopped out of the surrounding bushes, and having loped easily within a few yards of them, sat up and regarded them complacently.

"See, Mr. Dauntless," said Aileen, nodding towards the little animal, "there is Cucullain, my Chief Justice, Vice-Roy, and Chancellor, and though he is blind in one eye, poor thing, he is nonetheless a very sapient member of my council."

Harry observed that one side of the little animal's face was greatly scarred, and he therefore asked her how it had sustained such injuries.

"Years ago, when we lived at Glencairn," said she, "One of Florence's greyhound puppies struck him down almost at second panic and scattered immediately into irresolute groups; and if it had not been for the gallant Cartaret, who rallied them for the second time as valiantly as he had previously done in the glen, they would have fled from the insignificant force which had so demoralised them.

Dauntless heard the trumpets of his own party sound "the retire," and he turned around in order to follow his comrades, who were retreating in good order upon the infantry. Suddenly he was seized with giddiness, and, observing that a steady stream of blood was issuing from beneath his gorget, he realised stupidly for the first time that he had been wounded. As he struggled manfully against the deadly faintness which was overpowering him, he encountered one of Coote's retreating dragoons, and the Roundhead, observing his condition with a malicious grin, checked his horse and aimed a thrust at that space under his armpit which was undefended by his cuirass. The wounded man made a feeble effort to turn his enemy's point, but the trooper's sword slipped over his weak guard and ran through his ribs until it was stopped by the inner shell of the cuirass itself. Harry instantly dropped from his saddle with a faint prayer on his lips; and the Roundhead, not satisfied by this cowardly blow, leaned forward in his saddle and was about to deliver another thrust, which would have closed Cornet Dauntless's career on the spot, had not fate dropped on himself from a wholly unexpected direction.

Captain Cuttard, who had behaved on that day with the most remarkable bravery, had, for reasons best known to himself, ridden further in the charge than any of his companions. The fact was, the gallant soldier had observed a young Parliamentarian Cornet who wore a very handsome riding coat of blue velvet, and he had been seized with an ardent desire to possess it at all hazards. He had therefore hunted this unhappy young gentleman through the mêlée with the untiring patience of a bloodhound on the track of a runaway slave, and after a keen and exciting chase had succeeded in closing with his victim and disarming him in a pass or two. Deciding that a sword-thrust would be likely to injure the coveted riding coat, he stunned him with a blow of his musketoon, and having dismounted he stripped off the fallen man's cuirass in a twinkling and shook him out of the

"Harry instantly dropped from his saddle"

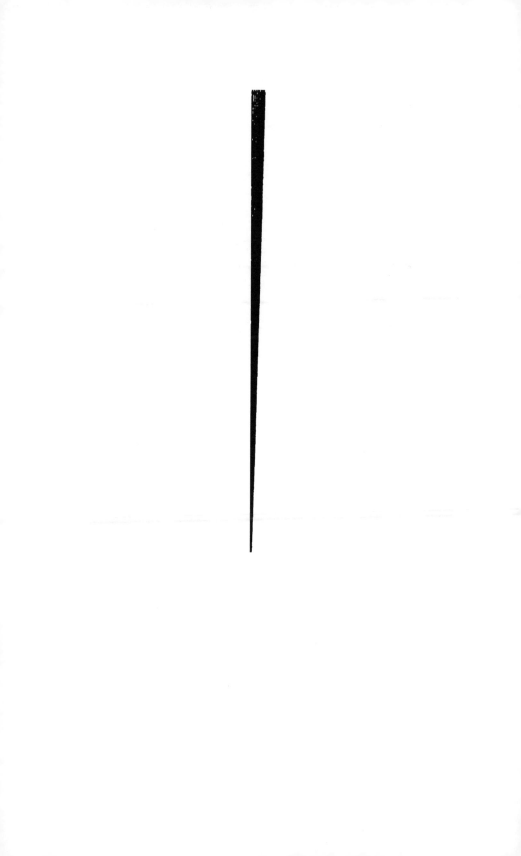

coveted garment with a dexterity perfected by many such experiences.

He was galloping back with his spoil, pursued at a discreet interval by two of his quondam comrades, when he perceived Harry lying on the ground with the dragoon in the act of giving him the coup de grâce. Notwithstanding that the spot was deserted by all of his own side and that three more dragoons had just then reinforced his pursuers, the troop-adjutant did not hesitate for a moment. He rode straight to the rescue of his officer, and brought down his musketoon on the dragoon's head with such force that the butt flew into pieces and the barrel nearly bent in two in his tingling hands. The steel helmet crumpled up like tin beneath that mighty blow, and the wretched trooper, with his skull fractured in a dozen places, dropped dead from his saddle without knowing what had struck him. His five companions, who came up at this moment, gathered fiercely round Cuttard; and although that gentleman defended himself, Harry, and the velvet riding coat with lion-like courage, it would have gone hard with all three had not Florence and half a dozen of his devoted clansmen rushed forward at this juncture and brought them into a place of safety behind the musketeers.

On account of the severe handling which both sides had received, neither Cartaret nor O'Donnell appeared inclined to renew the engagement, and accordingly the Irish fell back on the Lough with the captured cattle and left the road open for the Parliamentarians to resume their march on Enniskillen. At Butler's Bridge O'Donnell halted his command, inasmuch as his orders from O'Neill had placed that village as the Southern limit of the country he had given him instructions to patrol. He therefore detached a small party to convoy such of the wounded as could hobble along with the cattle by road to Clough Oughter, and he sent Cuttard in a small boat by water to the same fortress in charge of the still insensible Harry and three of the more severely wounded. Florence MacMahon, with a sorrowful expression on his face, watched the little boat glide down the Annalee, which at this point rushes in a strong and sinuous current to swell the waters of Lough Oughter and the Upper Lough Erne; and long after the boat and its melancholy freight had dwindled into a mere speck on the Lough, Cuttard observed his armour twinkling and flashing on the spot where he had left him.

in sore need of the aid which you could bestow if you were of the mind you profess to be."

"I cannot guess, by the wildest cast of my imagination," cried the bewildered Harry, "what malicious devil hath whispered to so many people that I am anything but what I profess to be, — namely, a poor country squire who doth not know at the moment whether the little he left behind him in Dublin is forfeited or not. Be assured, gentle Aileen, that I am what I am, — be assured, I am already embarked in the cause of my country as far as my poor means permit, — be assured, that if I could put a thousand men into the field I would do so to-morrow if it would gain me a smile from your lips to-day."

Aileen rose to her feet and smoothed her soft white dress in that feminine way which so closely resembles the fashion whereby a bird adjusts its ruffled feathers.

"Come," said she a little impatiently, "it grows late, and my aunt waits supper for us, and, as to the subject of our late conversation, believe me, Harry Dauntless, it were better for us both if we shall consign it to its proper grave in the lake and leave it there to rest in peace."

She stepped into the boat and as soon as Harry had taken his place in the stern she rowed him back to Clough Oughter. Between each dip of her oars she addressed some light remark to her companion; but, notwithstanding this outward show of carelessness, there was an aching feeling of sadness and desolation in her heart.

"I did not expect that he would have risked his fortune for the sake of a mere woman," she thought sorrowfully, "nor do I blame him for valuing his lands at a higher price than the love of a penniless girl; but, why — Oh! why, did he descend to such pitiable meanness as to lie to me about his true position in the world?"

young woman had been capable of hearing or understanding one half of what her assistant recounted, it is probable that she would have swooned outright. Fortunately for herself, Aileen had been so stunned by the ghastly appearance of Harry Dauntless and the discovery of her own secret feelings towards him, that the troop-adjutant's words made scarcely any impression on her sense of hearing; and, when she had finished dressing the wounds of the three men, Cuttard was obliged to speak twice to her before he could make her understand that Madame O'Neill required their presence above stairs. She declined the clumsily proffered assistance of his arm and ascended resolutely to the apartments where Harry had been conveyed; but once or twice on the way the sharp eyes of the adventurer observed her manifest symptoms of faintness, and he quietly spread out his arm behind in readiness to catch her lythe straight figure.

However, the moment she entered the chamber where Harry lay, she seemed to recover all her self-possession, although his appearance was even more ghastly than when she had first seen him in the guard-room. He was lying on a bed with his eyes closed, his arms stretched limply by his sides, and apparently insensible. His armour and coat had been removed, and his shirt had been ripped open already by Madame O'Neill, who had by that time succeeded in staying the effusion of blood from his wounds; but the blue mark of the musket-ball in his throat, the raw, red hole in his side, and the naturally fair skin of his breast which had turned as white as snow from loss of blood, gave him all the appearance of a corpse about to be laid out for the burial. Notwithstanding this trial to her fortitude, Aileen MacMahon executed such orders as her aunt issued with every outward symptom of composure; but a chance question that necessitated a reply on her part resulted in an incident which betrayed the highly strung state of her nerves.

At the sound of her voice Harry opened his eyes and looked on her with such an expression as one on the threshold of the grave might direct on some beloved object he was about to part from for ever. He struggled hard to utter some word which his white lips were unable to express, and, overcome with the effort, he sighed faintly and sank back unconscious. As his head rolled over on the pillow with a limp imprisonment in the Tower, had been executed at Tyburn just before the Ulster Army started for the North, and Florence had been so prostrated by the intelligence that it was some weeks before Aileen and Harry could succeed in rousing him out of the state of mournful apathy into which he had sunk.

As soon as the main body arrived at Clough Oughter, the soldiers were immediately set to work in putting up winter quarters along the Lough side, and their leaders assembled to consider by what means they would be able to maintain the army throughout the winter months and equip it for the campaign which the spring would bring about. Sir Phelim O'Neill, with the fierce impetuosity which characterised that unhappy and headstrong man, was for putting the surrounding country under contributions by force as the Scots had done in the North of England at the commencement of the Civil War; but Owen Roe sternly and decidedly refused to adopt such a plan, inasmuch as he declared that he would rather resign his command and return to Spain than put it in the power of his enemies to say that he had paid his troops with the edge of a robber's sword.

Every possible source from which arms, ammunition, or money could be procured was discussed and despaired of in turn. The gallant Montrose had suffered the crushing defeat of Philiphaugh, and the Covenanters held triumphant possession of Scotland. The King's party in England was at its last gasp and was utterly unable to help itself or afford aid to a party they had always regarded with suspicion. Ormond had parted with a princely fortune in his vain efforts to keep the Royal banner flying in the South of Ireland, and, although willing enough by this time to grant the terms which he had previously refused, was in even worse straits than themselves. The only leader who made no suggestion was the Bishop, but he was so restless, nervous, and irritable that it was quite patent to the remainder of the Council that he was in the throes of one of the many plots which seemed to be perpetually labouring in the good man's mind. He was continually seeking Harry's company, and he confidentially imparted to him so many wild schemes wherein Bearna Baeghail, the Ulster Army, the King, and a possible Baron's coronet for Harry himself were so inextricably involved that the young man began to fear that his hitherto level-headed kinsman was losing not only his worldly acumen, but his common-sense as well.

One afternoon he invited Harry to accompany him after a deer which he declared he had observed drinking on the shore of the neighbouring island of Eonish; and the young Cornet, who had by this time completely recovered from his wounds, slipped a hunting bandoleer over his shoulder, took a light gun in his hand, and stepped into the boat which the Bishop eagerly ordered to be manned. The boatmen pulled cautiously around the shores of several creeks indicated by the Bishop; but, notwithstanding the most careful scrutiny of the strand, Harry was unable to detect the slightest trace of horn or hoof. At first this absence of slot surprised him greatly, inasmuch as the shore was peat and was of so soft and spongy a nature as to have retained the imprint of even a smaller animal than a deer, but it was not long before the Cornet's attention was drawn to graver matters than sport.

The Bishop made so many rambling and self-contradictory statements about the exact spot where he had seen the deer that Harry began to eye him suspiciously, and the abrupt manner whereby the Bishop suddenly vetoed further search and ordered the boatmen to put about for Clough Oughter led the young man to the conclusion that Evir MacMahon was subject to hallucinations. These suspicions were exchanged for a pitying certainty that his kinsman had completely lost his reason, when the Bishop, after one or two wild plunges at the subject, suddenly asked him in a low voice for the loan of £1,000, which was greatly needed at that moment for the purchase of war material.

"One Thousand Pounds! Good Cousin!" cried Harry, blankly. "Where, in the name of Heaven, should I get One Thousand pounds unless by mortgaging Bearna Baeghail, and thou dost not surely think I would do that during my mother's lifetime? It is her jointure; the sole provision for her old age,—her only source of income; and though mine own interest in it hereafter is freely at the disposal of the King and the Confederate Army, yet let me tell thee, Cousin, that as long as God shall lend my mother to earth, I will never permit any man, be he King, Bishop, or Kinsman, to interfere with her poor fortune."

The Bishop, deprecating any such intention on his part,

then disclosed as much as he deemed fit of the history of that bond which he had so jealously guarded for over twenty years. He assured Harry that the entire sum of £10,000 was solely his own, begged him once more for the sum so urgently needed by the Ulster Army, and offered to engage himself for the repayment of the loan by a mortgage on his own attenuated estate.

By this time they were within a hundred yards of Clough Oughter, and the boatmen, in obedience to a signal from the Bishop, were pulling with a slow, dipping stroke, which urged the boat through the placid water with the gait of a weary living creature. Aileen MacMahon stood at the guard-room door shading her eyes with both her hands and looking straight across the sparkling wavelets at them. The evening sun levelled one of its shafts full into the guard-room arch and glorified the lythe, straight figure, which stood alone on the topmost step, and Harry turned away from the eager face of the Churchman and fixed his eyes steadfastly on that vision of womanly loveliness. He gazed silently on her for nearly a minute, and all that time a well-remembered sentence kept ringing in his head, as though it were being beaten on the drums of his ears to the timed stroke of a blacksmith's hammer: "I would love such a man! I would starve with such a man! I would die for such a man!"

"Do you mean to say, Evir," said he, faintly, after a pause, "that all this wealth is mine own, my very own?"

"Absolutely thine own, and apart from thy mother's jointure," was the reply.

The boat was by this time within a dozen lengths of the pier, and Aileen, nodding and laughing, descended a couple of the steps and asked Harry what had happened the deer which they had gone forth to kill. His ears were full of strange, roaring noises, and he did not hear and, therefore, did not answer her question; but his eyes were staring widely at her, and he thought how straight and round her leg was, as a sudden gust of wind whirled her dress to one side and displayed a momentary glimpse of her black silk and silver-striped hose.

Once more he repeated his last question in a low whisper and asked Evir MacMahon if he had the power to will this money to whomsoever he pleased.

"You could give it all to a beggar in the street," was the answer, "and no man could say Nay to you."

The rowers tossed their oars inboard, and the men who rowed bow oar stood up, boat-hook in hand, to catch the mooring ring at the pier. Aileen descended the steps to meet them, with her white robe fluttering about her slim little feet and the high-heeled, ruby-coloured slippers, which fitted them to perfection. Never had she appeared more beautiful than she did at that moment, for the cool evening breeze had given her a fresher colour than usual, and a merry air of gaiety had brightened her eyes with more than customary animation; but Harry Dauntless saw her but faintly, as through a mist, for his mother's spirit and his father's disposition were struggling hard within him just then. "Such a woman would die for you, if necessary," whispered one voice. "Wealth, Ease, and the respect of the World," whispered the other. The boat's gunnel rasped discordantly against the pier, and once more Aileen addressed Harry laughingly. Her voice broke the spell which held him tongue-tied, and he bent forward to his kinsman's ear.

"Take all, Cousin," said he, with a set look on his white face. "Take all of it and use it for the King's cause as you think best."

"*All!*" gasped the Bishop. "Do I hear thee aright, Harry, didst thou say—*All?*"

"Yes, all," said the young man, standing up in the boat and speaking in a tone of voice which, although low, was harsh and decided. "Bid Sir Phelim make out the necessary transfer this very evening, and I shall sign it in the morning."

The Bishop's gasping lips made an effort to frame a reply, but before he could utter a word, either of protest or thanks, Harry Dauntless sprang up the steps, bowed gravely to the astonished girl on the pier, and then disappeared under the arched entrance of the Castle. He made his way straight to the little room which he had occupied since the day he had been brought wounded to Clough Oughter, and when the Bishop followed him thither, half an hour later, he found the young man grimly silent. He curtly refused the Bishop's invitation to join the others at supper, on the excuse of feeling indisposed, and cut short his kinsman's melliferous expressions of gratitude by pleading a severe headache which nothing but solitude could cure. But when it grew dark he stole downstairs past the Banqueting Hall, whence came the sound of loud and jovial voices, and crept out into the little arbour, where he paced feverishly to and fro in an endeavour to calm his mind in the cool night air.

A light step on the gravel behind, and a low, sweet voice pronouncing his name, caused him to turn about with a quickened breathing; and, by the light of the stars, whose brilliancy was considerably enhanced by the lustrous, frosty atmosphere, he perceived Aileen standing before him, with her eyes full of tears, and her hands stretched out to him. They stood regarding each other for a second as though they were entranced, whilst the stars seemed to race round their heads and the lake whirled like a blue ribbon beneath their feet, and the next moment the two lovers were clasped in one another's arms in a perfect ecstasy of passion.

"Oh, Harry!" she sobbed. "How noble, how splendid, how generous of you to devote all your fortune to your Country on the very day that fortune came to you! How heroically unselfish you are, and how contemptible have I shown myself in my past estimation of your character!"

"Not so unselfish as thou mayst think, dear Aileen," said her lover, smiling down upon her, "for dost remember thy promise? As vulgar as poor Cuttard, as meanly born as a horse boy, and as ill-favoured as a hunchback,—and if I happen to be somewhat above any of the three, I shall hold thee, nevertheless, to thy bargain, dear heart."

Captain John Cuttard, who had ventured as far as the guard-room steps in order to see how the night went, stopped short at the threshold, on perceiving the two figures in the garden. His harsh, coarse features assumed a look of intense surprise, which was presently succeeded by a broad grin, and that, in turn, by a wink of supreme cunning which was specially directed to the constellation of Orion. Then he softly and discreetly withdrew to the guard-room, where he reseated himself among the soldiers, with whom he was a long-established favourite, and resumed an interrupted anecdote which afforded mutual gratification to the narrator and his auditors.

It was the history of a personal amour with a stout Flemish maiden who had acted as sutler to Meilleraye's regiment in the Low Countries. This incident had been a profitable, ell as a pleasant, event in the military experience of nultifariously employed troop-adjutant, inasmuch as Mr. ırd had been unable to consume all the beer and tobacco ı the lady was in the habit of supplying for his use, and he considerably augmented his income by the sale of such us luxuries among his less-favoured comrades. However, nteresting love affair was terminated by the gallant genın's own intemperate conduct. He became jealous of river of the lady's cart, challenged, fought, and wounded and was rewarded for this proof of his affection by being ɔff by the fair sutler, who married his vanquished rival as as that person could hop to church on a crutch.

[he moral whereof is two-fold, my good fellows," sentenʏ concluded the narrator, whose imperfect Gaelic and ' foreign affectations had rendered many of his most florid ds to be utterly unintelligible to his listeners. "And I aptly compare the deduction to the twin tines of a hayor, to use the language of Cavalieros, the double-headed which keepeth ward at the place whereto you are all likely) after death. Wherefore, if any of you honest fellows d happen to desire an easy acquaintance with wisdom, ı hath been sorely gained by men of experience, like lf, hearken carefully to my advice. *Primo:* If any of lads must needs fight for such toys as a woman's love, be you kill your rival, for if you spare him she will most edly wed him afterwards to spite you. *Secundo:* If any u should greatly desire to win a girl who is cold and coy, ourself in the way of sustaining some grievous wound, for, my words, there is nothing which appeals so much to a ın's heart as a wan face and an interesting languor, which eefiest-faced rascal amongst you can easily obtain by the ıf a couple of pints of his heart's best blood."

XXI

AS might be expected, there was an extraordinary sensation among the leaders of the Confederate Army when the Bishop communicated to them the decision of his young kinsman. Their own pressing need of money, the unexpected source whence it had come, the generous way it had been tendered, and the sum itself, which in those days, when money had a higher purchasing value than now, was a princely amount, all combined in affecting the excitable Ulstermen in an indescribable fashion. Consequently, on the following day Harry received such an ovation as was sorely trying to his shy and retiring nature.

Sir Phelim, who invariably assumed the initiative in all things except military affairs, which Owen Roe sternly reserved to himself, thanked the young Palesman in a speech which was an extraordinary mixture of fulsome affectation and bombast. O'Reilly, O'Donnell, and the lesser Chiefs expressed their sense of gratitude in speeches of varying emotional terms, and Florence, with his countenance lighted up with the fervour of an enthusiast, embraced him warmly and took occasion to add in a whisper how delighted he was to have learned from his sister of the prospect of being associated with him by a bond even more sacred than comradeship.

Owen Roe alone was calm and unimpassioned. He recommended Harry to reconsider his offer, hinted to him that decisions which were arrived at in moments of enthusiasm were often regretted afterwards, and quietly advised him to think over the matter for a week.

However, the Cornet protested so firmly that he intended to abide by his offer that O'Neill perceived that the young man's mind was made up, and accordingly thanked him in a short speech which was brimful of so much manly dignity and sincerity as to attach Harry more than ever to his General.

Evir MacMahon set out the next day no one knew whither, nor did any one in the Castle hear of his whereabouts for two months until Harry received a letter dated from London on the morning whereon he and Aileen were betrothed to one another in Clough Oughter.

The letter was brief and unimportant in itself and served merely to cover another from Lord H——, who was one of the King's confidential agents. The latter communication was a cautious assurance that Mr. Dauntless might consider His Majesty as being already his debtor, and that any advances made by him to the Royalist cause should be duly secured by an Exchequer Bill as soon as the money was forthcoming. Harry possessed enough of his father's insight to know the exact value of such a security, but he also possessed enough of his mother's nature to be able to contemplate his sacrifice without a sigh.

Therefore, his heart was light and his countenance reflected his inward happiness when he and Aileen plighted one another their troth in the Castle chapel on that bright March morning. The Betrothal, which consisted merely in an exchange of rings in the presence of the assembled relatives of the bride, was a rite then regarded as one scarcely less solemn than the marriage service itself. Harry had begged Aileen to consent to have the latter ceremony performed immediately after the betrothal, in accordance with the usual custom; but she had earnestly requested that this should be deferred until the return of the Bishop, and appeared to be so very desirous that her kinsman should officiate at the marriage that the bridegroom had been obliged to yield to her wishes.

The approach of Spring awakened the Ulster Army into a state of great activity for the forthcoming campaign; and Harry, aware that he might have to march off any week, spent every minute he could snatch from his military duties with his betrothed. One evening, as he and Aileen sat in the rose arbour with Florence stretched lazily in his mantle at their feet, Cuttard made his appearance and, having made an exaggerated bow to Aileen and leered familiarly at Harry, finally saluted Florence in the stilted way he was always accustomed to address that young gentleman.

There was mutual and openly displayed antipathy between the haughty, aristocratic Chieftain and the ill-bred, swaggering soldier of fortune. Florence never deigned to converse with Cuttard except in cold crystallised sentences, and Mr. Cuttard heartily reciprocated this feeling by treating Florence with a frigid punctiliousness whereby he inferred that their relations with one another were purely of a military character.

Consequently, when the troop-adjutant drew himself up stiffly, clicked his spurs together, and curtly informed Florence that the General desired to see him, there were few words exchanged between them. But when the young gentleman had sauntered off proudly with his chin in the air, he looked so gallant and soldier-like that Cuttard was unable to refrain from making an approving remark upon his appearance.

"A very tall and proper young gentleman," he said, nodding in the direction in which Florence had gone, "but — craving your pardon, Madame" (here he bowed profoundly and swept the grass before Aileen with his hat plume), "'t is a pity he is so impulsive, inasmuch as his hasty temper, which resembleth that of mine honoured friend and erstwhile Colonel, Prince Rupert, oft requites his native valour in a scurvy fashion."

Although Aileen shared a certain amount of her brother's high-bred disdain for the solecisms and vulgarity of the adventurer, she always treated him with a kindly air of friendship on Harry's account; and accordingly she smiled indulgently and bade him remember that her brother was a true-born son of Eire, wherefore it was natural to expect he should possess some of the most striking faults of his countrymen.

"True," murmured the troop-adjutant with a sigh; "true, that fact had escaped me for the moment — I have lived so long away from home, my Lady, that I am apt to forget, at times, the immensurable advantages which exist in the land which I have the honour to belong to and the misfortune to be exiled from; and, therefore, I often look for perfections which are rare even in England and impossible in this accursed country."

Aileen laughed and demanded a list of what he considered were the principal afflictions in Ireland.

"It should be a blessed land," answered Cuttard, kissing the tips of his gauntleted fingers and once more dusting the grass with his hat-plume. "A thrice blessed land, even if its sole claim to be happy were based on no other grounds than the fact that it had given birth to so fair and sweet a lady as yourself. It hath every gift to make it happy, but, alas, it is as you see — Its Ladies" (here the pantomime of the glove and plumed hat came in once more) "are as fair as they are virtuous — its Men are as valiant as they are hardy — and the Land itself is as beautiful as — its daughters" (another exaggerated bow). "But there is so much skimble-skamble and antiquated fancies of Old-World pride, Old-World folly, and Old-World traditions overcumbering the Island that (if I may be pardoned the phrase) if the Devil had it ready to his hand at the commencement of the World, he could have turned Eden into a howling waste through its instrumentality between drinking-time and drinking-time."

Aileen sat up very straight and asked how the possession of Ireland at that particular time could have benefited the Enemy to Mankind.

"Why, your Ladyship," replied Mr. Cuttard, with a grin, "all he need have done was to have waited his opportunity until the heavenly guards snoozed on their posts, which is by no means an unusual occurrence even among vigilant sentinels like the Germans. Then he could have slipped in a couple of your Irish Clans, two rival Chiefs, a dozen of your heathenish Sennachies and Pipers to whoop 'em on at each other; and, by my stainless honour, Gabriel, himself, would not have been able to part 'em once they were fairly started."

Harry and Aileen laughed very heartily at this new rendering of Paradise Lost; but the girl, like most of her countrywomen, was too warmly attached to her native land to suffer it to be attacked even in jest without a defence on her part.

"We are old-fashioned in our habits, our faith, and our traditions," said she, with a smile on her lip, but a combative expression in her eyes, "yet I challenge you, Captain Cuttard, to produce a single instance whereby our Old-World customs either offend or inconvenience any peaceable inhabitant of Ireland, be he Celt or Sassenach."

"Why, then, your Ladyship," answered Cuttard, readily, "I can give you an instance no later than last Sunday what time I attended Mass at Kilmore with my regiment. It will doubtless surprise your Ladyship that I, who am a poor but devout follower of the Church of England, should have been present at a worship which is so repellent to my belief; but I can assure your Ladyship that my sense of military uniformity is so delicate that I would rather wound my conscience grievously than not accompany my regiment to whatever Church it goeth. As I stood at the Church door smoking my pipe (for tobacco hath a most religious effect upon my meditations and I therefore invariably smoke it throughout a sermon) there cometh up unto me a saucy old beggarman. As the Church is a cramped little structure, the greater number of my men were kneeling outside in the graveyard as thickly packed as sheep in a pen; but this old rapscallion pushed through them as though he were a lord, and, notwithstanding his rags, my foolish fellows reverently yielded him room as though he were the General himself. I paid little attention to him, however, until he came to the door, when he fetched me a rap over my outstretched legs with his staff and bade me stand out of his way for a Sassenach dog. Your Ladyship can easily understand how a Cavaliero like myself sustained such an affront and I felt for the moment like quoiting the grey-headed old barbarian over the nearest tombstone. But the very instant I stretched out my hand towards him, about twenty of your Ladyship's gentle kinsmen started up with their hands on their skenes; and, as I had no liking to have so many hearty friends all sticking their daggers into me at once over such a trifle, I restrained my just anger and put up with the affront as best as I could.

"And now, your Ladyship, that is one of my grievances against the many Old-World fancies which obtain in this country to its hurt, for though I think it is very proper that grey hairs and ragged clothes should claim a share of our pity, that is no reason that insolent old rogues should be permitted to thrust their way through the King's troops, and rap honourable Cavalieros over the shins."

"I think I can explain that matter better than my sister," said a clear voice behind the indignant troop-adjutant, and Florence stepped in between him and Aileen with a pleased and exultant look on his face. He was booted and spurred and dressed as if for a journey, and the good-humour which possessed him was so great that it included even Cuttard within its genial limits.

"The reason so many people made way for that old hero on Sunday," said he, with a strange, proud smile on his face, "was because this incident took place in Ireland and not in England, where they manage things differently."

"That is just what I ventured to remark to the lady," said

Cuttard, drily; "but I fail to see why that should be a reason for showing so much deference to an insolent old beggarman."

"Listen, and I will tell you," said Florence, as he slowly drew on his heavy riding gauntlets and buckled their fastenings. "Forty-seven years ago that crabbed, bent old man, then as tall and proper a young fellow as ever braced on a target or swung a broadsword, was foremost in that battle of the Yellow Ford what time brave Harry Bagenal and the flower of England's soldiers went down before the might of the Red Hand.

"Now, Mr. Cuttard, during the three years I idled at Oxford and the two I wasted in London, if I did not amass much knowledge, I at least learned somewhat of the English character and the relations which exist between the English citizen and the English soldier; both when the latter is serving for pay and also when he is no longer required and is reformado or disbanded. I could tell you how the London citizens cheered themselves speechless when Buckingham's soldiers marched through the town on their way to the siege of Rochelle, and I could also tell you how I have seen some of those very soldiers, ragged, starving, and maimed by French shot and steel, beg for bread in those streets a year afterwards.

"I have no doubt you have seen such sights yourself, Mr. Cuttard, but let me tell you of an incident that I saw with these eyes at Oxford, which will convince you that we wild Irishers treat our maimed soldiers more humanely than your countrymen serve theirs.

"I saw an aged man — such a one as you encountered at Kilmore last Sunday — stand for an hour in the town pillory for vagrancy. He had lost a leg by a Spanish cannon-shot what time the Armada was on the seas and England's existence was in the scales, and yet — and yet such past services could neither afford that frail old cripple bread nor save him from the insults of the mob. Neither I nor my country owed him aught, and he probably had the blood of some of my kinsmen on his hand, yet — Faugh! it made me sick to see him hang there in agony and disgrace, whilst the tallow-brained country clowns hooted the man who had aided in securing them their liberties.

"Now, sir, compare that instance with the respectful conduct of our rough fellows on Sunday when they made way for that crabbed, snarling old man, and then prove to me, if you can, Mr. Cuttard, that your countrymen love their worn-out old soldiers better than we do ours."

The bitter truth of this speech disarmed the retaliatory answer that Mr. Cuttard would gladly have made. He looked down on the ground and shuffled his feet uneasily, muttered something about a few scurvy shopkeepers who battened on the hard services of honourable Cavalieros whom they undervalued and underpaid, and making a lame excuse to Aileen took a hasty leave. As soon as the troop-adjutant was out of hearing, Florence MacMahon bent forward and took his sister's right hand and her lover's left hand in either of his gauntleted ones.

"News! News! good news for both," he said. "The Bishop returns to Clough Oughter in six days from now, but you must defer your wedding for a little space longer. Three days — three little days after Evir's arrival — is all I crave of you two, and I promise I shall not spare either my horse or myself in the endeavour to be here before then if possible. I am post haste for Kilkenny with a written contract for Ormond's acceptance. He hath consented at last to Owen's terms, and as soon as he affixes his signature then we shall join armies and march on Dublin. They say that Blaney is in garrison there" (here a sinister expression lit up his face for an instant), "and if we should meet face to face on a fair field, I, at least, shall feel thankful."[1]

He embraced his sister affectionately, and bade her select and carefully reserve as his partner for the wedding dance the prettiest girl she could find in Ulster.

"No frail, courtly dame, mark you, Aileen," said he, merrily; "no delicate, town-bred damsel, but a straight, brown, agile daughter of the Mountains, one that is fit to face such a rout blythely until daylight; for, look you, Wench, on that night I intend to dance the soles off my new buskins."

He shook hands warmly with his prospective brother-in-law, and strode off gaily towards the guard-room steps, whistling

[1] Lord Blaney went out of his way to tender irrelevant but damaging evidence against Lord Conor Maguire at the State trial of that unhappy young peer. His testimony served little towards procuring a conviction, but the malignant ferocity he displayed on that occasion rendered his name odious throughout Ireland for many years afterwards.

"Planxty Sudley." As the boat which bore him to the shore shot out from the pier, Florence stood up and waved his plumed cap, whilst Harry, with one arm round his bride, waved his disengaged hand in reply; and the two young men smiled at one another, little thinking in what way they should next meet.

XXII

TRUE to the prediction made by Florence, Evir MacMahon arrived six days after the date of the young Chieftain's departure for Kilkenny. The three days that followed the Bishop's arrival was a trying period to the expectant bridegroom, who daily scanned the far-off road for a glimpse of the familiar cap-plume and mantle of his brother-in-law; but the third day came and passed without bringing Florence MacMahon. Early on the morning of the fourth day Harry mounted his horse and galloped off towards Cavan, in the hopes of either meeting Florence on the way or learning some news of him at that town; but he had not proceeded far through the woods of Killykeen before he encountered two horsemen, who, on closer inspection, proved to be a sergeant of O'Farrell's regiment in company with no other person than honest George Ledwidge.

The meeting between the young gentleman and his old comrade and servant filled them with so much mutual emotion that they were unable to interchange a word for some moments, during which time they silently wrung each other's hands. Before Harry could express in words those questions which his eyes asked so anxiously, the old man hastily assured him that all was well at Bearna Baeghail. *Herself* was in *elegant* health and spirits. Shanganagh was never so peaceful. There had never been a sign of a steel cap in the Valley since his honour had left it, barrin' Mr. Hooter and his troop of horse, and they had only stopped for a night and behaved like spring lambs; and, in short, there was not the slightest need for his honour to fear that he was the bearer of ill tidings.

Harry thereupon asked Ledwidge what had brought him so far North, and in reply the old man tendered him a packet which was superscribed in the well-known delicate Italian handwriting of his mother. As the young gentleman broke the seal and snapped the silk thread which bound the letter, he remarked to Ledwidge that he himself looked far from appearing well, but the old man stoutly protested that he was never in better health. He, however, confessed that old age and the wound he had received at Kilrush were commencing to tell on his bodily activity, and he sorrowfully added that his days as a horseman were over, and as soon as he returned home by easy stages he would hang up his saddle for good in the lumber-room along with his old steel cap and broadsword.

The young gentleman bade the Sergeant conduct the old man to Clough Oughter with an injunction to look after his comfort, and then shook hands once more with Ledwidge and resumed his journey towards Cavan. As he rode slowly under the rustling boughs of the forest, he spread out and commenced reading his mother's letter with every manifestation of pleasure; but, by the time he realised its import, his face became deadly pale and his hands trembled so much that he could scarcely decipher the last few lines. He pulled up his horse, read through the letter again, folded it up mechanically, and sat staring open-eyed at the ground.

A musket-hawk dashed down among the trees and some small bird screamed piercingly within a few feet of him, but he did not hear its cries, nor did he observe one of MacMahon's clansmen, in fluttering mantle and sparkling steel cap, who passed him by with a stare and a salute. A horseman overtook him, glanced curiously at his stooped figure, passed on, uttered an exclamation, and pulled up instantly. It was Evir MacMahon.

"What, Harry, what?" said he, anxiously. "No ill tidings of Florence, no bad news from Bearna Baeghail, I trust?"

Harry Dauntless straightened himself in his saddle and with a stern look of reproach handed him the letter and bade him read it. It ran thus: —

For the hands of Henry Dauntless, Esquire, Cornet in Colonel O'Reilly's Regt. of Horse — These — by the hands of George Ledwidge — Haste! Post Haste!

Our Lady's Day, 1646.

BELOVED SON, GREETINGS AND BLESSINGS, — I send this script by the hands of George Ledwidge, who will confirm the good accounts I send thee as to the excellent health, security, and prosperity I have enjoyed since we twain parted. The man Hooter, whom thou didst grievously wound, hath proved himself to be a more generous and forgiving character than thou didst appraise him. After he recovered from the effects of his hurt and left here he exerted himself very actively in our interests, and on more than one occasion saved me from the annoyance and expense of having soldiers billeted here at free quarters. It is indeed fortunate that such a man is disposed to make up for his former incivility by a display of friendly behaviour, inasmuch as his authority appears to be scarcely less weighty, now that Ormond is Viceroy, than it was when Borlase was in power.

However, such news is trifling compared with the matter which I desire to impart, and thou canst believe that I consider it to be a subject which nearly concerns the honour, happiness, and peace of thyself when I have not spared our faithful old servant so long and perilous a journey.

Two days ere the above date, a certain Master Quillett (an old and reputable friend of thy late father) came to Bearna Baeghail accompanied by one whom he introduced as his Clerk.

It was some while ere I could identify him, inasmuch as twenty years have passed since I last saw him, and time hath dealt as shrewdly with him as it hath with me; but I was scarcely recovered from the surprise of seeing him in Ireland than I was subjected to an even greater shock by learning the reason of his journey. He told me that the object of his visit was to beg us to suspend legal proceedings which had been taken in our joint names on a Bond which he held against a certain Master Wiltonholme. Now thou canst very well imagine, my dear Harry, how astonished I was to learn of the existence of such a bond and how indignant I felt at learning that any one had dared to institute legal proceedings in any matter without first consulting us.

I questioned Master Quillett angrily as to the nature of this Bond, the reasons why its existence had been hitherto kept from me, and the name of him who had dared to take such liberties with our concerns; but he stammered out several evasive answers and pleaded that these matters were not his own secrets. He assured me that the sum would be honourably discharged as soon as the gentleman came into a property which would become his on the death of an ailing Relative, and added if the proceedings in the Law Courts were permitted to go on that they would involve his Client in utter ruin. I was all the more offended with this air of Mystery, and I told the Lawyer roundly that if he did not answer the questions I had asked, I was resolved to find them out for myself. Thereupon Master Quillett and his Clerk conversed apart, and after a while the former reluctantly confessed that this Bond represented the price of an unfortunate young gentleman's ruin, which thine own Father — my tears blot the words as I write — thine own Father had accomplished at the gaming-table twenty-three years ago.

Oh, Harry, Harry, surely the vices and evil deeds of men lie dormant in their dead bodies and sprout up in a noisome harvest even from their graves to vex the world afterwards. Thou canst not think what agonising memories this resurrected and accursed Covenant awakened in me and how, in one short minute, I seemed to live once more through all those sorrowful nights when I held thy baby form in mine arms and wept to think that my husband was at that moment, perhaps, staking his last acre on a turn of a card. Oh, Harry, it was his sole vice, — he was kind, he was gentle, he was loving to us both, he was otherwise a very perfect man; but think what a heritage of suffering he left us twain on account of that one dreadful weakness.

I told the Lawyer that as far as it lay with myself I would never have aught to do with such unhallowed merchandise, and that I would add my prayers and entreaties to his in begging thee to abandon this wretched Law Suit. Whilst I did speak in this wise the Clerk bent down his head and wept bitterly; and, my suspicions being aroused, I pressed him shrewdly, whereupon he did confess that he was no other but Master Wiltonholme, himself; and some further questioning on my part drew from him the fact that the Bond itself was in the hands of my Cousin Evir. I bade him fear naught on thy account, inasmuch as I would stake my life upon thy refusing to take advantage of his folly and added that thy affection for me alone would make thee instantly withdraw this Law Suit if I so pleaded.

And now, dear Harry, let me not blush to learn that my poor boast was a vain-glorious one. Think how good Heaven hath been to us twain. Consider how our little Property hath escaped the ravening hands of both sides during these unhappy wars, and then reckon the number who have been stripped to their backs and in that fact recognise God's mercy to us. We have enough for our simple wants and do not need this accursed money. Therefore, do not have any hand in this Law Suit, bid thy Cousin Evir tear this wretched bond to shreds and, by doing so, grant Mercy to a Man who never injured thee, but who nevertheless pleads to thee as for his life, enrich thine own Conscience with Peace, and grant the first and only prayer of thy loving MOTHER.

Three deep furrows appeared on the broad forehead of Evir MacMahon as he read this letter, and when he had finished he handed it back to his kinsman and asked him unsteadily what he intended to do.

"What would you yourself suggest?" asked Harry, bitterly. "What would you counsel me to do? Should I follow the dictates of mine own conscience and spurn these infernal gains, or should I turn a deaf ear to my mother's prayers, bid this hopeless law-suit take its course, and so destroy this unfortunate wretch whose very name I was ignorant of until to-day? Mark you, now, I ask advice not of Evir MacMahon, the Confederate Soldier, but of Evir MacMahon, the Priest and Bishop. Ha! Cousin, ha! what is your rede?"

The Bishop turned away his face and did not reply, so his kinsman continued relentlessly, "This, then, was the fortune which you bade me possess myself of," he said scornfully. "This money, which represented another's destruction — this money, which you knew well was the eric of a young man's madness — for what is gambling for such monstrous sums but a form of insanity? And so you would not only have made me the participant in such tradings, but you would also have made me the instrument of stamping this poor fool into the dust. For shame, Evir, for shame!"

"I did suspect — I thought — I, at least, did surmise," said the Bishop, huskily, "that this sum was due on some gambling debt, but, as Heaven is my judge, I was not certain of it until this moment."

The young man asked the Churchman brusquely if the sums which Kathlyn Dauntless had received through him for the past ten years had been derived from this source. The Bishop's lips twitched themselves into two straight lines and a lump formed in his throat which prevented his replying, so he nodded silently and ruefully.

"Our poverty precludes immediate repayment," said Dauntless, gloomily, "and it may be years ere we can return all we have received; but I can, at least, prevent this matter going further, and we must therefore return instantly to O'Neill and explain why my offer must be withdrawn."

"No doubt my judgment was wrong," said the Bishop, sorrowfully; "but then, God help me, I am but a man, after all. Believe me, boy, what I did, I did with the best intentions, and my conduct throughout was guided solely by love for you and your mother. Do what you think is right, Harry, and may Heaven guide you and forgive me."

They rode back to the camp, where they sought out O'Neill and explained all to him, and the General, although obviously disconcerted by the news, took the matter very coolly.

"If it is against your conscience, Mr. Dauntless, to pursue this matter further," said he, quietly, "far be it from me to urge you to do aught than what seemeth best to yourself. You have given me the service of your sword and have behaved most becomingly under my command; and, therefore, if you can afford me no further aid than that, I am much beholden to you, for a man can give no more than all he hath."

When he left O'Neill, the Cornet wandered aimlessly about the lines on foot for nearly half an hour, but it was not long before he noticed that he was regarded with cold looks by his comrades, who, it was quite evident, had already heard of his decision and were disposed to attribute the worst motives to it. Angry, confused, and heavy-hearted, he turned away from the camp and sought self-consolation in the solitude of the woods of Killykeen, through which he walked gloomily for nearly a mile, until chance led his footsteps to a spot where he encountered the society he was so anxious to avoid.

He stepped suddenly into a level clearing by the waterside, where the short, sweet grass had been so closely mown and carefully rolled as to give it the appearance of a green velvet cloth set afloat on the lake; and on this delightful stretch of verdure he perceived half a dozen of O'Neill's younger officers who were being instructed in the Royal Game of Bowls by no worse a master than Captain John Cuttard.

It was too late to retreat, for the crackle of a fallen branch beneath his foot had caused all eyes to be turned in his direction; and, whilst he stood irresolute, two of the younger Chieftains, giving a view Hallo, ran forward laughing, and pinned him by the arms. They insisted, as that morning was the last day of his bachelor freedom, that he should join them in a game of bowls, and as he was too dispirited to resist their importunities, he yielded to their request. For the first half hour his carelessness and preoccupation were so evident that they evoked many sly allusions to his forthcoming wedding and the lovesick state of his mind, and this banter had the effect of rousing his emulation. He played more carefully and exhibited a marked increase in skill, and, as his interest in the game increased, his depression gradually faded from his mind.

His good spirits returned, his eye brightened once more, he had even laughed once or twice, and he was about to deliver a ball at the jack with a light jest upon his lips when suddenly he heard the hurried tramp of a horse in the woods, and Florence MacMahon, with his dress disordered and stained with the marks of travel, rode up to the bowling green and flung himself from his saddle without a word.

The young Chieftain's face was set, white, and haggard. His teeth were clenched hard, his eyes glared wildly, and there was such a distorted expression on his features that Harry shuddered involuntarily at the recollection of having seen such a look on his face when the drunken student had attempted to slap his face in Dames Street.

Dismayed by his friend's appearance, Harry dropped the bowl and advanced with his hand outstretched; but, to his amazement, the Chieftain, catching the proffered hand by the wrist, flung it violently from him, and said in a tone of suppressed passion, —

"Keep your hand for your weapon, Mr. Dauntless, for that is the purpose I intend you to put it to in a minute or so."

"In God's name," cried the bewildered Cornet, "have you taken leave of your senses, Florence, or is this some mad or drunken jest which you put upon me, to try my patience? If it is the latter, Cousin, I tell you that my sense of humour is so poor that I do not take such pleasantries in good part."

"You shall find it is a sorry jest, for one or the other of us within the next few minutes," was the fierce rejoinder. "I tell you, Henry Dauntless, in the presence of these gentlemen, that you are a villain and a traitor, and, if you have not lost all sense of manhood, strip and draw upon the instant."

"If you refer to that unhappy and accursed sum," said Harry, greatly pained and shocked by his friend's insane fury, "I beseech you, have patience but for one moment, and I shall fully explain."

"Damn you and your thrice accursed money!" cried the other, furiously. "Do you think I care the value of a rotten twig of heather about whether you give or withhold the wretched pelf? Let O'Neill and my priestly Uncle settle such base trash among them, but when the honour of a Lady of Glencairn is concerned, and that Lady is my sister, the matter brooks no other redresser than myself, though the whole Clan of Hy-Niall and the Hierarchy of St. Peter's itself stood in my way and bade me hold."

"What!" cried Harry, trembling all over with passion.

"'You shall not leave this spot without satisfying me'"

"This to me? This to your sister's affianced husband? By Heaven, Florence, wert thou not her brother —"

"Aye, I am her brother, and I shall prove that full soon," cried the infuriated Chieftain, stripping off his riding coat with such violence that he tore several buttons off the garment in the frenzy of his haste. "Thou shalt find that we people of the North do not brook a man engaging the affections of one of our women folk when he is already married to another."

"Good God!" faltered Harry, white as death. "Some enemy hath wrought this foul lie to my undoing. I beseech thee, Florence, listen to me for a moment."

"Draw your weapon instantly," shouted Florence, who now stood with his broadsword quivering in his right hand and his eighteen-inch skene in his left. "Draw your weapon, or, by the God who made you, I shall strike you dead where you stand. Juggle and palter, and plot with others as you will afterwards, but you shall not leave this spot without satisfying me first."

Harry turned a despairing look towards the surrounding chieftains as if to ask them to interfere in this unnatural quarrel; but the bystanders, surmising that some treachery had been practised on their fellow-chief, only regarded the Palesman with forbidding countenances, while Cuttard added the last straw by walking up jauntily to his Cornet, and, remarking that there was no help for it, bade him strip off his coat, and take to his iron with a cheerful heart.

"Keep thy hand low as thou lovest me, Harry," said he, in a whisper, "and I will engage thee to pink this young cock o' the mountains in the first veny, but beware of his left hand, for these Irishers have a trick of using their skenes for more than guarding."

The troop-adjutant then turned to his late pupils, and informed them pleasantly as he intended acting for his Cornet, he would be very happy to gratify any gentleman with a turn for fighting who might desire to represent Master MacMahon; but before he could complete this sporting offer, he was interrupted by the furious clash of swords behind him.

He turned around instantly, and cried out very indignantly: "For Shame, gentlemen, for shame, I protest I have not as yet given the word. Have you no sense of decency, that you should set to like a couple of market porters? Upon my stainless honour, this precipitance is contrary to all the established laws of the modern duello. Ha! that was a pretty thrust. Habet! Habet! right through the short ribs and into the brisket. Selah! Cavalieros. Selah!"

This last exclamation was evoked by the consequence of a sudden rush which Florence made on his unwilling antagonist, for Harry advanced his sword *en quarte* for the sole purpose of parrying the murderous cut aimed at him, and thus presented his point, upon which his assailant rushed in the blindness of his fury. The blade passed completely through the deltoid muscles of MacMahon's upraised sword-arm, and the shell of the hilt struck him with such violence on the ribs that he dropped on his knees as though the weapon had really passed through his body.

The wound, though by no means deadly, was so lacerated and agonising that, after one or two unavailing efforts to regain his feet, the young Chieftain swooned and fell, to all appearances lifeless; and the innocent cause of this tragical scene staggered back white and trembling to regard with horrified eyes the motionless body of the friend whose coming he had so affectionately looked forward to that morning.

While all around, now fully awakened to the repellent nature of this duel, remained fixed to the ground, O'Neill and Evir MacMahon, followed by three stout fellows bearing creels and fishing rods, made their appearance, and, like the remainder of the company, stood spellbound at the sight which met their eyes. Owen Roe was the first to recover his self-possession.

"What is the meaning of this?" he said sternly, regarding the guilty faces around one by one. "Is it possible there was so little reason among so many that it could not have prompted one of you to stay this act of criminal folly? Lift up Glencairn, Mr. Cuttard, and you, Evir, see if your nephew's hurts are like to prove mortal."

The Bishop made a hasty examination of his nephew's wound and answered quickly that he did not anticipate that it would have a fatal result.

"If it should," said O'Neill, with a look of unrelenting determination, "I shall hang the survivor, even though he be your cousin, for I am resolved that I shall not have a repetition of the sort of murderous folly which ran rife in our armies at the siege of Dublin."

He curtly ordered Harry to give up his sword, and the unfortunate young Cornet, who had been all this while standing as if in a trance, endeavoured to justify himself, but O'Neill cut short his speech with an impatient exclamation and a significant signal to the three gillies who accompanied him. These men, who happened to belong to Clan Mahon, and as might reasonably be expected, were full of burning thoughts concerning their fallen chieftain, fastened themselves zealously upon Dauntless. They would have gladly stabbed him on the spot, but the cold stern presence of O'Neill restrained them, and they were obliged to confine their vindictive inclinations to twisting the Cornet's sword from him, with wholly unnecessary violence.

In obedience to an order from their General, one of the men fetched a boat, and they conveyed their prisoner to Clough Oughter, where he was conducted to his own room and left there, with a couple of arquebusiers on guard outside his door. As soon as the door closed behind him, Harry dropped into a chair, completely unnerved, and remained in the same listless attitude as he had first assumed, for nearly half an hour. By the end of that time, he was roused from his stupor by hearing the voices of the sentinels raised in tones of deprecatory protest, such as they would have scarcely used towards a masculine intruder; and, guessing intuitively whom this visitor was likely to prove, he sprang to his feet once more, trembling all over.

His fears were speedily verified, for the door almost immediately flew open, and Aileen MacMahon, clad in the white silk robe which was to have been her wedding garment on that ill-fated day, appeared at the threshold, and, brushing past the two musketeers, closed the door haughtily in their faces. Her beautiful head and fine supple figure were drawn up to their full extent, her features were overspread with a flush of indignation, and her eyes, brimful of contempt, were fixed steadily on the shrinking face of her unfortunate lover. He stretched out his hands with a look of dumb entreaty, and murmured faintly, "Florence, Florence, is — is — he —"

"Not dead, but through no fault of yours, Mr. Dauntless," was the pitiless reply; "but I would to God that I had died ere I bound myself to such a one as you!"

"As Heaven is my judge," said the unlucky bridegroom,

"the quarrel was none of my seeking. I tendered thy brother fair words and offered to explain anything concerning myself that he might demand, but he would have nothing but my heart's blood. And yet, though he sought my life like a madman, I do protest, Aileen, that I still love him with a love that is little less than that I have for thee."

"Such love as you tender on the point of a rapier," said the girl, scornfully. "I prithee, keep such protestations of affection for whatever fools are likely to believe them. Love? the love of a traitor and a perjurer. Pah! I spit upon such contaminated love."

"Is all the world leagued against me," said the unhappy man, weakly, "that even you, Aileen, condemn me unheard? The worst criminal is entitled to a defence ere sentence is pronounced upon him, and you have not yet granted me that poor privilege."

"Even if you could clear yourself of treason to your country," said Aileen, relentlessly, "even if you could explain away your treachery to myself and the contemptible deception which you thought necessary to practise in order to gain my hand, there would still remain one incontrovertible fact, which in itself would give me grounds to hate you all the days of my life. My brother lies downstairs with a sword-thrust through him; it was your hand which drove that sword, and that is suffice for me. But all this talk is but child's prattle and hath no bearing on the matter which brought me hither. I have come, Harry Dauntless, to tell you of my changed feelings, not to discuss their merits, and in view of this change I want to know if you will restore me my troth and give your consent to our marriage being broken off forthwith."

Harry uttered a muffled cry of anguish and clasped one hand over his side.

"Oh, Aileen, Aileen," he faltered. "You cannot be so cruel, you cannot be so utterly heartless, as to cast me off unheard and unjustified, when my fault, if any, was unintentional?"

"Nay," said the girl, haughtily. "Do not impute a wavering faith to me, for, if plighted oaths are easily made and easily broken by the gentle Normans of the Pale, such conduct is unknown among us simple people of the North. You received my plighted word at the altar-foot, and this accursed band of gold binds me as securely to you as though I was loaded with all the gyves and fetters in Dublin Castle. You have my plighted word, — I will not break it, though the keeping of it should break my heart; but, if you insist upon the completion of your bargain, remember that you shall not claim a wife but a purchased slave, who will hate you as long as her life endures. Now speak, and let me know your answer."

"I cannot, I cannot," groaned Harry, covering his face with his hands. "I love thee, Aileen, better than I do my honour, my life, or my hopes of salvation. Command me to face death, and I shall court its presence with a smiling face; ask me to turn robber, and I shall be the veriest rapparee upon the high-road; bid me renounce my faith, and I shall risk Hell itself; but bid me not renounce thy love, for, if I did, I should go raving mad."

"Then you refuse," said the girl, coldly. "Well, I cannot cry out on my fate, inasmuch as I brought it upon myself; but you, at least, shall have no reason to reproach me in after years for having deceived you."

She turned her back upon him so swiftly that her bridal dress spun round her straight figure in a spiral curl and settled about her feet in such a way that she was unable to stir for the moment. Her lover dropped upon his knee and held out his hand in silent appeal; but she thrust aside the clinging folds of her robe with an impatient movement of her foot and walked out of the room without another word; and as the door closed behind her, it seemed to poor Harry that she was his good angel who had left him for ever.

XXIII

ON the following day O'Neill released Harry from arrest. All who had been present at the duel, including the wounded man himself, bore testimony to the Cornet's patience under affront and his desire to avoid a hostile encounter; and, consequently, Harry found himself once more restored to favour among a section of his friends and completely exonerated from blame by all his fellow-soldiers as far as the duel went.

The Bishop privately brought his nephew very severely to task, and the latter submitted to his correction meekly enough; for, in addition to being weakened and humbled by his wound, Florence was overwhelmed with a secret sense of shame and self-reproach. He listened very penitently to the Bishop's homily on Christian charity and the necessity of curbing one's temper; but he made a feeble effort to extenuate his conduct by pleading the provocation he had received on account of Harry's treatment of Aileen.

The wondering Churchman asked him to explain his words more fully.

"Why," said Florence, sulkily, "the fellow is as good as married already, inasmuch as he is fully betrothed to a young lady whom he betrayed and cast off in Dublin."

"From whom did you learn this foul lie?" asked the Bishop, in such a fierce tone of voice that his haughty young kinsman cowered down in bed like a whipped child. "Tell me instantly, Florence, who is this base traducer of your friend ere I wring the name out of your throat."

"I cannot tell you his name," said the younger man, with a shamefaced frown. "I promised I should not disclose it, but I shall tell you what he is and what he told me. He is an officer of high rank and repute in Ormond's army, and, in addition to being a former comrade of Harry, he is one who is highly esteemed by Mistress Kathlyn Dauntless. He shewed me several letters from her wherein she thanked him in moving terms for kind services he had rendered her son's estate, and he expressed such a warm interest in Harry's movements that I told him of what degree of relationship was about to be established between us. Then did he seem much discomposed, and he begged me beneath his breath not to speak of such a matter whilst I was South of Ulster, or it might lead to Harry's death. I pressed him hard to tell me wherefore such a thing should come about, whereupon he confessed with many sighs that Dauntless was betrothed to a young lady of Shanganagh; and added, that though it was a matter of indifference to him whether Dauntless made her an honest woman, or left her to mourn her too confiding trust in him, it would be a sore blow to himself if her relations found out her secret and slew his comrade for what he was pleased to term a trifling act of gallantry."

"Out with the name of this cowardly stabber of reputations!" cried the Bishop, fiercely. "Out with his name without further paltering; I charge you, tell me his name, by the virtue of my holy office."

"If you drive me thus," said his nephew, sullenly, "I suppose I must yield. He was a Colonel of Ormond's light-horse, and his name was Ephraim Hooter."

"Hooter!" almost shouted the Bishop. "Hooter! Hooter! The man whom Dauntless wounded when he defended Owen Roe and myself at the peril of his life and property. Upon my honour, Florence, thy sublime credulity passeth even the extent of thy folly. Hooter! Why, nephew, couldst thou not have guessed that he would have said nothing but what was injurious to the fair fame of Dauntless? and yet it was on the warrant of such a pitiful scoundrel that thou wouldst have slain thy brother."

"How was I to know that this man was the same whom Dauntless wounded?" answered Florence, petulantly. "You love to wrap yourself so much in mystery, Uncle, that one can never learn full particulars of the simplest tale you tell. You never mentioned the fellow's name to me in your account of the matter, and you may rest assured that he never told me anything about being shot by Harry on his own doorstep. All his conversation was nothing else but sugared compliments about his comrade, which praise you may be sure I greedily swallowed, wherefore, I deemed him to be a true friend to my friend, and accordingly had no other choice but to believe the infernal story which he told so lightly. Then, when I came home, the first words that greeted me were that Mr. Dauntless had withdrawn his proffered help on the morning of his wedding day; that Mr. Dauntless had but used it as a bait to catch Aileen; that Mr. Dauntless had entrapped his bird and withdrawn his lure; and then I went wholly mad,—and you know the rest."

The Bishop, with many asseverations as to the nobility of Harry's character, informed Florence of the true state of his friend's fortune and the reasons why he had withdrawn the offer he had formerly made to the Ulster Army. He did not spare himself either, and in a very humble fashion confessed how he had deceived and disturbed everyone connected with the unlucky Bond; which avowal was the more magnanimous on his part, as it was an open confession of a lack of *finesse*, which the good busy-brained man cherished as his darling talent. He gave his nephew a very severe lecture on the necessity of regarding the statements of chance acquaintances with cautious reservations, enlarged greatly upon the un-Christian sin of giving rein to one's evil temper, and finally insisted that Florence should see his injured friend immediately and sue him for forgiveness. At first the haughty young Chieftain made some unavailing objections to this proposal, then he begged for time for consideration, and, lastly, he implored a respite of a couple of days on the plea of his weak state; but the Bishop inexorably went off with his usual air of bustling importance and presently returned leading in Dauntless by the hand.

For a moment or two, Florence wrestled with his haughty nature and a humiliating sense of having shamefully wronged his friend, and then he commenced a halting and stilted form of apology. But when Harry threw himself beside the bed and begged *him* on his knees for forgiveness, all the innate generous warmth of his nature asserted its sway, and the wounded man threw his arms about his friend's neck and burst into tears. There is something inexpressibly touching in the reunion of two male bosom friends who have been parted and brought together again with a hoarded interest of affection to exchange; and Evir MacMahon, who loved them equally, felt that this scene was one that was too trying to regard with undimmed eyes.

He walked over to the window and looked out on the woods of Killykeen, which were full to their topmost boughs with rustling foliage, glowing sunshine, and all the warm, joyous life of a splendid day in June.

"I was distressed for Thee, my Brother Jonathan," he murmured softly to himself. "Very pleasant hast Thou been to Me — Thy love to Me was wonderful, passing the love of women."

The two young men spoke in undertones, and the greater part of their conversation was lost to the ears of the Bishop; but, when they parted later on, Evir MacMahon saw at a glance that the seal of affection which had bonded them comrades in the Chapter House of St. Mary's had been set once more between them; and it was destined to remain unbroken during the remainder of their earthly acquaintance. However, this reconciliation by no means dispelled a certain amount of antipathy towards Harry, which the duel and the cancelled loan had aroused among his comrades; and there were many of the Ulster Chieftains who shrugged their shoulders and smiled significantly whenever any of their companions endeavoured to justify his conduct.

Such persons remarked coldly that Mr. Dauntless was at perfect liberty to give or withhold his promised aid, and if O'Neill were satisfied, the matter was settled as far as they were concerned. Their friend, Glencairn, had brought some accusations against Mr. Dauntless as to his treatment of Mistress Aileen MacMahon, and Mr. Dauntless had proved he was in the wrong, according to the fashion whereby gentlemen decided such questions. Therefore, there was nothing further to be said concerning either affair.

Sir Phelim O'Neill was one of those who held such views, and he took considerable pains to demonstrate to Harry how intensely he disliked and distrusted him. Perhaps, a contempt for what he termed the Puritan-like severity of the young Palesman, perhaps, the undisguised admiration which Harry entertained for his General (whom Sir Phelim hated heartily), or it might have been the kindly interest which Owen Roe took in the young Cornet, had helped to stir up this antipathy still further. In any case Sir Phelim never lost an opportunity of making disparaging remarks about Harry; and, were it not for his intense fear of Owen Roe, which fear was accurately counterbalanced by a proportionate degree of jealous hate, it is quite possible that the big, foolish libertine would have thrust a quarrel upon the Cornet in order to provoke him to a duel.

However, the sneering remarks of Sir Phelim and the more covert dislike of the other Chieftains had little effect upon Harry, who was too much absorbed at this time in endeavouring to regain his lost position with Aileen MacMahon to be conscious of any other concern under the sun. The estrangement of Aileen from him, although suddenly effected, was such as was not to be repaired in the course of a day or two; and, even after her brother's complete recovery, she continued to treat Harry with undiminished coldness notwithstanding the *éclaircissement* which was offered her by Harry, the Bishop, and Florence himself. The fact was, that Aileen MacMahon, although perfectly assured after a few weeks of the innocence of Harry, felt that her awakening love was as yet not strong enough to melt the barrier of ice which had drifted so suddenly between them. She was one of those high-spirited and highly sensitive beings whose delicately poised emotions may be fitly compared to the dispositions of a strongly magnetised rod of fine steel.

Natures of this description love fiercely and hate fiercely. There are no intermediate degrees between North and South in the passions of such entities; and, though violence may deflect and even change the relative position of the poles for a while, if they are left to themselves, they are certain to swing back into their normal bearings in time.

If Harry had possessed more experience of human nature or less passionate love for his mistress, he would have left matters to right themselves and should have probably found himself re-established in her affections within a few more weeks. But, immediately after his reconciliation with Florence, the young man, brimful of devouring love and ineptitude, fled off to Aileen in order to sue abjectly for her love and pardon.

Now this was his first mistake. For if a man pleads to a woman for forgiveness for a fault which she is well aware he never committed, her first instinct is to assume that he must at least have possessed the desire to accomplish that harm which a mere accident has made him guiltless of. Aileen, therefore, commented very severely upon poor Harry's heinously bad temper, eulogised the natural patience, sweet disposition, and forbearance of her brother; and, impelled by that mischievous tendency to punish which sometimes makes women trifle with the love they feel assured of, bade Harry very gravely consider that he had lost her affection for ever.

Her lover remonstrated with her upon the folly of their being kept apart any longer, since all differences between Florence and himself had been adjusted, and took occasion to remind her somewhat sulkily that she was almost as good as married to him already.

This unlucky speech was his second and more grievous mistake.

All the fiery disposition of her nature flashed up at once at this allusion to her responsibility to him, and she scornfully told him that she understood he had been pleading for her love and not for her hand; but since he appeared to care so little for the former, he could claim the latter at any moment he pleased. She coldly reminded him, that on the occasion when she had seen her brother carried into Clough Oughter covered with blood, she had vowed to Heaven to strangle her love and would pray for strength to do so. If he claimed the fulfilment of his bargain, she would make good her word, but, as for promising him her affection, she declared she would not go out of her way wantonly to break a covenant with Heaven, especially since she had successfully taught herself to regard him with indifference.

The Bishop and Florence afforded their intemperate partisanship to Harry, and had two or three fiery interviews with the young lady, which only resulted in making matters worse for the unlucky bridegroom. They assailed her with angry arguments, and she answered them with haughty obstinacy. They ordered her to fulfil her engagement immediately, and she replied that Mr. Dauntless could claim her whenever he pleased. They bade her fix a day for the postponed wedding, and she foiled them by assuring them that she was indifferent whether it took place next month or the following year. Finally, they commanded her imperiously to wed Dauntless offhand or restore him his troth, and to the latter part of this proposal she expressed ready acquiescence.

Dauntless, however, would not give his consent to this

alternative. Her troth was his last anchor, and he felt himself utterly incapable of severing the cable which still bound her to him. He left Clough Oughter, however, and took up his quarters once more in the camp, where he sulked about by himself for a week. It was the wisest decision he had as yet adopted, and, if the Army had remained another week by the Lough, it is very likely that Aileen would have missed, pined for, and received back her lover within that time; but fate willed it should be otherwise.

One night a ragged, mud-stained creature appeared in the Camp shortly after midnight. He gave a secret password and a letter enclosed in a roll of wax to the officer on guard, who chanced to be Florence, and the young Chieftain no sooner heard the one and received the other than he instantly jumped into a boat and crossed over to Clough Oughter. He returned in half an hour in company with O'Neill, and, ten minutes after the latter set foot on shore, the drums beat to quarters and the pipes snarled out the gathering. There was no time for leave-takings and little for dressing and arming, and, consequently, Harry was obliged to take his place with his regiment and march off with it half an hour later without the sad consolation of a farewell interview with Aileen.

As the Ulster Army crept softly over the hills and wound in and out among the hollows by the Lough side, it appeared to two weeping women, who watched it from the battlements of Clough Oughter, to be some iron-scaled monster which was wriggling slowly along under the starlight.

The elder of the two women stood erect and regarded it proudly through her tears, but the younger turned away despairing and buried her streaming eyes on the other's bosom.

"Oh, Rose! Rose! my dear gossib Rose!" she sobbed. "He is gone away, perhaps, to his death without a look or a word, and I myself would not send him even a message when Florence asked me a while ago if I had any token I wished him to bring back to the Camp. Oh, *Wirrastrue! Wirrastrue!* I am more than punished for my folly, for, even if I am blessed with a sight of him again, I feel that I have lost him for ever."

XXIV

THE little army marched all night in a Westerly direction and at daybreak found themselves about twelve miles from the lakes in a wild part of the County, where they established a temporary camp. Owen Roe's forces consisted of 5000 foot, which was composed of picked men of the Northern Clans and a small body of Scotch Highlanders under the command of Alexander MacDonnell of Antrim. His cavalry barely numbered 600 men, who were chiefly recruited from the Clans of O'Reilly of Cavan and O'Donnell of Tyr-Connell, two septs long famous for the excellence of their horsemen; but it was on his carefully trained infantry that the soldier of Arras mainly depended.

They remained two weeks in this camp with a jealously maintained screen of pickets guarding their repose, and every day the regimental officers put their men through a severe test of efficiency and drill under the unsparing eye of Owen Roe himself. No one knew the real cause of this sudden advance, for O'Neill, though accustomed to ask and listen attentively to the counsel of those under him, was not in the habit of affording the slightest clue to his own plans; but it was generally believed among the lesser chiefs that this expedition was being organised against Coote, who still held the strong town of Enniskillen.

As this rumour gained ground, Captain Cuttard evinced the liveliest sense of gratification, which feeling Harry was at a loss to account for until the stout troop-adjutant disclosed the following secret to him in a burst of confidence.

Some time before he accompanied the Ulster Army to the siege of Dublin, Mr. Cuttard had the unblushing effrontery to despatch a letter to Sir Charles Coote, wherein he informed his late commander that upon casting up his accounts, which had been somewhat neglected lately, he had discovered that the Scots Parliament were indebted to him to the extent of £6. 9. 6½ Sterling, English Money. "The latter item of which," observed the Captain, mournfully, "I went to the pains of underlining in red ink lest he should send me the sum in your cursed Irish currency, which hath proportionately a lower value to our Christian English coinage, as your infernal system of mileage hath a higher standard than ours."

The answer to this unparalleled emanation was a very polite letter written by Coote himself wherein he acknowledged the accuracy of the Captain's memory and book-keeping. Payment, however, was deferred until such time as the writer should have the honour of presiding over Mr. Cuttard's trial at a drum-head court-martial, after which he would have much pleasure in handing him the amount, which he hinted the gallant gentleman might employ very usefully in a subsequent interview with the hangman.

"Which base and contemptible breach of faith, look you, Mr. Dauntless, is not to be borne by honourable Cavalieros," said the troop-adjutant, swelling with rage, "considering it hath always been a principle among honourable commanders, from time immemorial, to regard the back pay of a soldado as sacredly exempt from all claims and stoppages. Wherefore, I am rejoiced to hear that we are for Enniskillen, inasmuch as a personal encounter with Colonel Coote would be an immense satisfaction to my outraged feelings, and young Master Swizzletail (from whom you may remember I stripped this coat at that affair at Glencairn) can assure Sir Charles that when Cut-and-Thrust-and-Come-again Cuttard singles out a man, he is like to get within half-sword distance of him even if he stood in the centre of a battalion."

Mr. Cuttard's hopes of an encounter with Sir Charles were, however, frustrated, inasmuch as a few days afterwards O'Neill led his army in a Northerly direction, which made it apparent to all that Enniskillen was not his objective. They crossed the Blackwater at a ford near Aughnacloy and halted for the night close by the ruins of an ancient Castle, wherein O'Neill took up his quarters while his army lay bivouacked around it in their mantles.

It happened on this particular night that Cornet Dauntless had charge of the Cavalry picket which O'Neill had ordered to be posted in advance of the musketeer sentinels, and about two hours after midnight he set out in company with one of those inferior officers, who were then termed "Gentlemen of the round," in order to visit his guard. It was a pitch dark night, and consequently the two horsemen had some difficulty in finding their way, and it was almost three in the morning by the time they reached the picket. The corporal reported that all was still in front, and Harry was about to return to the Camp when one of the sentinels close by challenged abruptly, and the Cornet, bending low in his saddle and sweeping his eyes along the sky-line, observed the dark figure of a man on foot floundering slowly towards him through the long, rank grass.

The sentinel challenged again at the same time, blowing ominously on the match of his carbine, and the advancing figure answered in a low weak voice that he was a friend and a comrade, but unacquainted with the word, whereupon Harry recognised the voice as that of a corporal in his own regiment who had been sent out the previous day in company with three troopers on a scouting expedition. As soon as the man approached, he informed Harry that his party had been surprised by some of Munroe's Cavalry and his companions killed and himself taken prisoner at a spot some six miles East of Armagh. He had succeeded in giving his guards the slip and effecting his escape on foot, and he brought back such information that Harry deemed it of the greatest importance to bring him immediately to the general.

On approaching the tumbled down ruin wherein Owen Roe had taken up his quarters, Harry was greatly surprised to observe a light shining through the cracks in the shattered door, and, encouraged by this evidence of the General being awake, he knocked boldly on the rotten panels. The door was opened by an old soldier who had served with O'Neill in the Low Countries, and this personage, confronting Harry and his companion with a forbidding expression, asked him ungraciously what they wanted at that unusual hour. Before the Cornet could explain the object of their visit, the General's voice within bade them impatiently enter, and the two accordingly crossed the threshold and found themselves in a miserable little arched vault.

The accumulated rain of the previous spring, which dripped down through the cracked roof, had formed two or three fetid pools on the bare broken floor, and these pools were still further augmented by several sluggish streams of noisome water exhaled from the foul and glistening walls. O'Neill, clad in a complete under-suit of chamois leather, much frayed and stained by long contact with his armour, sat at a table with a compass in his hand and a vast heap of cypher-books, maps, and military sketches before him. A lamp burned brightly at his side and showed plainly every detail in this wretched apartment. Half a dozen freshly cut hazel pegs stuck into various crevices of the sweating walls supported his helmet, breastplate, pauldrons, tassets, and gauntlets, along with a riding coat and a heavy frieze cloak. There were a couple of horse rugs spread in the only dry corner of the vault, with an inverted demi-pique in lieu of a pillow, a military treasure chest on which was laid the remains of a frugal supper, a small leather travelling-valise, a few cooking utensils, and that was all.

"And it was for such a lodging," thought Harry, "that this man voluntarily relinquished a palace in Spain."

At first O'Neill regarded the intruders with a look of mingled weariness and annoyance; but, when he learned the reason that had brought Harry thither and heard the man's account of what he had that day witnessed, his face gradually assumed a look of keen excitement which was rarely seen on those quiet, melancholy features.

"Can you tell me, Corporal," said he, breathing hard, "how many colours of infantry and guidons of cavalry were in the Roundhead army when they marched into Hamilton's Bawn this morning?"

"Aye, that I can, your Excellency," replied the trooper. "They passed me by, rank by rank, while the lobsters who had charge of me waited for Munroe himself to come up with the rear guard, and I counted sixty colours of foot, six cavalry standards, and seven pieces of artillery."

"Sixty Colours," murmured O'Neill, softly, to himself, "means 6000 foot; six standards, 600 horse; and seven guns, including their gunners, matrosses, engineers, and fireworkers, at least 400 more; in all, Seven thousand of the best-trained soldiers of the Continental Wars."

He bent across a map, compass in hand, and rapidly compared a couple of spaces on it with the scale marked at the foot. Then he looked up swiftly, and Harry observed that his eyes were even brighter than before.

"Tell me, Corporal," said he, "didst thou hear where their next march was likely to be towards?"

"I heard those who did hold me in ward say that they were for Armagh in the morning," answered the man, "and after that they were bound for Glasslough, where they expected to meet Munroe's brother, who is coming with a great power of cavalry from Coleraine."

O'Neill sprang to his feet with a triumphant exclamation and dashed down the compasses with such violence that one of the steel legs of the instrument pierced through the parchment map and stuck quivering in the table.

"At last!" he cried, "at last! I have thee, Robert Munroe, where I shall put thee to the test as to whether thou or I be the better soldier. We have met, time after time, in foreign lands, and thou didst always succeed in giving me the slip; but here on my native soil thou art not to escape, and I am prepared to undergo the assay even in the teeth of the two thousand men wherein thou art alone superior to me. Give this good fellow a rummer of brandy, Cathal. What, only half a flask left? then give it all to him, for you know I never drink the stuff, and add my last silver drinking cup for the welcome news he hath brought. Mr. Dauntless, fly to Colonel O'Reilly and bid him and the O'Farrell get their regiments of horse under arms within an hour, for they are to set out immediately to intercept George Munroe, on his way from Coleraine. Corporal, you to my cousins Tirlough, Bryan, Hugh, Art, Cormac, and Con, and bid them attend me thither at once. You, Cathal, to MacDonnell, Maguire, Magennis, MacVay, the Bishop, and his nephew Glencairn. Tell them all to rouse their men, and arm themselves ere they come hither to receive my orders, for, as soon as I dismiss them, our signal trumpets shall blow, and we shall march on to Benburb and Victory."

The mingled notes of trumpets and bagpipes, the tramp of armed men, and the neighing of horses resounded through the camp within a few minutes, but there was no unnecessary noise, and an utter absence of confusion in the manner in which the officers and soldiers assembled. Within half an hour, the cavalry selected to intercept George Munroe were armed, mounted, and away through the grey mist in the direction of Dungannon; and, as the sun peeped over the hills, the remainder of the Confederate army fell in and commenced their march on the fateful village of Benburb.

The Clan of Florence formed portion of the advance guard, and a small party of horse had been detached under Dauntless to support it, so the two friends were therefore close to one another on the march. MacMahon was overflowing with violent excitement. His eyes glittered with a light that almost approached delirium, his cheeks were flushed with the anticipation of battle, he sang light snatches of song, and, as he walked by his friend's stirrup, he trod the ground as though his feet spurned it in sheer exuberance of spirit. He looked singularly handsome in his bright armour, and his straight slim figure and clear-cut animated features reminded Harry so forcibly of Aileen that the recollection swelled the Cornet's bosom and for the moment depressed him. Florence, however, bantered him so unmercifully upon his gloomy appearance, and assailed him with so much light-hearted persiflage, that his good spirits also inspired Harry with a responsive feeling of airy gaiety that continued throughout the remainder of the march.

But the Clansmen of Glencairn who tramped steadily behind the two friends regarded this light-hearted excitement of the Chief with other feelings, and they whispered to one another that such mirth was unlucky and unnatural. One or two exchanged uneasy looks, and muttered beneath their shaggy beards that it seemed to them as if the Taioseach was Fey; while Cormac, who, as Foster-Brother and Henchman to the Chief, consequently bore his standard, observed with a start of superstitious terror that the light morning breeze which waved the banners of the other Clans behind failed to stir the folds of his master's, that hung heavily on the standard shaft with the weight of its own gold embroidery.

However, neither the dark looks of the Clansmen nor the muttered forebodings of Cormac MacMahon were observed or heard by either of the two young gentlemen who at the head of the advance guard entered the little village of Benburb shortly before sunset. An hour later the main body entered the village, and the whole army encamped for the night on those heights where the ancient stronghold of the O'Neill family looks down majestically upon the foaming Blackwater, which chafes the base of the steep cliff whereon the Castle is built.

Owen Roe, in company with Evir MacMahon and Sir Phelim,

supped in one of the apartments of the Castle, and Harry and Florence withdrew to the quarters in the village which had been assigned to the former and his troop-adjutant. This last worthy was absent from supper, for it was his invariable custom to celebrate an exchange of billets in a convivial manner that was particularly gratifying to himself and the choice friends who shared his pleasures on such occasions. However, it must be confessed that his company was not very much missed by the two young gentlemen, and as their supper was good, their appetite and spirits vigorous, and their flask of Canary excellent, the evening passed very pleasantly without Mr. Cuttard's assistance until the hour came when they were compelled to part company for the night.

Florence, who had contributed greatly to the conviviality of the evening by innumerable jests, songs, and sallies of wit, bade a more than usually affectionate farewell to his friend and then sauntered off whistling "Argan Mor," in the direction of the heights where his Clan were bivouacked under the stars; while Harry, overcome by that pleasant languor which follows a long journey that has been crowned by good wine and a good supper, lay down half-dressed on a little settle bed, and immediately fell fast asleep.

He had not slept long, however, before he was rudely awakened by a thundering knock on the door, and, assuming that it heralded the arrival of his missing troop-adjutant, he rose sleepily, and, with a hearty malediction upon the convivial habits of that gentleman, relit a lamp on the table and crossed the room to admit him.

He opened the door with an angry speech ready upon his lips, but he started back silent and astonished, for, instead of the tall, cadaverous form of the jovial troop-adjutant, he encountered Florence MacMahon, who was clinging to the door-post like a drunken man.

His eyes were staring open with the glassy look of a dead man's, his mouth was pinched up in a grotesquely horrible fashion, his dark curling hair hung limply on his white temples, and his whole countenance exhibited such a look of dreadful pain that when Harry could recover his voice he asked him hurriedly if he were ill, for that from his appearance he looked as if he had lately seen a ghost.

"So I have," was the reply, in the low, tremulous voice,

"or Something very near akin. For God's sake let us withdraw within doors, the Night is full of Shadows, and if I added another minute's experience to what I have suffered during the last six hours I should go mad."

The solemn sound of the Church clock of Benburb striking the hour of Four confirmed the space of time which had elapsed since they had parted, and before the last stroke knelled out, Florence staggered past his friend into the room and dropped down on the bed whence Harry had just risen. He turned his ghastly eyes upon Harry with such a wild and vacant stare that the latter shrank back horrified and beat his breast softly as the awful conviction seized him that his friend had lost his reason.

They regarded one another in painful silence for some minutes, and then the young Chieftain suddenly shuddered violently, folded his arms upon his cuirass, and leaned forward with his elbows on his knees and his eyes fixed on the tiled floor.

"Thou wilt very likely think I have gone crazy, Harry," said he, in a low monotonous voice, "when I tell thee what I have to tell. But, as I feel I must tell some one of what I have been the unwilling witness of, or go mad in very earnest, I shall confide my experience to thee, even at the risk of exciting thy ridicule or worse." He paused for a moment, as if to collect his self-control, and then continued in the same low tone of voice: "When I left thee, Harry, and went down the street, I perceived, almost at the moment wherein you closed the door, One, armed and clad like myself, pass me and walk on some dozen paces ahead. I thought nothing of this figure, whom I surmised carelessly was some belated clansman, like myself returning to his quarters, until he passed a window in which a light was still burning brightly, when I saw that not only did he wear the colours of my clan, but he also displayed the gold crest and eagle's feather, which, as thou art aware, Harry, is the reserved privilege of the head of my house, alone, to assume. I was very indignant at this assumption of an honour which belonged to myself alone, and I hurried after the daring pretender with the intention of plucking the plume out of his cap, and thrashing him soundly for his impertinence, but before I could catch up with him, he suddenly turned the corner of the street, and when I hastened up to the spot where he had disappeared, I found the only human beings in sight were a picket of O'Farrell's Horse, who were sitting round their watch-fire. I addressed myself to them and asked what direction the stranger who had just passed had taken, but the fellows stared, and evidently thought from my excited manner that I had been dipping too deep into the wine cannikin. They answered me very civilly that no one had passed their post for the last two hours, and I was half inclined to believe that mine eyes had played some prank upon me until I left the village, when I saw the same mysterious figure pass straight across my path and disappear into a thicket where it would have been impossible for me to have found him, if he were willing to avoid me. I was by this time furious at what I took to be the drunken freak of one of my own clansmen, and, fully resolved to search out and severely punish the offender on the morrow, I made my way to one of the watch-fires, where my clan were bivouacked, and lying down by my foster-brother's side addressed myself to sleep.

"Scarcely had I adjusted my mantle about my limbs, when I perceived the same figure which had hitherto eluded me approaching the watch-fire, where I lay; I instantly started up in a fit of anger, and was about to call upon the sentinel to seize the insolent intruder, when it advanced into the full glare of the firelight, and, turning towards me, froze the words upon my tongue and the marrow in my bones—Arms! Dress! Figure! Features! were mine own—*It was my Fetch.*"

Florence, as if overcome with the horror of his experience, covered his face with his hands and shuddered, while Harry, who was but imperfectly acquainted with this prevalent superstition of the North of Ireland, struggled hard against his own sense of fear in an endeavour to seek an explanation in some other source than that of the supernatural.

"It was some trick of thine eyes, Florence," he said, "some vague and impalpable mockery of thy intelligence, which fatigue or perchance our late merry supper summoned up in delusion of thy tired senses."

"Delusion?" echoed the Chieftain, with a ghastly smile. "I tell thee, Harry Dauntless, I saw every feature on Its face, every button and buckle on Its dress, every trifle of Its accoutrements, down to the very dint upon the chape of the broadsword scabbard which I crushed against my heel, a week ago. I saw All, as though I saw myself in a mirror. Aye, and my wolf-hound, Brendan, that would face an unchained bear, saw It too and shared my fear, for he crawled as far from It as he could and cowered all a-slobber with terror against my breast."

"Then it was some silly jest," said Harry, white to the lips and trembling, despite his words, "played by some idle fool, who, relying on his likeness to thee, and tricked out in thine own garments, took this opportunity of startling thee and others."

"I tell thee, man, It was nothing human," said Florence, steadily, "for I saw the sentinel pass and re-pass It thrice within an hour, and the fellow never glanced aside or ceased the song he hummed, although his beat was scarcely an ell from where It stood in the full glare of the watchfire."

He paused again and then continued: "Truly, Harry, I never believed that I possessed the dreadful gift of the Spae-man, for my reading at Oxford taught me to despise such phenomena, which are so firmly trusted by my simple fellow-countrymen of the North; but I have seen such sights to-night that have convinced me of the shallow impertinence of so-called human philosophy. I have often heard Brian, our old Sennachie of Glencairn, say in days gone by that dying eyes can see into the future, and I have as often laughed heartily at his tales and remarked that I would give my best horse for such a peep, if it were possible; but little did I know then that such prevision was to be granted, and still less did I think how it would affect me. Oh, Harry, it was an experience that was calculated to scorch up the eyeballs, sear the heart, and craze the mind of the Seer, and during the awful time which elapsed since I accepted the Message sent me, I felt such agony that made me think that the sharp wrench which divorces the soul from the body had been spun out into one long thin thread of the most exquisite torture. Death!" cried he, with a burst of fiery scorn, "Death! consider how bravely the meanest Kern can face it, and do not think so poorly of me, dear Harry, that because I know my time is come, I shall meet it less resolutely to-day than the occasions wherein I have already dallied with its presence. But, Oh, the horror, Brother, Oh, the horror, of witnessing the future of others, without the power to avert their fate as well. Oh, the anguish of knowing that my poor foster-brother, Cormac, who lay sleeping by my side, was among the destined Few. The poor soul is betrothed to the Forester's daughter of Clough Oughter, and thou canst not think how it plucked my heart-strings to see him smile in his sleep and hear him mutter his colleen's name whilst I sat beside him, and watched the hag-light dance upon his healthy face. Oh, Brother, it was horrible. Horrible, truly horrible!"

And the young man covered his face with his hands, whilst the perspiration trickled slowly through his loosely knotted fingers.

"All this vision of Death may be a warning a long while in advance, Florence," said the Palesman, with a shaking voice, "for who can say that this battle will take place at all? Munroe hath the reputation of being one of the most cautious, as he is one of the most experienced, soldiers of the Parliament, and when he sees how strongly we are posted at Benburb, he may decline to fight altogether."

"It is not at Benburb where I see the Eagles and the Wolves gathering to the feast," said the Chief, sitting up rigidly and taking his hands from his eyes, which once more stared horribly on vacancy, as though he had relapsed into the state of catalepsy which he had probably experienced on the heights of Benburb. "It is not at Benburb where the Skenes and Broadswords are destined to be reddened. It is a place I have never seen before, with a River on the left and a little stream flowing into it before us. There is a high hill in our rear, the sun is in our eyes, and the Roundheads' pikes glimmer on the hills opposite. Blaney, the accursed Blaney, is among them, there is a look of triumph in his face, though the corpse light dances before him too, and the Scottish pikes waver behind him and go down, down beneath the Broadswords and Skenes of Clan Colla. Down goeth the Banner of Glencairn in the hour of its triumph, but, alas! its Children are left desolate as the sheep of a dead shepherd of the mountains. They melt, they fade, their name is past and gone. Woe! Woe! to Eire, I see a figure laid out upon a bed for the burial and the lycht-wake — past and gone! past and gone, when most required. Then it is my brother Harry, standing before a Gross Fat Man, with a file of Sassenach musketeers standing behind with lighted matches; but, Courage, brave heart, Courage, thy time hath not yet come. But beware when thou dost stand upon a crumbling wall. I hear the English cannon roar around thee, — I see the English pikes coming slowly, slowly up beneath thy feet, and, then, my Brother! Oh, my Brother! my more than Brother — "

And at this point the Seer fell heavily to the ground, where he lay struggling and foaming at the mouth in a violent fit.

Dauntless in a state of great agitation ran to his aid, lifted him up, opened his jacket and the collar of his shirt, and laid him on the bed. He fetched some wine, which still remained in the flask they had opened for supper, and, forcing open MacMahon's clenched teeth with a spoon, poured some down his throat. In a few minutes Florence sighed heavily, opened his eyes, and, catching sight of Harry's frightened face, smiled faintly and asked him in a low voice to sit down on the bed and talk to him.

He was quite composed and rational and talked quietly and even cheerfully with his friend. By and by he sat up and asked Harry if he would mind his stopping with him the remainder of the night as he was unwilling to return to camp at that hour (here he shuddered slightly), and added in a feeble tone of assumed lightness that there might be accidents on the morrow which might separate them, if not for ever, at least for some time.

It was quite clear to Harry that all recollections of what he had recently spoken had vanished from his mind during his brief syncope, for after a while he chatted gaily upon various incidents connected with the term of their friendship. He reminded his friend how they gave the Dublin mob the slip when Harry first befriended him at Dames Gate, dwelt at much length on their coursing matches, hunting parties, and other daily amusements at Clough Oughter, recalled to him the incidents of their first skirmish at Glencairn and how Cuttard had replenished his wardrobe at the expense of the Roundhead Cornet, whereat he laughed heartily, and remarked that Cuttard was a droll fellow. Once, and once only, he betrayed a glimpse of the inward belief he had in his own approaching death, and that was when he referred sorrowfully to their first and only estrangement. He expressed a very earnest wish that the morrow had come and gone ere that day had dawned whereon he had drawn his sword upon his brother and preserver, and he once more begged his loving forgiveness in so self-humiliating and touching a fashion that Harry felt the tears start into his own eyelids as he grasped his hand and swore that Florence had been the chief sufferer.

They sat on the bed chatting to one another until Cuttard, who had been spending the last twelve hours in an all-night sitting with two other gentlemen of similar tastes, sneaked into the house with a very shamefaced expression and informed the two young gentlemen that the trumpeters were about to sound "the rouse."

Florence sprang to his feet instantly, buttoned his jacket, resumed his scarf, and adjusted the Limerick lace ruffle at his neck.

"What, Harry, what," said he, gaily, "thou hast made me spend such a rousing night that I had almost forgotten my duty, and if that had been neglected there would have been an indelible stain upon my name, for what would all Clan Colla have said if Glencairn had been found lagging when the bagpipes blew on such a day?"

He embraced Harry in the French fashion, and then, turning to Cuttard, utterly confounded that worthy by asking forgiveness for some trifling sharpness he had exhibited to him a few days before. He said, laughing, that as they were going into battle within a few hours, soldiers should leave no debts of ill-will behind them on such an occasion, and he shook hands so heartily with Mr. Cuttard that that gentleman became quite affected, and felt it incumbent on him to go off immediately afterwards and drink a stiff rummer of usequebaugh to the health not only of Florence, but also to all Irish Cavalieros, in whom, he swore, there was much hidden grace when all was said and done.

XXV

WHEN the Irish army fell in at daybreak they found, early as it was, that the Parliamentarians had been no sluggards either, on that bright June morning, for a long hedge of sparkling pike-heads and a row of waving standards on the horizon announced that Munroe and his Seven thousand veterans were marching forward on Benburb.

The advanced videttes of the Irish fell back towards the river as the Roundhead cavalry trotted briskly forward, and presently the foot and artillery of the latter debouched from the hills and formed up facing O'Neill's army; however, the manifestly strong position of the Irish troops did not by any means please the cautious Scotch General, for shortly afterwards his entire army halted as if undecided what plan to adopt.

"Ha, thou hast heard of Beal-an-the-Buighe, Munroe," murmured O'Neill, with a grim smile, "and thou hast no liking to cast the dice on such an ill-omened spot. So thou wouldst turn Southward and cross at Kinnaird. Well, it is of little moment, for I have thee at either spot in the palm of my hand."

The Parliamentary Army had turned abruptly to their left as O'Neill spoke these words to himself, and were now directing their march along the Eastern bank of the Blackwater as if in search of a ford; so the Irish General sent forward a strong body of cavalry under the command of his brother-in-law, and followed himself, with the main body of his army, for six miles along the river bank, moving flank to flank with Munroe and keeping a sharp watch on his movements.

When the rival armies reached that turn in the Blackwater which is now known by the name of Battleford, Munroe again halted, as if he meditated forcing a passage at that spot; but the serried ranks of the Irish army and the wholesome respect he entertained for his old adversary of the Continental Wars made him abandon that project, and he once more resumed his march Southward.

In front of the Royalist Army lay the high conical knoll which is now locally known by the name of Thistle Hill, and, leading his army round this elevation, Owen Roe formed them up on its Southern base in that little triangular stretch of ground which is formed by the junction of the Oonagh with the Blackwater.

He drew up his infantry in three lines with a squadron of horse in support on the flank of each Clan, and massed the remainder of his cavalry on the right; and as soon as his forces were disposed in the order in which they were to fight, he rode to the front of his little army and addressed it in a speech that was pregnant with fire.

He warned them that they were about to fight, not merely for their King and their Country, but their Faith, their Wives, and their Children. He impressed upon their minds that they were as well armed and as carefully trained as the troops with whom they were about to engage, bade them think little of the two thousand men which the Roundheads outnumbered them by, as such advantage was nothing compared with the sanctity of their own cause, which armed each man of Ulster with a twofold strength, and, last of all, he told them with impassioned eloquence that the man who faltered in his duty on that day was deserting not only his Country, his King, and his Colours, but also his own fellow-soldier, himself, who had trained him.

Amazed by the fiery periods of their leader, who was at all times remarkable for his unimpassioned calmness and silent melancholy, the Clansmen of the North remained staring blankly at one another for a full minute after he had finished speaking; and then with one accord the battle slogan of Hy-Niall burst forth from Six thousand hairy throats, and the shout of "*Lambh Derg an Uachtair*,"[1] reached the ears of Munroe, who was then crossing the river at the ford of Kinnaird some four miles further up.

O'Neill sent forth Colonel O'Farrell with a body of horse for the purpose of delaying Munroe's advance until the sun was in a less unfavourable position in the heavens, and then bade his men lie down and take what rest they could until the enemy came in sight, when they were to rise and await his orders with courage and confidence.

[1] "The Red Hand uppermost."

Florence MacMahon and his Clan were on the extreme left of the line, and Harry Dauntless and his troop were on their flank, so when the order to lie down was given and his own men had dismounted and slackened their horses' girths, the Cornet strolled over to his brother-in-arms.

The Chieftain stood in advance of his Clan. His clasped hands were resting on the hilt of his sheathed broadsword, his bright eyes fixed smilingly on the green hills in front, his lips were moving, and as Harry approached he heard him murmur softly to himself: —

"Yes, it is the Spot. The little Stream in front, the River on the left, and the Sun shining in our eyes. It only wants the Roundhead pikes on yonder hill to make the picture complete."

He greeted Harry cheerfully, and talked and laughed as though he had completely forgotten the incidents of the previous night; but his companion, notwithstanding the strenuous efforts he made to appear as cheerful, felt his own heart overwhelmed with a weight of superstitious horror. Far from appearing concerned about himself, Florence chatted lightly, not only with Harry, but with such of his Clansmen as happened to be close by, and when one big fellow expressed a hope that he would fall in with a Roundhead of the same tremendous girth about the chest as himself, in order that he might fit himself out with a cuirass, the young Chief cried out gaily that he himself would not be better armed on that day than any of his faithful kinsmen.

Then, despite the entreaties of his foster-brother, Cormac, he insisted on stripping off his cuirass and embroidered buff-coat, which he tossed down recklessly on the heather, in company with his morion and gauntlets; and when Harry remonstrated with him upon such proceedings, he laughed merrily, and said it was a hot day, and in any case a man would fight better in his shirt and truis than under a stone weight of iron. He evidently entertained some design of getting his foster-brother out of the way, inasmuch as he made some trivial excuse about sending him back to the village of Benburb, but the poor fellow exhibited such heartfelt anguish on hearing this command, and begged so piteously for his right to carry the standard of Glencairn, that Florence reluctantly yielded to his prayers, and muttered that what was to be would be.

Presently the sound of heavy firing in the woods in front informed all that O'Farrell was engaged with Munroe, and half an hour afterwards the cavalry, sent out to delay the approach of the Parliamentary troops, appeared, and slowly retired on their main body, disputing to the last every hillock and clump of trees which afforded them a temporary shelter. Just as O'Farrell's cavalry crossed the Oonagh and rejoined their comrades, who were by this standing to their arms, Robert Munroe's artillery, preceded by a cloud of cavalry, wheeled into position on a high hill to the right of the Royalist army, and shortly afterwards the Puritan infantry, debouching from the woods and forming with admirable precision, took up their position on a high hill facing them.

The battle commenced with a heavy cannonade from the right of the Puritan forces, and then Munroe endeavoured to entice his wary enemy by one or two feints into an advance which would have placed him at his mercy. Seeing that it was hopeless to draw O'Neill from his position, Munroe threw his splendid cavalry forward against his right, in the hopes of turning that flank, but the steady ranks of pikemen hurled back the Puritan horsemen as though they were unarmed children. Another desperate charge of Munroe's pikemen, supported by Lord Blaney's regiment of horse, failed to make any impression on the centre; and as the discomfited Puritans fell back in an orderly fashion which spoke highly for their discipline, a hot and grimy messenger spurred up to Owen Roe, and gasped out that O'Reilly's cavalry, who at the moment were barely visible on a distant hill, had completely routed George Munroe's horse on their march south.

Just at this time, a company of the Parliamentary musketeers had succeeded in creeping up to a strong position on the extreme left of the Confederate line; and O'Neill, observing that Lord Blaney's cavalry were preparing to return to their support, sent word to Florence MacMahon to attack and drive back the musketeers before their advancing comrades could come to their assistance.

Up to this part of the battle, O'Neill had been acting strictly on the defensive, and the prospect of having the honour of striking the first blow appeared to the impetuous Chieftain like a glimpse of Paradise. According to the wild code of warfare that obtained among the Clans, it had always been deemed a privilege of the highest order to open the attack, until Owen Roe and his system of trained warfare had abolished its honourable significance for ever; but the traditions of its glory were sufficient to throw Florence into an ecstasy of glowing pride and enthusiasm.

He rolled up his shirt sleeves above the elbows, bound back his dark, curling hair into a Coolin with a silk point torn from his discarded buff-coat, drew his broadsword and skene, and then turned to his Clansmen with blazing eyes.

"Hear Ye! Ye Children of Glencairn," he cried out, in the Gaelic tongue, in tones which vibrated like the summons of a silver trumpet, "hear Ye, of the honour done our Sept by Hy-Niall, which this day relinquisheth its place in the battle to Us. Oh! be valiant, ye Clansmen of Glencairn, as your Fathers were in ages past, and be mindful of the honour done ye to-day. Strike up, Pipers! Advance, Banner! and follow me, Ye Cherished Ones of Clan Colla."

The pipers burst into the "Royal Hunt," the White and Gold standard flew onward like a swooping sea-eagle, and, shouting the slogan of his Clan, Florence MacMahon rushed forward upon the Puritan musketeers, who were so close to the Irish lines that Harry could hear the nasal tones of their officers' voices as they bade their men await their orders coolly, and then to fire low upon the accursed spawn of Belial.

The Clan followed their Chieftain with quick, stealthy steps. They did not shout nor break into that furious rush wherewith their race closes with an enemy, for that final phase of the charge was yet to come; but they moved over the undulating ground with an ominously quickening pace, which gave them the appearance of an advancing ocean billow, to which the deep, hoarse murmuring of the men themselves and the shrill treble of the pipes imparted an additional resemblance.

Coolly and steadily the Parliamentarians awaited their coming until they were barely thirty paces distant. Then the smoke rolled lazily over the meadow in front of those stern, close ranks, and a murderous volley saluted the Clansmen of Glencairn. A score of writhing bodies dropped upon the grass, the White and Gold banner reeled for a moment in that tempest of blood, but immediately swept on, followed by its devoted retainers, "*So dorn don a dubh fuiltibh*" split the air above and the powder smoke below with one terrific yell, and then that living wave overwhelmed the Parliamentary ranks. The broadswords and skenes leaped up and down like piston rods in the bright June sunlight, — one moment bright and cold-looking, the next red and smoking, — there was one brief, bloody, gasping interval, and then the Puritan musketeers broke and fled madly in every direction.

Harry watched this terrible sight from start to finish in rapt excitement, but as soon as the musketeers fled, he drew a breath of thankful relief on perceiving the well-known figure of his comrade still erect and apparently unhurt. He was facing his Clan, his arms outspread to restrain them from pursuit, for the Parliamentary cavalry, led by an officer in splendid armour, was trotting down the hill towards the Oonagh, too late to succour their comrades, but in good time to avenge them if the impetuous Ulstermen should give them the chance.

However, the Parliamentary horsemen were denied the gratification of charging, for the broken musketeers rushed wildly into their ranks and threw them into immediate confusion. The cavalry hesitated, drew rein, and commenced to look back suggestively; and, notwithstanding that their leader dismounted for the purpose of rallying the broken infantry, all the while cursing them both for being dismayed by a handful of naked savages, the troopers continued to rein back their horses still more, and look oftener behind them each moment.

The quick eye of O'Neill observed this indecision, and he immediately ordered a general advance. The cavalry were instructed to accompany the infantry side by side until the order to charge was given, when they were to wheel round the right of their comrades, and fall upon the left flank of Munroe. So the word to advance was passed rapidly from unit to unit, the *Fear-Brataighe* of each sept darted forward, standard in hand, to the head of his company, and with the united pipes of the Clans screaming "Planxty Sudley," the Irish army crossed the Oonagh and advanced steadily up hill.

As the main body drew near to the spot where Clan Mahon still maintained their ground, Harry again caught sight of Florence. His sword-blade was red from point to guard, his shirt torn and blood-stained, and, as he pressed forward through his disorganised enemies, with his loosened hair tossing wildly about his face, he looked like some frenzied Bacchanal of slaughter. He was cutting his way step by step towards the dismounted leader of the Puritan cavalry, who was yet endeavouring to rally the flying musketeers. Two of the latter threw themselves bravely across the Chieftain's path, but Florence ran one through the body, and then turned and fractured the skull of the other with a tremendous blow of his sword-hilt. He stepped lightly over the body of the fallen musketeer, and confronted the Puritan officer, who by this time stood alone and unhelmeted.

The two regarded one another for one silent moment of unexpressed hatefulness, and then Florence addressed him with a fierce joy that was uncanny to witness.

"Ha, my Lord Blaney," said he, "I have awaited this hour more eagerly than ever a lover looked forward to his wedding-day. Stand on your guard, my Lord, for you cannot look for quarter from a kinsman of the murdered Baron of Enniskillen."

"Ere you talk of offering terms," was the reply, which was accompanied by a look of scarcely less bitter animosity than that which confronted him, "you must first wait, young Sir, until I sue for quarter from malignant rebels to the Parliament of England. But boast not of your power to give or withhold, for this day is not yet over, and you and your friends may sing to a different tune before the sun goeth down."

"Then be assured, my Lord," said Florence, gripping his sword so tightly that the bones of his hand stood out through the skin like ivory, "that one or the other, or both of us, shall sing no more on this earth, at least."

"You never spoke a truer word, Mr. MacMahon," said Blaney, with a vindictive grin, and as he spoke he drew a petronel from his belt and cocked and presented it with one motion. Cormac, who had followed Florence through the thickest part of the battle, was close beside his Chieftain, and, with a touch of that devotion by no means uncommon among Irish foster-brothers, threw himself straight upon Lord Blaney the moment that the trigger was drawn; however, this heroic action afforded little benefit to his master, for the heavy two-ounce ball, passing completely through his body, not only killed him instantly, but desperately wounded the object of his self-immolating zeal.

Florence knew he was mortally wounded, yet his indomitable courage nerved all his fleeting strength to accomplish one last superhuman exertion. Gripping his broadsword with both hands, he struck his enemy such a terrible blow that the blade sheared the head in two from the crown to the teeth and stuck fast in the Baron's skull. Blaney dropped dead on the instant, and Florence, after a feeble effort to recover his weapon, relaxed his grasp on the hilt and then sank down dying himself; but, even in that moment of agony, a triumphant smile lit up his face, for he heard the yell of his retainers as they dashed on ahead of the other Clans to avenge him, and he saw a prevision of the victory, of whose glory he was already a participant.

Harry saw Florence drop, with a dull sense of horror, but he had no opportunity of going to his assistance, or even of ascertaining whether he was not already dead, for at that moment the command was transmitted to the cavalry to perform the pre-arranged movement of wheeling round the flank of the infantry, who were then closing with the enemy, and he was obliged to accompany his comrades as they swung down on the left flank of Munroe.

He had a dull, confused sense of hearing the deep, drumming thunder of the horse's feet underneath him, and the shrill clang of the cavalry trumpets sounding the charge behind. He felt a stifling flavour of powder smoke in his throat and nostrils; then he saw a row of white, stern faces above a row of pikes in front, and the next moment he was in among them, cutting and thrusting as though he had been carried forward on the crest of a huge wave. There was every phase of feeling in the white, upturned faces which surged around him knee-high on every side,—hate, stern resolution, abject cowardice, scorn, and agony,—but there was one predominant expression which was marked on all features, and that was an overwhelming look of despair. A blood-red veil flickered before his eyes, and in his ears rang a horrid medley of groans, oaths, shrieks, curses, deep-fetched gasps, and the click of the broadswords as the point or edge encountered steel cap and breastplate.

He was never able to say how long this dreadful carnage lasted, for carnage it had now become, as the battle had by this time been completely decided. Crushed by the irresistible hedge of steel which slowly pushed them up hill, hemmed in by the deep river on their right and overwhelmed by their own broken left, which had crumbled beneath the headlong fury of the Royalist Cavalry, Munroe's fine army had been already annihilated.

Here and there, in broken but resolute knots, some of the most desperate of the Puritans still maintained a hopeless resistance, and, sustained by the dogged courage of their race or the fanatical spirit of their party, fell one by one, refusing quarter to the last. Harry was sick of the butchery which falls as the unavoidable lot to the Cavalry of a victorious army, even in these days of humane warfare, and was only too glad to avail himself of less repellent work, which presented itself to him shortly after the ruin of Munroe's army was assured.

He saw a young Puritan officer, mounted on a fine horse and more handsomely dressed than the austerity of his party usually permitted, burst suddenly through the Royalist horsemen and set off at a headlong gallop, with a cavalry guidon tightly clasped to his breast. Harry was mounted on a fine, half-bred horse, which, though inferior to that of the flying Puritan, was far fresher; and he accordingly set his teeth and started in pursuit, with the determination of making the capture of the officer and the standard his own affair.

After a hard gallop of a mile or two, Dauntless gained sufficiently on his quarry almost to touch him, and though he could easily have disposed of him with a sword-thrust, his natural generosity prevented his adopting such a means of stopping him. He called twice upon the Parliamentarian to surrender, but on the second summons the runaway turned in his saddle and discharged a pistol almost in his face. The ball whistled so closely overhead that it scattered the white and green plume in his helmet to the winds; but, before the Puritan could draw a second pistol, Harry gripped him firmly by the collar, and the two clung desperately to one another, while their uncontrolled horses galloped on, side by side, for a hundred yards or so.

"Too much powder, Mr. Dauntless," shouted a familiar voice, "but a miss is as good as a mile;" and at the same moment Cuttard appeared on the far side of the Puritan, with whom he grappled vigorously, and the three men fell to the ground in one fierce, clinging embrace.

"Halves!" gasped Cuttard, as soon as he could recover some of the breath which the violence of their fall had knocked out of all three. "Halves, you know, between us, Mr. Dauntless, like honourable Cavalieros. Be quiet, my Lord Viscount Montgomery," he added angrily to the young Puritan, who was making a violent effort to rise. "Be quiet and resigned, my Lord, like a good Christian and a valiant soldier. I have no desire to put a pistol-hole through your head, because prisoners with such blemishes have but little market value, but I tell you, upon my stainless honour, that —" here he hesitated for a suitable threat — "I shall certainly slap your Lordship's ears if you attempt to draw that pistol."

"I surrender! I surrender!" gasped the fallen youth. "I tell you I surrender, and therefore take your knee off my heart, for God's sake, as you are killing me."

He gave up his sword and the coveted standard very sullenly to Harry. Cuttard went in chase of the horses, who, tired by the furious pace at which they had been ridden, allowed themselves to be caught with very little trouble; and as soon as they were secured the two Royalists turned back with their prisoner in the direction of Thistle Hill. The young Viscount walked beside Harry, who carried the captured standard, while Cuttard followed close behind, leading his own horse and that of the prisoner. On their way back, Cuttard, who never permitted himself to lag more than a yard or two from the young lord, continued to make several pleasant conjectures to Harry as to the probable amount they would be likely to screw out of their prisoner for ransom; and, in order to silence these unfeeling remarks, Harry very angrily bade him keep all the ransom, whatever it might be, provided he instantly held his peace and permitted him to retain the captured standard.

"Why, Certes," was the cheerful reply of the worthy soldier, who possessed about as much delicacy of feeling as a Lapland savage, "you are welcome to the flag if you have a liking for such gauds, though, for my part, if I had any mad desire to use such a thing for a napkin, I should buy a square yard of much handsomer and brighter-coloured stuff for a couple of gold pieces. Natheless, Mr. Dauntless, touching the matter of our friend's ransom, I tell you I will not take advantage of your generosity, for, mark you, I did stipulate that we should go halves, and I do intend to abide by my bargain as steadfastly as I should have expected you to have done if our places had been reversed."

When they reached the top of the hill, on which Munroe had taken up his position that morning, the battlefield, with all its grim adornments, lay before them, and the sight silenced even the callous remarks of the soldier of fortune.

The Irish troops had already withdrawn from the actual battlefield, and had fallen into their ranks some distance from it in an orderly fashion. Their restrained behaviour spoke well for their discipline, for, next to a defeat, a decisive victory over a wealthy enemy is perhaps one of the hardest tests to which soldiers can be subjected, and Harry proudly drew Lord Montgomery's attention to the absence of any indications of pillage and the orderly guards that had been already established over the baggage, artillery, and treasure-chests of the vanquished army, as well as the eight hundred prisoners who had sullenly yielded at the close of that tremendous struggle. The field itself was deserted, except by a few straggling figures who wandered among the heaps of lifeless bodies in search of some missing friend or comrade; and as Harry and his companions approached the Oonagh, they encountered a group of the Clansmen of Glencairn who were standing on the spot where Harry had seen their Chieftain fall.

Making his way hastily through these faithful retainers, he found Evir MacMahon kneeling beside the still breathing body of Florence. The Chieftain's eyes were closed and his hand rested lightly on the neck of the great deer-hound, Brendan, that had been his constant companion in sport, and who now pressed whimpering up against his dying master in a state of pitiable anguish. Close to Florence, poor Cormac lay where he had fallen, with the White and Gold standard still clasped under his faithful body, and beyond him crouched the stiffened corpse of Lord Blaney with his head supported against the neck of a dead horse. The eyes of the latter were wide open and staring straight in the direction of Florence; and, though the broadsword yet stuck in the hideous wound it had made, the dead man's face still retained the expression with which he had died, and seemed even in death to regard his expiring enemy with hate and derision.

Harry approached the Bishop, who had rushed down into the thick of the battle, at the imminent risk of his life, to stay the slaughter, and knelt down beside him. He observed a slight pulsation under the torn and blood-stained shirt of his friend, and asked the big Churchman if there was any hope, but his kinsman shook his head sorrowfully and replied in a low voice that the bullet, which had broken a rib and pierced the lungs, had inflicted a mortal wound, and that Florence was already bleeding to death internally.

At the sound of their voices the young Chieftain opened his eyes and, looking up at Harry with an expression of the most affectionate pleading, intimated by a slight gesture that he desired to speak to him. The Cornet bent down to listen, but Florence spoke with such difficulty that he had to place his ear almost against those dying lips in order to catch the whispers they breathed so painfully.

"So, Harry, So," he gasped, "The Visions of the Morning are fulfilled ere Evening — Closer — and yet closer, Harry, for I can scarcely see thee — My love, my last, fond love to Aileen and, Oh! Brother, cherish her for *My* sake, even if she should ever fail to value thee as thou deservest — Bid mine Uncle Owen take my deer-hound and care for him well. I know he values a good dog, and I therefore trust Brendan to his care — my Brendan, my brave, fleet, gallant Brendan, I know he will miss me — and Harry — Remember — Remember —"

He paused and sighed gently, closed his eyes quietly, and said once more and yet more faintly, "*Remember.*"

Observing that his lips moved again, Harry bent down once more with a suffocating feeling in his throat and remained thus straining every nerve to catch another word, whilst the deer-hound, raising up his muzzle and stretching his neck after the fashion of his kind when affected, howled long and piteously. Harry felt a touch upon his shoulder. He looked up stupidly and encountered the Bishop, whose tearful eyes were regarding him with a wistful look of sorrow.

"Rise, Harry Dauntless," said he, with a little choke in his voice. "Thy Brother's earthly pains are over. Cover him with his flag and leave him for the present to his Clansmen's hands to straighten for the lycht-wake. Oh, Florence! Florence! Beloved pulse of my heart! though I would have freely offered my old and worthless life in lieu of thy fair and blooming existence, yet, if I had thee back again, I could not wish thee a better end than on such a field and on such a day."

XXVI

FOUR days after Benburb a small party of the dead Chieftain's friends and Clansmen, under the protection of a safe conduct from Coote, arrived at Enniskillen with his dead body and proceeded to Devenish Island, where the hoary monuments of long-forgotten ages of piety look down on, perhaps, the most ancient and beautiful place of Christian sepulture in the world. The boat which conveyed the coffin was dressed out with cypress streamers, a knot of the same mourning material was festooned around the banner of the Embowed Arm and Sword, which waved from the bow, and the hereditary piper of Glencairn sat in the stern whilst he played the lament for the last Chieftain of his House. The firing party destined to pay the last tribute of military respect to the dead man followed in the next boat. They were all picked men of Glencairn, and as they rowed slowly in the wake of the funeral barge, they chanted in a low, solemn tone the *Tuiream*, which kept a melancholy accompaniment to the measured plunge and creak of their oars. The next boat contained the principal mourners, including Owen Roe, Evir MacMahon, and Harry Dauntless, and the fourth and last boat was occupied by no less than Captain Cartaret, himself, who, having been formerly acquainted with the young Chieftain, had taken this opportunity of showing his esteem for his memory by attending his funeral with six trumpeters and as many drummers from the neighbouring Puritan garrison of Enniskillen.

At the sight of the stern but sympathetic face of the Roundhead officer who stood bareheaded by the grave while the Bishop read the last service over it, Harry thought with a long-drawn sigh of his first skirmish with Cartaret in the grey of that summer morning at Glencairn; and he remembered sadly that Florence had said on that occasion he would recover his lost patrimony of Glencairn or would fill the last place for the last coffin in the vault of his ancestors on Devenish Island. Nevertheless, as he stood by the grave of his departed friend,

Harry felt that he could not have wished him a happier death. He had fallen in the glorious intoxication of victory, at a time when the Cause he so ardently loved was at the zenith of its success, and he had been spared the pain of seeing any possible misfortune threaten it afterwards. Therefore, when the three rounds had been fired over the grave, with a long roll and flourish of Coote's drummers and trumpeters between each volley, Harry bade a loving farewell to his spirit and sorrowfully resigned the body of his once fiery-souled comrade to its quiet resting-place among the mountains he had loved so well.

After the death of Florence, as he himself had foretold in his ecstasy at the village of Benburb, his Clan, now that it no longer possessed a leader, broke up and melted away. Those members of it who desired to retain their name attached themselves to the MacMahon of Dartry, who was the head of the parent branch of their late Chieftain's Sept, and those who preferred joining other Clans adopted the names of such Chieftains, to whom they transferred their allegiance, and in consequence of these changes the name of Glencairn as a separate Clan became nothing more than a memory within a week after its last Chieftain fell at Benburb.

Two months passed before Harry had an opportunity of seeing Aileen again, and then it was but for one brief day, on the occasion whereon he was sent to Clough Oughter with the troop that escorted young Viscount Montgomery of the Ards and fifteen other prisoners of rank to the island fortress. It was a painful meeting for both, inasmuch as Harry shrank from renewing his suit so soon after his mistress's bereavement, and the grave, silent manner whereby he endeavoured to express his sympathy with her was very easily mistaken by Aileen for courteous reserve.

The poor girl, as might be expected, had been prostrated by the death of her brother; but, like him, she possessed that type of fate-defying spirit that impels its owner to smile outwardly on the curious world, although it is inwardly bleeding to death. She was fully conscious, poor Soul, of her love, grief, and weakness, but she was resolved that not even Harry should detect them in her outward appearance. Consequently, whilst he refrained from intruding his love upon her sorrow, little knowing in his simplicity that it is on such occasions that a woman's heart most yearns for a man's affection, she imposed a still further barrier on his lips by the assumption of a cold, calm demeanour towards him. The result of this unhappy want of mutual confidence was, that Harry rode away the next day to join O'Neill at Kilkenny with the despairing reflection that Aileen was resolved to continue the self-imposed feeling of dislike which his encounter with Florence had evoked; and Aileen, whose womanly pride had been grievously wounded by what she assumed to be cold indifference on his part, at first reproached herself bitterly for having been the cause of this estrangement, and then humbly accepted the decree of fate which had not only taken her beloved brother, but had, seemingly, robbed her of her lover also.

With this unhappy cloud between them, Aileen and Harry parted; and in the meantime events took place which still further helped to deepen the misunderstanding between them.

The victory of Benburb shook off at one exertion the heavy grasp which the Parliamentary party had hitherto maintained on Ulster, and the Confederate Council of Kilkenny ordered Owen Roe to abandon that Province in order to march against Lords Broghill and Inchiquin, who had completely routed Ormond in Munster. This move of the Ulster Army placed the Puritan garrison of Dublin between it and Clough Oughter, and the consequence was that for nearly two weary years the Clans were as much cut off from their homes as if they had been on the other side of the world.

However, if the Confederate Council had hoped that the brilliant success which had followed O'Neill's march across Ulster would continue to attend his banners in Munster, their own incompetence and intestine jealousy were destined to frustrate such expectations. Once more, Preston and the other Confederate Generals hampered Owen Roe as they had previously done at the siege of Dublin. Once more, titled incompetence took charge of affairs and arrogantly prevailed over the actions of the experienced soldier of the Continent. Mismanagement, lost opportunities, and useless moves resulted in universal disaster, and in addition to these annoyances the health of the great Ulsterman began to fail rapidly under the influence of a then little understood form of rheumatism.

Worn out with suffering and disappointed with a harassing campaign in which neither side had gained any advantage, O'Neill led his army back to the North for the purpose of going into winter quarters near Londonderry. He had advanced as far as Limavady when the tidings of the King's murder at Whitehall overtook him like a thunder-clap. The news was conveyed to him in an incoherent letter from Ormond. The Marquess informed him that Prince Charles had been already proclaimed King in every town in Ireland except Dublin — the whole of the South and East were up in arms for God and King Charles the Second — all the country was drunk with loyalty; and he implored O'Neill not to be behind the rest of his countrymen in devotion to the King, but to prove his zeal forthwith by marching South to join his army.

Immediately upon the receipt of this summons, O'Neill set out to encounter Cromwell, who had recently landed in Dublin. On the first day's march, however, he was seized with a return of the mysterious malady which had previously attacked him in his last campaign, and after a short journey he was compelled to stop.

He lay in camp for ten days in the greatest suffering, but he continued to attend to the daily duties of his position, although it was even then apparent to all his officers that he was dying. At the end of the tenth day Daniel O'Neill appeared with another letter from the Marquess, and the impatient tone which pervaded it roused Owen Roe to a superhuman effort to prove the sincerity of his good faith. He ordered an immediate advance, and though he fainted twice in his saddle during the earlier part of the day, insisted, as soon as he recovered consciousness, in remounting his horse and resuming the march until a third seizure later on completely prostrated him, whereupon Evir MacMahon instantly ordered a halt of the entire army.

Six days afterwards, Daniel O'Neill again appeared with another imploring letter from Drogheda, and as his inferior officers dared not withhold such communications from him, it was reluctantly brought Owen Roe by the Bishop.

It excited the dying man into one last effort, which affords a pathetic example of the ascendancy of a gallant spirit over the frailty of the body it is about to part from. He directed his attendants to construct a light litter, upon which he bade them lay him in full harness with his sword and leading-truncheon in either hand, and in this fashion Owen Roe took his place at the head of the Clans, who once more resumed their march towards the South.

That journey was an event which was full of sorrowful recollections to all the followers of the expiring hero, and Harry Dauntless could never recall it to memory in after years without feeling considerable emotion. The dying man, clad in his armour, with the sweat and pallor of approaching death upon his features, the silent ranks of horse and foot which followed behind with hushed voices and gloomy faces, the absence of the song, the merry whistle, and the jest wherewith the Irish troops cheer the long marches for which they are to this day famous, and the soft, hollow tramp of the buskined Clansmen, whose measured footfall on the heather sounded like the roll of muffled drums, invested the whole scene with the melancholy appearance and associations of a vast, military funeral.

By the time they reached Cavan, Owen Roe was in a state of coma; and Evir MacMahon, who had assumed temporary command of the army, directed the Clans to march forward to their old camping-ground round Lough Oughter, while he himself rode forward to acquaint Madame O'Neill with her husband's melancholy condition and to make preparations for his reception.

He was carried to the room which he had formerly occupied in the days when he had superintended the first steps of his infant army, and here he recovered consciousness. Rose O'Neill, who was weeping softly by his bedside, was the first person whom his eyes lighted on; and though the poor lady struggled hard to conceal her agony, his quick eye detected and recognised in her despair his own hopeless condition. He gently chided her for her grief, reminded her of all the dangers he had safely passed through during the time they had been separated from one another, and begged her with a quiet smile that she would share some of his gratitude to Heaven for being permitted the happiness of dying in her arms.

The Bishop made a silent gesture to Daniel O'Neill, and the two, withdrawing into an adjoining chamber, left the dying man and his wife to themselves.

When the door of communication was closed between the sick-room and the antechamber, the two men regarded one another steadily for a minute without saying a word.

Daniel O'Neill was the first to speak.

"How long?" asked he, abruptly, with a searching look of inquiry into his uncle's face.

"A day — two days — perhaps, three — but not longer than six or seven at the most," was the troubled reply.

His nephew sighed deeply, and leaning out of the window fixed his gaze moodily on the hills and woods of Killykeen, which were fading into blurred shadows as the gloom of the September evening closed over them, while the Bishop paced from end to end of the room, in the restless fashion peculiar to him when under the influence of any uncommon agitation. Presently the door opened, and a flood of light streamed softly into the darkened room, whereupon both men turned towards the entrance, where their eyes encountered the thin figure of Owen Roe's old soldier-servant, Cathal, who at that moment entered with a lighted lamp in his hand.

The meagre cheeks of the old man, which extreme age and long exposure to wind, sun, and rain had given the appearance of much-worn leather, were still more wrinkled by the intensity of his grief, and, as he placed the lamp upon the table, his hands shook so violently that the two kinsmen expected to see him overset it in his agitation. He asked in a choking voice if their honours desired any supper, but a hasty reply in the negative from both gentlemen did not, however, dismiss him, for he made a pretence of setting to rights a few ornaments about the room, and at length faltered out an inquiry if his Grace thought any better of his Excellency's condition.

The Bishop shook his head without venturing to trust to his voice.

"Ah, Sirs," said the old man, "if you had seen him, as I have on the Continent, when the Frenchman's bullets filled the air with the sound of a tempest overhead, and the ground seemed to fly upwards as they struck underneath, — if you had seen him then, as I have often seen him, with the standard of Hy-Niall in his hand leading us on while his men dropped around him like October leaves, you would have verily thought that Owen Roe O'Neill was immortal. Ah!

Vhoe! Vhoe! Vhoe! that I and other old toothless hounds who have followed him through so many bloody huntings should be spared, while the Princely Forester lieth on his death-bed with five thousand of his name around who would give their heart's best blood to ransom him off it."

The old man turned away with the tears running freely down his withered cheeks, and shuffled out of the room with the gait of a sick old dog to which he had aptly compared himself.

"Poor, faithful heart," murmured Daniel O'Neill, softly, as the door closed behind the old soldier, "thou art but a type of thousands of others not less devoted than thyself. Tell me, Uncle, if thou canst, what subtle magic lurks in the arrangement of the letters whereby this same name of O'Neill can be made a spell in this country of Ireland to witch men into such a state of voluntary servitude? Is there no other name under which men will carry on the work which Owen O'Neill commenced, or must the harvest, after all the sweat and labour of the husbandman, fall to the earth to rot there too along with him?"

"It shall not rot if you consent to garner it," said the Bishop, looking steadily at his nephew, who started violently, turned pale, and shook his head. "And wherefore not? You are the trusted agent of Ormond and the English Royalists alike, — the confidential favourite of Charles of England, as you were his father's before him; as near the Royal stem of Hy-Niall as any in the land; and I can promise you the leading staff of the Ulster Army to-morrow on one condition."

"I know what you would say, Evir," answered the young man, frowning slightly, "but I would not accept such conditions. No! not even to seat my Royal Master on his rightful throne. Good Uncle, allow me but a small share of the consistency which you claim for yourself, and consider how useless it is to try and tempt me. I have been brought up in the faith of the Church of England, to which I am as much attached as you are to your own belief; and, therefore, suppose our conditions were reversed and I offered you such a bribe, think what your own reply would be, and so consider it as my answer."

"Well, they may dub thee Subtle by name, but friend and foe must own thou art ingenuous by nature," said the Bishop, sighing and smiling at his own feeble wit. "I cannot enter on a duel of casuistry with a man who disarms me before I have drawn my spiritual weapons; however, for all that, may peace go with thee, Dan, for I respect and love thee all the more. Yet, tell me, good nephew, what hand among the men of the North is fitter to take up the fallen truncheon than thine own?"

"My Cousin Hugh," was the ready reply.

"What, Hugh Dhu?" said the Bishop, contemptuously. "That gloomy, awkward, silent misanthrope? Why, he is but a paltry Captain of foot—Tush, Dan, Tush—such a fellow would never do to lead the Clans."

"Awkward he may be," was the dry reply, "but then the manners of a Courtier do not go much towards making a general, if your Grace is to judge by Lord Castlehaven's performances. He is gloomy; but a noisy, roaring emptiness does not make a leader in the council, if we are to take our worthy kinsman, Sir Phelim O'Neill, for an example. He is silent; but so was his uncle under whom he was trained in the Low Countries. If he be silent, awkward, and gloomy, he is nonetheless a very perfect soldier, he is of the Royal line of Niall of the Hundred Battles, and is such a one as the Clans would follow to the rampiers of perdition itself if he would lead the way."

As Daniel O'Neill was thus enumerating the good qualities of his absent cousin, O'Reilly appeared and informed the Bishop that Owen Roe required his attendance.

The sick man was still very faint, but on the appearance of the Bishop he roused himself instantly from his listless state of weakness and asked with all the querulous irritability of sickness how it was that the trumpets had not sounded, although it was long past the hour appointed for the setting of the Night Watch. Evir MacMahon answered in a soothing fashion that he himself had given orders for the omission of this military formality, lest the sound should disturb him, but this reply appeared to exasperate him more than the neglected ceremony itself.

"Send forth, Evir, and bid them sound at once," he said angrily, "for I shall have no departure from the usual routine of my troops so long as I command them."

A messenger was instantly sent to the camp with the dying General's last command, and a few minutes afterwards the kettledrums of O'Donnell's cavalry beat a long rolling accompaniment to the shrill flourish of the trumpets. The strains of the latter instruments leaped from note to note and tone to tone in that sharply irregular cadence which stirs some hearts more profoundly than the sweetest music, — at first deep and brazen, then richly mellow, then soft and swelling, and then they climbed by a rapid and melodious scale to one long, lingering note of sweetness. They ceased, and their echoes died away into a sigh amid the woods of Killykeen, and then the united pipes of the Clans played the first few bars of "Planxty Sudley." The long, plaintive notes of the pipes came in wailing accents across the lake and seemed to the watchers as though they were the sounds of the Banshee mourning over the greatest member of the princely House of Hy-Niall, but they appeared to act on the sick man like a refreshing stimulant.

His voice recovered its former vigour, his eyes their wonted light, and, pushing back the bed-clothes from his chest, he sat up and bade his nephew bring writing materials. His wife and Evir MacMahon both feared that his mind was beginning to wander and endeavoured to persuade him to defer his correspondence until he should feel stronger.

"Go to! Go to!" he said petulantly. "Is it because I would take advantage of this brief spell of strength that you deem my mind as weak as my poor carcase? It is the duty of the Master Mariner to look out for the crew and freight when he is assured that the ship is sinking, and he should provide for their safety before the water has crept as far as the lower gun-ports.

"I know full well, Alas! that I cannot hold a pen, far less write a letter, but you shall be my scribe, Evir, and when you have taken down the last letter which Owen Roe O'Neill is ever like to send to man, I shall lie me down quietly and commend myself to God."

Writing materials were accordingly brought, and the Bishop, sitting close beside the bed, wrote at his dictation that pathetic letter wherein Owen Roe bade farewell to Ormond and resigned to him that trust he had so well maintained. He told the Marquess that he was sending the Clans forward under the command of his nephew, Hugh Dhu, whom he considered the fittest person to lead them. He commended his army to the honour and care of Ormond and exhibited such a touching solicitude for the welfare of his rough, true-hearted soldiers that Evir MacMahon's hand shook once or twice as he wrote and his eyes grew dim for the moment.

When the letter was finished, Owen Roe read it himself. He made one or two querulous objections to a word or two, and then bade the Bishop hold his hand while he added his name at the foot. The irregularly-traced characters, utterly unlike his usual firm, neat writing, straggled painfully under the Bishop's guidance across the page. The pen dropped from his nerveless fingers. He sank back on his pillows with a sigh and turned away his face. It was the last signature of the bravest, the simplest, and the noblest soldier that his country ever produced.

XXVII

ALTHOUGH the following three days was an epoch of general depression in the Ulster Army, Harry Dauntless had reason to feel this universal sorrow even more acutely than the generality of his comrades.

From the day whereon he joined the Ulster Confederates, the Palesman had entertained a sincere admiration for the genius, modesty, and nobility of Owen Roe, and during the years they had been associated with one another, Harry had become profoundly attached to the quiet, dignified soldier, partly, on account of the chivalrous purity of O'Neill's character and, partly, on account of the many kindly words and benefits he had received from him. Therefore, it was with more than ordinary anxiety that he turned his eyes nightly towards the light that shone as of old in the third story of Clough Oughter, and when each morning dawned, he was almost afraid to look on the Castle lest he should perceive the Bloody Hand displayed at half-mast on the flag-staff.

On the third evening after Owen Roe had dictated his last letter to Ormond, Harry was sitting moodily in his tent when Daniel O'Neill suddenly appeared before him. The face of Infallible Subtle wore such a look of intense distress that the Cornet sprang to his feet and asked in a faltering voice how the General was, fully expecting to receive the news that he was already dead.

"As near death as the frayed thread of life can support him," was the answer. "He hath been raving these last two nights there is nothing more to be done here in Ireland and that he must set out for the Holy Lands to fight the Turk. At times he hath intervening periods of reason — brief upward leaps of the flame ere it goes out for ever — but such intervals of reason are more trying to us than his ravings, as we durst not then cross his slightest whim for fear of stirring up fits of most extraordinary passion. When I left him, some few minutes since, he was quite collected and sent me to fetch you to him, so, I prithee, come incontinently, as he waxes exceedingly fretful at any delay in the execution of his orders."

On entering the sick man's room Harry's first impression was that he had arrived too late, for the gaunt, moveless figure on the bed and the sorrowful faces of those around made him think that Owen Roe O'Neill's pains were over. Rose O'Neill knelt by one side of the bed, and Philip O'Reilly stood behind her. At the foot of the bed, in buff and breast-plate, stood Hugh Dhu O'Neill, who had come to receive his last instructions about the Ulster Army, and at the far side, close to Evir MacMahon, stood Aileen. She was weeping softly when Harry entered and was unaware of his presence until his sword happened to tap lightly against a chair, whereupon she raised her eyes and recognised him with a sudden start. She flushed painfully, made a slight inclination of her head to him, and then covered her face with her kerchief; yet, notwithstanding her grief and the short glimpse he had of her face, Harry instinctively felt that the past two years had but added further tributes of grace and beauty to her former charms.

O'Neill asked who it was that had just entered, and Harry, who had expected to have heard the thin, piping whisper of one choking in the agonies of death, was startled by the clearness of his voice. Some one told O'Neill that it was Master Dauntless.

"Come hither, Boy," said he, in a calm, stern voice, "close, close, nay, more, to the foot of my bed, so that I may see thy face, for I take more heed of what a man's eyes say than the words his lips utter."

Harry stepped close to the bed and hoped sincerely that his Excellency felt more at his ease.

"It was not to hear you talk of myself that I sent for you," was the peevish answer, "so a truce to such idle queries. I have always found you to be a pattern of truthfulness and honour, Harry Dauntless, and I want to put a question to you now which requireth nothing more than a truthful Nay or Yea. Are you prepared to grant me such a favour?"

Harry bowed and murmured that his Excellency could depend on his honour as he could upon his life.

"Then answer me in all truthfulness," said O'Neill, with a piercing look, "and do not, because you are speaking to a sick man, affirm with your lips what your heart inwardly denies, with any base intention of comforting and deceiving alike. Do you still entertain the same love which you formerly professed for my god-daughter, Aileen MacMahon? Yea or Nay, Harry Dauntless, Yea or Nay?"

Harry Dauntless drew himself up with a certain amount of haughty dignity, for he little knew to what this conversation was tending.

"God knoweth, your Excellency," said he, somewhat coldly, "I have never given Mistress MacMahon any cause to think that my feelings were ever changed towards her."

"Then, ere I leave this world," said O'Neill, faintly, "I shall at least do one good action in my lifetime. I love you two wayward souls as though you were mine own children, and I shall not permit you to wreck each other's lives for the sake of a foolish lover's quarrel, in which each is unwilling to condone the fault of the other. Aileen, thou silly wench, I know thy heart's true disposition towards him who, in the sight of Heaven, is already thy husband, and, I tell thee, I will not have thee act so wickedly and foolishly as to refuse my request."

Aileen, throwing herself on her knees, kissed the thin, bony hand stretched out to her from among the bed coverings, and murmured through her sobs that his will was hers in all things. Harry sighed deeply at this ambiguous answer, which he remarked sorrowfully she had not vouched for even by a glance in his direction. But the next words spoken by the dying man struck a cold chill into the hearts of both the lovers.

"You hear, Evir, what these foolish children say," he said, in a tone of command which there was no gainsaying, "therefore, in God's name, buckle them fast in marriage now, before my eyes, or some other act of moonstruck folly may again separate them."

Aileen and Harry glanced at one another's faces, with a furtive look of amazement and terror. To Harry such an union seemed fraught with the horror of being immediately and indissolubly bound for life to a woman who was determined to hate him; and the shrinking terror on his face conveyed to the half-distracted girl the still more dreadful agony of shame which a high-spirited woman might reasonably be expected to feel, when she finds herself being forced on the love of a man who is indifferent to her.

The consternation reflected in each other's faces confirmed the inward dread each one had of the other's feelings, and they both turned with a faint look of appeal towards O'Neill. However, the dying man shook his head impatiently; and, as there appeared to be no help for either, Harry took the hand of Aileen in his, while the Bishop, hastily assuming his stole, commenced reading the marriage service.

And never was marriage solemnised with more depressing surroundings or under more extraordinary circumstances. The gaunt, motionless figure that lay already in the passing agony upon the bed, and the silent group of sorrow-stricken witnesses who stood half-revealed in the diffused light of the flickering candles, rendered the scene inexpressibly mournful, whilst the two agitated principals in this sombre drama, who loved each other so passionately in secret, but who nevertheless felt that each faintly murmured response they uttered was an added bar to all mutual affection, were invested with such agony as might be felt by two criminals whom some barbarous sentence has compelled to be active assistants in their own execution.

As soon as this ghastly ceremony was concluded, Owen Roe commenced an affectionate exhortation to the newly wedded pair; but, before he had spoken half a dozen words, he was seized with a dreadful spasm and dropped forward in a deathlike swoon. Hugh Dhu O'Neill and Harry ran to his assistance, while Rose O'Neill administered a restorative, and after a few minutes he groaned feebly and breathed once more. Presently, he recovered semi-consciousness, and the two young men resigned him to the care of his wife and drew back mournfully. Hugh Dhu plucked Harry by the sleeve and nodded significantly towards the door, whereupon the latter became aware for the first time that during the short interval they had been bending over the unconscious man the other occupants of the room had silently withdrawn. Hugh Dhu glided softly out of the apartment, and Harry turned to follow, but at the foot of the bed he paused for a moment to take a farewell look at his beloved commander.

Close by the spot where he halted stood a little table upon

which were displayed a few cups, vials, and such like accessories of a sick-room, and amongst this litter lay the helmet and gloves of the dying man. A single green, ostrich feather, that had become detached from the plume-socket, lay limp and draggled among the cups and medicine glasses; and as Harry Dauntless stopped to regard the white drawn face on the pillows before him, he picked up this solitary feather and thrust it into the bosom of his doublet before he left the apartment.

In after years he often congratulated himself on having secured even this poor memento, for, living or dead, he never saw Owen Roe O'Neill again in this world. He made his way downstairs to the deserted banqueting-hall, where he flung himself down into a chair in a state of lethargy such as one might feel a stunning blow that has completely benumbed all sense of where and how it has been inflicted.

Gradually, and with more and more painful distinctness, the realization of his position came, piece by piece, to his bewildered brain. Married! Married! Married! He was married to the woman he would have risked his prospects of Paradise to have love him, and yet, by that very ceremony, was placed beyond the pale of her love for ever.

He strove hard to persuade himself that, as he had not insisted upon the fulfilment of Aileen's promise, he had surely no reason to fear her reproaches; and then he argued with his despairing inner self that his marriage with the woman he adored was surely not a matter to repine over; yet strive as he would to persuade himself that their marriage was a predestined union, wherein neither his bride, nor himself, had any volition one way or the other, an ever busy fiend seemed to whisper in his ear that Aileen, like her dead brother, was possessed of an intolerable spirit of haughty pride, which would rather ruin the life of the owner than yield in any matter of expressed opinion.

"If she is proud, why, so am I," he muttered with a groan, "and, by Heaven, she shall learn that I have as lofty a sense of honour now as she had when she so scornfully bade me not fear that she would withdraw her plighted word, once it had been given to me. She hath been forced into my arms against her will, but she shall be as free as if this marriage had never taken place; and as for me, alas! I shall be resolute even though my heart should break."

A step behind caused him to start up and turn about, and he confronted Evir MacMahon, holding a small travelling valise in one hand, and leading Aileen by the other.

She was dressed in a dark blue riding-skirt and jacket, a velvet barrad of the same colour was set on her soft, dark curls, and her face was concealed by a small black satin riding-mask, such as ladies of that time assumed, when travelling, for the purpose of guarding their complexions from the effects of sun and wind.

But other reasons than the care of a complexion, which she had never troubled herself to preserve, had caused Aileen to assume this last article of disguise. Beneath its protecting shade her cheeks burned vividly with the agonising fire which outraged womanly pride and dignity had kindled within her, and this feeling of shame so overpowered her spirited nature that, notwithstanding the sustentation afforded by her mask, she was barely able to keep herself from swooning.

The Bishop released her hand, in order to withdraw from the bosom of his rochet three sealed letters and a small sheaf of papers; and, as soon as the poor girl was deprived of his support, she sank down trembling on a chair, and turned away her despairing face from the scarcely less miserable one of her husband. The Bishop handed the letters and papers to Harry, and the latter perceived, by the sickly light of the dawn, that two of the letters were addressed to Ormond, and the third to himself, whilst a single glance at the papers showed him that they were four safe conducts verified by the well-remembered signature of the Marquess.

"The Shield of the Mighty is cast away utterly," said the Bishop, in accents which seemed to Harry like the measured tolling of a funeral bell, "and all is now at peace with Owen Roe O'Neill. Come, Harry, the day breaks, and it is necessary that you should be presently on your way in order to carry out his last commands. In the packet addressed to yourself, you shall find instructions as to the delivery of the letters addressed to the Marquess. The safe conducts are for yourself, Aileen, your serving-man, Shane MacAfee, and John Cuttard. I filled in the name of the latter at his own request, and, though I, myself, deem him to be a sorry rascal, I had not the heart to refuse the earnest petition he made to be permitted to accompany you. And now, Harry, your horses stand saddled already by the Lough side, and nothing remains but to conduct Aileen to your mother's house, where you must leave her until it please Heaven to grant such peaceful times as shall enable you to return to her arms again."

The two kinsmen led the trembling girl downstairs through the guard-room, out through the tiny rose garden, where the withered leaves lay as dead as Harry's own sad hopes, across the soft, short grass which was glittering with night dew, and down to the little pier alongside, where lay a boat manned by two soldiers. One, who had been a follower of poor Florence (although long since transferred to another regiment), still wore on the bosom of his weather-stained buff-coat the Embowed Arm and Falchion of Glencairn; and, at sight of this emblem of her dead brother, Aileen's bosom swelled with a stifled sob, and two tears gushed from the eyelet holes of her riding-mask, and rolled slowly down its black satin cheeks. The Bishop embraced his two young kinsfolk with an emotion not less poignant than their own, and then handed Aileen to her seat in the stern of the boat, where she was presently joined by Harry. The men at the oars looked interrogatively from Harry to the Bishop; but the two kinsmen were so full of distressing thoughts that neither of them felt capable at the moment of giving the word for departure.

Evir MacMahon stood upon the topmost step of the little pier, with the tears running undisguised down his broad, bearded face. Twice did he stretch out his hands in blessing over the heads of the two young people in the boat alongside, and twice did the swelling heart of the big, loving, impetuous man prevent him uttering a word.

The lake lay black and sullen around the Castle, and the steaming mists of morning hung over every distant object like a funeral shroud. The leafless woods of Killykeen stood like an army of spectres along the shore. The banner on the top of Clough Oughter hung dead and dripping, and the gaunt figure of the sentinel, who stood beneath it, leaning pensively on his arquebuse, appeared to share with those below upon the pier this universal depression of nature.

Suddenly, a thrush in the woods burst into a sweet flood of song, wherein she seemed to promise hope, comfort, and joy to her despondent fellow-mortals, and this natural hymn of gladness broke the sorrowful spell that bound them.

Harry nodded to the boatmen, who instantly gave way, the boat leaped towards the shore, and the Bishop, falling on his knees, turned his streaming eyes to Heaven, and invoked a tremulous blessing on the heads of the two beings he loved most upon earth. When the boat had gone half a dozen lengths, Harry ventured to turn his head. The Bishop was still kneeling on the pier, with clasped hands and quivering lips, and that was the last sight he had of him on earth, for the bloody fate that Evir MacMahon was destined to undergo was even then close at hand. That parting was always a sorrowful and depressing memory to Harry Dauntless; and, when he was compelled to revisit the North in after years, he was careful to avoid Clough Oughter, whose walls formed so melancholy a tomb for many broken hopes and friendships.

On landing they found Cuttard and MacAfee standing by the horses, and, having assisted Aileen to her saddle, her husband mounted his horse, and the little party set forward on their journey. Harry and Aileen rode in advance, side by side; both silent and occupied with their own sad thoughts. Cuttard and MacAfee followed some twenty yards behind; and, as the latter knew absolutely no English, and for some private reason chose to misunderstand the barbarous Gaelic of the troop-adjutant, the conversation between the travellers was limited to monosyllables.

They rode on all day without drawing bridle, and, not daring to pass through Trim, which was then held by the Cromwellian troops, halted late at night at a little wayside Inn, some fifteen miles South of that town. Harry and his wife were accommodated with a couple of boiled chickens, and a side of smoked bacon, in the private parlour of the Hostess; but, though their long journey should have given them a good appetite for much simpler fare, they each felt unable to eat more than a couple of mouthfuls.

The Hostess, who was one of those elderly, garrulous, good-natured busybodies that sometimes succeed in making eminently uncomfortable those whom they most delight to honour, was unceasing in her attentions to the young couple. She hardly left them to themselves for a moment, and, when not actually talking to them, talked at them, whilst she set dispensable dishes, glasses, and other articles upon the table or busied herself about wholly unnecessary trifles in the room. She also bombarded Aileen with a variety of simple dainties in a determined but misdirected effort to make her eat against her will; and, when no persuasion could prevail upon the young lady to touch any more food, she made sure that the poor dear lamb was ill and insisted upon her trying many sovereign cordials and remedies. These well-meaning offers were also firmly declined, but the good, dense soul continued to press the poor girl so determinedly that at length her victim faintly confessed that she was over-fatigued, and begged earnestly to be conducted to her room, as she felt weak and ill.

Her husband was deeply moved by her obvious faintness, and he started up from the table to offer her his assistance. But she rose so hurriedly when he approached, and shrank back so timidly from his proffered arm, that he resigned her to the care of the Hostess, with whom she left the room as unsteadily as if she were being led to execution.

Harry Dauntless stood by the table, mute and rigid, until the door closed behind the two women; but the moment that he was left alone, he uttered a deep sigh, and, pushing back his chair, subsided into it in an attitude of profound misery. There was a squat little Dutch clock upon the mantel, and he stared for a long while alternately at it and the peat fire on the hearth, without noticing how the time was speeding with the one, or how slowly the other was decaying at his feet.

Suddenly he was roused by the entrance of the Hostess, and at the same moment he noticed with a start that the stumpy hands of the little clock were already folded over the hour of midnight. The talkative old woman had come to still further increase his torture; for, quite unconscious of the effect she was producing on the wretched young man, she proceeded to give him a long account of the state of mental anguish wherein she had left his wife.

She told him with a great deal of sighing and much uplifting of her plump, red hands and watery eyes how the swate young crathur was nigh kilt by her long journey; described how very wake she was, how very, very bitterly she had wept on her own ample bosom, and yet how very obstinately she had refused to confess what ailed her gentle heart; and finally the old lady implored Harry not to think of setting out on the morrow, as such another day's journey would just murdher the purty bird outright.

Harry replied in a choking voice that their setting forth at daybreak was a matter of absolute necessity, and begged her to leave him to himself; but his tormentor was not to be dismissed without inflicting some further rankling wounds.

"Ah, yes, Avourneen," said she, sympathetically. "Shure, it is meself that can undherstand the dhreadful plight ye are in. I knew the very minnit I set eyes upon ye that ye were wan iv the King's ossifers who 've been juking around the counthry iver sence the bloody massacree o' Tredagh;[1] for me husband — God be good to him for a dhrunken blaggard — was a Corpperil in the Earl o' Wentworth's Horse, and I consequently know the luk iv a soldier-ossifer whiniver I see wan. There was such a wan as yerself, wid just such a purty colleen iv a wife as yer own, who stopped here in me house after Trim was tuk be Gineral Jones (May the foul Fiend fly away wid the black-hearted reiver). It made me heart bleed, so it did, to see the poor gintleman sittin' here all night long in this very room wid his soord and pistols on that table, there, forenent ye. Not a wink o' slape would he take that night, at-all-at-all, and whin I begged him to lie down be the fire for even an hour, he laughed a quare wild laugh and sez, sez he, 'Iv I had only meself to think iv, me good woman, I 'd slape as calmly as a babe in its mother's ar-rums; but, whin I 've such a charge above stairs to luk afther, it is me duty to remain on guard wid me weepons ready for the inimy.' Ah, Sir! Sir! yer good lady should set a high value by ye for — God be good to us — it is in such sore times as these that the love iv a good, thrue man is proved."

She set a couple of tallow candles, whose wicks were composed of peeled rush-pith, on the table, and with the remark that his honour's room was the first on the right above stairs whenever he felt inclined to retire, withdrew and left the unhappy man to his own reflections.

"It is in such sore times that the love of a true man is proved," he muttered to himself with a groan. "Yes! you foolish, chattering *caillagh*, you utter more truth than you are aware of, and at the same time point me out the course I must adopt, but, God help me! it is a hard trial, a hard, hard trial for a man to undergo."

The lamp was guttering on the table for lack of oil, the fire

[1] Drogheda.

was subsiding for want of fuel, so he lit the tallow candles with a fir splinter kindled at the hot embers, and flung some billets on the smouldering peat. Then he reseated himself once more before the hearth and watched the logs as they crackled joyously and spurted forth little jets of fragrant smoke and fitful tongues of fire, whilst the squat clock upon the mantel slowly marked the hours of his misery.

Once he started to his feet and crossed the room with a feverish step. He stretched out his hand to open the door; but, the moment his fingers touched the handle, he recoiled from it as though it were burning brass, and, returning to his seat, once more sank down into his former attitude of dejection. The little clock ticked on, serenely indifferent to his anguish, the burning logs in the grate changed one by one into glowing charcoal, which in turn faded into white ashes. The mud that caked his dress, boots, and spurs turned from black to yellow, the wretched tallow candles grew fainter and fainter as the dim, grey light stole gradually into the room; and still Harry Dauntless sat staring, staring into the ashes until the red flush of morning shone full on his haggard face and told him that his wedding night was passed.

XXVIII

ALTHOUGH they were but an easy day's journey from their destination, the fear of falling in with any prowling body of Cromwell's troopers made the travellers anxious to get beyond the dangerous zone of Dublin as soon as possible; and, accordingly, they resumed their journey shortly after daybreak, and rode forward at a pace that forbade any continuous conversation. On two or three occasions Harry asked Aileen gently if they were not travelling at too rapid a pace, and once he begged her to alight and rest a while; but, as her only reply to these questions was the same faintly spoken but decided negative, they shortly afterwards relapsed into silence and continued on with unrelaxed speed.

But when the little party reached the borders of the Dublin Mountains, whose loneliness promised security to them for the remainder of their journey, they all drew rein instinctively before they plunged into the dark defiles which lay before them. The spot where they halted was half-way down a little green *boreen*, where the banks sloped upwards about the height of a horseman's shoulders, and here they dismounted and slackened their horses' girths before they essayed the rough mountain road that lay before them.

Suddenly a sound came across the meadows, at first faint and distant, and then growing more and more distinct and immediate each moment, and the three men instantly recognised its import and exchanged a swift look of consternation. It was the measured throb of kettle-drums, as they beat time to the trot of a cavalry regiment, which was evidently approaching rapidly in their direction.

Cuttard was the first to recover his presence of mind.

"Stand by your horses' heads," said he, in a low voice, "and be ready to stuff your cloaks into their nostrils if they make any attempt to whinny."

Then he flung down his steel cap on the grass and clambered to the top of the bank, where he crouched down stealthily with one hand stretched out behind him to enjoin silence on his companions.

"From their Red coats and the White and Orange sashes of their officers, I take them to be a troop of Reynolds's dragoons," he whispered hoarsely. "They are making towards the road which runs parallel to this, a musket-shot off, and if their horses do not get wind of ours, they are like to pass us unnoticed. Be secret and silent, on your lives."

Harry, who stood holding two of the horses' bridles, felt a slight touch upon his arm, and turning his head found Aileen close beside him.

He could not see her face, for it was concealed by her mask, which she had not discarded even at supper on the previous evening, but her fine eyes shone through the eyelets of the visor with a dark splendour which reminded him of happier days in Clough Oughter.

"Harry," she said in a calm, resolute whisper, "if it should happen that we are discovered, will you promise the last favour that you can bestow on me?"

She laid her hand significantly on the butt of one of the two pistols in his belt; and the gesture so unnerved him for the moment that he felt unable to reply, so he merely bowed his head and turned his face away.

After a few minutes of agonising suspense the clatter of the passing cavalry was lost on their ears, and gradually the throb of the kettle-drums died away into a tinkle as faint as the chirp of a distant grasshopper; but none of the three fugitives in the lane below dared move a limb until Cuttard, turning round a face as white as its natural yellow would permit it to assume, slid down the bank and wiped the sweat off his brow.

"I am not much of a praying man, myself, Mistress Dauntless," said he, with a ghastly grin at Aileen, "though I have gone through a good course of 'uplifting of the spirit' under Hugh Peters at the leaguer of Bristol and Basing House what time I served with the Eastern Associates; wherefore I must delegate you to offer up a portion of your devotions on my account. Heaven be praised, Madame, you did not know the danger you stood in when yonder devils were passing, but I knew, alas! for my regiment served with Reynolds's at the storm of Bridgewater, and I remembered — Faugh — what made me queasy to think of. Therefore, Madame, as I cannot very well tell you what deeds those gentry are capable of, I suppose you must only take my word that you have every reason to say a few extra prayers to-night on your own account."

They resumed their journey thankfully; and Harry, taking the lead, conducted them across the mountains by the least frequented road he knew. His bosom swelled with long dormant memories as he recognised each well-remembered spot which was associated with his own lonely but happy boyhood. There was the sea shining as brightly blue as ever with its snow-white border of sand. Nearer lay the sweet green fields over which the long shadows stretched in grotesque forms, and right and left appeared one by one every familiar gorge, rock, watercourse, and scaur among the purple and gold of the flowering heather and furze. That little hill to the right was where he had shot his first woodcock under the tuition of old George Ledwidge; yonder was the pool where he had killed the monster trout (which in after days appeared never to have exceeded half a pound); there was the spot whereon he had so often paused to look upon Carrickmines, and last of all came the hump-backed hill of Ballycorus, beneath which Bearna Baeghail lay in the bright, frosty sunshine.

As they approached the Castle, Harry saw a great, hulking figure digging in the garden and instantly recognised it to be Con MacGauran. He called him by name; but the idiot, far from being reassured by the sound of his voice, flung down his spade with a wild cry of terror and bolted in doors like a rabbit at the sight of an agile terrier. By the time that Harry reached the entrance, the gate was already closed, and MacGauran's voice was bellowing the cheering intelligence to all the inmates of the Castle that "de Sassenach Soldiers was come at last to cut all our troats."

Harry flung himself from his horse to knock; but, before he could raise his hand, the muzzle of a gun was thrust through one of the lower windows, and the stern voice of old Ledwidge bade him stand back on peril of his life as the garrison were well armed and prepared to defend their trust to the last. His master smiled faintly at the old man's vaunt, and explained in a few words who he was, whereupon Ledwidge, shouting out the news to "*Herself*" at the top of his voice, stumbled down the turret stair and had the gate unsparred almost as soon as Harry had assisted Aileen to dismount.

The moment the gate was opened, Kathlyn flew out and clasped Harry in her arms. She held her son for a full five minutes against her breast, laughing, weeping, and praying alternately over him, and during that rapturous interval was quite unconscious of there being any witnesses to this scene, although Cuttard and MacAfee were scarcely ten paces off, and Aileen, herself, stood trembling by her husband's side.

At length Harry succeeded in extricating one of his hands from hers, and he stretched it out and drew Aileen forward.

"Dear Mother," he said, "when I set forth from Ulster I knew that I must part from thee as suddenly as I returned, and, therefore, I brought thee a daughter who will console thee in my absence and will share my place in thy affections."

Aileen timidly removed her mask, and the eyes of the two women met. They exchanged one flashlight glance, and in that moment read each other's disposition in that intuitive fashion whereby women so accurately gauge the character of one of their own sex.

Kathlyn stretched out her arms immediately towards her daughter-in-law, and the poor, tired, heart-broken girl threw herself spontaneously upon her gentle breast and burst into tears. The elder woman experienced a happy thrill as she realised how beautiful the young girl was, for the pride which a mother takes in her son is scarcely greater than her triumph when she learns that he has secured a prize worthy of him, and she therefore raised up the lovely face which cowered on her bosom and pressed two quick kisses on Aileen's mouth and forehead.

"Dear wife of a dear son," said Kathlyn, tenderly. "Until this moment I had always deemed my cousin Evir to be a just and warm-hearted man, but the praises I have heard of thee from his lips fall so far short of thy true self that I must henceforth doubt either his judgment or his generosity. Sweet slip of the Royal Line of mine own dear Sept, and fairest daughter of Clan Colla, why dost thou weep? Hast a lurking fear I shall not value thee at thine own true value? if so, my beloved one, fear no longer, for, henceforward, thou shalt be as dear a daughter to me as Harry is a son."

"Dear, kind Mother," sobbed Aileen, as she hid her face again in the elder woman's bosom, "thou shalt find out for thyself, too soon, how unworthy I am of thy love and praises; therefore, let me, like an unwilling impostor, enjoy such sweets until time shall prove how unworthy I am of them."

"Thou art as modest as thou art beautiful," said Kathlyn, smiling, "and I have no doubt thy other qualities keep step with these two best attributes of womankind. But why do I stand chattering here, for you tremble, my pretty one, like a bird in a net, and the air without doors is eager, notwithstanding the sunshine on the mountains. Come within doors, my Daughter, and thou, Harry, lend thou an arm to either of us, and let George and thy companions look after the horses."

"I cannot tarry for a single hour," said her son, in a choking voice, and looking down upon the ground to conceal the agitation on his face. "My orders forbid me to rest night or day until I deliver the despatches of which I am the bearer, and, therefore, dear Mother, I must to horse and away without going further than the threshold."

For a second the widow's face was wrung with a look of anguish, but the spirit of her martial family came bravely to her assistance, and she drew herself up as resolutely as a Spartan mother might have done when she gave her son his shield and bade him return with it, or on it.

"Heaven forbid, dear Harry," said she, simply, "that either wife or mother should withhold thee from the path of honour, even for an hour. Therefore, my beloved Boy, if thou must needs leave us now, go forth under the care of Him to whom we two poor women shall pray nightly on thy behalf, and bearing in mind that thou mayst walk through a fiery furnace unsinged if it is His will that it should be so. Depart, my Son, and fulfil thy duty like a gentleman and a soldier."

For a minute husband and wife stood regarding one another white to the lips. One word from either would have dispelled for ever the barrier which stood between them; but self-pride interposed, and the word remained unspoken.

Harry advanced slowly towards Aileen, who stood clinging to his mother's arm. He had a passionate desire to take her in his arms and tell her, even in the presence of so many spectators, how much he loved her; but a sinking fear of being repulsed if he attempted to embrace her made him hesitate; and whilst he regarded her in this miserable state of indecision, Aileen slipped down quietly in a dead faint as suddenly as a daffodil whose stem has been shorn through by the mower's scythe.

"Weak from fatigue and grief at thy departure," said Kathlyn, hurriedly, as she loosened the garments of her daughter-in-law. "No! Harry, no! do not carry her within doors; I prithee leave that office to me and Maureen. Go! Go! my Boy, go! in God's name — Go, ere she comes to, for it is better — Oh, believe me, it is far better — that ye twain should part thus."

Harry took off his hat, and, bending down over the unconscious girl, pressed one fierce kiss upon her forehead. Then he straightened himself and embraced his mother in a state of distraction which she attributed to the fact of being so soon parted from his wife.

"Farewell, Mother, Farewell," he murmured huskily, "and bear in mind this, my last message to Aileen. Do not add one word to it. Do not, as thou dost love me, forget one word of it. Entreat her, dear Mother, to write to me — as she loveth me — *as she loveth me* — and tell her that when she sends me such a letter as she knows I long to receive, I shall come back to her, even from the ends of the earth."

The next moment he was in his saddle, and, without waiting to thrust his feet into the stirrups, urged his horse at full gallop down the bridle path and along the high-road. He was blind, wild, and deaf with grief. He hardly knew or cared whither he was going, and rode on with such reckless haste that his two discontented companions had great difficulty in keeping him in view. The troop-adjutant and the serving-man had been looking forward to a long sojourn in comfortable quarters, and were very much disappointed at being compelled to resume their journey. Mr. Cuttard was particularly mortified, inasmuch as he had been very favourably impressed by a brief glimpse of the trim figure and comely face of Maureen, and had been promising himself a very agreeable stay at Bearna Baeghail.

Consequently, their journey South was by no means a cheerful experience. Harry was too sadly preoccupied to notice either of his companions, MacAfee had become more sullenly taciturn than heretofore, and Mr. Cuttard, deprived of the consolation of having some one to whom he might confide his disappointment, swore softly but soulfully the whole way at the haste of certain Cavalieros and the universal insolence of latter-day serving-men.

On the third morning after their departure from the Valley they surmounted a high hill, and saw Waterford lying before them in the bright November sunshine. Each of the three travellers instinctively drew a breath of relief, notwithstanding the fact that the most perilous stage of their journey had now been reached. The town was their destination, and they were cheered at the sight of its walls, although Ormond and his army were shut up within them on the South side of the river, and the Parliamentary troops lay between them and their friends.

Warned by the sullen boom of the English cannon, which were battering the town from the Northern bank, they turned abruptly to the West in order to avoid Cromwell's videttes and crossed the river some five miles higher up at a ford that was guarded by a strong body of the Royalist cavalry. Harry briefly stated to the officer in command he was the bearer of important despatches, and that person, after a suspicious scrutiny of his passes, detailed a Cornet and two troopers to accompany him and his companions to the city. This escort was sent for the ostensible purpose of shewing them the way; but, from the sulky reserve of the officer who kept company with Harry, and the affectionate fashion whereby the two troopers rode stirrup to stirrup with Cuttard and MacAfee, the three travellers had little difficulty in seeing that they were being regarded more in the light of prisoners than comrades.

A ride of an hour's duration brought them to the gates of the town. Here they dismounted, and the officer led them on foot through several narrow streets, wherein they speedily recognised how closely the place was being invested. Nearly all the houses were shut up, most of them were sorely battered, and every man they encountered was armed. The far-off sound of the Parliamentary cannon was being answered round for round by the louder detonation of the Royalist artillery along the river front, and now and then a vibrating hum in the air overhead, a shower of tiles and coping stones upon the pavement, or an occasional crash of heavier rubbish, intimated in an unpleasant fashion to Harry and his companions with what accuracy the Cromwellian gun-layers were addressing their pieces.

The officer conducted them into a noble old tower, whose massive walls, raised by the Danish King Sitricus, had proved their strength fifty years before Hastings was fought. The venerable old fortification stood as stoutly as it does at present, and seemed, even in that dire period, to defy the combined efforts of man and time to humble it. It had been a favourite mark for the Puritan cannoneers throughout the siege, and was therefore honeycombed on the river side with hundreds of deep indentations; and even as Harry Dauntless entered, a heavy shock on the outside, that caused the whole structure to shake and groan like an aged prize-fighter who has received a telling blow from a younger antagonist, marked the fresh impact of a heavy shot.

There was a shower of small pieces of mortar, which clattered on the stone floor as noisily as if they were flint pebbles, and through the haze of whitewash dust that was exhaled from the walls Harry discerned the pale face of a man regarding him intently. It was Lord Castlehaven, who immediately held out his hand and welcomed him effusively.

"I am truly glad to see you, Mr. Dauntless," said he, gasping and coughing as the fine particles of dust penetrated his eyes, mouth, and nostrils. "Prut! Tut! but I thought for the moment that the old tower was about to come tumbling down about our ears. I trust you shall prove a harbinger of better fortune than that we have lately experienced, and that your coming is an earnest of many days of comradeship."

Harry explained in a few words how he was a volunteer as well as a bearer of despatches, whereupon Castlehaven, with many friendly assurances, led him to an upper room, where they found Ormond bending over a large military plan, which he was studying as composedly as though he were in the peaceful seclusion of his own country house. The Marquess looked up as they entered, and greeted Dauntless with a cold nod, and Castlehaven with a look of polite interrogation.

"My Lord Marquess," said Castlehaven, "I am sure it shall be scarcely less pleasant for you to hear than it is for me to relate, that I bring a volunteer as well as a messenger from Ulster."

"They both bring their own welcome," said Ormond, with

a somewhat supercilious smile upon his handsome features. "May I ask, Mr. Dauntless, to what circumstance I am indebted for this offer of your sword? Have you already grown aweary of the service of your Ulster General, or have you awakened to the fact that the King's interests are little served by the policy of inactivity which O'Neill has been pleased to assume lately?"

"My Lord," said Harry, flushing at the covert sneer, "I know you are too generous to wound the reputation of those who are unable to defend themselves, and these letters shall convince you that you not only slander the living, but the dead."

"The dead?" echoed Ormond, letting the packets slip from his fingers to the table. "Good God! Mr. Dauntless, you do not surely mean to say that Owen Roe is dead?"

"Even so, my Lord," answered Harry, with a low bow, "and judged these four days past for his merits and demerits by a tribunal where human testimony is regarded little one way or the other."

Ormond in great agitation broke the seals of the letters and read them hurriedly. The first he opened was from Bishop MacMahon, and when he finished reading it he handed it without comment to Castlehaven. The other letter was that which the heroic Ulsterman had dictated during the brief spell of energy which his expiring vitality had summoned up; and during the perusal of that melancholy letter Ormond turned his back upon his companions and withdrew into the recess formed by one of the little barred windows, as though the light was insufficient elsewhere; but, when he turned once more to Castlehaven, Harry noticed that his eyelashes were draggled as if with tears.

"Great Heaven!" he cried passionately, "to what Devil of Discord hast Thou given over this unhappy Country that never begets any purpose, howsoever promising, but is doomed to be strangled ere its birth? Once it was I who could not yield to this man's terms; then, when I was empowered to grant them, it was his turn to hang back and temporise; and now, when we had at last agreed to terms, and were about to join hands, — Death intervenes, and forbids the union of our swords."

"Good, my Lord Marquess," said Castlehaven, to whom

this, the news of O'Neill's death, had but little concern, as their joint services at the beginning of the Civil War had but resulted in mutual dislike. "You appear to overlook the most important part of the Bishop's letter. He says most distinctly that 5,000 picked men of the Clans are already on the march to join us, and with such an addition to our powers it would be a marvel if we were not able to shake the soldiership of Cromwell to its centre. Why, your Excellency, I consider that the death of this gloomy, over-cautious man is rather to our gain, for he was ever a breed-bate unless he held uncontrolled management of affairs; and if we get the pick of his men, unencumbered with his presence, I do think we are better off than if he came to us alive at the head of twice as many."

"The times have changed, Castlehaven," said Ormond, with a gloomy frown, "since a thousand men pitted against a thousand others decided the fortune of a field merely by push of pike. War, nowadays, hath become a coy mistress only to be won by patient devotion to her service, and can no longer be wooed in the light-o'-love fashion whereby you and I, and, indeed, most of his Sacred Majesty's officers have paid court to her. We are but simple gentlemen, who have been summoned to military positions which we would relinquish to-morrow if we could sheathe our swords honourably. We are not soldiers ourselves, and have hitherto despised the professional fighting-man — I know not why — perhaps, on account of his inherent poverty, perhaps, on account of our ignorance of his true value; but we want such a one now, Castlehaven, and, Lo! we are in the position of a country clown who hath flung some pretty pebble into a deep river, and learns, when too late to profit by it, that he hath thrown away a ruby."

"Methinks, your Excellency," said Castlehaven, with a twitching mouth, for this tribute to his dead rival was extremely galling to his petty soul, —"methinks, your Excellency places too much stress on the importance of the formalities which it was the glory of this same Ulster precisian to observe."

"If there is such little value in military studies," said Ormond, with a piercing look, "tell me, Castlehaven, how it is that the King's arms have had such continuous ill-fortune whenever they have encountered Cromwell's? Our numbers are as great if not greater than his; our men as brave and well armed as his, — and I do not vainly boast when I claim for myself a courage not inferior to that of the studious boor of Huntingdon. No! No! my Lord, it is you who are wrong in underrating the value of one trained to his trade, and such a one as Owen Roe O'Neill would be of more avail to the King's cause at this moment than twice the number of his men who are now marching to our aid."

The Marquess crossed the room and opened a little court-cupboard, from which he took a couple of sealed warrants. He returned with them to the table, and, planting one booted knee on a chair, bent down, hurriedly filled in some blank spaces in the parchments, dashed some sand over them from a little brass pounce-box, and handed them to Castlehaven.

"Find me a reliable and speedy messenger," said he, quickly, "and bid him ride post-haste with this commission to Bishop MacMahon. The Bishop hath little skill in soldiership, but he is at least brave and honourable, and shall serve to keep up a bustle in the North. He may prevent Coote advancing to join Cromwell, and even if he is unable to do us any good, it were better to entrust the command of the remainder of the Clans to him than to that noisy, blustering fool, Sir Phelim O'Neill. I shall require another messenger of like prudence and speed to anticipate Hugh Dhu O'Neill ere he arrives with the Clans at Clonmel. That warrant is his authority to assume the governorship of the town, which will thus menace Cromwell and his Northern supplies. Wherefore, if we can manage to cut off the Roundheads from Dublin, and you can succeed in relieving Duncannon to-morrow night, we shall — *Marte Volente* — have Master Oliver and his army in our hands like a basket of apples."

The Earl and Harry bowed and were about to withdraw, but Ormond stopped them with a gesture.

"One moment, Mr. Dauntless," said he, with a glimpse of his winning smile. "You have been good enough to offer me the service of your sword for the second time, and I am afraid I was not only rude enough to forget my thanks but my manners likewise. I therefore beg you to pardon me, and I shall consider it as a token that you have forgiven and forgotten my distempered words, if you will tell me now in what capacity you would like to serve the King under my command."

"Your Excellency is extremely kind," said Harry, with a bow, "but I cannot claim a greater honour than being permitted to resume the saddle of a private gentleman in your own regiment of Life-Guards."

"I think I can offer you something better than that," said Ormond, smiling. "There is a vacant troop in my Lord Castlehaven's regiment of horse which I think I can promise you in exchange for the Lieutenancy you lately held from O'Neill, that is" (he continued, nodding to Castlehaven), "if your Lordship is willing to take the recruit which you, yourself, already have enlisted."

The Earl answered with a warmth unusual in his listless manner that he desired nothing better, and, having acknowledged his sense of gratitude for Ormond's kindness, Harry once more bowed and withdrew with his new Colonel.

In the lower room they found Cuttard and MacAfee, and Harry having mentioned to Castlehaven the rank of his dependents and their willingness to take service under him, the Earl commented very favourably upon the appearance of these two additional recruits.

"Sir," said Cuttard, majestically, with a flourish of his gauntlet and a dip of the hilt of his spadroon for the purpose of displaying the embroidery on his cuffs and the scarlet silk lining of his cloak, "I have had the extreme honour of serving under the banners of three Kings, six countries, and twelve generals, and I therefore trust that your Lordship will not take as flattery what is merely a frank avowal. My Lord" (a deep bow), "I esteem the honour of serving under so distinguished a general as yourself" (a still deeper bow) "as an additional distinction in the career of a blunt but honourable Cavaliero like myself" (a still more elaborate bow than before). "Sir!" (very fiercely and standing up very straight), "I am your Lordship's own from the comb on my steel cap to the mud on my under spur-leather."

Castlehaven, although notoriously one of the most incompetent of all the incompetent generals of the Royalist party, had the most touching belief in his own military abilities, and the gross flattery of the soldier of fortune had its own sweet effect. The result of this favourable impression was, that not only did he take occasion to remark to Harry several times during the evening what a remarkably soldier-like and intelligent person Mr. Cuttard appeared to be, but, on the following afternoon, when the two troops were assembled for the relief of Duncannon, he also ordered one of the troop-adjutants to fall out, and bade Cuttard take his place, although every man in the party had been carefully selected by himself for this expedition fully two weeks before.

XXIX

IT was almost sunset when the party detailed for the relief of Duncannon stole out of the Southern Gate of Waterford and rode cautiously along the right bank of the river in the direction of Credan Head. They halted on the summit of the cliff which shelters the tiny village of Passage; and while the troopers dismounted and lay down to await further orders, Castlehaven and Harry went forward to reconnoitre the scene of their intended movement.

Down beneath them swept the magnificent river on its march to the sea, and opposite lay the fort of Duncannon on that steep rock which sentinels the white scythe-like expanse of sand curving round to Hook Head. On the hills beyond the fort the white tents of the Cromwellian troops lay like a fall of snow, and among the mounds which marked the position of their batteries an occasional puff of smoke and a sulky rumble that was answered by a like appearance and sound from the fort showed how determinedly the siege was being carried on by both sides. Some two miles down the river and well out of the range of the heavy seaward guns of Duncannon, lay five English ships of war with the ensign of the Commonwealth displayed from each of their foretops. They were detained at anchor by the commanding position of the Royalist fort, which could have easily sunk them one by one, if they should attempt to pass; and it was quite apparent to Harry that the reduction of Duncannon would be followed by the appearance of the men-o'-war before Waterford and the ultimate fall of that important town.

As soon as night fell and the cannonade of both besiegers and besieged had ceased, two red lamps appeared on the seaward bastion of Duncannon. It was the pre-arranged signal to Castlehaven that the garrison were ready to receive the expected reinforcements, so he ordered ten of the troopers to lead their horses down to the boats which were to ferry them across. There were but four wretched skiffs in all, each capable of bearing no more than six men in addition to the oarsmen; and as soon as the men had taken their places, the Earl and Harry assumed charge of a boat apiece, and set off with the horses swimming behind them.

After a long and anxious pull across the dark water, which is nearly a mile broad at this point, they arrived safely at the foot of the rock. They led the shivering horses over the soft, white sand, and, starting and halting at every faint sound, made their way cautiously up the steep path to the fort, where they were silently but joyfully admitted by the Governor, who was that Bayard of the English Royalists, Colonel John Wogan.

He shook hands warmly with Castlehaven and drew him apart, and, while the two conversed in a low voice, Harry superintended the stabling of the weary horses. It was fully an hour before another boat brought the next small detachment, and by this time Castlehaven had worked himself into a fever of anxiety. As he felt that nothing but his own presence on the other side of the river would facilitate matters, he started back for Passage in one of the returning boats and left Harry behind with orders to bring him any report which might bear upon the scheme for that night.

Notwithstanding the bustling haste of Castlehaven, it was eight weary hours before the last boat-load came to the fort, and it was almost dawn by the time the last horse was led under the gate.

"That makes the eightieth,' said Wogan, as he carefully uncovered a lantern in the dark angle of the sally-port; "take my compliments to Lord Castlehaven, Mr. Dauntless, and tell him that with the aid of the horses he has sent me I shall make Master Ireton raise the siege by daylight or shall request my second in command to shoot me and send me pickled to old Noll himself. Tell his Lordship, as I have more mouths than I can well feed at present, I am sending him back ten of his troopers. I am sure he will be glad enough to get them and I can very well dispense with them, for I have plenty of stout knaves among my foot, who, like most of these Irish fellows, can wind and manage a horse with any dragoon in the land."

Harry, well aware of the fretful irritability of Castlehaven, and anxious to protect himself, begged Wogan to write a note to that effect. The latter assented very good-humouredly, tore a leaf from his tablets, and, resting it on the head of a drum, knelt down and scribbled a few lines; and, whilst Harry waited for this necessary billet, Cuttard was despatched to the boats along with the ten men who were not required.

As soon as he received the note, Harry exchanged a warm grasp of the hand with the gallant Governor, and then stole out through the sally-port and made his way cautiously down the rocks to the spot where his companions were awaiting him. He had drawn near enough to distinguish the dark outlines of the boats and the cowering figures of their occupants huddled together like cattle for mutual warmth, when he was suddenly startled by seeing the tall bony figure of Cuttard standing on the sand with a stranger sitting dejectedly at his feet. He was still more astonished, on drawing nearer, to perceive by the dull, leaden light of the approaching dawn that the latter figure was that of a young Parliamentarian officer with a pair of very sloping shoulders and a pale, gentle face which was overclouded with a look of mortified shame.

Harry asked in a low voice what the Roundhead's presence meant.

"Came upon us in the dark," answered Cuttard, cheerfully, "and walked up with a pious exhortation to watch and pray on the muzzle of my spanned pistol. What shall I do with him, Captain?"

"Do with him?" repeated Harry, in some surprise. "Why, bring him along with us, of course. His person, in accordance with the usual custom in such cases, shall stand some of us in good stead for ransom or exchange some day or other."

"When we two have taken our places," remarked the troop-adjutant, coolly, "you would not be able to squeeze a marmoset aboard those wretched cockle-shells, which, like everything else in this accursed country, are narrow — damned narrow, antiquated, and uncomfortable."

"Then bring him back to the fort to Colonel Wogan," said Harry, impatiently. "I have no doubt he can find a use for him, and let us be gone as soon as you return."

"It is too late to return to the fort now," said Cuttard, tersely, and pointing to the sky-line, where some ten or twelve Cromwellian troopers had at that moment appeared with their armour shining dully in the young light of the morning.

"There is but one way, Captain Dauntless, to dispose of such encumbrances; so stand to one side, if you please — and you, young Sir, take off your lobster-pot."

"God's Will be done," said the young Puritan, removing his helmet deliberately, and looking up with all the devotion which a brave and sincerely religious man might assume when the hour of his death is come. "Good friend, I prithee, shoot me through the breast and do not mangle my face, for I have a young wife" (here his voice faltered a little) "who would doubtless wish the poor privilege of kissing it ere she committeth my body to its last bed in pleasant Cambridgeshire."

Harry caught the petronel which Cuttard was fingering with brutal indifference, and took it instantly from his hand.

"Thou Shalt not do Murder," he said, after a choking pause. "Put that weapon back in thy belt, Jack, and get on board immediately. As for you, young Sir," he added to the prisoner, "go in peace, and if at any future time it should be your lot to do some unfortunate comrade of mine a like service, remember that there are among the followers of the King some men who love their wives as dearly as you do yours."

The young officer, who looked scarcely more than a boy, made an effort to speak, but his emotion was too great for utterance, so he pressed his enemy's hand hard and turned away his face. Harry disengaged his hand quickly and stepped on board one of the boats. The other, under the charge of Cuttard, was already twenty lengths away, and Harry bade his men pull for their lives; for the Cromwellians, who had been regarding them for some time in puzzled indecision, were already trotting forward from the sandhills, unslinging their carbines as they advanced.

The rowers required little encouragement to bend on their oars with a will, and as the tide was flowing like a mill-race after a flood, they were far out on the river before their enemies reached high-water mark; and the next moment a grey bank of sea mist crept down upon the two boats and covered them with its friendly ægis.

In less than half an hour they arrived safely at Passage. Here Dauntless and Cuttard remounted their horses and set out together for Waterford, which they reached a couple of hours before midday. Without delaying to change their dress, they set off, as soon as they had stabled their horses, to report to Lord Castlehaven the successful transport of the entire reinforcement, and at the entrance to Reginald's Tower encountered the Lord Lieutenant in company with Castlehaven and the ubiquitous Daniel O'Neill.

Harry took off his hat with an anticipatory smile, but, instead of returning his salute, Ormond fixed his eyes with a stern, steady look upon Cuttard, who started violently and shrank back with a modest diffidence wherewith that gentleman was not often afflicted. The Marquess then turned his back coldly on the astonished Cavalier and spoke a few words to his companions in a tone of voice too low for the former to overhear. Whatever he said appeared to cause the Earl the most exquisite pain, and Daniel O'Neill the most intense amusement, for the former turned white and scarlet alternately, and the latter laughed in a noiseless and convulsive fashion which had an unpleasant effect upon the nerves of both Harry and his abashed companion.

Dauntless, whose astonishment was gradually giving way to a feeling of indignation at this behaviour, felt a hot flush creep over his face, which was intensified when Ormond asked him in a cold tone if he regarded Cuttard in the light of a personal friend.

"Considering, your Excellency, that he saved my life at the peril of his own," said Harry, with a frigid bow, "I may say he is entitled to lay such a claim upon me. If your Excellency is prejudiced against him on account of his having served in the ranks of the Parliamentary army, I do most earnestly assure you that his fidelity to the King has been tried on a hundred occasions since he joined the Ulster Army, and I will gladly stake my life upon his good faith."

"It is not my intention, Captain Dauntless," said the Marquess, coldly, "to suggest to any man what friends he should keep, and whom he should eschew, therefore, I leave such matters to yourself; but as for you," he said, turning to Cuttard with a set mouth which carried with it a more threatening import than his words, "I shall not do justice upon you, as you deserve, so long as you discharge your duties to the satisfaction of my Lord Castlehaven; but, mark my words and chew upon them well, my friend, — that the first indication I observe of misconduct either as a soldier or a private subject of King Charles, and, by the God who made you! I shall send you dangling from the top of Reginald's Tower. Do you understand me, Mr. Cuttard?"

Mr. Cuttard very meekly expressed his sense of the perfect clearness with which his Excellency conveyed this communication; and, with a cool nod to Dauntless, Ormond walked off with his two companions, leaving Harry petrified with astonishment, hat in hand, and Cuttard smiling very feebly and adjusting his rich lace cravat with trembling fingers, as though it already felt uncomfortably tight about his neck.

Before Ormond had gone many yards, he evidently sent O'Neill back, because that young gentleman returned, and, drawing Harry apart from Cuttard, advised him with one of his inscrutable smiles to drop that gentleman's acquaintance as soon as he conveniently could.

"Why, in the name of reason," asked Harry, angrily, "should I cast off a man to whom I am so much indebted, merely because he has served the Parliament?"

"Well, you see, my dear Dauntless," said O'Neill, regarding him with his strange, mirthless smile, and tapping him on the cuirass to accentuate each word, "your friend has not confined himself entirely to the profession of arms; and his Excellency hath a foolish prejudice to officers of his army contracting bosom friendships with gentlemen who make travellers on the King's highway serve as their bankers."

"Why not say out at once the usual term, Highwayman?" said Cuttard, who, unobserved by both, had approached near enough to overhear the last words uttered by O'Neill. His face was contracted as in some spasm of agony. His white lips, drawn back into two rigid lines, disclosed his yellow teeth set fast like those of an animal; and Harry, with a rising fear of what he dreaded was about to happen, prepared to throw himself between the contending rapiers the moment they should be drawn.

"Ah, the gentleman hath taken the very word off the tip of my tongue," said O'Neill, nodding affably to the troop-adjutant. "Yes, Highwayman is the plainer word; and if you desire any satisfaction, Mr. Cuttard, and can find a *gentleman* in Waterford willing to bear your message, why, my dear Sir, my address is 'The Falcon,' in Bakehouse Street," and with another smile to Harry, Infallible Subtle walked off cheerfully.

"Come, Captain Dauntless," said Cuttard, hoarsely. "Come to our lodgings; I have somewhat of business to transact with you."

Divining immediately that he was about to be made the bearer of a challenge from one friend to another, Harry disconsolately accompanied Cuttard to their lodgings, which were in a comfortable little inn in Lady Lane. As soon as they entered the room which they shared in common, Cuttard went to a cabinet and produced from it a small steel casket, which he always carried strapped to his saddle bow on the march and secured every night under his saddle flap when in camp. He unlocked this casket and very gravely set to work to count from it the gold pieces which it contained. Harry conceived an uneasy feeling that this was the preamble to a will, in view of what appeared to be an inevitable encounter; but he nevertheless made a shambling attempt to hint that the words used by O'Neill might not have been intended in the sense wherein they had been accepted, and that, perhaps, an explanation might avert the impending duel.

"Duel," repeated Cuttard, in a very composed voice, though his eyes bore a strangely wild look, "there is not going to be any duel, inasmuch as Mr. O'Neill stated what was no more than the bare truth."

"What!" cried Harry, falling back in his chair aghast. "Do I understand you aright, Captain Cuttard?"

"Perfectly, Captain Dauntless," answered his companion, harshly but coolly; "and lest Mr. O'Neill did not make himself clear enough, I think it is right you should now hear from myself what I really am."

He paused for a moment and then went on in a low monotonous voice, and with his eyes fixed on the wall behind his friend's head, as though he feared to meet his gaze: "I am no Captain, Harry Dauntless; nor had I, until I joined Owen Roe O'Neill's army, ever served any general in a higher capacity than that of a private trooper. I confess to all that Dan O'Neill hath charged upon me—Aye! and more, for this time I intend to make a true avowal of my character. I have been a bully of Alsatia and the Mint in London, a paid government spy in Spain, a hired bravo and duellist of such Parisian gallants as were too dainty to soil their white hands with a rapier hilt, and all over the world I have been a cardsharper, a swindler, a thief, and — and — no other man durst say it but myself — and a liar —

"I have no claim to gentle blood or breeding, though" (with a touch of his never-failing vanity) "one might think I had lived all my life among the highest of the land; and my only acquaintance with your father was the one occasion wherein I cogged him out of twenty gold pieces by the aid of doctored dice. And now, Mr. Dauntless, since I have told you so much of my character, let me tell you why a fellow like myself should be so cast down at the prospect of our parting.

"When I heard at Clough Oughter that you were the son of the gallant, sprightly ruffler, Walter Dauntless, I felt a sneaking kindness towards you. He was the first to detect my earliest and clumsiest attempt at cheating, and yet he let me keep his money and also spared me the shame of exposure, for, though you may scarcely credit it, I did own some sense of self-respect at that time, Captain Dauntless. Wherefore, in my poor way, I resolved to do you some good turn as a set-off against your father's generosity; but you, yourself, increased the obligation I intended to pay, and so left me as much in debt as ever. What you were pleased to regard as a service, but which was no more than I would have done for any fellow-comrade, was the main cause of this; for you did appraise my behaviour so much above its value, and were so untiring in acts of kindness out of all proportion to my deserts that — that I grew to love thee, Harry Dauntless, better than any human being I have ever known since the time I broke my father's heart."

He paused again as if to allow his companion an opportunity to speak, but as Harry still remained silent, he resumed with an air which was half insolent and half defiant: —

"There is about £160 there on the table, Mr. Dauntless. One hundred pieces of it is your share of the ransom of young Lord Montgomery of the Ards; the remainder, whatever it is, is all that survives of my portion — owing to silk cloaks, laces, gloves, and such gauds coming so expensive in this accursed country. Add twenty more pieces to your share, as conscience money for what I cozened your father out of, and then let us part. But if it were not a great inconvenience for you to withdraw to another Inn, I would take it as a last favour not to turn me out of this one, as, indeed, the sack and the hostess and the attendant wench are all very much to my liking."

During the time that the troop-adjutant rambled on through this speech, Harry Dauntless sat far back in his chair. A mist hung before his eyes, and out of this shadow Cuttard talked raucously; but the only thing the younger man was conscious of was a vision of the entrance to the Valley of Glencairn on that summer morning when he lay faint and gasping on the heather, surrounded by the murderous faces of Coote's dragoons, whilst Cuttard stood over him with his sword in one hand and the blue velvet riding-coat in the other. His eyes were full of moisture and the muscles of his larynx were contracted as he rose to his feet and pushed back his chair.

"No, Jack Cuttard," said he, unsteadily, "neither thou nor I shall leave this Inn so long as it suits us both; and if thou wilt give me thy word of honour to reform thy life, I am damned if O'Neill or Ormond or the King himself shall part us twain as long as we live."

For a moment the troop-adjutant stared blankly at his companion and held back from his outstretched hand; then he averted his face, covered it with his left arm, and stretched out his gaunt, muscular right hand in search of the friendly, generous one that met and clasped it.

"God bless you, Mr. Dauntless," said he, in a broken voice. "You are the first honest man who has ever taken my hand after learning what I am; and yet, Harry, and yet you may be proud of what you have effected thereby, for you have done what never a priest, preacher, or prester John of them all could do, and that is, — you have made an honest man of Jack Cuttard from henceforward."

When he grew more composed, he told Harry briefly the story of his life. It was pitiable in its sordid simplicity and differed very little from thousands of similar instances that are as common now as they were then. His father, a small shopkeeper of Northampton, had saved a little money, and with a commendable ambition had resolved that his son should have an opportunity of rising higher in the world than himself. John Cuttard was therefore sent to London and articled to a lawyer; but the unaccustomed freedom, the friendliness and inexperience, of the country youth soon led him into the destruction he was only too anxious to meet half-way. Cards, the all-devouring passion of that time, came first. Then came drink with all its attendant vices, and within a year after he left his home, London had swallowed up his little patrimony and left him nothing but the maddening lust of vicious poverty. Cheating at cards, dice, and games of skill was followed by more hardened methods of obtaining money, and then the Law stretched out its hand to seize him, and he fled to the Continent. He wandered from country to country eking out a desperate existence, sometimes at cards, sometimes by highway robbery, sometimes by hiring his sword to titled ruffians, too cowardly or fastidious to undertake themselves the brutal work he did for bread, and sometimes serving as a soldier, which was the only honourable vocation he had ever practised, and wherein, he carelessly added, his courage and military talents had never been questioned. Two or three times he had attempted to start a fresh lease of honesty among strangers, but his own evil past had followed him like a spectre, and each time he had been driven back by society on his former hopeless course. He concluded his autobiography with the gloomy remark that fate had once more chased him down, for the fact of his having robbed Ormond himself on the Curragh of Kildare some years back did not afford him any brilliant prospects for remaining with the Royalist army.

Harry reminded him of his own assured friendship, and begged him to forget his past and show by his future what true stuff he was, whereupon Cuttard swore vehemently he would prove himself worthy of such a friend, and during the next two weeks was continually on the lookout to intercept anything ranging from a troop of horse to a single Puritan trooper who might appear to threaten the person of his friend.

In the meantime, Ireton, startled by the appearance of cavalry in Duncannon, which, as he was well aware, had been hitherto deficient in this branch of an army, was under the impression that they represented a portion of a much larger reinforcement. He accordingly raised the siege and ordered the ships to weigh anchor and stand out to sea, and a few days after the batteries on Mount Misery suddenly ceased fire and Cromwell retreated from Waterford.

The appearance of Hugh Dhu O'Neill at Clonmel and the

failure to reduce Duncannon had cut off Cromwell alike from his supplies and the aid of his fleet; but, if Ormond had calculated upon such checks staying the victorious career of the great Regicide, it was not long before he was undeceived. Three weeks after the withdrawal of Cromwell, O'Neill, at the head of the remnant of the garrison of Clonmel, entered Waterford, having made the most memorable and gallant defences of a walled city that has been recorded in the entire history of the Civil War in Greater Britain.

The Clans were greatly thinned, but when Harry saw them coming swinging into the town to the shrill screaming of their war-pipes, he thought their step was as light and their bearing as jaunty as when he first saw them in the North years before. The Parliamentary army investing Clonmel had made six desperate but unsuccessful assaults, three of which Oliver had led in person; and when one portion of the walls was so battered as to be absolutely untenable, the baffled Puritans found on entering the breach that an inner wall of even greater strength than the former had been built by O'Neill during the night. Even the resolute spirit of Cromwell was checked by this unforeseen obstacle; and as two thousand of the flower of his Ironsides lay dead in the breach, he offered very favourable terms, which were immediately accepted. It was not until he entered the town that he learned that O'Neill had in the meantime slipped out with his army during the night; and although he was extremely mortified at the way he had been hoodwinked into granting such good terms to an untenable post, it is recorded, to the eternal honour of Cromwell, that he scrupulously adhered to the terms he offered.

XXX

A FEW weeks after O'Neill entered Waterford, the united armies of Cromwell and Ireton appeared once more on Mount Misery and resumed the siege of the now doomed city. As affairs by this time appeared hopeless, Ormond invested Castlehaven with the Vice-Royalty, sent Hugh Dhu O'Neill with his army to Limerick, and then took shipping for France, in order to represent personally to Charles the futility of continued resistance in Ireland.

From the day whereon Ormond left the Kingdom, an era of disaster and incompetence set in. Castlehaven, better fitted to be a monk than a soldier, completely lost his head from the outset, and behaved more and more wildly as Cromwell deliberately closed in on the Royalist forces. He shamefully abandoned Waterford to its fate and led his army into the West of Cork, where he frittered away his own time and the energies of his men in the reduction of several petty garrisons, until a rumour that Cromwell was following him up from the East chased him from that quarter in a wild state of panic. He crossed the Blackwater at a ford near Fermoy, and led his dispirited troops Northward in the hope of evading his terrible enemy among the Tipperary mountains.

It was early in December. The snow lay thick beneath their ill-shod feet, and a bitter wind penetrated through every hole in their rags as they slouched along over the mountain solitude of Kilworth. They were half-starved, wet, miserable, and bewildered by the inexplicable movements of their leader, and it would have needed some stronger character than the vacillating, excitable Castlehaven to have roused them into anything like a fighting spirit in case they had been attacked on the way.

Harry's troop of horse rode some two miles behind the rear-guard as a protecting screen, for several small bodies of the Parliamentary Cavalry had been observed hovering round the Royalist Army in the earlier part of the march, and appeared to be waiting an opportunity to swoop down on the straggling wretches that limped painfully in the rear. Accordingly, both Harry and Cuttard made every effort to rouse their companions to a sense of the proximity of their danger, but the men appeared to have lost all heart and rode with dejected faces as if they were utterly indifferent to their fate.

About midday they arrived at that part of Kilworth where the mountains glide abruptly down to Mitchelstown, and at that spot where the first sight of the little town is caught by the traveller, the troop drew rein. Before them rose the towering peaks of the Galtees, and beneath them lay one of the finest scenes in the South of Ireland; but little did either Harry or his men think of the view as they halted, cold, hungry, and exhausted on the frozen ridge. There was a deserted windmill close by, and he bade his men dismount and rest themselves for a while in its lower story, whereupon the troopers flung themselves from their horses, and, leaving them standing on the road indifferent as to whether they stayed or strayed, entered the mill and dropped down sullenly on the floor.

Harry would have had them search the upper stories and would have established sentinels, but the selected troopers flatly refused to obey his orders, and told him that he might pistol them where they lay, as they preferred to be rid of their misery at once rather than undergo additional suffering. As it appeared to be hopeless to maintain discipline among men so far gone, Harry very prudently left them to rest themselves, and sat down by the door to watch the horses himself; but, as he was quite as exhausted as his companions, it was not long before he found his own head rocking on his breast in a state bordering on sleeping and waking.

He was thinking drowsily how the strong soul of Owen Roe had enabled these very men to weather even worse circumstances, when he was startled by hearing the unmistakable sound of scabbards clashing against stirrups, and, opening his eyes, perceived a body of Parliamentary dragoons galloping up to the mill from the road. He instantly sprang up, drew his sword, and shouted out to his men that the enemy were upon them.

Cuttard was by his side in a twinkling, and some of the troopers rushed forward to support their officers; but the majority looked at one another in sullen indecision, and before they could make up their minds as to what they would do, a volley was suddenly fired down from the rotten floor overhead, and nearly half their number dropped dead or wounded on the ground. The survivors ran to the door, sword in hand, but only to find themselves hemmed in in that quarter by a row of levelled carbines.

"Surrender at discretion," shouted the Parliamentary leader, "or my men shall pour their shot among you ere I count ten."

Every man among the dispirited Royalists knew well that a surrender to Cromwell's troops did not always entail immunity from the gallows afterwards; but, as they were hemmed in by unknown enemies above and confronted by instant death in front, they unhesitatingly chose the least objectionable course that was open to them, and dropped their weapons on the ground.

A score of dragoons, who had been up to this moment concealed in the loft above, clambered down the rotten ladder that communicated with the ground-floor, and their leader, a grim-looking Corporal, approached and saluted the officer.

"I did not altogether carry out thy commands, Colonel," said he, in a strong, nasal drone, "inasmuch as I bade my comrades tarry in the deliverance of their fire when I saw your helmets over the ridge, deeming, thereby, to encompass these sons of Bashan the more surely, in order to utterly destroy and exterminate them. Yet, peradventure, if I have offended by this exercise of my poor judgment, my men are already loaded again, and it costs but the word and a few charges from their bandoleers to complete the good work."

"By no means, Corporal Oh-Let-Me-Be-Thankful Foster," replied the officer, in a voice which made Harry start and wonder where he had heard it before. "Thou hast done best by following thy own counsel, inasmuch as these men might have been tempted to offer more resistance if they had been driven out into the open, and in that case there would have been undoubtedly more effusion of blood."

The Corporal, who was apparently one of that severe class of fanatics, groaned dismally and remarked that it was lamentable that any of the uncircumcised should have survived the volley poured down from above.

"Thou shouldst bear in mind, Corporal," said the officer, gently, "that the Lord who hath delivered us out of Egypt hath also commanded us to shew mercy to the stranger within our gates and the captive of our bow and spear."

"Yea, Colonel," answered the Corporal, brightening up at the prospect of a religious argument; "but it is also written that the Captains of the tens, who, I take it, are men such as I, and the Captains of the thousands, who are of like rank to yourself, shall show no mercy to the Amorite, the Canaanite, the Perizzite, the Hivite, nor the Jebusite, and that the swords of the chosen of Israel shall devour all such and their eyes shall not pity them."

"Yea, truly, Corporal Foster," replied the officer, dropping the argumentative tone and resorting to one of sharp command; "but it is also written that thou shalt pay dutiful homage to the lawful rulers set over thee, and therefore see that the wounds of these unhappy men are attended to forthwith, the prisoners sent back to Fermoy under a sufficient escort, and prepare to accompany me with these two gentlemen within half an hour to the Lord General's quarters in Youghal."

The officer then dismounted and raised his barred face-guard, whereupon Harry recognised him to be the same young Parliamentarian whom Cuttard had taken prisoner two months before at Duncannon.

"War plays wanton tricks with men's destinies," said he, with a grave bow, "but I little thought, Mr. Dauntless, I should have had the honour of meeting you so soon and under such circumstances. My only regret is that I am unable to offer the same chivalrous terms which I lately received; but when I represent to the Lord General what obligations you have both laid me under" (here he bowed stiffly to Cuttard), "I have little doubt His Excellency will grant you conditions little less generous than your own."

Harry smiled grimly, and remarked that his late prisoner appeared to be very confident of either the merciful disposition of his General or his own influence over him; but, as for himself, he could not help having uncomfortable recollections of Drogheda and Wexford.

"I know that my father is little loved by the followers of the Man Charles Stuart," said the young Parliamentarian, flushing scarlet at the taunt; "I know that it is their habit to fetter the name of Oliver Cromwell with the most hideous lies ever invented; and so I do not expect to learn that you are well disposed to him. There is never a man of your party killed in a fair field whom he has not personally murdered — never a battle fought but he is charged with killing his prisoners after they had been admitted to quarter — never a common criminal punished with his just deserts whom he has not martyred. I have no doubt, Mr. Dauntless, that you do sincerely believe all these tales; and yet, I suppose, you have never even seen Oliver Cromwell, much less experienced what humanity he is capable of. Wherefore, Sir, until you have a better opportunity of judging personally, take it from me, his son, Henry Cromwell, that the Lord Governor of Ireland is a human being, — a living man, Mr. Dauntless, such as you are, with flesh, blood, heart, feelings, sorrows, joys, sympathies, failings, aye, and even virtues, — and is not a mere iron Moloch of blood, fire, and cruelty."

Harry bowed gravely and silently; and the young Colonel, who had worked himself into a high state of excitement during his speech, walked up and down the mill as if to calm himself. By and by, the Corporal entered and held a brief conversation with his officer, and the latter signed to Harry and Cuttard to accompany them outside, where they found four horses waiting for them.

As soon as they were mounted, they set off rapidly in a westerly direction; Harry and young Cromwell in advance, and Cuttard and the Corporal riding close behind. About sunset, they arrived at Cappoquin, and, riding down straight to the river, pulled up and dismounted on a little wooden pier. There were several labourers, sailors, horse-dealers, porters, and two or three better-dressed men lounging about; and the young Puritan officer and his Corporal drew one of the latter apart and held a long conversation with him, whilst Harry walked to the extremity of the pier in order to regard more closely a six-oared *Cot* that lay alongside.

It was the first time he had seen one of those curious craft that are still used on the Blackwater, and he was musing on its unusual build and the little spade-shaped paddles lying across the knees of the men on board, when Cuttard, who had been sauntering jauntily about by himself, approached and plucked him by the sleeve.

"Hist, Harry," said he, in a low voice, "yawn, and look unconcerned, but hearken. I have been pumping the Corporal on our way hither, and learned incidentally that young Bottle-Shoulders intends to leave the horses here and cart us twain down to Youghal by water. Now, I have met an old friend among yonder horse-copers, and have come to a certain little understanding with him whereby I hope to give our friends the slip lower down. Wilt join me, Harry?"

Although the young Puritan had neither asked nor received parole from his prisoners, Harry by no means favoured this project, and he endeavoured to transmit some of his own lately acquired trust in Cromwell's humanity to the troop-adjutant, but that gentleman shook his head in a superlatively cunning fashion.

"Whatever chance of mercy you may have at the hands of that bloody-minded old tyrant," said he, "I am quite assured I would have none. I have very many private reasons to avoid an interview with Old Copper Face, and therefore intend to part company with his amiable young son when I can, and if you will take the advice of an old campaigner you will just pop overboard along with me when I say good-bye."

At this moment the approach of the two Puritans interrupted the conversation of the prisoners. Henry Cromwell pointed to the *Cot*, whereupon Harry took his place in the stern, while Cuttard, with an assumption of great modesty, took his far forward in the bows; and as soon as Colonel Cromwell had seated himself beside Harry and the Corporal had scrambled beside Cuttard, the oarsmen pushed off and swung the boat with a strong dip of their paddles far out into the middle of the Blackwater.

As they sped down the river, whose densely wooded banks were rendered darker by the gathering shades of the winter evening, the boatmen raised one of those low, melancholy, Gaelic chants such as their ancestors had very likely sung a thousand years before, and which the stray English tourist of these days may hear their descendants sing in the summer evenings. Harry and the Puritan Colonel were silent and thoughtful, for the deep shadows on the river, the dip and gurgle of the paddles, the plaintive chant of the boatmen, and the low solemn tones of Cuttard and Corporal Oh-Let-Me-Be-Thankful Foster, who were engaged in a deep religious controversy, were accessories well calculated to sober the most frivolous nature.

By and by, the moon swung out its great silver shield upon the clear frosty sky; and, just as it rose, they glided by an island, bordered with white sand and densely fringed with pine-trees that nodded and sighed mournfully in the sharp night breeze. Then the stately tower of a great Castle rose up almost from the water's edge on their right; and the young Puritan, indicating it with an air of scarcely concealed triumph, informed his prisoner that it was Temple Michael. Harry, already acquainted with the gallant effort which its last proud possessor had made to withstand the march of Cromwell, sighed as he beheld the ragged gap in its massive walls; and the boatmen, whether from respect to the once mighty family that had lately held it, or from some secret arrangement, suddenly ceased their song and rested their paddles, while the *Cot*, impelled solely by the current, floated slowly past.

"How now, knaves," said the young Colonel, "what means this? it is not such a long pull from Cappoquin, that you should require to rest at a spot where the tide flows least?"

"It is not on that account, your honour," said the chief boatman, who, being a descendant of one of the Elizabethan Planters, consequently spoke English perfectly, "but we are unwilling to row past Garrett's Ferry with song and stroke at this hour."

"If this is the spot which the malignant, Garrett FitzGerald, used as his ferry when alive," said Henry Cromwell, "I do not see how that fact should make you fear to row by it now that he is dead and unable to do further harm."

"I do not know whether the Geraldine used this spot as his ferry or not when he was alive," was the sullen reply, "but I know that he uses it now, to the destruction of anyone daring enough to row in it after nightfall."

The young Puritan scornfully bade the man explain his words more fully.

"Why, Sir," said the boatman, looking fearfully about him, "when your honour's father knocked the old walls about and drove Garrett Cromagh out of Temple Michael, they say it broke his heart in pieces. His clan buried him in Ardmore, but his soul does not rest easy there and must needs wander until his body is brought to the North Abbey in Youghal. Men say he wishes to lie with his own kith, and a voice which is not of this world cries aloud to every boat which dippeth oars in these waters after nightfall to beg a ferry for Garrett; and every boat's crew that hears that hail cometh to misfortune ere a month is past. Therefore as we do not wish to risk either our boat or our lives by awakening such unearthly passengers, we will not wet a paddle until we are clear of this uncanny water."

The boat continued to drift along with the tide for some distance until the young Puritan gentleman, overcoming the uncomfortable feeling which the superstition of the age and the melancholy surroundings had imposed even on his rigid spirit, bade the oarsmen give way, as they were already beyond the limits of the water of Temple Michael. Just as the stroke raised his paddle, a voice, so appealing, so melancholy, and so unearthly that it froze the blood of those who heard it, cried out from the willows on the left bank of the river:—

"*Garrath a Harrowing! Oh! an Garrath a Harrowing!*"[1]

Young Henry Cromwell dropped back aghast in the stern, and Harry, scarcely less startled, shrank up against him. The boatmen cowered trembling over their oars with a terror which was very real or excellently assumed, and the Corporal, shutting his eyes close and opening his mouth wide, bellowed out:—

"Into thy Hands, Oh Lord! Into thy hands I commend my spirit. Be thou my buckler against the snares of Sathan and all his false gods."

The only person who appeared unaffected by this apparently unearthly summons was Cuttard, who, rising up in the prow of the boat, bade Harry jump for his life, and sprang overboard in the twinkling of an eyelid.

Although he was heavily accoutred in horseman's boots and buff-coat, it is quite possible the bold renegade would have escaped, if he had only succeeded in disarming the soldier-like vigilance of Corporal Oh-Let-Me-Be-Thankful Foster in the same easy fashion as he had dispelled all doubts about the state of his soul. But that saintly warrior, well aware of the military and spiritual advantages to be obtained by those who

[1] "A ferry for Garrett! Oh! give Garrett a ferry."

watch as well as pray, no sooner heard the splash over the side when he opened his eyes very wide indeed, shut his mouth immediately, and, wresting a paddle from one of the boatmen, struck Mr. Cuttard on the head as soon as he rose from the surface. The blow, which was delivered with the edge of the paddle, was sufficiently heavy to have split any ordinary skull in two; but it had no worse effect upon the thick head of Cuttard than to render him unconscious, and, as he drifted by, Cromwell and Dauntless dragged him over the side and laid him bleeding and shivering at the bottom of the boat.

As soon as he came to, he gasped out a request for his late assailant.

"Corporal," said he, faintly, "touching that flask of brandy which you told me you carried as a corrective to the noxious drinking water of this infernal country, I beseech you give me a sip for the sake of good King Lemuel, who said, give strong drink unto him who is ready to perish and wine unto him who is heavy of heart."

The Corporal, in obedience to a gesture from his officer, crept aft among the rowers and put the neck of his canteen to the lips of the semi-conscious prisoner. Cuttard's teeth chattered round the tin nozzle of the flask; but, though he was suffering intensely from the combined effects of cold and shock, he smiled sweetly up in the grim face of the Corporal and whispered. "*Nunc est bibendum nunc pede libero*, as that dear merry-hearted gentleman of Rome used to say," and then held on to the flask so lovingly that Corporal Oh-Let-Me-Be-Thankful had to use considerable force to take it from him after a long, sweet, gurgling interval.

"What doth he say?" asked Cromwell, bending forward to catch the faint accents of the half-unconscious man.

"Please your Honour, I do not quite understand," said the Corporal, in some perplexity; "but from the word '*est*,' I do think that the obscene beast was saying the Mass, so, if it please you, I shall transfix him with my dagger through the fifth rib, even as Abner smote Ashael by the pool of Gibeon."

"On thy life, do him no harm," answered his commander, hastily. "All I lay upon thee is not to suffer him to make another attempt to escape, for even if I were to offer the poor wretch his liberty on condition of swimming ashore he would perish ere he had gone a dozen yards in those bitter cold waters."

The Corporal remarked with a dismal groan that such whitewashed sepulchres of Sathan ought to be levelled with the ground, and looked extremely disappointed at not being permitted to carry out that pious work on the earthly habitation of whatever represented Mr. John Cuttard's soul. However, he consoled himself by sitting as closely to his religious apostate as he conveniently could, and kept his strong hand firmly clenched on Cuttard's sodden belt until the boat arrived at the Water Gate of Youghal.

Here, Cuttard was taken in charge by two musketeers of the guard, who assisted him ashore; then, the young Parliamentary Colonel conducted his prisoners along the deserted moonlit street, and, turning abruptly up a very narrow lane, brought them into a tiny little square formed by three or four ancient houses on the right, a fine fortified dwelling-house on the left, and a venerable old Church in front.

In this little square a sentinel stood, with his armour gleaming in the full light of the moon, and young Henry Cromwell stepped aside, to exchange a few words with him in an undertone. The man pointed to the Church, whereupon his officer nodded and led his prisoners round to its Western front and through a low, arched doorway.

The roof had been stripped off and the moonlight shone through the arches overhead and the bare, black oak rafters, as through the ribs of some gigantic skeleton. There were a number of horses tethered on either side to the beautiful old oak stalls. Six soldiers sat smoking composedly on the stone floor around a fire, and the fragments of rich old carvings that smouldered on the latter, the horses, and litter, showed with what indifference the followers of Cromwell had appropriated the sacred building for the joint purpose of a guard-room and a stable.

Passing by the guard, the Parliamentary Colonel turned abruptly to his right and stopped before a tall oak screen, over which a red glare wavered from some strong light within. He opened a door in the screen and disclosed to Harry's eyes the only uninjured portion of the building. It was that Southern transept of the venerable old church of St. Mary's, which is known as the Chapel of the Saviour, and, by the light of half a dozen torches stuck in various corners, Harry saw a sight which was fated to be impressed on his memory as long as he lived.

A big, heavy man, wearing a tarnished cuirass and a dirty buff-coat, sat with his back to Harry at a little table in the centre of the Chapel. Before him stood a little, squirming man dressed in a respectable suit of black broadcloth. To the right of the table and at the foot of a splendid tomb of coloured marble, surrounded by a beautiful, wrought-iron railing, was a black, gaping space in the pavement, and a heap of black, greasy-looking clay, with a pile of bricks and some freshly made mortar, left little doubt as to what this excavation was intended for.

The young Parliamentary Colonel raised his hand, and Harry and his companions stopped short, while the man at the table spoke as follows to the little, squirming man in broadcloth:

"Now, Master Crutchett, I shall feel greatly beholden to you if you will remember this, my message, to the worthy but misguided gentleman who has heretofore held forth in this steeple-house which he is pleased to call his church. Tell him that we poor wanderers from Egypt have already found ministers in the wilderness, and though, perchance, they may not be so cultured as he, nevertheless, they are chosen instruments of the tribe of Levi and well fitted to perform the work which the Lord hath laid upon them. Methinks I have already told Mr. Hoyte that my poor, silly soldiers are too simple-minded to appreciate his learned discourses; but, alack-a-day, he evidently will not take my poor word for this, and must needs send you to me with a message about his right to officiate in his own church, with other skimble-skamble and prelatic nonsense. Now, hark ye, Mr. Crutchett, do not forget to impress upon Mr. Hoyte, with my sincere love, that if he has the presumption to appear to-night at the obsequies of our dear departed brother, I shall set him in the stocks to-morrow for two hours, though he were the highest Jack that wore a surplice among the Steeple Men of the Church of England. Do I make myself plain, Mr. Crutchett?"

The agonising wriggles of the little man in black could not be mistaken for anything but a sign of the most perfect comprehension, so the man at the table continued:—

"Now, as to his formally cited objection as to our depositing the remains of our late brother and co-worker in the regeneration of England in the vault of the Boyles, whom carnal men term Earls of Cork, let this same meddling gentleman know, that if it were My Will to lay the corpse of the humblest soldier who ever carried a pike in the Cause of the Commonwealth of England by the side of a King, I would have no saucy priest that ever wore bands talk to Me of desecration, for I consider such dust sufficient to ennoble the vain ashes they would mingle with. Therefore, Master Crutchett, I prithee beg your worthy pastor not to send me any more messages about rights to officiate, faculties for opening graves, and such matters, which, if you will pardon me for so describing them, appear to my poor understanding to be very tiresome and silly. And now, my dear friend, although I am as much your servant as my humble position maketh me, I prithee remember there are many who have equal claims upon my time, so, if you have no further business with me, I entreat you to allow me to attend to the affairs of others."

The poor little man in black needed no second hint to tell him that the interview was ended, and, looking more dead than alive, he backed out hastily through those who stood at the screen doorway. Henry Cromwell walked over to the table, made a military salute, and, bending down, said something in a low voice to the last speaker.

"Bring them in front of me, so that I may see their countenances," said he, in a deep but not unpleasant voice, and Harry stepped forward, whilst the troopers assisted the faltering steps of Cuttard to a spot beside him.

The man at the table raised his head and looked from one to the other with a sharp look of interrogation, and Harry regarded him, in turn, with a feeling of breathless awe.

There could be no doubt as to the identity of that harsh, keen, thoughtful countenance; no doubt as to the being who owned those clear, perceptive, hawk-like eyes, the stern mouth under its tuft of bristling grey moustache, the deep, determined furrows which ran in straight lines from the coarse nostrils to the grimly set lower jaw, the thin, iron-grey hair which straggled over the muscular neck. It was Oliver Cromwell, the late Brewer of Huntington, and at that moment the virtual King of England.

XXXI

WITHOUT moving his terrible amber eyes from the faces of the prisoners, he asked his son, in the drawling tones affected by his party, if they had been taken in arms.

"Yes, your Excellency," was the nervous reply, "but the obligations under which I stand to these gentlemen are of so great a nature that I took upon myself to transgress your commands in order that you might deal with them yourself."

"Ah, Harry, Harry!" said Cromwell, with a sad smile and a half-reproachful look at his son. "Dost thou too shrink from the duty which the work of the Lord hath laid upon thee? Alas! that mine own son, in common with so many faint hearts, should wish to transmit all the doubt, the responsibility, and the answering for blood upon me, and say thus to thyself: 'Lo! My Father's shoulders are broad enough to bear the share of the burden which I dare not essay to claim for my portion.' Well, Boy, well, if thou hast transgressed thy explicit orders to mete out death to the leaders of the Malignants, far be it from me to unsheathe the slaughter weapon which thy hand has not been resolute in holding forth, inasmuch as the Parliament of England, in whose great hands I am but a humble instrument, is very just and very, very merciful, being, as it were, an exceeding gentle Mother who desireth the repentance and amendment of the lives of her froward and unruly children, rather than their condign punishment. Wherefore, if the answers of these twain shall satisfy me as to their fitness to be regarded in the light of misguided, but otherwise blameless characters, I can doubtless find them places on board a ship bound for the Barbadoes and now lying weatherbound at the Cove of Cork."

Barbadoes! The word pierced Harry Dauntless like a wound. It meant lifelong slavery under cruel taskmasters in the plantations. It meant an unhealthy climate and banishment from all he held dear. Barbadoes! It seemed worse than death itself.

He was roused from his state of stupefied despair by the voice of Cromwell, asking him what rank he and his companion held in the Royal Army.

The tones, although nasal and affected, had nothing in them to indicate the blood-thirsty ferocity such as party hatred had attributed to the questioner, and Dauntless accordingly told him composedly what position he and his companion occupied.

"Verily, subordinate, but nevertheless honourable positions," was the comment, with a drawl of affected humility, "inasmuch as we read that the mighty Thirty so beloved of David attained to no higher rank than such as you hold. Tell me, young Sir, from whom you received your commissions?"

Harry felt the cold wet hand of his companion laid on his wrist with a clutch such as a drowning man might have exerted, but as he expected nothing more from Cromwell's mercy or vengeance, he answered without hesitation that their commissions were from the Supreme Council of the Confederation of Kilkenny.

At this moment a gust of night wind, which found its unobstructed way through the broken windows and ruined walls of the adjoining church, blew in the door of communication. The piercing wind stirred the tattered banners hung aloft in the little Chapel of the Saviour, and brought a faint smell of earth from the open grave at the foot of the marble tomb on his left. The flames of the candles wavered and burned blue for a second, and a thin stream of melted grease ran round the stem of that on the table like a winding-sheet. Cromwell rose from his seat, kicked to the door with his heavy boot, and then turned round and regarded his prisoner with such a look as made the latter feel he had never been in closer company with Death than at that moment.

"Verily, unhappy young man," said he, with a terrible expression on his harsh face, "out of thine own mouth hast thou condemned thyself." His son gasped as if he had received a sudden blow, and commenced a supplication on behalf of the prisoners, but Cromwell stopped him by raising one large, grey-gauntleted hand in rebuke.

"Nay, Boy," said he, sternly, "plead not for them, for it is not meet or fitting that mine own son should try to let and hinder the course of retributive justice merely because these obscene ministers of Sathan have laid him under obligations. The same Voice which commands us to have pity upon the vanquished hath also laid upon us as a statute and an ordinance to our generation for ever that those who have committed murder and idolatry must answer for their crimes with their life blood. These Confederates have shed the blood of the Saints at Benburb, Newry, Athlone, and elsewhere; and therefore their name, like the remembrance of Amalek, must be blotted out from under the vault of Heaven without pity or remorse. Peace, Boy, peace; I say these men must die, for they have wrought much folly in Israel. Corporal Foster," — the Corporal stepped up to the table and raised his hand to the rim of his steel cap in salute, — "how many men keep guard by the horses in the steeple-house?"

"Six, an' it please your Excellency," was the answer.

"Fetch two more from the Corps d' Garde in the College," was the stern command. "Bid them all load with ball ammunition and then lead out these men and shoot them to death. The moon shineth fairly enough against the Southern wall to enable them to fulfil their orders."

"Father, I beseech thee, hear me," began the young Colonel, imploringly, but Cromwell stopped him again.

"I tell thee, Harry," said he, with a frown, "that this mistaken chivalry on thy part shall avail these fellows little good and thyself still less credit. They own to being Confederates, and I tell thee that if Castlehaven, their arch priest in wickedness and idolatry, stood along with them, he should also sup the bitterness of death."

"Then," said Cuttard, hoarsely, "if die we must, let me prefer a last request."

He shook off the hold of the two soldiers who had up to this been holding him loosely, and, staggering over to the table, laid both his hands upon it to prevent himself falling. His wet clothes clung so miserably on his bony frame that he looked like a scarecrow after a thunderstorm, and his eyes peered forth from under his blood-matted hair with so wild and animal-like an expression that Cromwell involuntarily started back and drew a pistol from his belt.

The two musketeers instantly sprang upon the troop-adjutant and dragged him violently back from the table; whereupon Cromwell, as if ashamed of having shown any symptoms of fear of such a wretched-looking being, returned the pistol to his belt and asked Cuttard sternly what statement he desired to make.

"A favour, Noll, a favour," said Cuttard, thickly, for the blow on his head and the brandy he had drunk had affected his speech. "A favour to a friend, for the sake of old times."

Cromwell regarded the unsteady figure with a look of scornful contempt.

"The man is drunk," said he to the Corporal, in a tone of unutterable disgust. "Put him and his companion in ward for the night, and, if the brute is sober enough to meet his end by noon to-morrow, see that my orders are then carried out."

"I never was so sober in all my life, more is the pity," interposed the prisoner, sorrowfully; "and, I prithee, Noll, for the sake of our old friendship listen to me for a moment."

"How, now, you brandy-smelling disgrace to manhood," said Cromwell, in a voice that sounded like the growl of an angry mastiff. "Tell me who you are at once, or I shall have you triced up and flogged with ramrods until the blood squirts into your boots."

"Why, Old Rakehell," said Cuttard, thrusting back his matted hair from his face, "dost not remember John Cuttard of Northampton, thy old pupil at tuck, primero, and brag? Ah! Noll, Noll, many a time have we two seen the morning-light coming creeping through the windows of thy chambers over the Gate in Lincoln's Inn, aye! and many a time have we missed its coming altogether, when we sat all night in the Painted Wine-Vault of Mother Mercer in Alsatia. Lord bless us both! how often I have sat with thee learning those lessons which have since so benefited me in the world, and yet, and yet, thou dost pretend to forget me. Well, Noll, well, I do forgive thee, for thou wert a sportsman and a jolly companion at that time, though I suppose thou wouldst not undertake to tell the difference between a dice-box and a wine-cup now, but if there is any corner left in thy heart for the memory of those merry, waggish old times, grant me a request before I die."

Cromwell, who had not moved a muscle of his face throughout this wild speech, continued to regard Cuttard with an unchanging look of disgustful contempt, but his fingers closed convulsively within his soiled, grey gauntlets as though he were endeavouring to strangle some painful recollection by mere bodily exertion.

"What not a word, my gay old ruffler of the Inns?" said Cuttard, with a drunken leer. "Well, silence gives consent, so here is my request; namely, complete what thou didst begin and take a carbine and join the firing party thyself. Ho! but we three should make quite a striking tableau. Thou, the Chief pillar of the Temple, this young gallant, the son of our old friend, Dashing Dauntless, and I, thy loving pupil and companion. Why, it would be the making of one of the best farcical tragedies ever produced within the walls of a theatre. Ha! Ha! Ho! Ho! Ho!"

Cuttard leaned up easily against one of his guards and burst into a fit of laughter so horrible and nerve-jarring that Harry's blood curdled at the sound. The young Puritan Colonel stared at the troop-adjutant with amazement and indignation depicted on his face, and the two musketeers glanced threateningly at him, but the prisoner laughed on for a full minute notwithstanding this discouragement and the additional menace conveyed by the Corporal, who drew off one of his gloves and deliberately rolled it up into a compact ball about the same calibre as Mr. Cuttard's open mouth.

Cromwell, himself, maintained the same appearance of unruffled composure wherewith he had regarded Cuttard from the first. The steady amber-coloured eyes never wavered for an instant or showed any indication of anger or agitation, the stern mouth continued to keep its rigid curl of scorn; but the brown face lost somewhat of its colour, and the clenched hand in the grey gauntlet closed tighter and tighter on the table each moment.

As soon as the last echo of Cuttard's unnatural merriment had died away, Cromwell turned to his son and asked how the wretch had come by the drink that had so brutalised him. His voice was perfectly natural and controlled, but the pallor of his face became even more pronounced as he spoke. Henry Cromwell commenced a hurried account of Cuttard's attempted escape, and had got as far as the incident wherein the Corporal had played so leading a part when he stopped suddenly, and at that moment Harry observed the big, grey-gauntleted hand slip off the table and swing down heavily at arms-length by the side of the chair.

Cromwell sat back and pressed his hand in a troubled way to his forehead, whilst his son with a look of deep concern bent down and asked him tenderly if he were ill.

"Somewhat faint and giddy," was the low reply. "Lend me thy arm, Boy, and lead me to my lodgings in the College. I would fain lie down a while, Harry; I would fain take a little rest. I have been overtaxing my poor frail carcase beyond its strength, and if I did deceive myself by treating it as though it were iron, this moment of giddiness hath reminded me I am but poor flesh and blood like other men."

He rose ponderously to his feet, gave some directions to the Corporal in a low voice, and then left the Chapel, leaning on the arm of his son.

As soon as father and son had withdrawn, the Corporal conducted his prisoners to a coffin-shaped aperture in a corner of the Chapel, and led them up a very narrow stone stair into what had been in former times the organ-loft, but which was then a wilderness of debris. Notwithstanding its ruinous condition, it made a very secure prison, for the floor, in addition to being thirty feet from the ground, overhung that portion of the Chancel where the stable guard sat round their fire.

Harry and his companion were treated much better than they expected, for, later on, the Corporal carried up to them a couple of rations of boiled beef dressed with a thick, white sauce made of flour and vinegar, and one of those generous earthenware jars known as a "Youghal dandy," which proved to be full of excellent ale. He likewise brought a change of dry clothing for Cuttard, — an attention much appreciated by that gentleman, who took occasion to remark cheerfully that his mind now felt perfectly at rest as to the morrow, as he no longer had reason to fear an attack of rheumatism, which he considered one of the most painful disorders wherewith flesh could be afflicted.

The Corporal stood apart in grim silence until they had finished their supper, when he collected the platters and the dandy (which Cuttard took good care to see went away empty), posted a sentinel at the foot of the stair, and left the two friends to reflect upon their equivocal position.

As soon as they were alone, Harry asked his companion eagerly what had induced him to use such extraordinary language to Cromwell, and if he could explain why they had not been immediately shot in consequence.

"Why, Harry," mumbled the troop-adjutant, sleepily, for the fumes of the brandy still lurked in his head, and his supper had imparted a blissful sense of peace towards all living creatures, "it was my last card, but whether it will prove a trump or not, we shall find out for ourselves in the morning" (a prodigious yawn). "There is generally a spot in every man's life whereby he can be jogged at will, provided" (yawn) "you know where to lay your finger; and as Noll's secret spring is remorse for his early roistering" (yawn), "I pressed it with what result you have already seen — Y-e-e-o-w — I wish the Corporal had left the jug, for even though it were empty, it was a pleasant sight to contemplate."

Harry asked him how he hoped to benefit by such a questionable method of attracting Cromwell's sympathy.

"Why," said Mr. Cuttard, rolling himself up in his borrowed cloak, which was much too short for him, "Noll may be the master of many men, but he is the veriest slave to his own conscience. May the devil fry the tailor that made this cloak, for a parsimonious sneak-cloth! I have known Cromwell return money that he had won at play twenty years before. Aye, and it was given back in hard times too, when he was on his way to Virginia, and if he insisted upon men receiving back sums which they neither wanted nor remembered losing, why, it would puzzle the nicety of his conscience to shoot an old friend like myself whom he himself had helped to the Devil" (prolonged yawn). "Not that I blame Noll for my downfall, for if he had not been in the way, I would have found plenty of others to shew the path I was seeking myself."

Harry next enquired if his own father and Cromwell had been intimate during the days of their studentship, but he was unable to get much information on this subject, as the troop-adjutant was almost asleep.

"Can't say," he grunted drowsily. "Only once saw 'em together — time I jockeyed Walter Dauntless. Noll twigged loaded dice too (Honk) 'ceedingly 'shamed of me to do him justice — would have cast me off (Honk) if I had let him" (self-satisfied chuckle) "knew too much to let him do *that* (Honk) gave me two chances to reform (Honk) not all iron-heart — Noll — be all ri-ght morning (Honk)."

And after two or three more premonitory rasps, Mr. Cuttard was snoring like a saw-pit in full operation.

Harry, much too agitated to sleep, lay for some time listening to the subdued murmur of the stable guard, who kept watch in the Chancel, while his thoughts dwelt mournfully on Shanganagh, his mother, his wife, and his own unfortunate love. Ever since his arrival in the South he had daily looked for a letter, a message, even a token, which would have revived his dying expectation, but the long-continued silence of Aileen had so affected his sensitively affectionate nature that love and hope seemed moribund already in his heart.

He had lain for some hours in a state of wakeful wretchedness when he was suddenly startled by hearing the measured tramp of armed men filing into the Chapel of the Saviour, followed by the jar and clatter of musket butts striking on the tiled floor. His first surmise was that the firing party had come to execute Cromwell's suspended sentence on them, and he sat up with every nerve tugging in his body for a few minutes; but as the time passed and no one appeared, he regained his composure. His next thought was that some guard was being posted or relieved below; however, the continuous tramp of rank upon rank, which continued to enter the Chapel, soon dispelled that assumption, as his own military experience suggested that so many men were not likely to be employed for such a duty.

Half-way down the stairs was a little unglazed window overlooking the Chapel, and curiosity induced him to steal down the steps and peep through.

The building below was filled from end to end with closely packed ranks of red-coated soldiers. Each one wore a knot of green and black mourning ribbons in his helmet, each one leaned on his reversed musket, each stern, clean-shaven face exhibited a differently expressed look of dignified sorrow. A hundred flambeaux lit up the little Chapel of the Saviour with a glare brighter than that of a tropical sun at midday, and the resinous exhalations of the torches streaming overhead in a thick unguent vapour settled in the groining of the roof like a funeral pall.

By the side of the grave he had previously observed at the foot of the beautiful marble tomb of the Cork family lay a common deal coffin, and, even from where he was, he could distinctly read on the lid in plain white letters the name and date of the decease of its occupant. Harry Dauntless started and held his breath. It was the funeral of Michael Jones, who had died on the previous morning at Dungarvan.

Six officers of the deceased General's regiment lowered the coffin into its place; and when they had rendered that office, Harry observed Cromwell step forward and take his place at the head of the grave.

He was in buff-coat and breastplate, booted and spurred as if he were about to take the field. His hands were clasped behind his back, his legs spread far apart, and his chin bowed down on his breast; but, though his pose was inelegant and his covered head gave no indication of any outward show of respect, there was something about the stoop of those broad shoulders and the pensive hang of the massive head which betokened a sincerer sorrow than falls to most men for the loss of a mere comrade. He raised his head abruptly and drew from his pocket a small, travel-stained Bible. Then he slipped his sheathed broadsword from the frog of his shoulder-belt, and, leaning on it as though it were a cane, commenced to read a verse from the book in a droning, affected fashion.

He took as his text, "Know ye that this day there hath fallen a Prince of Israel;" and as soon as he had concluded, he replaced the book in his pocket and burst forth into one of those incoherent rhapsodies which at that time were considered by the enthusiasts of the Independents' party as the acme of religious eloquence.

His discourse embraced so many wild hyperboles and allegories, and his zeal, or rather religious frenzy, lured him into such extraordinary flights of fancy, some of which soared little short of actual blasphemy, that if Harry had not known the reputation for abstemiousness and keenness of intellect for which Cromwell was renowned, he would have thought that the preacher was either raving drunk or insane. But the remainder of Cromwell's auditors were obviously impressed with other and very different sentiments. Every countenance exhibited an universal look of fervour which varied only in degree according to the temperament of each. Grim faces lighted up here and there under their steel caps with the fierce eagerness of fanaticism, many marked their approval of certain periods of the funeral sermon with gloomy nods of approval, deep-drawn sighs from sturdy chests marked the emotion of some, and a choking gasp here and there indicated others even more affected; while none betrayed for a moment the least diminution of attention to the seemingly interminable flow of nonsense which Cromwell continued to pour forth until he was compelled to stop from sheer vocal and bodily exhaustion.

He wiped the profuse perspiration from his face with the cuff of his grey gauntlet and made a sign to his staff of officers. One by one they passed by the open grave, each one stooping and casting in a handful of clay in the coffin below; and then, rank by rank, the soldiers filed slowly by and trampled out through the chancel, through the nave, and so into the night. In a few minutes the Chapel of the Saviour was deserted by all except Cromwell and a couple of gravediggers and masons, and the former walked gloomily backwards and forwards while the gravediggers filled in the clay, and the masons replaced the brickwork and flagging. When they had finished their work, they withdrew, and Cromwell stood alone and thoughtful for a few minutes by the freshly mortared flagstone. Then he sighed, took up the solitary lantern, and stalked off also into the night, and the Church was once more left in silence and darkness save for the red glow of the watch-fire and the measured pace of the sentinel in the chancel below. Harry retraced his steps softly to the organ-loft, rolled himself in his cloak, and almost immediately fell asleep. He was roused some hours after by a heavily booted foot being thrust into his side, and, opening his eyes with a start, perceived it was already daylight. A soldier, closely wrapped in a large watch-cloak, stood beside him; and, assuming that he was about to be led out to die, he asked the man in as composed a manner as he could assume if that were the reason of his appearance. The soldier shook his head and then nodded successively in the direction of Cuttard and the staircase, so Harry laid his hand upon the troop-adjutant's shoulder, whereupon that person snorted, stirred, sat up, and, after regarding the muffled soldier with one swift look of intelligence, instantly arose and made his way down the stairs, closely followed by Harry.

The sentinel at the foot of the stairs had been withdrawn, and, finding a side door open, Cuttard and his companion stepped out into the Churchyard, and walked on boldly to the head of the street, until a warning cough made them look back to the cloaked soldier, who intimated by a sidelong gesture of his head that they were to direct their steps towards the left.

The three men entered that ancient garden wherein Sir Walter Raleigh had so often lounged away the pleasant summer evenings with Edmund Spenser long, long before. It was covered with hoar-frost then, however, and every detail in the delightful old pleasaunce looked dead and bare. They passed down a narrow, box-bordered path, whose vista was terminated in the grey wall of the town rampart, and walked on, crunching the frozen pebbles beneath their heavy horsemen's boots until they stopped before a strong, iron-clenched door. The man who had hitherto followed them at some distance now brushed roughly in between them, and, after some fumbling in the folds of his heavy cloak, produced a key wherewith he opened the door and motioned them to pass through.

Outside the immensely thick walls they found two horses tethered to the wheel of a broken caisson, and without further comment Cuttard unfastened their bridles and swung himself up into the saddle of one, while Harry followed his example and mounted the other.

There was an embarrassing pause for a moment, and then Harry ventured to ask if they were free to depart; and, if so, might they not also have their weapons returned to them for their personal protection?

The man in the cloak silently handed two neatly folded papers to Dauntless, and the latter felt a tremor run through him on observing that the hand that delivered them was covered with a greasy, grey gauntlet.

"I think, young Sir," said he, drily, after a pause, "that you shall find that paper will afford you more protection than a thousand soldiers at your back. Do not ask why such favour hath been shown, and place no vain hope in its availing you beyond the limit set forth, so make what use you can of it ere its virtues wax cold. As for you, unhappy man," he continued, indicating Cuttard with one thick forefinger, "regard not this favour as a charter for the continuance of your evil ways, but merely as a chance of amendment, which, if not availed of, shall prove no more than a brief suspension of the sentence that must otherwise overtake you ere long. Once more, both of you, take heed of my words, for they come from one who doth not usually warn twice." And with these words Cromwell withdrew inside the postern door, which he immediately closed and bolted.

The two friends sat staring at one another for some minutes, overcome with awe of the terrible man in whose hands the lives of princes and nobles were as indifferent as those of the humblest labourers. A sentinel appeared on the great wall above, and in a sharply pitched London accent bade them begone, at the same time blowing in a menacing way upon the match of his piece, so they turned and rode up the steep hill that overhangs the town. On the summit they drew bridle and looked back.

Below them nestled Youghal in the cold light of the winter morning, with its encircling battlements as defiantly raised as they are at present, and beneath their walls curved the Blackwater, like a great Scimitar of Syracuse workmanship that had been laid by some protecting giant between the town and the firm, white sands of Ballinatray on the Eastern shore.

Harry slowly unfolded the papers, and read their contents with a mournful smile. One was a pass for Cuttard to Virginia, the other was a protection for himself and his family, with liberty to proceed to any port or ports in England or Ireland, and thence to any port abroad within the next thirty days. Both protections were written, signed, and sealed by Cromwell himself.

"At another time," murmured Harry, softly, "I would have cheerfully parted with all my worldly gear in exchange for such a favour; but now it seems as vain and trifling as the fortune which my fatuous kinsman, Evir, once promised me on the assurance of a worthless gambling bond. Come, Jack, come," he added aloud, and there was a bitter ring in his voice. "We have both been made a present of our valuable lives, and so let us be jogging towards Killaloe, where we can consider at our leisure what is to be done with them."

At that very moment, when the two comrades turned their horses' heads westward, a horseman rode out of the gates of Dublin, and trotted briskly along the Athlone road. That horseman was Con MacGauran. In his goatskin wallet the simpleton carried a sealed safe conduct for his own person doubly secured by the signatures of the Parliamentary Commissioners of Dublin and the Marquess of Ormond, and shuffling about in the wallet in company with this document were two letters addressed to Harry Dauntless. One ran as follows:

For the hands of Master Dauntless, Captain of Horse in the Southern Army of the Young Man, Charles Stuart, these.

THE CASTLE AT DUBLIN,
30th Dec., 1649.

SIR, — These, by the hands of your own domestic, will, no doubt, surprise you, coming as they do from one whom you have never met, but who, nevertheless, has much reason to be beholden to you. Some time since, you were pleased to do me a great service at the cost of what must have been a grievous sacrifice, and my recollection of your generosity can never lose the sweetness of its savour. Though I can never expect to repay you in full, Mr. Dauntless, I rejoice exceedingly that the Lord hath just now put into my hands an opportunity of doing some service both to yourself and to those whose love must be ever precious to you, and on that account I hope that you will therefore accept my help now, in order that I may in a little measure repay somewhat of the debt I owe.

Yester morning, one of our Leinster pickets conveyed a young woman prisoner to Dublin Castle. She was brought before me, charged with the offence of attempting to pass through our lines to the rebel camp, and on questioning her as to her motive for essaying this hazardous and impossible feat, she confessed that it was in order to join her husband, who was among the followers of the Young Man, Charles Stuart.

My heart was touched with pity on hearing this story of wifely devotion, and I offered her a safe conduct, which she did very gladly accept; but whilst making out the necessary form, I learned her identity, and so changed my plans. Oh, Sir, you can now guess whose name I am about to write ere you read further, for she was no other than your own loving lady, Mistress Aileen Dauntless.

You may be sure, Mr. Dauntless, I was greatly startled to learn this (for she was but meanly dressed as a dairy wench, in order that she might the better hoodwink our sentinels), and I asked her if you were aware of her perilous venture. She blushed and answered in some hesitation that she feared you knew nothing of her undertaking, as you had failed to answer any of the many letters she had despatched to you, and on that account had resolved upon the desperate course of journeying a-foot through a hostile country in order to be with you. Thereupon I did what I deemed best for you both.

I made a show of severity, pretended that I had changed my

mind, refused the pass altogether, and said I would detain her in custody until I had proved the truth of her story. Then did she fall down before me, and never did man or woman so pray for life as she prayed for liberty, in order that she might imperil it again in seeking you. Her entreaties wrung my very heart-strings, and I had much ado to maintain the stern attitude that I had resolved to adopt towards her; however, I succeeded in winking back my tears, and ordered her to be lodged in safe ward, where she was to be permitted to have everything suitable to her rank and sex except her liberty.

And now, Mr. Dauntless, my great desire is to learn what is your will in this matter. Surely, you cannot be so fond as to imagine that the cause of the Young Man, Charles Stuart, is anything but a trembling ruin, already toppling to its foundations. Surely, you must know that the presence of Mistress Aileen Dauntless in a besieged city, or with the rear guard of a broken army, would be fraught with every danger to her life, and I cannot believe that you would wish her to be exposed to such perils.

If you will give me your undertaking not to bear arms against the Commonwealth for a twelve-month, I can easily procure your pardon and the secure protection of your property; but if you are so enamoured with the false glamour of the Stuarts as to desire death in their service, let me beseech you not to drag down your fair young wife to the same fate.

I shall anxiously await your reply by the hands of your servant, MacGauran, and assuring you of my heartfelt love for your person and my eagerness to perform all things according to your wishes, I write myself,

Your sincere friend and well-wisher,

RICHARD WILTONHOLME.

The other letter was from Aileen. It was dated likewise from Dublin Castle, and, though hastily written and almost incoherent in some of its passages, conveyed more passionate love in its margins than ever found expression on similar space through the cold, dead medium of ink and paper. It was blotted with tears. It was tearfully eloquent in its artless supplication for love and pardon. It was like the cry of some hungry creature begging for the food without which it must sink and die. I cannot set it down, for there are some phases in a woman's soul which are desecration to lay bare, and every word in that piteous letter had leaped there warm and glowing from the inmost cell of the writer's heart.

XXXII

A WEEK later, Dauntless and Cuttard rejoined the Royalist army at Killaloe and were received by their friends as though they had returned from the dead. Cuttard had obstinately refused to avail himself of his pass unless his companion also left the country; but as Harry, torn in two by his own secret sorrow, insisted on remaining on for the present, the two friends accordingly sought the only asylum that their party offered.

During the next three weeks Harry looked hourly for news from home, resolved that if he should receive the slightest encouragement from his wife during that period, he would resign his commission and withdraw with her and his mother to Virginia. Ireland was by this time no longer a country capable of either living in or being served any further; and none but the most desperate or enthusiastic of the Royalist party contemplated remaining on to encounter the final catastrophe.

The days dragged on painfully and hopelessly. Each day some friend bade him farewell and then fled abroad. Each day he saw the inevitable draw nearer, and at last in his despair he wrote to Aileen. He told her of Cromwell's merciful but conditional pardon, whereof he would avail himself or not according to her decision. He begged her therefore not to be less merciful than his late judge, and assured her that, as life without her love was unendurable, he would tear up the protection and share the fate of his other desperate companions unless she would consent to pity him.

But scarcely had he despatched this letter when all his pride returned. He had been guiltless of any wrong to her, he thought, and yet he had already humbled himself before her more than ever a man had done before woman. He had been repulsed with coldness and hatred, and now he was crawling once more to whine at her feet, perhaps, to be humiliated by some fresh insult — Perish the thought! His mother could not possibly have failed to transmit his faithful, loving message; and if Aileen had wanted him or his love, she would assuredly have written long before.

So he mounted his horse and rode at the peril of his life across country after his messenger, whom he overtook the next day at Athlone. Then he bade the astonished man return him his letter; and when he had torn it and Cromwell's protection into shreds, he returned sullenly to Castlehaven's army and his fate.

The following month Cromwell left Ireland, and his son-in-law, Ireton, set himself to dust off the country which his great relative had so thoroughly swept. Coote closed in from the North, driving his scattered enemies before him step by step; and Ireton, equally successful in the South, pushed them West; so that between the two Puritan armies the broken remnants of the Irish Cavaliers were gradually herded into Limerick, which by this time represented the last important stronghold in the two Islands still flying the ragged standard of King Charles. As ruin closed in slowly on him, Castlehaven lost whatever poor faculties of administration he ever possessed, and after one or two futile efforts to dam the advancing tides, threw one-half his foot into Galway and, retreating down the Shannon with the remainder of his infantry and all his cavalry, resigned them to Hugh Dhu O'Neill and then immediately fled to France.

The meeting between Hugh Dhu O'Neill and Dauntless was brimful of emotional feeling. It brought back to O'Neill all the memories and hopes that had been buried with his uncle, Owen Roe. It revived a thousand recollections in Harry's sad mind connected with the springtime of his love, the summer of his wooing, and the dead, cold winter of his unhappy marriage.

All who had started out so bravely in their company were dead or banished. Owen Roe lay in his unknown grave in Cavan Abbey; Florence MacMahon slept peacefully on Devenish Island; Evir MacMahon, the impetuous soldier-Bishop, and the foolish Sir Phelim O'Neill were broken fugitives, hiding no one knew where; Ormond and Castlehaven were at the Court of the exiled King in France, almost starving for lack of the common necessaries of life; and the indefatigable Daniel O'Neill was lurking in England, still hatching desperate plots among the English Royalists. The two reunited friends were well aware how precarious was their own present position, how hopeless their future; and, following the instinct of men drawn close together in times of deadly peril, they renewed their vows of comradeship and resolved to fight and fall together.

Almost the first person Harry encountered after leaving O'Neill was Hooter. This amiable person, although holding a colonel's commission from Ormond as a reward for his previous treachery to Parsons, was by no means an enthusiastic unit of the Royalist army. Indeed, he would have very gladly gone back to his first love, the Parliamentary side, if it had not been for a shrinking diffidence as to how his late friends might receive him, and on that account had elected to stay with the side which was as yet not inclined to hang him.

Before Harry was aware of his identity, Hooter rushed up to him, beaming all over, and grasping him by the hand saluted him in the most effusive manner. As soon as Harry recovered from his amazement, he shook himself free from the ex-pirate's grasp as though he were plague-stricken, and, stepping back with a look of overpowering disgust, peeled off his glove from the hand which Hooter had clasped so warmly.

"What, Captain Dauntless," said Hooter, with a look of good-humoured deprecation, "is not seven years enough to forget and forgive an incident wherein I was the worst sufferer? Fie! Fie! that is carrying a grudge beyond the limit that either a soldier or a gentleman should set. Come, Sir, come, let us shake hands and drown all unkind remembrances in a friendly glass, and if you will take my arm, I shall conduct you to a tavern wherein they keep some noble Madeira."

Harry dropped his glove on the ground as though it were infected and stepped back another pace.

"Colonel Hooter," said he, as calmly as he could, "you murdered one of my friends, nearly succeeded in making another of my friends murder myself, and, worse than all, your foul tongue mortally stabbed the happiness of my life. The cause which we are both sworn to sustain forbids my demanding now the only reparation you can ever make; but rest assured that the moment I am free I shall endeavour, Sir, to the best of my poor ability, to kill you; and until that fortunate time arrives, I trust we shall meet as seldom as possible."

He carefully gathered his cloak about him as if to avoid brushing against his enemy and deliberately crossed the street and walked on. Hooter stood regarding him with a look of the most malevolent hate and trembling all over with passion.

"Some seven years ago you took the same high tone to me, my gay young Captain," he muttered between his locked teeth, "and since then I have been the means of plucking a few plumes out of your tail feathers. Damned fool! Do you think I will risk my life for the pleasuring of a landless puppy like yourself, Pah!"

He spat furiously on the ground, and at the same moment switched the glove which Dauntless had dropped into the middle of the street with his walking cane. As the glove fluttered through the air, a small, bright object dropped out and rolled tinkling over the cobblestones; but before it had travelled far the worthy Colonel pounced on it, and after a brief examination transferred it to his pocket-book. He then flicked the empty glove to a convenient street culvert, and, having poked it down into this receptacle, carefully raked some garbage over it.

"My dear young Sir," he whispered as he directed a benevolent nod in the direction that Dauntless had gone, "you have never sailed among the Antilles, and therefore may not have heard of the *Guantes Españoles*.[1] However, I may soon have an opportunity of affording you a practical illustration of those dainty specimens of hand-gear, and if I am to be your glover on that occasion, I can assure you that I shall take more off your fingers than signet rings."

A month after this interview, Hooter abandoned his post at the Pass of Killaloe and fell back on Limerick before the advancing army of Coote; and a week after that event Ireton, who had been slowly working his way from Cork, drew in and invested the city on all sides.

One need only stroll around the ancient walls and count the long, green mounds which to this day mark the investing batteries, to learn how long and how fiercely were the dying fortunes of the Stuarts upheld in the "Citie of the Ships." Night and day the scarcely ever ceasing cannon of Ireton

[1] "Spanish Gloves." A horrible torture practised by the buccaneers. It consisted in winding a lighted musket-match around the fingers of the victim, whose hand was thus slowly reduced to cineration.

bellowed round the ramparts, creeping nearer and nearer each morning, and gradually reducing the stone fortifications to the consistency of bloody mortar; yet night and day the guns upon the walls answered shot for shot with dogged regularity, although the plague had appeared among the garrison, and was already playing as much havoc among them as the Parliamentary guns. There was no faintness of heart now, no thought of surrender, although the position of the garrison seemed hopeless in the extreme, for the remainder of the Clans, who formed the bulk of the defenders, freed from the depressing authority of Castlehaven, and once more under the leadership of an O'Neill of the Bloody Hand, faced death and disease with like unflinching courage.[1]

The first attack began upon the gate-house which defended the Clare end of the historical bridge. After three months' bloody fighting the Cromwellians fought their way sufficiently close to it to enable them to use their howitzers with effect. Two days' incessant cannonading reduced this strong little outpost into a heap of rubbish; but just as the Puritan forlorn hope scrambled over the ruins and were on the point of delivering the long-deferred assault upon the Castle, the remnant of the heroic defenders of the gate-house blew up three arches of the bridge, and thus isolated Limerick as effectually as the friends of Horatius had cut off Rome from the Etruscans when that other famous bridge went down into the Tiber.

A gallant attempt on the part of Ireton to breach the city from the King's Island was as gallantly disputed by the garrison for three more weary months; and as it was by this time October and the plague had moreover spread to the Cromwellian camp, it looked for the moment as if the Royalists had made good their position. The besiegers, who by this time were greatly thinned by casualties and disease, thought so too, and Ireton had actually decided upon raising the siege when treachery within the walls effected what cannon had so far failed to bring about outside.

It was on the morning of the 21st of October, and Dauntless had called upon O'Neill for the purpose of laying before him

[1] Ludlow, in his memoirs of this Plevna of Ireland, mentions that he saw several of the garrison fall down dead in the ranks from sheer exhaustion and disease.

the usual daily report, when Cuttard burst in upon them white and wild-eyed.

"Your Excellency," he gasped, "we are undone; the villain Hooter hath delivered up the Gate of Saint John, and the Roundheads are already in the city."

O'Neill sprang to his feet and ran to the door, closely followed by his two companions, but only to be confronted by a strong body of red-coated musketeers led by a Parliamentary officer. The brave Governor turned white and reeled up against the door-post with something like a sob in his throat.

Drogheda, Clonmel, Waterford, Wexford, each with a record of unavailing heroism written in blood, had succumbed to the overwhelming genius of the Commonwealth generals, and Limerick, the last sad hope of the Country, the only place in Ireland that had baffled the enemy, was now fallen in the hour of its hard-won triumph, betrayed by one of its own garrison.

The officer advanced to take their swords; and as he drew near, the three Royalists perceived he was their old adversary of the North, Captain Cartaret. Harry gave up his sword with grave courtesy, Cuttard delivered his with an assumption of insolent defiance, but O'Neill drew his sheathed rapier from his shoulder belt and, holding it with the point in his left hand and the guard in his right, regarded it for a moment in silent anguish.

Then he pressed his lips to the hilt and bent the weapon across his knee with such violence that the broken shivers flew out through the burst leather of the scabbard and tinkled on the cobblestones at his feet; and then the silent, patient soldier turned away and covered his face with his hands to conceal the grief that was rending his heart in two.

"Come, Colonel O'Neill," said Cartaret, kindly, "take heart of grace and bear yourself blythely yet. Methought the Hugh Dhu O'Neill whom I knew in the North was made of harder metal than this and could take evil fortune as sturdily as the good luck which hath followed him so long. Remember that the sun shone on your side of the wall for a long while, so wherefore repine that it should favour us now?"

"It is not that I grieve over the fortune of war," said O'Neill, in a broken voice, "but, Oh, Captain Cartaret, it is a bitter blow to be deprived of my trust through the base treachery of mine own side."

"Treachery may have robbed you of your right, but nothing can ever rob you of your reputation," answered the Parliamentarian, with a grave bow. "Believe me, Sir, there is scarcely a man in our army, much as it hath suffered at your hands, who doth not hold you as a gallant and honourable gentleman. Yet you must acknowledge that this intaking, although effected by questionable means, will prove to be the best matter that could happen this distracted country, inasmuch as a temporary success on your part would have only resulted in another siege and more bloodshed later on, without benefiting you or your party in the long run."

Cartaret promised that every courtesy due to his rank and worth should be paid to O'Neill, and, for his sake (here he glanced with a meaning look at Cuttard, who winced and cocked his hat defiantly), he would also see that his companions were no worse treated than himself. So he permitted the three comrades to retain their lodgings near St. Mary's Church, and, on receiving their parole not to leave the house, marched off his men without leaving even a single sentinel outside their door.

During the following two days the prisoners were visited by several of the Parliamentary officers, and the respectful attention they received from these stern visitors encouraged them to anticipate better terms than they had hitherto hoped for. However, on the third morning of their imprisonment, as they sat at breakfast, Harry and O'Neill were startled by the ominous tramp of many armed men passing the house, and after a pause they heard a long-drawn groan as of a multitude suddenly and painfully affected, mingled with a deep roll of drums which seemed to be beaten with a different object than of encouraging men on the march.

The two friends exchanged a look of uneasiness, and presently Cuttard entered the room with a portentous look of dismay on his thin, sharp features.

Harry, still more discomposed by the troop-adjutant's appearance than the disturbance in the street, jumped up and asked him hastily if he knew what had happened out of doors.

"Aye, that I do," was the gloomy answer. "That raddledaddle of drums which you heard but now was the first tick in the list, wherein I fear we ourselves are already set down. In short, Cavalieros, the Bishop of Emly and Colonel Purcell are already hanging dead at the corner of the street, and there is an escort under our old friend, Corporal Foster, — whom you may remember we last had the pleasure of seeing in Youghal, Captain Dauntless, — waiting for us three at the door, so, I suppose, we may consider ourselves as good as gibbet tassels already."

"What?" cried O'Neill, aghast. "Hang us for doing our duty like soldiers and without the semblance of a trial?"

"Nay, your Excellency," answered Cuttard, with a grin such as a fox might assume when the leading hound snaps at him, "it appears we are to have the full benefits of martial law, for we are to be tried by no less than Ludlow the Commissioner, Waller, the new governor, and Ireton himself. No formality is to be omitted; all is to be done in strict accordance with the law, judges, hearing, conviction, and hangman all provided free of charge. Waller and Ludlow may be what they will, but they must dance only on whatever spot it pleases their colleague to jerk 'em to; and, as I can commend Ireton with great confidence for being the bloodiest-minded hypocrite either in my own or this accursed country, I take it that we are as good as convicted already."

O'Neill laughed mirthlessly and remarked that they should not abandon hope as yet, inasmuch as they had not been arraigned so far.

"The only hope that *I* have," remarked Mr. Cuttard, dolorously, "is that Ireton may be in a good humour, in which case he will adjudge me to die before a platoon of musketeers; but, as he hath a naturally parsimonious mind, I fear he may grudge a poor distressed Cavaliero like myself the expense of a few ounces of powder. However, die all, die merrily, as the fellow in the play says; and, if you gentlemen will excuse me for a few minutes, I shall go upstairs and make a change in my attire, inasmuch as I have a quaintly beautiful suit of sky-blue taffeta with silver passementerie on the cape and cuffs, wherein I fancy I shall cut a pretty figure even if I have to take a dive and a dance on nothing at the end of a vile penny cord."

The tidings brought by the troop-adjutant affected the two

friends differently. O'Neill was indignant and yet uncomfortably conscious that the renegade had not spoken idly, for he was well aware that the conditions offered by Ireton previous to the treacherous surrender of the town had specially excluded himself, in revenge for his heroic defence of Clonmel. Dauntless received the news with listless tranquillity. He had once rejected mercy, and he knew well that the Commonwealth was not in the habit of pressing their pardon on an enemy a second time. However, his life seemed so hapless and joyless that the prospects of death dismayed him as little as it would one whose vitality had been gnawed through by some wasting disease.

Accordingly, when Cuttard reappeared a few minutes later in a dress fitter for a masquerader than for one about to undergo trial for his life, he found Harry calmly passive and O'Neill proudly indignant; and, as soon as the three were conducted into the presence of their judges, the latter could not detect any other expression but that of resolution on their countenances.

Ludlow, a grave but not unkindly looking person, sat on one side of a table covered with writing materials, and opposite to him sat Waller, a courtly, handsome man whose curling brown hair, twisted moustache, and clear-cut, aristocratic features gave him the appearance of one of the Cavalier party. At the head of the table, leaning on the rail of a high-backed chair, stood the president Ireton. He was a tall thin man with colourless features, black, piercing eyes, and a coarse, straight-haired moustache under which his pale lips were stretched in two straight, cruel lines. In one hand he held a little red leather-covered book to which he occasionally referred while he addressed irregularly put questions to the prisoners in a soft, murmuring tone of acquiescence that reminded Harry vaguely of the purring of a cat. Between his queries he alternately stretched his large-knuckled, venous hands to the fire that roared behind him, and stamped with his spurred feet on the floor as if he was chilled by the approach of death, which, unconscious to himself, had already laid its hand upon his shoulder.

When asked what defence he had to offer for his life, O'Neill, in a very dignified and manly speech, claimed, first, that his birth, as a citizen of Spain, placed him beyond the jurisdiction of an English Court of Law, and, secondly, that his conduct throughout the war had been consistently that of a soldier and a man of honour, who had always treated any of the officers of the Commonwealth, fallen into his hands, in accordance with the usages of civilised warfare, even though they were fighting against their lawful prince.

"Verily, verily, Colonel O'Neill," said Ireton, softly tapping the book he held in one hand with the loosely closed knuckles of the other, "verily, if thou hast placed thy trust on such poor foundations, thou hast built the walls of thy refuge upon the sand; for know from me that the aristarchy of England, mighty, merciful, and incorruptibly just, still holdeth forth at all times its buckler over the innocent and oppressed, or smiteth the guilty with the edge of the sword, regardless of the frown or blandishments of the Perizzite or Jebusite. If thou hast no better defence to offer than thy Spanish citizenship against the blood which crieth out in testimony against thee, then —" here the half-closed fingers straightened out, for the cat nature within him had changed suddenly to the rending humour,— "thy fate is sped, and thy place shall know thee no more."

He drove one of the brands deeply into the heart of the fire with the heel of his heavy horseman's boot, and, after glancing into his little red leather-covered book, turned his head sideways on his shoulder, and regarded Harry with a gentle look of deprecation.

"And you, young Sir," said he, dropping once more into his former unctuous tone of voice, "what folly or wickedness tempted thee back once more into thy evil courses, — thou, who hast been once already the pitied object of the Commonwealth, which bade thee, in its mercy, go forth and sin no more? What hast thou to say in thy defence?"

"Naught, your Excellency," answered Harry, with a weary sigh of resignation, for the mockery of this court of justice was weighing heavily on his saddened spirits. "Since you have been pleased to daff aside the higher claims which my General hath offered for your consideration, I acknowledge myself to be a subject of England, and the fact of having drawn my sword on behalf of my lawful prince can find but little favour with one like your Excellency, who was mainly instrumental in sending him to the block."

"Alas for thy enthusiasm!" snuffled Ireton, with a sigh of affected commiseration. "Such misdirected zeal, which prompted thee to turn thy weapon against the breast that felt pity for thy folly, might have placed thee in the foremost rank of the saints. And yet, young Sir, methinks that not all of the sin lieth at thy door, inasmuch as the late dead Tyrant, and the lascivious wanton, his Son, seem to have been gifted by their master Sathan with some devilish lure to draw weak souls into their nets; wherefore, I take it, that answering for some of the guilt of such misguided men as thyself must lie at the heads of these false gods of Dagon, now so happily overthrown. But you, fellow," said he, turning quickly on Cuttard with a sudden ferocity, "you, who ate the bread and wore the coat of the Parliament,—what have you to urge in defence of your contemptible life?"

Cuttard, who had been adjusting his ruffles, cravat, and cloak during the examination of his companions, with little furtive twitches and shakes, trembled, for a moment, at the unexpected vehemence of his questioner; but all the brazen hardihood of his nature came to his assistance instantly, and he assumed an attitude of insolent defiance, which, he secretly flattered himself, gave him an appearance of noble dignity.

"Because, please your Excellency," said he, coolly, "as an honourable cavaliero must live by bread, I was forced to offer my sword to the Confederates, inasmuch as the Parliament would have none of my humble aid."

"Aye, Certes, if thou wert a liar from thy birth, thou hast spoken truth at last," answered Ireton, grimly, as he turned over the leaves of his little red book. "I have some memoranda here concerning thee. Ha, yes! Bristol, April, 1643. Convicted, by a martial court, of drunkenness and profane language, for which thou wert compelled to ride the wooden horse with a musket at each heel, followed by thy discharge from Captain Reynolds's troop. Again, at Nantwich in the following October, a certain Thomas Heavy-in-Spirit (whose description appeareth to have a remarkable resemblance to thine), was brought to the halberts—"

"If it please your Excellency," interrupted Cuttard, with a considerable amount of uneasiness, but with no trace of shame, "I remember it very well, *that* was for that little affair of the Earl of Manchester's saddle-cloth. However, as all these little matters are so very well impressed on my memory, and appear to be equally well known to your Excellency, with all respect to your Excellency's honoured judgment, it appears to me to be but a waste of time to recount to all these worthy gentlemen my little acts of weakness; but, if you can recollect any act of soldiership, such as my recovery of the Earl's standard at Devizes, or other similar behaviour, which it doth not become me to vapour about myself, let me prefer some claim as to the choice of my death, for, although I am but a humble soldier of fortune, I can boast of some gentility, and would, therefore, have a very natural leaning to be shot instead of scragged."

"Pah! sirrah," said Ireton, contemptuously. "Dost think the Parliament of England would stoop at such gutter sparrows as thyself? Go, poor tosspot; amend thy ways, if possible, but beware lest thou shouldst dare to impose thy drunken company again among our cleanly living soldiers, or I shall have thee beaten to death with stirrup leathers." Without taking further notice of Cuttard, who was as much astonished by this unexpected act of leniency as another might be on hearing a wholly unjust and unmerited sentence, Ireton closed his book with a sudden snap, and addressed himself to the other two prisoners.

"Hugh Dhu O'Neill and Henry Dauntless," said he, regarding them with his cruel eyes half closed, "on your own pleadings, you stand convicted of waging war against the Commonwealth of England, with no better warrant than that given by the arch traitors of these realms. It is, therefore, my duty to pass sentence of death upon you, in reparation of the blood which your hands have spilt, and I hereby advise you to set your souls in order, to meet your punishment on the bridge of Thomond ten days from hence."

Neither of the prisoners spoke, but Ludlow sat up erect in his chair and exchanged a look with Waller. His colleague shook his head and shrugged his shoulders with a slight frown, and Ludlow thereupon wrote something hastily on a sheet of paper and handed it to Ireton. The president glanced over it, folded it carefully, and then dropped it into the fire, whence it was whirled in a flash up the chimney.

"It may not be Civil Law, your Excellency," said he, blandly, "but it is good, sound, military justice. One persisted in holding out an untenable post, in spite of due warning, and thereby caused the deaths of eight thousand of God's Saints by plague, shot, and sword, and the other forfeited his life irreparably by resuming arms against the Parliament which had previously admitted him to pardon. Therefore, there is nothing more to be urged on their behalf."

Ludlow seemed troubled and confused. He was a slow-thinking, honest man, with no experience of soldiership, and though his position as Deputy Lieutenant gave him a superior rank to the purely military one of his colleague, at that very moment the army was beginning to assert itself in such a way as to make the Civil power uncomfortably conscious of the strength of the monster they themselves had created. He was indignant at the cruelty of his co-partner, but too perplexed and fearful to oppose him openly.

There was an uncomfortable silence, which was broken by a muffled cough, something like the distant sound of a culverin, and Cuttard, who had taken this method of attracting attention, smiled feebly at Ireton, and, after giving fire to a second and more subdued bronchial explosion beneath his hand, begged his Excellency for a boon. Deeming his companion was about to make a vain entreaty for his life, Harry felt his eyes gradually fill, and he turned to Cuttard with a look of pitying affection; but that gentleman was too much occupied with his own affairs to notice anything but the cruel eyes of the President.

"A boon, fellow!" said Ireton, sharply. "What more do you want than your own worthless life?"

"A little scrap of a protection, signed by your Excellency," said Mr. Cuttard, with an insinuating bow, "for your Excellency is doubtless aware that a poor reformado Cavaliero like myself would have but a parlous time travelling without it, since your Excellency's excellent soldiers occupy every road in the country."

Ireton scribbled the necessary passport on a sheet of paper, and tossed it scornfully across the table. The renegade pounced upon it with trembling fingers, and, mumbling some incoherent thanks, backed out of the room in such haste that he neglected to bid farewell, even by so little as a nod, to his two less fortunate companions.

XXXIII

INSTEAD of being sent back to the lodging which they had previously occupied, the two condemned prisoners were conducted from the council chamber to separate apartments in the Castle, and were thus deprived of the last poor consolation of each other's society.

Harry's prison was in the basement of the great round tower that flanks the bridge across the Shannon. The room had been formerly used as a magazine on account of its proximity to the battery defending the river-gate; but, as this spot had been more fiercely attacked than any other during the siege, all the ammunition had been long ago carted off by the gunners, who, no doubt, had rendered a good account of it among the Cromwellians. Projecting almost into the centre of this room was a wide-mouthed fireplace whose splayed chimney-shaft, tapering up to a bare square foot above, looked like a great drunken obelisk leaning up against the stone wall. The window, narrow, heavily grated, and partially sheathed with iron plates, blinked down like a half-closed eye on the great, pulsing river, which at this point assumes one of those turbulent phases so common in its upper waters. A chance shot had deflected one of the bars and burst a concave jagged aperture in the sheathing, thus affording a peephole through which the prisoner could survey the opposite shore and the silver-laced water of the Shannon as it spouted in long glassy shoots through the blackened gaps in the bridge.

Into this apartment Corporal Oh-Let-Me-Be-Thankful Foster conveyed a table, a couple of chairs, and a truckle-bed, and, having stacked up and set light to a generous supply of firewood in the grate, he left Harry Dauntless to his own reflections.

Now that Death had drawn so close as almost to become a materialised presence, the higher spiritualism common to all thoughtful natures roused itself in Harry's mind and overcame that languid acquiescence with fate which the doctrine of Predestination had so far imposed upon him.

He had hitherto believed that his love, true, passionate, and devoted as it was, had been fated to wither away in mockery of his legal and moral possession of Aileen. Now it appeared to him in the clearest light that nothing but his own haughty pride and reserve had been the cause of losing her and his own life together, and he sighed heavily as he recalled to memory that fateful letter he had torn up so passionately along with Cromwell's protection. In the early selfishness of his manhood he had come to regard himself as a political martyr who had been singled out by a malignant destiny for exceptional sacrifices; but now, in the solitude of his prison, he remembered hundreds of long-departed comrades who had eagerly offered to their country what he had so grudgingly brought, and he felt humbled at the recollection of his own tardy patriotism. As the days passed on, so slowly and yet so dreadfully swiftly that he had already lost count of them, the sullen heathen stoicism which had up to this time supported him became transmuted into the chaster spirit of Christian resignation, and even his bitter disappointment in Cuttard softened into a magnanimous feeling of pity and affection.

"Poor Jack," he murmured to himself with a smile, "thou hadst more reason to fear Ireton and far less sorrow to endure than I have, so why should I feel aggrieved because thou wert in such a red-hot hurry to be gone from the presence of that bloody-minded Regicide? Still, I should have liked a parting clasp of thy hand, doubtful moralist as thou art, for I had come to love thee more than I knew myself, and perhaps, better than thou hast deserved."

Although a better nature was being thus swiftly developed within Harry, he allowed the days to drift on without making any attempt to set his spiritual or worldly affairs in order. True, he endeavoured to read the well-thumbed military Bible which Corporal Oh-Let-Me-Be-Thankful Foster had left ostentatiously on his table, and he also made some attempts to write letters of farewell to his mother and Aileen; but he felt that his mind was not yet calm enough to draw consolation from the one or transmit it through the medium of a coherent letter to those he loved, and so the days passed on and death drew near.

Beyond a listless interest which he took in the repair of the Thomond Bridge he was unable to concentrate his thoughts upon more serious matters; and he might have continued in this diseased state of mind until the hour wherein he was to die, had not the erection of a scaffold on the Bridge, with all its gaunt accessories of steps, gibbet, and ladder, roused him one evening to his true position.

This grim appearance at the Clare end of the Bridge braced up his flaccid nerves like a sharp tonic; and when Corporal Foster appeared with his midday meal, he asked him with the composure of one who has dined well, and who has plenty of money to discharge the debt, what amount he stood indebted to him for his maintenance up to and including the morning.

"Not very much, your honour," answered the Corporal, with a solemn stare, "for what wine you had to your meals was sent from Sir Hardress Waller's table. If I remember rightly, there were four capons — but they are cheap — say three pence apiece, and sauce, say sixpence, and bread, a shilling, pepper, salt, and other condiments another shilling, batatas I got for nothing, as they are as plentiful as skenes among these accursed children of Ammon, therefore, I should say ten shillings or thereabouts."

Harry laid two gold pieces upon the table.

"I have no change," said the soldier, austerely, "and I am averse to trading upon the misfortunes of a brave man like your honour; wherefore keep your money for the present, and I shall set before you my account with all the items duly set forth in due time, inasmuch as this is but Friday, and your honour does not suffer until Monday morning."

Dauntless asked for whom the scaffold was destined, whereupon the Corporal smiled sourly.

"Methinks you will grieve but little over the punishment of him for whom that gibbet is set up," he answered grimly. "Nor do I see why any of the chosen of Zion should lament him either, seeing that it is written that when Rechad and Baanah came to David with their hands red with the blood of his rival, he slew them with the edge of the sword for the murder and bade no one pity them. That gibbet is set up for Ephraim Hooter, whilom Colonel in the service of the Young Man and his carnal servant Ormond."

"What?" cried Harry, in astonishment, "Hooter, he who rendered the Saint John's gate into your hands? Methought the villain deserved better treatment at your hands than this."

"Even Hooter," was the unconcerned reply; "true it was he did some service to the army of the Lord, but then it was for the purpose of saving his own base carrion. Ah, verily, verily, he fished between two pools, but in setting his angle in the one, stepped unwittingly into the deeper water of the other."

Later on in the afternoon, Sir Hardress Waller entered with a troubled look on his handsome features.

"Mr. Dauntless," said he, in a tone of hesitation, "it is my duty to inform you that the sentence previously passed upon you by the martial court has been confirmed, and that you are to be shot to death in the market-place at high noon on Monday. If there is any last service which I can render, you can command me freely with the assurance of my ready wish to aid you as far as my duty permits."

Harry bowed, and quietly asked for the attendance of a priest, but Waller raised his eyebrows with a comprehensive twitch and shook his head. "All of such profession who have been caught have been long ago hung or shot," said he, shortly, "nor do I think that any who may yet lurk in disguise would dare to acknowledge themselves to such of my men as I could send in search of them."

The prisoner next begged for an interview with his comrade-in-arms and fellow-sufferer, Hugh Dhu O'Neill.

"That is also out of my power," was the reply, "inasmuch as General O'Neill departed this morning under charge of the escort which conducted the dead body of our late general to London."

"Is Ireton dead?" asked Harry, startled at the brief measure of life that had been meted out to his judge.

"Aye, dead of the plague this two days," was the grave reply, "and by so much longer has your own lease of life been extended. The court which assembled to consider the sentences passed upon you and your General commended him to mercy, but could find no such favour on your behalf. I trust you will bear your fortunes with a constant mind, remembering on what insecure tenure we poor mortals hold the commission of our lives, and that, short as it is, your own term may outlast mine, and so, Mr. Dauntless, I bid you farewell."

"Farewell, Sir Hardress," said Harry, gravely and earnestly, "and in a happier and more peaceful world I hope to acknowledge your courtesy in this uncertain and turbulent one."

Harry slept so tranquilly that night that it required a rough shake from Corporal Oh-Let-Me-Be-Thankful to rouse him in the morning. The Corporal bade him dress himself, as there was one outside who desired speech with him. He had lain down to sleep partially dressed, so he turned out of bed drowsily and stumbled across the room in his shirt and hose to the open doorway. Here he was confronted by two halberdiers, who supported a third man between them in such a disordered state of mind, body, and clothing that for a moment or two he was unable to identify him until the man twice pronounced his name in a tone of pitiful entreaty.

It was Hooter with his unwashed and unshaven face turned the dusky grey of lead which has been some time exposed to the weather. His mouth was gaping open, his eyes were fish-like and stupid, and his limbs were twitching and straightening with that all-devouring fear which turns men's bowels into water. Fully awakened and not a little indignant, Dauntless would have turned away, but the ex-Commissioner, slipping from the hands of his guards, clutched hold of him and lapsed in a quivering heap upon the bare, stone floor at his feet.

"Don't turn away, Mr. Dauntless," cried the trembling wretch; "don't desert me in my peril. Mercy! Mercy! Mr. Dauntless, for the sake of the mercy you may needs plead for yourself ere long."

"What folly is this, Mr. Hooter?" said Harry, sick with disgust, and endeavouring to extricate the grimy hands which clung so desperately to him. "Let go my shirt, I tell you, and get upon your feet— Faugh! take heart and die like a man."

"Nay, never think I fear to die, Mr. Dauntless," cried Hooter, wildly. "Never think I fear to meet death. I have often encountered it upon the sea in storm and battle, on a fair field in front of a platoon of musketeers, and even at the end of a rope, but those were times when I had bargained for it, and none could say I flinched then; but, in this instance, I am being murdered. Murdered! I tell you, Mr. Dauntless, for Ireton did promise me 1,000 pounds in return for the Gate of Saint John, and now they tell me that the money is to be crammed into my pockets at the gallows' foot. There is some terrible mistake; I know if Ireton were alive he would not permit this cruel outrage. I prithee, Mr. Dauntless, send for Sir Hardress Waller; you have more influence with him than perhaps you wot of, and I am sure he will listen to you. Beg him to reassemble the court and reconsider my sentence; at least beg him to put off my execution until Monday, when I shall not feel so lonely in dying in your company. It is but for three days — three little days — and in that time a reprieve may arrive from Dublin, and you would have the blessed satisfaction of knowing, even if you had to die alone, that you had saved a fellow-creature's life."

"What influence do you think I have," said Harry, who was weakened by the loathsome cowardice of the condemned man as with some deadly miasm, — "I, who, like yourself, am already as near the grave as you are? Turn to your prayers, man, and peace go with you."

Corporal Oh-Let-Me-Be-Thankful tapped the miserable man on the shoulder, and Harry tried to disengage the hands which clung so wildly to his garments.

"Don't leave me like that!" cried Hooter. "Don't, for your own peace of mind. Don't let us part until you forgive me, for I have injured you grievously. No! No! don't look at me like that, for the love of Christ; you bring to my mind one whom I made walk the plank in the Caribbees, and who cursed me silently with such a look in his eyes. Say you forgive me — say it with your eyes as well as with your lips, and I may yet do you a good turn you cannot compass by the wildest dream of imagination."

"I forgive you freely for the misery you have caused me," said Harry, suddenly extricating himself from the hands of the abject being at his feet and stepping back instinctively. "I forgive you as freely as I hope to be forgiven myself when my time comes on Monday morning, and so depart in peace."

"Don't leave me yet!" shrieked Hooter, shuffling across the rough pavement on his knees. "Let me remain, Corporal, for an hour — half an hour, then fifteen minutes longer. A reprieve may arrive even while we are talking; it may be even now in the Governor's hands, and if you drag me away now, my blood will be upon your head. Ask these men for a little grace, Mr. Dauntless, ask them in pity's name, and they will not refuse you — gain me a quarter of an hour's time longer, and I will tell you a secret for which you would barter your own last two days in order to learn."

Corporal Oh-Let-Me-Be-Thankful made a scornful gesture of his head to the two soldiers, who immediately seized Hooter under the armpits and jerked him to his feet. He struggled with them like a wild beast, snapping and rending at their buff-coats with his teeth, but they dragged him fiercely to the doorway. Here he clung like a limpet for a moment to the doorpost, but the Corporal hammered on his hands with his bunch of heavy keys until the blood started from his bruised fingers, and then the halberdiers with a sudden wrench tore him struggling and growling from his hold. The impetus carried them all three to the head of the stair, down which they went stumbling and clinging to one another, whereupon Hooter, conscious of the futility of resistance, rolled back his head until his chin pointed to the roof, and, fixing his staring eyeballs upon Harry, gave breath to a shriek as dreadful as that which was wrung from Faustus when the fiends started up to pluck his limbs asunder. The Corporal swung to the iron door and locked it, thus mercifully shutting out those awful cries, but Harry staggered blindly across to the window for air, and was further tortured by the scene without.

On the far side of the river he saw the gibbet with the dark figure of the hangman sitting close under the angle-beam. The thin, slimy rope swayed in festoons from its projecting arm like some horrible gossamer in the bright sunshine, and the repulsive form of the executioner, crouching on the top-most round of the ladder, looked like a species of noisome spider that had spun some unholy web across the quiet beauty of the morning. The riverside and bridge were paved with white upturned faces that seethed and heaved like an unquiet sea, and through them a narrow lane, fringed with a double row of pike-heads, led to the gallows' foot. Presently he saw a compact knot of musketeers issue out of the Thomond Gate and wriggle slowly down this narrow passage, and at that moment a cry of execration arose which made him sick and giddy.

Only those who have heard an assembly of Irish men and

" They dragged him fiercely to the doorway "

women greet one whom they regard as a spy or a traitor can understand the thrill which such a sound conveys. It has nothing of the deep-tongued bellow that denotes the anger of an English mob, nor the shrill, hysterical note that marks the fury of a Continental one. Hoarse, murmuring, and disgustful, it swells from one low cry of horror into a higher one of contempt, and then sinks to swell out into a long-drawn yell of hate and loathing. It is a dreadful cry, and is not easily forgotten by anyone who has once heard it.

Harry stared at this little party of musketeers, wondering why they should be greeted with such obloquy. However, his attention was soon attracted to the centre of the party, where a couple of twinkling halbert-heads rocked to and fro with measured regularity, and between them he observed a flaccid shape drooping forward and swinging backwards at each step, which he recognised immediately as the already half-dead body of Hooter. He heard him cry out once with a shrill intensity that pierced the low thunder of the mob like the scream of a drowning sailor in a tempest, and, unwilling to see the last pitiful spectacle, he turned away from the window. He thrust his fingers into his ears to shut out the roar of the mob, sat down on his bed, and remained in this position for nearly half an hour; but, when he arose, some morbid instinct drew him to the window once more and in one brief glance he saw what he had so earnestly hoped was already over.

Hooter had succeeded in postponing his fate by one miserable pretext after another until that moment. He was crouching like some misshapen monkey on the top of the ladder. The rope was round his neck, his hands were bound behind him; yet, even at that stage of hopelessness, he was struggling hard to prolong his existence. Two soldiers upon the scaffold were thrusting at him with their pikes; but the shafts of their outstretched weapons were barely long enough to reach his body, and consequently the tortured wretch yet contrived to cling on to the ladder, notwithstanding their efforts to force him into that last fatal jump.

Just as Harry glanced out, the soldiers lost patience, and, handing their weapons to a couple of their fellows, seized hold of the ladder, and with one strong heave shook the ex-pirate off it as one might shake a drowning rat from a stick. Down shot the miserable man feet foremost among the crowd, who shrank back with an audible gasp. The coiled rope straightened out and vibrated, and the body, checked by the sudden tension of the cord, bounded upwards like some horrid puppet, spun round once or twice, and then settled down into the last awful convulsions.

Harry recoiled from the window, made his way unsteadily across the room to his bed, and sat down on it sick at heart. Contact with an abject coward has its own insidious effect even on the valiant. It infects strong hearts with a momentary weakness, and, though its results are evanescent, the bravest cannot escape its sickly contamination.

Until that morning, Harry had confronted his fate with calm resignation, but the pitiable cowardice of Hooter and that last dreadful scene had shaken him to the core. Hooter, brutal ruffian as he had been, had often proved his animal courage on past occasions; yet the prospects of death at a fixed hour and in a pre-arranged form had reduced his spirit to the consistency of a wet rag. Was he too contaminated with this degrading virus, and would he falter also when his time came? He shuddered and flushed crimson, but the thought spurred his blood into a red hot gallop through his temples and pulses, and his spirit rose once more within him. Thank Heaven, there was a considerable difference between his position and that of Hooter! Hooter had overreached himself in craft, and the unexpected judgment of Ireton had overwhelmed him body and mind; he, on the other hand, had never expected mercy and had no such trial for his fortitude. Hooter had gone to his death with innocent blood upon his hand, and the curses of the wretched peasantry, whom he had robbed, upon his soul — while he had no such burdens on his mind. Hooter, tricked by a mightier villain than himself and driven to madness by the bitter mockery of being paid first and hanged afterwards, had died despairing and dishonoured; but he himself was to be accorded the death of a soldier who had fought in a noble cause. No crime oppressed his conscience at that moment, no dishonour would stain his memory when he was dead, and under the influence of these reflections he recovered his former firmness.

He was in almost a cheerful mood by the time the Corporal brought him his supper; and, having obtained writing material and additional candles from that sombre person, he spent the night writing letters of farewell to those he loved most. The first was to Aileen; and as he proceeded to unfold to her a tender assurance of his never-failing love, he discovered fresh and hitherto undiscovered well-springs of passion that rose up within him and swelled the full tide of burning love, which ran through every sentence he wrote. He wrote on for several hours without either raising his head or pausing for a word, though the candles before him were more than three quarters wasted and the hoarse voices of the sentinels throughout the city had long since proclaimed that midnight was past. Suddenly, a key clicked in the lock, the hinges whistled discordantly as the door swung open, and Corporal Oh-Let-Me-Be-Thankful, accompanied by a dejected-looking figure, appeared at the threshold.

XXXIV

THE Corporal thrust his companion with very little ceremony into the centre of the room, and Harry saw that he was a tall, straight boy dressed in the variegated truis and long riding-boots of the better class of peasantry; but as he wore his blue barrad pulled low down over his forehead, and had one end of his crescent-shaped mantle muffled across his chin, he had little opportunity of judging his age.

"I am sorry to incommode your Honour by herding such cattle with you," said the Corporal, indicating the peasant with his lantern; "but as the worshipful Governor remarked that this fellow would be left here no longer than daylight, you must make shift to put up with him till then."

Harry smiled faintly and replied that even if they were to share the remainder of their lives together, they would have little time for quarrelling; he then turned to the young peasant and asked him kindly what crime he was charged with.

"*Na ha Sassenach,*" muttered the prisoner, indistinctly, into the folds of his mantle, and turned away sullenly from the lantern which the Corporal advanced towards his face.

"Waste no English upon him," said the Corporal, sourly, "for he is one of those dogs who speaketh no tongue but that of Egypt — I know not what he is charged with, but as he looks too slender to be a fighting man and too young to be a Popish priest, methinks he is a suspected spy, in which case, I can assure you, your Honour's meditations shall not be disturbed by his presence after sunrise."

With this grim admonition the Corporal withdrew, and the boy, sinking down upon a bench in the angle formed by the projecting fireplace, covered his head completely with his mantle in the fashion which the Irish peasant assumes in grief or pain, and leaned back against the wall while his fellow-prisoner resumed his writing. Harry wrote on eagerly until the wavering struggles of the last half-inches of his candles compelled him to bring his labours to a conclusion;

and, as he laid down his pen, the sounds of the town clock tolling four and the voices of the sentinels repeating the hour and the number of their posts in varying tones, according to the distance they were posted from the Castle, recalled him to the fact that he had but barely thirty hours to live. He proceeded to fold and seal the letters to his wife and mother, when, happening to glance across to the deeply shadowed angle where his fellow-prisoner crouched, he saw that his body had contracted to half its size and was quivering in silent but unmistakable agony.

"I wonder," thought Harry, "if there is any spell about this accursed dungeon which robs all its inmates of their manhood." He rose and walked over to his companion with his heart full of pity, for the boy appeared to be bravely struggling against his terror.

"My poor boy," said he, kindly, "has life been so pleasant that thou shouldst fear so much to part with it? Then, more happy in thy fate than I, learn from one who like thyself hath but a little measure of life, that death is not a greater pang to bear than those griefs which troop around a disappointed manhood. Hast thou a dearly prized ambition — hereafter it might have crushed thy heart in more mature years. Hast thou a dearly prized friend — his ingratitude might have soured thy heart. Hast thou a dearly loved sweetheart — she might have broken it. Better to die at thy age, boy, ere disappointment has had time to curdle the sweetness of thy delusions, than live long enough to learn that we poor mortals are but the fools of our young hopes."

Harry spoke in Gaelic, the mother language of sad poetry, and the words he spoke almost unconsciously trended into a melancholy sweetness which no mere English translation could convey. His companion was now sobbing undisguisedly, although he had muffled his lemon-coloured frieze mantle closer about his mouth.

"Thou hast very likely a clearer conscience than I," said the boy, between his sobs; "but I, who have done grievous wrong, can look on neither death nor life with any other feelings than those of fear."

"If thou hast wronged anyone on this earth," said Harry, gravely, "make thy peace with him, and then address thyself to death with the consolation that life is scarcely brighter than yonder poor, struggling candle which the light of day will soon render futile."

"Ah, but he whom I wronged would have forgiven me long ago," muttered the boy, with a fresh paroxysm of weeping; "but a wicked pride forbade the confession, and when I humbled myself, he would have none of my penitence."

"Then ask thy pardon from God alone," said Harry, quietly, "and reserve thy pity for him thou hast wronged, inasmuch as his cruelty shall weigh down his head with its own heaviness."

The flames of the two candles, which had been fluttering in and out like the breath of an expiring man, at this moment fizzled, gasped, and went out extinguished in their own grease, and there was a long silence during which Harry raked the embers in the grate together and threw on some fresh fuel. Presently the wood caught fire and burst into a blaze that half-lighted the great gloomy apartment.

"Come, lad," said Harry, gently, "sleep is as good as food to a tired heart, and we cannot spend the remainder of the night in a better fashion. I am older than thou and perchance more used to the rough chances of a soldier's life, therefore, take thou my bed and I shall lie down before the fire."

The boy negatived this proposition by a silent but emphatic shake of his head, whereupon Harry lay down on his bed dressed as he was and almost immediately fell asleep. His rest was disturbed by dreams, wherein the horrors of the day recurred again and again, and after a couple of hours' uneasy slumber he was awakened by a horrible sensation that a steady rain of human blood was falling upon him. He stirred and groaned, and at that moment distinctly felt a drop of some warm liquid fall upon his cheek, whereupon he started up wide awake.

By the faint light of morning that mingled its ashy shades with the rose-coloured glow of the wood brands on the hearth, he saw his fellow-prisoner rise suddenly from beside his bed and draw back guiltily. Surmising he had been attempting to pick his pocket, Harry stretched out his hand to seize him; but the suspected thief retreated towards the fireplace, all the while spreading his hands before his face and shrinking as if from an expected blow. Harry followed him angrily and was on the point of closing and thrashing him soundly, when the door suddenly opened, and, turning his head, he perceived the Corporal and a stout, bearded gentleman dressed in a black riding-suit appear on the threshold.

The boy immediately availed himself of this unexpected diversion. He sprang under Harry's outstretched hands, whipped round the table like a greyhound, and flung down upon the letters a heavy sealed packet. Then he threw himself into the arms of the gentleman in black and cried out pitifully, "Take me away, take me away! For God's sake take me away any place — any place so long as it is away from here."

At the sound of those words spoken in English, the ground appeared suddenly to become unsteady under Harry's feet. His throat, ears, and brain instantly became congested with the blood which rushed into them, the inside of his head seemed to be flying round like a potter's wheel at work, and, though he tried to speak, his voice wheezed in his throat like the gasping efforts of a drowning man, and no word issued from his trembling lips.

The man in black gently disengaged the clinging arms of the supposed boy from his neck and very gently pushed him back towards the trembling prisoner, who managed to find his voice with an effort and utter with a great cry of love, eagerness, and wonder, "Aileen! Aileen! my beloved wife." She turned and snatched the barrad from her beautiful hair, which fell in a soft dusky cloud about her upturned face, and then fell upon her knees before him as if to entreat for her life.

The stranger took the lantern from the Corporal's hand and laid it silently upon the table. He made a sign to his gaping companion, who muttered something under his bushy moustache about the twenty-second chapter of Deuteronomy, and that it was an abomination for a woman to wear the garments of a man, and the two withdrew into the passage.

"Pardon, Harry, pardon," cried the sobbing woman at his feet, who clung to his knees despite his efforts to raise her. "If I have wilfully disobeyed thy commands, forgive me for the sake of my great love. I did but purpose to gloat upon thy face in secret for a few hours, but my tears and my womanhood betrayed me."

Harry raised her to her feet and held her tightly to his

heaving bosom. He was too dazed to comprehend what had happened, too wildly excited to understand her meaning; but his incoherent words of endearment, the fervid look of his eyes, and the loving pressure of his arms conveyed to Aileen more than any eloquent speech how dearly she was beloved; and then, because she was so certain of that happiness, she buried her face in his bosom, and, twining her arms about him, proceeded to upbraid him in true woman fashion.

"I knew thou wouldst repent that cruel message," said she, punctuating each phrase with a little sob, "I knew thou couldst not hold to the wicked pact. And yet I did merit it, for I was foolishly wicked and wickedly foolish, and did deserve to lose thee for my folly. Still, it was a monstrous punishment, Harry, out of all proportion to mine offence, which I had long before expiated in a gale of sighs and a sea of tears; and, indeed, Harry, methinks that some of the blame belongs to thee, for if thou didst possess but a tithe of the experience I gave thee credit for, thou shouldst have known thou didst possess enough power to whistle me to thy hand long ago."

"Answer? Compact? Punishment?" faltered Harry, with a blank look of mingled fear and astonishment. "I sent thee no answer, dear Heart, inasmuch as I received no letter from thee. I made no compact with thee save the one whereby I pledged myself to love thee until Death shall part us, from which contract I have never swerved for one moment, and, as for punishment, I never devised a greater one than the leaden weight of mine own awkward affection."

Her feet, which touched his heavily booted ones, remained close to his; but her body from her hips upwards swung back to the full limit of her outstretched arms, and her eyes, swimming in a mist of ineffable love, fixed themselves on his with a look of questioning wonder.

"Didst thou not send thy signet ring by Con MacGauran, in earnest of the receipt of my last pitiful little letter?" she said in accents that were fetched from the bottom of her heart. "Didst thou not charge me on peril of my proper life never to attempt to see thee nor write to thee again?"

The slow and painful shake of her husband's head filled her with a fierce joy.

"I did write thee thrice to Waterford," she said rapidly,

"thrice, in accordance with thy mother's precepts, and when I received no answer judged that my letters had miscarried. Then did I procure a special pass for MacGauran, to ensure the safe delivery of my last letter, wherein I expressed penitence for my folly and begged leave to be permitted to follow thee, even as a horseboy. In reply, I received that message which was vouched for by the unequivocal surety of thy signet ring, and then I deemed in my despair that thou wert lost to me for ever."

"The fellow lies wilfully and maliciously, or is madder than ever I took him to be," answered Harry, white to the lips and trembling violently. "I swear I never received any such letter, nor have I laid eyes on MacGauran since I was last in Shanganagh. As for my signet-ring, it was stolen from me some months ago; but how it ever got into his hands and shackled with such a monstrous lie, is more than I can dare hope to know in this life."

"It matters little to me now," cried Aileen, joyously, as she clung to him like a woodbine on an oak. "It matters little how he became charged with such a cruel message, since you deny it. No longer, no longer, my beloved, can any malignant cloud come between us, and our existence henceforward shall be one long summer day."

"Alas, dear Heart," said he, sorrowfully, "you forget that my hours can now be counted almost on my finger tips; for to-morrow — to-morrow at noon — shall see my last day on earth, and yet these hours seem the sweetest I have ever known."

"No! No! No!" she cried wildly, "there are happier days in store for both of us, thanks to Providence, which hath raised up a friend to thee out of the measure of thine own good deeds."

She was holding him with a fierce strength, such as one of the Jewish mothers might have put forth when the soldiers of Herod appeared to drag her babe from her arms. Her grey eyes were dilated, her breath came and went in husky struggles, her voice betrayed incipient hysteria, and Harry, with a smile of mingled love and pity, shook his head, but nevertheless held her closer and more lovingly to his bosom.

"Thou dost not understand," she said in broken little periods of alternate tears and laughter. "Thou dost not know how a good action beareth twenty fold its seed. Dost remember Mr. Wiltonholme — he whom my poor uncle, Evir, pressed thee to sue upon thy father's bond? He is a commissioner of the Parliament in Dublin, and hath as much power in Ireland as Cromwell hath in England. I was his prisoner in Dublin for a month, under the charge of his wife, Mistress Barbara Wiltonholme, a most lovable gentlewoman; and when he heard of thy peril he straight procured thy pardon. Before he set out with it himself, he and his wife acquainted me with the object of his journey, and told me, moreover, the reason why I had been so long restrained in prison, whereupon I resolved to see thee if it should cost me my life. Both he and Mistress Wiltonholme would have dissuaded me, but partly by storming and partly by entreaty, I had my will, and so accompanied him hither. But that dreadful message rankled in my heart, and notwithstanding my longing to look upon thee, I feared a repulse, which would have been worse than death itself, and so — and so I donned this disguise, resolving to go away quietly afterwards and so leave thee free to go what way thou wert pleased. But, Oh! Oh!" she cried, starting and pulling her boy's cap down over her brow, "whom have we here?"

Mr. Wiltonholme, in his plain black riding-suit, and Sir Hardress Waller, in buff and breastplate, stood in the room.

"Madame," said Sir Hardress, with a courteous and solemn bow, "there are horses waiting for you and your husband whenever it should please you to set forth, and my lady begs to offer the use of her chamber and wardrobe," here he glanced doubtfully at Aileen's doublet and hose, "in case you should wish to change your garments for others more suitable for travelling."

He offered her his arm, which she accepted shyly, and then she went forth with him, hanging down her head in pretty confusion at her boy's dress, for there were four or five people standing in the passage and regarding her curiously.

The moment she was gone, the ground once more appeared to become unsteady under Harry's feet, so Mr. Wiltonholme slipped his arm around him and led him to a chair. Corporal Oh-Let-Me-Be-Thankful Foster brought him a cup of water, which he drank greedily, and then he recovered his composure and endeavoured to thank his benefactor, but that worthy person ridiculed his gratitude and declared he himself owed Harry a debt that he would never be able to clear.

Outside in the passage there was a sound like the bleating of a distressed sheep, and presently Harry caught sight of an unsteady figure in a suit of sky-blue taffeta that swayed about among two or three scandalised Parliamentarian troopers.

"Cuttard!" he cried hoarsely, "Cuttard! — my dear old friend."

A tall, bony figure, dispelling a palpable vapour of fermented spirits, lurched heavily into the room and threw a pair of sinewy arms around him with all the fervour of an amorous polar bear.

"The same, Harry, the same, or all that 's left of him," said he, thickly, "for I have been in the saddle nearly the whole time since I saw thee last, and have foundered two horses and nearly killed a third. Alas! Harry, I have to confess I was compelled to revert to my unregenerate ways the day after I set out. My horse was worn out — no money to buy or hire another — so was compelled to cry 'stand' to a fat little farmer, and help myself to both his purse and nag; but it shall never happen again, Harry, never again; and besides, Harry, dost remember what thy own jack-priests say about a case of necessity as to baptism or marriage or some other ceremony — in a Case of Necessity — Mark you, Harry, — in a case of necessity — any lay man or woman, etcetera, etcetera."

There was blood upon his clothes, and his face was more than usually cadaverous, so his friend asked him anxiously if he had sustained any hurt on his journey.

"Mere nothing," he mumbled, "a mere nothing — Before I made the acquaintance of this Cavaliero" (unsteady bow to Mr. Wiltonholme) "went to lodgings of our friend Colonel Cromwell at three in the morning. I hammered so hard at his door that the sentinel at the corner of the street took me for a robber and put a pistol bullet through me before I could succeed in getting young Master Bottle-Shoulders out of his bed — but it is a trifle, Harry, a mere nothing, for Heaven be praised for my leanness, the ball went through me and made a nice clean hole, which will mend fast enough when I have leisure to rest and eat somewhat again, for I have been in such haste, Harry, that I have not had time to eat, and so was compelled to confine my bevers to what I could drink in the saddle."

It was quite evident from his appearance that the renegade did not exaggerate the haste in which he had journeyed. From spur-rowel to forehead he was plastered with the mud of every county between Dublin and Limerick, and the sky-blue taffeta suit cried Ichabod, for in verity its glory had departed beyond recall. Nevertheless, it took some persuasion on the part of Mr. Wiltonholme to dissuade him from accompanying Harry on his homeward journey, when a few minutes afterwards Aileen, all smiles and blushes, and arrayed in a riding-habit of blue cloth trimmed with silver lace, made her appearance and was assisted to her saddle by her husband.

"I shall not say good-bye," said the Commissioner, as he held Harry by the hand, "inasmuch as I hope to see you and your good lady at my house in Merchant's Quay ere many weeks are past, and that reminds me of the greetings and good love which my dame charged me to deliver to you when I met you."

"It was very kind of Mistress Wiltonholme to send so kind a greeting to one who is a stranger," answered Harry, somewhat surprised. "Kindly commend me to her and assure her of my desire to become better acquainted with her as well as with yourself."

"Nay, you are not such a stranger, perhaps, as you may think," said the Commissioner, with a quiet smile, "for my good dame Barbara was a while a neighbour of yours and tells me you were at one time wont to count her as a friend. She hopes that you can still retain some corner in your affection for one who hath never ceased to regard you as a dear brother, and as a token bade me tell you that though she was too late to dance at your wedding, she at least looks to sup with you and your wife some day ere long at Bearna Baeghail."

Harry and Aileen trotted out across the courtyard; and as they passed beneath the archway, they turned to wave their hands to the little group they left behind them. Sir Hardress Waller, hat in hand, stood with his stately head inclined in farewell; beside him stood the stout Commissioner with a smile on his plump bearded face; Cuttard leaned against the doorway and wiped his eyes with what appeared at that distance to be a pocket handkerchief; while the stern face of Corporal

Oh-Let-Me-Be-Thankful Foster loomed under the arch behind with his grim features softened into what bore a close resemblance to a smile.

Their direct road to Dublin lay across the Thomond Bridge and from thence through Killaloe; but, recollecting with a shudder that the corpse of Hooter was still dangling on the gibbet at the far side of the bridge, Harry took the longer route through the far side of the City which led to the Clonmel road. Once clear of the ill-omened gate of St. John and the dismantled Black Battery, they trotted forward side by side over the rising ground, until they reached the great mounds and trenches, where the cannon of Ireton had roared night and day for eight dreadful months.

Each, as if reading the other's wishes, drew rein, and both turned their horses round. Before them rose the stately tower of Saint Mary, the massive, clustering buildings of the Castle, the ancient town walls and fortified gates all battered, shattered, and dismantled, but still sturdy and looking like wounded but unconquered soldiers in the saffron flush of the rising sun. Two or three strayed sheep cropped the short grass around the scored trenches, a few wandering fowls clucked cheerfully as they scratched at a rotting nose-bag full of sodden corn, which some trooper's hand had flung among a litter of other military rubbish, and on the broken limber of a dismounted gun a magpie and his mate sat side by side. Their horses stood very quietly side by side, with the reins lying slack upon the saddle bows, and husband and wife with one accord leaned sideways from their saddles, and clasped one another in a loving embrace. They kissed each other very tenderly, and then turned their faces Eastward, with the sun of a new day on their countenances and a new-found life quickened into a radiant glory in their hearts.

It took nearly a week's crafty cross-questioning before Harry and Aileen succeeded in obtaining from MacGauran a solution of the mysterious message which had caused them both so much pain. At first, MacGauran doggedly refused to give any information, and, when Harry pressed him sternly, broke down into such a pitiable state of imbecile terror that humanity forbade continuing that method of inquisition. But, eventually, Aileen, with the insinuating tact of a woman, succeeded in coaxing the idiot into an admission that he dared not reveal

Captain Hooter's secrets on peril of his life, and in this admission she instantly found a key to the mystery.

On being solemnly assured of the death of Hooter, MacGauran confessed with much fear the history of the ring and message. The poor fellow had conscientiously chased the flying army of Castlehaven step by step through Munster in accordance with his instructions. He had been suffered to pass and re-pass unmolested through the Commonwealth troops, owing to the powerful safe conduct with which he was armed, but, when he finally reached the Royalist outposts at Killaloe, he met with an unexpected check. The officer before whom he was brought for the purpose of having his pass *visèd* was no other than Hooter, and the recognition between the two was mutual, for the one tremblingly remembered Hooter as the person who had frequently horsewhipped him at Bearna Baeghail, and the other instantly recognised the half-witted servant of his enemy.

The ex-commissioner had little difficulty in worming out of the frightened simpleton the object of his journey, and the possession of the two letters that he carried; and, having read them both with every symptom of satisfaction, he ordered the messenger to be hanged forthwith. On second thoughts, however, he changed his mind by the time two of his musketeers had half strangled MacGauran, and, being well aware of the fashion whereby communications were impressed on the poor fellow's weak mind, proceeded to repeat over and over again to him the message which was supposed to have been given to him by Harry. Then, having satisfied himself as to MacGauran's acquaintance with the part he was to play, he entrusted him with Harry's signet ring, and, threatening him with the most awful tortures if he should fail to deliver the message or should reveal the true personality of the sender, sent him off more dead than alive on his return journey to Shanganagh.

It is almost needless to say that Aileen and Harry exonerated the poor creature from all blame in the matter; but Cuttard, who arrived a few days after these disclosures in a state of tolerable sobriety, was of a different mind. The worthy soldier was of opinion that a dose of stirrup leather judiciously administered to poor MacGauran would prove of incalculable benefit to his mind and morals, and was extremely disappointed because Harry did not agree with him.

A cherished design of returning to Limerick for the purpose of stealing Hooter's skull off the spikes on the Cork gate, and transferring it to the top of Bearna Baeghail, also met with firm opposition, and in consequence of this rebuff Mr. Cuttard sulked for a day or two, but at the end of that time recovered his usual good spirits.

"After all, Harry," said he, confidentially, "I believe you are right. We should be generous to others in our prosperity, and, though I have no doubt it would be a monstrous pleasing ornament for you and Mistress Dauntless to contemplate, yet we should remember that the worthy citizens of Limerick as well as ourselves had a few grudges against Hooter, and it would be hardly fair to deprive them of the pleasure of looking at the dead villain's noddle now and then."

Not many months after the fall of Limerick, Cuttard was installed by some mysterious means into the position of Deputy Keeper of the State Records of Dublin Castle. The cheerful soldier of fortune continued to maintain to his dying day that this office was bestowed upon him as a reward for some of his notable services to the Parliamentary Army; but Harry had a shrewd suspicion that the uneasy conscience of Cromwell had prompted him to take this means of once more setting his former dupe in the way of making an honest livelihood. Being eminently unsuited for such a post, he reduced all the documents connected with it into the hopeless state of confusion which they continued to remain in until quite recently; but, notwithstanding his incompetence, Mr. Cuttard continued to hold his appointment, to the great satisfaction of himself and the despair of generations of antiquaries, until the day of his death, which happened at a very advanced age.

Few of the other officers of Owen Roe O'Neill's great Ulster Army were so fortunate as Harry and Cuttard.

Poor, hasty, scheming, warm-hearted Evir MacMahon fell fighting gallantly in the North against Coote; but his impetuous soul was spared the cruel indignities that fell to the lot of his vain and foolish companion, Sir Phelim O'Neill.

After the fall of Limerick, Sir Phelim dragged out a wretched existence for two years, hunted from hiding-place to hiding-place like a wild animal until he was captured on one of the lakes in Tyrone. He was brought to Dublin, where he was tried and condemned to death by his old enemies, the

Puritan faction, and, though offered his pardon on condition of incriminating the late King with his own mad schemes, steadily refused to buy his pardon at such a price. He was followed, even to the scaffold, with offers of life and property, if he would but acknowledge the genuineness of the commission which he had forged in the King's name: but with a gallant chivalry which more than redeemed his past follies, Sir Phelim bade the executioner make haste and do his office in order that he might be rid of his tempters.

Philip O'Reilly and his sister, the noble Rose O'Neill, withdrew to Flanders, under the protection of a special safe conduct from Cromwell, and their graves are still to be seen carefully tended by the loving hands of their countrymen in the Irish seminary of Louvain.

Hugh Dhu O'Neill, whose gallant conduct at Limerick and Clonmel had gained him the admiration and sympathy of the English Royalists and the grim respect of Cromwell, was released after a short imprisonment in the Tower of London, and, returning to Spain, passed the remainder of his life in honoured retirement.

His cousin, Daniel, the incomparable Subtle, followed the fortunes of the exiled Charles into France when he recognised the futility of attempting to overthrow the might of the Commonwealth with his restless plots in London. On the Restoration, he benefited by the change in the government. He became the first Post-Master General (an office specially created for him by the King), married a countess, amassed an enormous fortune, and succeeded in retaining the affectionate confidence of his fickle master to the hour of his death, which event drew tears even from the eyes of the capricious Charles.

Mr. Wiltonholme and his wife continued to be firm allies to their old friends of the Valley all their lives, and it was through their influence that the lands of Harry Dauntless were preserved to him and his latter-day descendants from the rapacious agents of the Commonwealth.

For the race of Dauntless still hold fast to the ancient patrimony of their fathers in that lovely Valley of Shanganagh, with all the tenacity of their ancestors, and the loving prophecy which Kathlyn made to her son and daughter-in-law on her death-bed has been silently confirmed by five succeeding generations.

"Many, many of thy race shall follow these link by link," whispered the old woman, as she smiled on the blooming faces of her surrounding grandchildren, "and amongst them many hitherto unknown names; but there shall be many Harrys and many Aileens too, my beloved ones, for those two names shall for ever endure in the race of Dauntless with a fragrance sweeter than roses."

THE END

L. C. Page and Company's Announcement of List of New Fiction.

Philip Winwood. (50th thousand.) A SKETCH OF THE DOMESTIC HISTORY OF AN AMERICAN CAPTAIN IN THE WAR OF INDEPENDENCE, EMBRACING EVENTS THAT OCCURRED BETWEEN AND DURING THE YEARS 1763 AND 1785 IN NEW YORK AND LONDON. WRITTEN BY HIS ENEMY IN WAR, HERBERT RUSSELL, LIEUTENANT IN THE LOYALIST FORCES. Presented anew by ROBERT NEILSON STEPHENS, author of "A Gentleman Player," "An Enemy to the King," etc.

With six full-page illustrations by E. W. D. Hamilton.

Library 12mo, cloth decorative, 400 pages . . . $1.50

"One of the most stirring and remarkable romances that has been published in a long while, and its episodes, incidents, and actions are as interesting and agreeable as they are vivid and dramatic. . . . The print, illustrations, binding, etc., are worthy of the tale, and the author and his publishers are to be congratulated on a literary work of fiction which is as wholesome as it is winsome, as fresh and artistic as it is interesting and entertaining from first to last paragraph."— *Boston Times.*

Breaking the Shackles. By FRANK BARRETT.

Author of "A Set of Rogues."

Library 12mo, cloth decorative, gilt top, 350 pages . $1.50

"The story opens well, and maintains its excellence throughout. . . . The author's triumph is the greater in the unquestionable interest and novelty which he achieves. The pictures of prison life are most vivid, and the story of the escape most thrilling."— *The Freeman's Journal, London.*

The Progress of Pauline Kessler. By FREDERIC CARREL.

Author of "Adventures of John Johns."

Library 12mo, cloth decorative, gilt top, 350 pages . $1.50

A novel that will be widely read and much discussed. A powerful sketch of an adventuress who has much of the Becky Sharpe in her. The story is crisply written and told with directness and insight into the ways of social and political life. The characters are strong types of the class to which they belong.

Ada Vernham, Actress. By Richard Marsh.

Author of "Frivolities," "Tom Ossington's Ghost," etc.

Library 12mo, cloth decorative, gilt top, 300 pages . $1.50

This is a new book by the author of "Frivolities," which was extremely well received last season. It deals with the inside life of the London stage, and is of absorbing interest.

The Wallet of Kai Lung. By Ernest Bramah.

Library 12mo, cloth decorative, gilt top, 350 pages . $1.50

This is the first book of a new writer, and is exceedingly well done. It deals with the fortunes of a Chinese professional story-teller, who meets with many surprising adventures. The style suggests somewhat the rich Oriental coloring of the Arabian Nights.

Edward Barry: South Sea Pearler. By Louis Becke.

Author of "By Reef and Palm," "Ridan, the Devil," etc.

With four full-page illustrations by H. C. Edwards.

Library 12mo, cloth decorative, gilt top, 300 pages . $1.50

An exceedingly interesting story of sea life and adventure, the scene of which is laid in the Lagoon Islands of the Pacific.

This is the first complete novel from the pen of Mr. Becke, and readers of his collections of short stories will quickly recognize that the author can write a novel that will grip the reader. Strong, and even tragic, as is his novel in the main, "Edward Barry" has a happy ending, and woman's love and devotion are strongly portrayed.

Unto the Heights of Simplicity. By Johannes Reimers.

Library 12mo, cloth decorative, 300 pages $1.25

We take pleasure in introducing to the reading public a writer of unique charm and individuality. His style is notable for its quaint poetic idiom and subtle imaginative flavor. In the present story, he treats with strength and reticence of the relation of the sexes and the problem of marriage. Certain social abuses and false standards of morality are attacked with great vigor, yet the plot is so interesting for its own sake that the book gives no suspicion of being a problem novel. The descriptions of natural scenery are idyllic in their charm, and form a fitting background for the love story.

The Black Terror. A Romance of Russia. By John K. Leys.

With frontispiece by Victor A. Searles.

Library 12mo, cloth decorative, 350 pages . . . $1.50

A stirring tale of the present day, presenting in a new light the aims and objects of the Nihilists. The story is so vivid and true to life that it might easily be considered a history of political intrigue in Russia, disguised as a novel, while its startling incidents and strange dénouement would only confirm the old adage that "truth is stranger than fiction," and that great historical events may be traced to apparently insignificant causes. The hero of the story is a young Englishman, whose startling resemblance to the Czar is taken advantage of by the Nihilists for the furtherance of their plans.

The Baron's Sons. By Maurus Jokai.

Author of "Black Diamonds," "The Green Book," "Pretty Michal," etc. Translated by Percy F. Bicknell.

Library 12mo, cloth decorative, with photogravure portrait of the author, 350 pages $1.50

An exceedingly interesting romance of the revolution of 1848, the scene of which is laid at the courts of St. Petersburg, Moscow, and Vienna, and in the armies of the Austrians and Hungarians. It follows the fortunes of three young Hungarian noblemen, whose careers are involved in the historical incidents of the time. The story is told with all of Jokai's dash and vigor, and is exceedingly interesting. This romance has been translated for us directly from the Hungarian, and never has been issued hitherto in English.

Slaves of Chance. By Ferrier Langworthy.

With five portraits of the heroines, from original drawings by Hiel.

Library 12mo, cloth decorative, gilt top, 350 pages . $1.50

As a study of some of the realities of London life, this novel is one of notable merit. The slaves of chance, and, it might be added, of temptation, are five pretty girls, the daughters of a pretty widow, whose means are scarcely sufficient, even living as they do, in a quiet way and in a quiet London street, to make both ends meet. Dealing, as he does, with many sides of London life, the writer sketches varied types of character, and his creations are cleverly defined. He tells an interesting tale with delicacy and in a fresh, attractive style.

Her Boston Experiences. By MARGARET ALLSTON (nom de plume).

With eighteen full-page illustrations from drawings by Frank O. Small, and from photographs taken especially for the book.

Small 12mo, cloth decorative, gilt top, 225 pages . $1.25

A most interesting and vivacious tale, dealing with society life at the Hub, with perhaps a tinge of the flavor of Vagabondia. The story has appeared serially in *The Ladies' Home Journal*, where it was received with marked success. We are not as yet at liberty to give the true name of the author, who hides her identity under the pen name, Margaret Allston, but she is well known in literature.

Memory Street. By MARTHA BAKER DUNN.

Author of "The Sleeping Beauty," etc.

Library 12mo, cloth decorative, 300 pages $1.25

An exceedingly beautiful story, delineating New England life and character. The style and interest will compare favorably with the work of such writers as Mary E. Wilkins, Kate Douglas Wiggin, and Sarah Orne Jewett. The author has been a constant contributor to the leading magazines, and the interest of her previous work will assure welcome for her first novel.

Winifred. A STORY OF THE CHALK CLIFFS. By S. BARING GOULD.

Author of "Mehala," etc.

Library 12mo, cloth decorative, illustrated, 350 pages . $1.50

A striking novel of English life in the eighteenth century by this well known writer. The scene is laid partly in rural Devonshire, and partly in aristocratic London circles.

At the Court of the King: BEING ROMANCES OF FRANCE. By G. HEMBERT WESTLEY, editor of "For Love's Sweet Sake."

With a photogravure frontispiece from an original drawing.

Library 12mo, cloth decorative, 300 pages $1.25

Despite the prophecies of some literary experts, the historical romance is still on the high tide of popular favor, as exemplified by many recent successes. We feel justified, consequently, in issuing these stirring romances of intrigue and adventure, love and war, at the Courts of the French Kings.

God's Rebel. By HULBERT FULLER.

Author of "Vivian of Virginia."

Library 12mo, cloth decorative, 375 pages . . . $1.25

A powerful story of sociological questions. The scene is laid in Chicago, the hero being a professor in "Rockland University," whose protest against the unequal distribution of wealth and the wretched condition of workmen gains for him the enmity of the "Savior Oil Company," through whose influence he loses his position. His after career as a leader of laborers who are fighting to obtain their rights is described with great earnestness. The character drawing is vigorous and varied, and the romantic plot holds the interest throughout. *The Albany Journal* is right in pronouncing this novel "an unusually strong story." It can hardly fail to command an immense reading public.

A Georgian Actress. By PAULINE BRADFORD MACKIE.

Author of "Mademoiselle de Berny," "Ye Lyttle Salem Maide," etc.

With four full-page illustrations from drawings by E. W. D. Hamilton.

Library 12mo, cloth decorative, gilt top, 300 pages . $1.50

An interesting romance of the days of George III., dealing with the life and adventures of a fair and talented young play-actress, the scene of which is laid in England and America. The success of Miss Mackie's previous books will justify our prediction that a new volume will receive an instant welcome.

God — The King — My Brother. A ROMANCE.

By MARY F. NIXON.

Author of "With a Pessimist in Spain," "A Harp of Many Chords," etc.

With a frontispiece by H. C. Edwards.

Library 12mo, cloth decorative, 300 pages . . . $1.25

An historical tale, dealing with the romantic period of Edward the Black Prince. The scene is laid for the most part in the sunny land of Spain, during the reign of Pedro the Cruel — the ally in war of the Black Prince. The well-told story records the adventures of two young English knight-errants, twin brothers, whose family motto gives the title to the book. The Spanish maid, the heroine of the romance, is a delightful characterization, and the love story, with its surprising yet logical dénouement, is enthralling.

A Gentleman Player. (*Thirty-fifth Thousand.*) HIS ADVENTURES ON A SECRET MISSION FOR QUEEN ELIZABETH. By ROBERT NEILSON STEPHENS.

Author of "An Enemy to the King," "The Continental Dragoon," "The Road to Paris," etc.

Illustrated by Frank T. Merrill.

Library 12mo, cloth decorative, 450 pages . . . $1.50

"A thrilling historical romance. . . . It is a well-told tale of mingled romance and history, and the reader throughout unconsciously joins in the flight and thrills with the excitement of the dangers and adventures that befall the fugitives." — *Chicago Tribune.*

"'A Gentleman Player' is well conceived and well told." — *Boston Journal.*

Rose à Charlitte. (*Eighth Thousand.*) AN ACADIEN ROMANCE. By MARSHALL SAUNDERS.

Author of "Beautiful Joe," etc.

Illustrated by H. De M. Young.

Library 12mo, cloth decorative, 500 pages . . . $1.50

"A very fine novel we unhesitatingly pronounce it . . . one of the books that stamp themselves at once upon the imagination and remain imbedded in the memory long after the covers are closed." — *Literary World, Boston.*

Deficient Saints. A TALE OF MAINE. By MARSHALL SAUNDERS.

Author of "Rose à Charlitte," "Beautiful Joe," etc.

Illustrated by Frank T. Merrill.

Library 12mo, cloth decorative, 400 pages . . . $1.50

"The tale is altogether delightful; it is vitally charming and expresses a quiet power that sparkles with all sorts of versatile beauty." — *Boston Ideas.*

Her Sailor. A NOVEL. By MARSHALL SAUNDERS.

Author of "Rose à Charlitte," "Beautiful Joe," etc.

Library 12mo, cloth decorative, illustrated, 325 pages $1.25

A story of modern life of great charm and pathos, dealing with the love affairs of an American girl and a naval officer.

"A love story, refreshing and sweet." — *Utica Herald.*

"The wayward petulance of the maiden, who half-resents the matter-of-course wooing and wedding, her graceful coquetry, and final capitulation are prettily told, making a fine character sketch and an entertaining story." — *Bookseller, Chicago.*

Pretty Michal. A ROMANCE OF HUNGARY. By MAURUS JOKAI.

Author of "Black Diamonds," "The Green Book," "Midst the Wild Carpathians," etc.

Authorized translation by R. Nisbet Bain

Illustrated with a photogravure frontispiece of the great Magyar writer.

Library 12mo, cloth decorative, 325 pages . . . $1.50

"It is at once a spirited tale of 'border chivalry,' a charming love story full of genuine poetry, and a graphic picture of life in a country and at a period both equally new to English readers." — *Literary World, London.*

Midst the Wild Carpathians. By MAURUS JOKAI.

Author of "Black Diamonds," "The Lion of Janina," etc.

Authorized translation by R. Nisbet Bain.

Illustrated by J. W. Kennedy.

Library 12mo, cloth decorative, 300 pages . . . $1.25

"The story is absorbingly interesting and displays all the virility of Jokai's powers, his genius of description, his keenness of characterization, his subtlety of humor, and his consummate art in the progression of the novel from one apparent climax to another." — *Chicago Evening Post.*

In Kings' Houses. A ROMANCE OF THE REIGN OF QUEEN ANNE. By JULIA C. R. DORR.

Author of "A Cathedral Pilgrimage," etc.

Illustrated by Frank T. Merrill.

Library 12mo, cloth decorative, 400 pages . . . $1.50

"We close the book with a wish that the author may write more romances of the history of England which she knows so well." — *Bookman, New York.*

"A fine strong story which is a relief to come upon. Related with charming, simple art." — *Philadelphia Public Ledger.*

Omar the Tentmaker. A ROMANCE OF OLD PERSIA. By NATHAN HASKELL DOLE.

Illustrated by F. T. Merrill.

Library 12mo, cloth decorative, 350 pages . . . $1.50

"The story itself is beautiful and it is beautifully written. It possesses the true spirit of romance, and is almost poetical in form. The author has undoubtedly been inspired by his admiration for the Rubaiyat of Omar Khayyam to write this story of which Omar is the hero." — *Troy Times.*

"Mr. Dole has built a delightful romance." — *Chicago Chronicle.*

"It is a strong and vividly written story, full of the life and spirit of romance." — *New Orleans Picayune.*

Manders. A Tale of Paris. By Elwyn Barron.

Library 12mo, cloth decorative, illustrated, 350 pages $1.50

"Bright descriptions of student life in Paris, sympathetic views of human frailty, and a dash of dramatic force, combine to form an attractive story. The book contains some very strong scenes, plenty of life and color, and a pleasant tinge of humor. . . . It has grip, picturesqueness, and vivacity." — *The Speaker, London.*

"A study of deep human interest, in which pathos and humor both play their parts. The descriptions of life in the Quartier Latin are distinguished for their freshness and liveliness." — *St. James Gazette, London.*

"A romance sweet as violets." — *Town Topics, New York.*

In Old New York. A Romance. By Wilson Barrett, author of "The Sign of the Cross," etc., and Elwyn Barron, author of "Manders."

Library 12mo, cloth decorative, illustrated, 350 pages $1.50

"A novel of great interest and vigor." — *Philadelphia Inquirer.*

"'In Old New York' is worthy of its distinguished authors." — *Chicago Times-Herald.*

"Intensely interesting. It has an historical flavor that gives it a substantial value." — *Boston Globe.*

The Golden Dog. A Romance of Quebec. By William Kirby.

New authorized edition.

Illustrated by J. W. Kennedy.

Library 12mo, cloth decorative, 620 pages . . . $1.25

"A powerful romance of love, intrigue, and adventure in the time of Louis XV. and Mme. de Pompadour, when the French colonies were making their great struggle to retain for an ungrateful court the fairest jewels in the colonial diadem of France." — *New York Herald.*

The Knight of King's Guard. A Romance of the Days of the Black Prince. By Ewan Martin.

Illustrated by Gilbert James.

Library 12mo, cloth decorative, 300 pages . . . $1.50

An exceedingly well written romance, dealing with the romantic period chronicled so admirably by Froissart. The scene is laid at a border castle between England and Scotland, the city of London, and on the French battle-fields of Cressy and Poitiers. Edward the Third, Queen Philippa, the Black Prince, Bertrand du Guesclin, are all historical characters, accurate reproductions of which give life and vitality to the romance. The character of the hero is especially well drawn.

The Making of a Saint. By W. Somerset Maugham.

Illustrated by Gilbert James.

Library 12mo, cloth decorative, 350 pages . . . $1.50

"An exceedingly strong story of original motive and design. . . . The scenes are imbued with a spirit of frankness . . . and in addition there is a strong dramatic flavor." — *Philadelphia Press.*

"A sprightly tale abounding in adventures, and redolent of the spirit of mediæval Italy." — *Brooklyn Times.*

Friendship and Folly. A Novel. By Maria Louise Pool.

Author of "Dally," "A Redbridge Neighborhood," "In a Dike Shanty," etc.

Illustrated by J. W. Kennedy.

Library 12mo, cloth decorative, 300 pages . . . $1.25

"The author handles her elements with skilful fingers — fingers that feel their way most truthfully among the actual emotions and occurrences of nineteenth century romance. Hers is a frank, sensitive touch, and the result is both complete and full of interest." — *Boston Ideas.*

"The story will rank with the best previous work of this author." — *Indianapolis News.*

The Rejuvenation of Miss Semaphore.

A Farcical Novel. By Hal Godfrey.

Illustrated by Etheldred B. Barry.

Library 12mo, cloth decorative, 300 pages . . . $1.25

"A fanciful, laughable tale of two maiden sisters of uncertain age who are induced, by their natural longing for a return to youth and its blessings, to pay a large sum for a mystical water which possesses the value of setting backwards the hands of time. No more delightfully fresh and original book has appeared since 'Vice Versa' charmed an amused world. It is well written, drawn to the life, and full of the most enjoyable humor." — *Boston Beacon.*

The Paths of the Prudent. By J. S. Fletcher.

Author of "When Charles I. Was King," "Mistress Spitfire," etc.

Illustrated by J. W. Kennedy.

Library 12mo, cloth decorative, 300 pages . . . $1.50

"The story has a curious fascination for the reader, and the theme and characters are handled with rare ability." — *Scotsman.*

"Dorinthia is charming. The story is told with great humor." — *Pall Mall Gazette.*

"An excellently well told story, and the reader's interest is perfectly sustained to the very end." — *Punch.*

Cross Trails. By Victor Waite.

Illustrated by J. W. Kennedy.

Library 12mo, cloth decorative, 450 pages $1.50

"A Spanish-American novel of unusual interest, a brilliant, dashing, and stirring story, teeming with humanity and life. Mr Waite is to be congratulated upon the strength with which he has drawn his characters" — *San Francisco Chronicle.*

"Every page is enthralling." — *Academy.*

"Full of strength and reality." — *Athenæum.*

"The book is exceedingly powerful." — *Glasgow Herald.*

Bijli the Dancer. By James Blythe Patton.

Illustrated by Horace Van Rinth.

Library 12mo, cloth decorative, 350 pages $1.50

"A novel of Modern India. . . . The fortunes of the heroine, an Indian nautch-girl, are told with a vigor, pathos, and a wealth of poetic sympathy that makes the book admirable from first to last" — *Detroit Free Press.*

"A remarkable book." — *Bookman.*

"Powerful and fascinating." — *Pall Mall Gazette.*

"A vivid picture of Indian life." — *Academy, London.*

Drives and Puts. A Book of Golf Stories. By Walter Camp and Lilian Brooks.

Small 12mo, cloth decorative, illustrated, 250 pages . $1.25

"It will be heartily relished by all readers, whether golfers or not." — *Boston Ideas.*

"Decidedly the best golf stories I have read." — *Milwaukee Journal.*

"Thoroughly entertaining and interesting in every page, and is gotten out with care and judgment that indicate rare taste in bookmaking." — *Chicago Saturday Evening Herald.*

Via Lucis. By Kassandra Vivaria.

With portrait of the author.

Library 12mo, cloth decorative, 480 pages $1.50

"'Via Lucis' is — we say it unhesitatingly — a striking and interesting production." — *London Athenæum.*

"Without doubt the most notable novel of the summer is this strong story of Italian life, so full of local color one can almost see the cool, shaded patios and the flame of the pomegranate blossom, and smell the perfume of the grapes growing on the hillsides. It is a story of deep and passionate heart interests, of fierce loves and fiercer hates, of undisciplined natures that work out their own bitter destiny of woe. There has hardly been a finer piece of portraiture than that of the child Arduina, — the child of a sickly and unloved mother and a cruel and vindictive father, — a morbid, queer, lonely little creature, who is left to grow up without love or training of any kind." — *New Orleans Picayune.*

Lightning Source UK Ltd.
Milton Keynes UK
UKHW020109140219
337249UK00009B/355/P

9 781527 658721